W9-AAO-169

Lamb in Love

Also by Carrie Brown

Rose's Garden

Lamb in Love

A NOVEL

BY

Carrie Brown

Algonquin Books
of Chapel Hill
1999

7 Brown

Published by
Algonquin Books of Chapel Hill
Post Office Box 2225
Chapel Hill, North Carolina 27515-2225

a division of
Workman Publishing
708 Broadway
New York, New York 10003

Printed in the United States of America.
Published simultaneously in Canada by
Thomas Allen & Son Limited.
Design by Anne Winslow.

This is a work of fiction. While, as in all fiction, the literary perceptions and insights are based on experience, all names, characters, places, and incidents are either products of the author's imagination or are used ficticiously. No reference to any real person is intended or should be inferred.

Library of Congress Cataloging-in-Publication Data
Brown, Carrie, 1959–
Lamb in love : a novel / by Carrie Brown.
p. cm.
ISBN 1-56512-203-8
I. Title.
PS3552.R68529L36 1999
813'.54—dc21 98-44580
CIP

10 9 8 7 6 5 4 3 2 1
First Edition

For John

and for

Helen and Sandy McCully

for taking me there

If love be good, from whennes cometh my woe?

Geoffrey Chaucer, *Troilus and Criseyde*

Lamb in Love

PRELUDE

HERE'S VIDA NOW, passing through the faint bars of afternoon sunlight striping the lane, come to meet Manford. High above her head, in a perfect proscenium arch, the boughs of the oak trees rise and fall on the wind. Pairs of clouds slide by, soundless against the blue sky. Vida's long shadow trails behind her over the grass.

To Norris Lamb, the postmaster who has hidden himself behind a nearby horse chestnut tree, Vida's passage takes a church-like eternity, and his ears fill with the deafening sound of his own racing pulse.

But at last she arrives. Not twenty-five feet from Norris's position behind the tree, Vida Stephen takes her place quietly on the bench fitted into the alcove of boxwoods, folds her hands, and turns her chin slightly to face the vanishing point on the curve of the lane.

Manford, Vida's poor charge, will be along now any moment.

IT IS A warm afternoon, the last day of July. It has rained each morning over the last week, but in the afternoons the weather has cleared. By five—customarily the hour when Vida leaves Southend House to walk down the lane to meet Manford—the light is low and devotional, finely particled as though you could sift it through your hands.

Vida and Norris wait there now, one upon her bench, her hands motionless in her lap, the other hidden behind his tree. Minutes tick past. Norris feels his diaphragm expand and fall with each breath, his heart steadying now after the first excitement of seeing Vida again. Then, as if at a signal from an unseen hand, the silent air around them ignites with the rise and fall of buzzing sound. Swarms of dragonflies—devil's darning needles, Norris calls them—lift from the tall grass and veer down the lane. Vida raises her head at the purring their wings make.

Despite her gravity at this moment, her patient attitude, her careful clothes, Norris sees Vida as something wild, something barely contained—something greater, perhaps, than she is. After all, she might protest, what *is* she but a middle-aged woman (forty-two in December), not very striking in any way? Though with lovely chestnut hair—everyone in the village agrees about that.

What else can be said of her that they might all agree upon?

That she has been loyally employed for nearly twenty years now as nanny to the retarded son of an expatriate American architect. That she was an undistinguished girl, whose constancy with Manford has shown her to better advantage than her neighbors might have predicted. That she wears a hat to good effect. That she—well, they cannot think of anything else. And then perhaps they are surprised to realize they don't know anything at all about her, really.

But now it is Norris's privilege and pleasure to see her as no one else does, for he has been struck by love for Vida. And in his eyes, under the transforming inspection of his gaze—well, who can tell? Vida *may* become something other, something *more* than she appears at this very moment, waiting quietly on her bench, the world breathing delicately around her.

A FEW DAYS ago—on July 20, 1969, Norris's fifty-fifth birthday, in fact—American astronauts landed on the dusty ridge of Mare Tranquillitatis and planted a flag atop an atoll on the moon's marvelous ashen desert.

Late that same night, after sitting for nearly two hours in front of the BBC, watching the snowy footage of Neil Armstrong advancing slowly as a mime across the moon's surface, Norris went out for a nocturnal stroll, awed to find himself alive—indeed, celebrating a birthday—at a time when such a thing as a man's landing on the moon might be possible. He'd gone out just to have a look at the *real* moon, as he thought of it, and had stood for a while in the middle of the Romsey Road, his head craned back. Then he'd walked out across the fields under the stars and paused by a silvery, moss-covered stile to stare up into the sky. And at last he found himself led as if by habit onto the lawn at Southend House; he had walked there often in the past, to admire the architecture of the gardens. The moon hung high in the sky above him, and Norris had stared up at it, distracted and amazed, thinking there could be no greater miracle.

And then he had seen Vida.

Not for the first time, of course; they'd known each other for forever.

But he'd never seen her like that before. He'd never seen *anything* like that before.

And you don't see a nearly naked woman dancing in the moonlight in a ruined garden and then just go on about your business as though nothing has happened, do you?

VIDA, OF COURSE, had watched the moon landing, too. That's how it happened.

After hours of the proceedings on the telly, when she was sure it wouldn't be a moment longer before they actually set foot on the moon itself, she ran upstairs and woke Manford. She helped him into his dressing gown, hurried him back down the stairs and through Southend House's interminable passageways, back to the sitting room off the kitchen.

But no matter how hard she tried, she could not keep Manford awake. She told him it was an important moment, a historic moment. But he wanted to lie down on the floor or to put his head in her lap. He put his hands over his ears and closed his eyes and rocked back and forth and yawned like a hippopotamus, and at last she gave up on him, let him have the sofa, and sat cross-legged tailor fashion by herself on the floor in front of the set. Once she reached out and touched the picture before her; a shower of tiny electrical sparks met her fingertips.

She was disappointed not to have company for the event; even Manford's company would have been better than nothing.

When the program reverted to the commentary again, she realized how late it was, and yet how strangely alert, how alive, she felt. Manford still lay curled on the sofa, his face turned away from her, his hair standing up in the back.

She stood and crossed the room to look out the window.

The casement was ajar. It was a warm night, and from below, the bright, souring scent of grass and boxwood drifted up to her nose. She looked up at the moon. And it wasn't enough then, being there inside the house. She wanted to be outside, nothing between her and the moon. She wanted to be standing there on the lawn in the moonlight. That one night, she wanted nothing between her skin and the world, nothing, at last, to come between what she wanted and what, in the end, she would discover she had.

THIS LOVE FOR Vida has swept over Norris, overtaken him after a lifetime of crisscrossing the same streets as she, going in and out the same doors, conducting their business over the same counters.

Oh, Norris knows how silly it looks, how they'd laugh, all his neighbors, if they knew. He knows he is a victim of a delicious assault, a caress from a lion's paw.

In his better moments, his braver moments, his love for Vida inspires joy in him—now, at last, at such an age, he has fallen in love. But it fills him with terror, too. How unlikely his prospects are. He could stay up half the night worrying about how it will all come to nothing, or worse—to ruin. To humiliation. But sometimes he grows nearly hysterical with the pleasure of his fantasies.

Norris is postmaster for Hursley, a small village a few hours southeast of London in the county of Hampshire. He is also, not surprisingly, a philatelist, a collector and admirer of stamps. As such, he carries in his head a mental reel of images not unlike that of the serious scholar of art history. Both may see the past as one of those shutter books one flips with one's thumb to make a motion picture, time streaking forward, image by image.

So when Norris dwells on Vida, it is often through the world of his stamps. He sees her masquerading in all the stamps he knows and loves so well: in a severe white uniform, holding aloft a beaker of some foaming substance, a look of serious and intelligent consideration on her face—this from the Christmas Island stamp celebrating the phosphate industry. Or in a glowing and bristling headdress of beads and feathers, from a definitive series issued by Papua New Guinea. He sees her face where the Madonna's should be, eyes downcast, in the cracked pigment of the image reproduced in a commemorative stamp for St. Thomas. And sometimes, though it seems a bit absurd, he finds her features arranged under the queen's crown and demure coif, her face etched in purple or blue or forest green.

Yet, released from time to time from his library of stamps, he finds himself surprisingly—uncharacteristically, he would say—inspired. Closing his eyes, he imagines Vida without her blouse, her hair unwound, flying from the prow of a ship—a figurehead. He sees her all in white, ministering to a fallen soldier (himself, of course) safeguarded in a ruined Italian convent serving as hospital; her hands are infinitely gentle on the man's broken limbs. He sees her dreamy and restful, her arms bathed in soapsuds, washing up his dinner plate. He even sees himself, bearing her in his arms onto an endless crescent of shore from a limpid, gaseous ocean; his own bathing trunks are dark blue, and his physique, very manly. This fantasy feels faintly apocalyptic to him. He couldn't say where it comes from.

LEANING AGAINST HIS horse chestnut tree, trying to breathe quietly, Norris travels over his image of Vida, so restful and patient now upon her bench. Why is he so sure that some recklessness resides within her, some capacity to surprise him, surprise them all? He is slightly shocked to realize that he can imagine claws retracted inside the soft pad of her foot, her teeth buried within her still and watchful face.

Perhaps it is just the fact of Manford, her poor charge. Nothing should ever happen to Manford. Norris understands that Vida would, at all costs, prevent that.

Although Manford is not young now. Not anymore.

In light of that truth, that Manford is now a man himself, Norris sees as he never did or cared to before what Vida has within her. All along she has been faithful steward to Manford. She has prevented every accident, every misfortune—and certainly if ever there was a person who needed protection, Manford is it. Norris himself is quite overwhelmed by the notion of children, all the dangers waiting to befall them. Sometimes he finds himself almost intimidated by Vida, as if she has already seen right through him, seen how nervous children make him, how inept he becomes in their presence.

He tries to see Vida now first as he thinks others must see her: As a pleasant woman with quiet manners, attractive, though not in any way you might consider showy. A woman who's done her duty. And she's grown into such a capable person—no one would have pegged her as someone to last with Manford Perry. Not that he isn't sweet; it's just—well, how dreary it must be sometimes. With no one to talk to.

For Manford is not only retarded, but mute, too. Though perhaps it's for the best—think what he might say if he *could* speak. Nothing but gobbledygook, likely. From their own doors and windows on the Romsey Road, the neighbors watch Vida pass down the street, Manford beside her, Vida chattering away happily as if they were actually having a conversation, her hands busy describing shapes in the air. And Manford himself squinting at the sun, shaking his head, running a hand over his hair, distractible as a dog. Almost no one can remember Vida as a girl anymore, when she ran errands for her mum at the shop, up and down the Romsey Road, those long braids flying out behind her, pink in her cheeks. Now the gestures of her youth, once so fluid and excitable, appear careful, economical. Vida is almost old enough now to be considered a spinster. And no one has ever known her to have a young man.

What a pity, people say. She might have had children of her own.

But Norris knows—he believes he alone knows—what is still there to be rescued and revived. He imagines that he sees what others, lacking the wondrous prism of his passion, cannot. She has been waiting, he thinks. All along, she has been waiting. And now, could she love him? Could she?

Impossible, he thinks, closing his eyes against the surge of disappointment, the embarrassment. But then he reels, steadies himself against his tree, rights himself, his heart: I will love her so well, he thinks, that she will have to love me back. That's the way it works.

ONCE IN HER life, a long time ago, there was a spell when Vida was wild to get away from Manford, wild to be with people like her, to have what she used to think of as a "normal" life. It was almost as if she could see her life trailing away like a distant curl of smoke, going on without her. Her desperation lasted a little while—she had fits of weeping, wrote many letters of resignation to Mr. Perry that she tore up into tiny bits. And then somehow, one day, it was gone, and she felt like a person who has had a very high fever for several days and then wakes one morning to find the world calm and dry, a sparrow singing at the windowsill, a kettle blowing a shrill whistle from the kitchen downstairs.

Sometimes, though she cannot say why, she finds herself blinking away tears—it happens occasionally when she sits quietly like this, waiting for Manford. She has a sudden apprehension, so quick and sharp that it feels like pain, of what she thinks of as the world's transparency, the way everything is held together so loosely, so delicately, so impossibly—raise her hand, she thinks, and it will all fly apart; she will lose it forever.

One

SOMETIMES, WHEN HE is hiding behind the horse chestnut and spying on Vida, Norris dares to lean slightly to the east and watch for Manford.

Since he has been pondering Vida and the circumstances of her life, Norris cannot decide for himself whether Manford is blessed or cursed. Certainly Manford has been lucky to have Vida, he thinks, though of course it is an unwelcome blessing to need a nanny all your days, no matter how charming and dependable she may be. And blessed, too, after a fashion, by his state of permanent innocence. But surely in all other ways it is a curse to be as dim-witted as Manford, unequipped to consider the marvelous complexities of the world, to tarry awhile in the amusing company of one's own thoughts and the genius of society's inventions. Does Manford, grown to manhood now, a strapping twenty-year-old fellow recently employed at Niven's Bakery to stuff the doughnuts with jam, have even a single thought? Something that might be described as having a beginning and a middle and an end, with a little flash of revelation glowing in the center of it? What does he think as he fills those doughnuts? Norris can't say for certain that Manford thinks anything at all, and the notion perplexes him.

Whenever he's there in the lane, hoping to catch sight of Vida, Norris prepares himself for the sound of her voice, for the frisson of delight that runs over his body. He hears *her,* of course, for Manford does not speak, has never been known to speak. Every time, Norris listens for the receding murmur of Vida's voice as she receives Manford's staggering embrace and inquires after his day (but isn't it pointless to ask if you can't be *answered?*) and leads him back down the lane to Southend House.

At that moment, after they've gone, Norris always thinks: It is so pretty in the lane. And he raises a hand delicately as if toward a work of art.

ALONG WITH SERVING as Hursley's postmaster, Norris is also amateur organist for St. Alphage, an entirely voluntary situation inherited from his grandmother, who, until she lost her sight, was pleased to be the only woman in Hampshire, she imagined, to hold the position of organist. As a consequence of her gender, she had begun offering her abilities free of charge, some vague understanding between her and the church committee that hers was a temporary service until the original organist was returned—safely, they all prayed—from the war. He was not, however. And by the time Norris was sufficiently proficient, the job was thought to be a sort of family office. He's never had a shilling for all his Sundays, though his repertoire is, he acknowledges, somewhat limited.

A philatelist and bachelor and collector of obscure reveries, Norris has never in his whole life had what might be described as a love affair. But he still remembers the name—Mary—of the sweet-faced girl who sat in front of him in the third form and whom he tried to kiss one day after school, darting out from behind a monkey puzzle tree and grabbing her to him. He remembers the feel of her upper arms within the circle of his hands, the slight yield of her flesh. But the girl had pulled away from him in horror, wiped her hand across her mouth, and burst inexplicably into tears, a response that mortified Norris so powerfully that the memory of it haunted him forever after, the scene replaying itself over and over again in excruciating detail, just when it seemed he might be free of it.

There was that one other time, the sad and mysterious incident with the weeping woman. Why *do* they all always seem to cry?

This woman's father, a postmaster in Winchester and an acquaintance of Norris's through the stamp league, had asked whether Norris wouldn't play escort to his daughter at a dance held at the St. Jude Hospital, where she was a nurse; her boyfriend, the father intimated, was a doctor who'd recently given her the brush-off. Norris, though nearly sick with anxiety, had dutifully presented himself to the girl at her flat. They had a cup of Pimm's at the dance, meanwhile watching other couples go round and round the large, empty room with its green walls and white plumbing. A steady rain beat dark against the windowpanes. Norris, his heart racing, had asked the young woman to dance—she was quite pretty, after all. But once in his arms, she had wept so profusely and with such ferocity that she had soaked the shoulder of his suit coat. Eventually, with dismay, he had managed to steer her outside, still pressed to his shirtfront. He had driven her home and there he had left her off, still crying so hard that he could understand nothing of what she said other than, "Do forgive me."

Afterward the woman's father had been oddly nervous around Norris, as though they shared some terrible complicity. So, women—well, until Vida, it all seemed simply too complicated, too important, for words. He has made do without, pushing the idea of the fairer sex, as he refers to them, far, far to the back of his thoughts. He knows other men who seem always to be on their own—Sir Winstead-Harris, for instance. *He's* done all right, Norris thinks. Pots of money, anyway.

So. He is just a fifty-five-year-old stick whom his neighbors consider a confirmed bachelor. Terrified of women, perhaps? Or maybe a queer? (So careful with his appearance, etc.) He strikes some, in fact, as having the vulnerability of certain animals, the dolphin, perhaps, with its high, blunt brow and the dignity of a captive. With his mournful eyes and sometimes distracted manner, he is a fellow to be pitied, in a way, though he seems satisfied enough, always busy at the post office, full of helpful advice about the mails and so forth. Still, one does feel sorry for him; he's exactly the sort you expect to be taken by surprise by a sudden myocardial infarction. Or to be bitten by a rabid dog. One senses—vaguely—some harm speeding toward him, its target certain, its course unswerving.

But he is more than that now, Norris thinks, walking through Hursley, opening up the post office, mounting the steps to the organ on Sundays, doing his wash or his gardening or his sweeping. He is more than any of that. No one has the slightest idea who he *really* is, what he's capable of.

He can often be heard singing as he goes about his work these days.

He's happy.

For the first time in his life, he thinks, he isn't harm's foolish target, the idiot about to be turned tail over teacup, the one with egg on his face. He's standing directly in harm's way now, isn't he? He's brave as a soldier, fully prepared. He has everything to risk, and everything to gain.

He is Norris Lamb in love. Lamb in love.

BUT HOW REALLY does Norris understand Vida? For that matter, Manford Perry?

Nowadays it's no longer proper to call them idiots or fools, these souls with the strange air of the savant behind their otherwise childlike expressions. Handicapped is how Norris has overheard Vida describe Manford.

"He is *neither,*" Norris once heard Vida say, "a spastic *nor* a vegetable. Those are two different things *entirely.*"

At the time, Norris took no special notice of her remark, beyond the upsetting nature of its context. It was near Christmas, well over a decade ago, at the annual children's party at the vicarage. The little children were playing pop goes the weasel, all of them arrayed in an uneven circle in the small wooden chairs carried over from the Sunday school into the parlor at the vicarage. The horsehair sofas, the ottomans, and the slipcovered chairs had been pushed back against the wall. The dark glass before the gloomy pictures—of rained-on moors and ruins and abbeys and so forth; what a sad lot of pictures the vicar surrounded himself with, Norris thought—held the reflection of the wavering spire of the Christmas tree. Yellow and red and blue bulbs threaded through the boughs glowed dully. The stiff faces of little wax dollies hanging from its branches, the spheres and spirals of the ornaments, the woolen mittens, the toy autos and lorries parked beneath—all this could be seen in the glass of those dreary pictures.

The children had just finished trimming the tree. The vicar himself balanced atop the wobbly ladder affixing the angel, meanwhile adjuring the children to take their places for the game.

Just over a quarter century before, this same room had been employed during air raids as a general shelter. Then, too, the furniture had been pushed back against the walls in precisely the same way, to make room for them all and provide a sort of buffer against explosion, Norris had thought, imagining feathers and horsehair drifting over their heads in the aftermath of impact. Norris himself had been refused by the British military service thanks to poor eyesight and a weak back, a rejection he'd taken very hard. As a consequence, however, he had remained in Hursley for the war and thus remembered the black shades at the vicarage pulled down before the windows, the yellow lamp shade shrouded in a dark cardboard sheath, so that only a small saucer of honey-colored light fell on the tabletop. Kneeling there beside his trembling neighbors, Norris had made himself believe that the church would deflect a bomb by virtue of its very holiness, that his mother and grandmother and all their friends would be safe. And, in the end, his prayers were answered, for Hursley itself was completely untouched by the war, though it suffered heavy losses among sons and fathers overseas. Norris's own father, Terry Lamb, was killed while on patrol in Winchester with the Dad's Army, when he was struck by a grief-stricken woman on a bicycle bearing home to her children the news of their own father's death in France. In his fall to the pavement, Terry Lamb suffered both a heart attack and a massive blow to the head, though either injury alone would have been enough to kill him.

Though no one ever suggested it, something about his father's death always felt ignominious to Norris. During the war years, no death, unless it was in direct service to the war effort itself, seemed quite justified. Ordinary passings on—by accident or by disease—even seemed vaguely embarrassing, a slacking off, as it were. Though there was a small service held for Terry Lamb at St. Alphage, and enough men were rounded up to carry the coffin, Norris would always remember the occasion as a family humiliation.

A decade went by; much changed in the village. But on the occasion of Vida's comment about Manford and spastics and vegetables, the common room of the vicarage looked very much as it had when the Germans had been bombing London and Norris had been bowed, cheek by jowl, beside his grandmother and a lot of other old pensioners, their anxiety perfuming the close air of the crowded room with a sour potage of fear and apology.

On this particular afternoon, the afternoon of Vida's remark, the vicarage had been stiflingly hot. The radiators hissed and steamed in a musical way. The vicar, perspiration running down his temples and into his clerical collar, had been anxious to move the festivities along. From his place near the Christmas tree, where he was cordoned off now by the circle of children, he held up his hand and raised his index finger, nodding vigorously at Norris. Taking the vicar's cue, Norris bore down on the piano. It was horribly out of tune, as usual, Norris noted, with that same stubborn resistance to the pure tone, especially the sharps.

As the music began, one little boy, young Davey Horsey, jumped up and began to race round the circle of children, stopping at last behind Manford's chair to pat him on the head. At Davey's touch, Manford looked up, his expression one of happy surprise, as though a star had perhaps just fallen and lighted on his head, twinkling there and pirouetting on one delicate point. But when he failed to jump up and give chase to Davey, the boy gave him another tap on the head—harder this time—and then again and again as Manford simply continued to sit there, his expression evolving to anxiety, young Davey walloping away stubbornly at Manford's head.

Manford had raised his arms protectively and cowered in his chair, his mouth wobbling with dismay, tears springing from his eyes. Lacey Horsey, Davey's mother, had rushed forward and slapped her boy. Taking him roughly by the arm and putting her mouth close by his face, she said to him in a loud whisper, "Not the spastic vegetable, Davey! Can't you see he doesn't know how?"

By then a good number of the other children were in tears,

too. Davey's assault and Lacey's reprimand and Manford's weeping had upset them all. Mothers hurried into the circle to comfort their children. And so Vida's fiery rebuke to Lacey—about Manford being neither a spastic nor a vegetable, but only a little boy, *for God's sake*—was lost perhaps to everyone but Lacey and Norris himself, his hands poised above the keys in midphrase.

The mothers hushed their children and led them back to their seats to begin the game again. Vida turned away from Lacey, went to Manford in his chair, and wiped his face with the white cuff of her shirtsleeve. She knelt before him, looked into his face, and said his name quietly. When he raised his gaze, she reached out and touched his cheek. "Mind me now, Manford," she said. "It's easy as anything. When someone taps you on the head, you must stand up and run right after them fast as you can. Run, Manford. That's all you have to do." And then she gave him a brilliant smile and a hug and stood up.

Norris had been watching her. She walked briskly back to the edge of the room, where she turned to stare out the window into the darkness of the cemetery beyond the vicar's famous Christmas garden, the bare trees there bedecked with ghostly gray suet shapes for the birds. Norris had found himself staring at her back, but when she turned to face the room again he hurriedly averted his gaze. And as he sat there stupidly at the piano, a memory of an illustration from a picture book he'd had as a child came into his head. The painting had been an allegorical representation of the virtue Mercy, a towering female figure turning the brilliant benediction of her smile on a pastoral depiction of the harvest. In her pale-as-plaster hands, Mercy cradled a young calf; at her knee a tiny farmer had put aside his knife and embraced the lamb. The scene had been painted in minute, exquisite detail, like an illuminated manuscript, and had fascinated Norris. But one day, months after first opening the book, he discovered that one detail had escaped his notice: despite the figure's patient smile, despite the gamboling lambs freed from the farmer's knife, one damning, crystalline tear hung quivering at the figure's eyelash. Norris struggled with the presence of this tear. When he put his own fingertip to the page, he half expected to see the tear come away, with a little shine of wetness. That tear—somehow so real, so necessary—complicated the picture beyond his understanding.

But on the afternoon of pop goes the weasel, when Norris looked up from where his hands rested on the piano keys, the vicar, signaling firmly, caught his eye. And Norris shook himself free of his reverie and set to playing.

Round and round the mulberry bush.

From time to time, he saw Manford's eyes stray hopefully to Vida's back. But no one hit him for pop goes the weasel again. A shame, Norris thought.

Still, he wondered: If not a spastic or a vegetable . . . then *what?*

NORRIS SEES HOW Manford, grown into adulthood, has become a handsome man in a way, though he appears like a child in most other respects.

Vida, who began as Manford's nanny when she was twenty-two, has been looking after him his whole life, twenty years, Norris calculates. Before starting work at Niven's, Manford had spent all his time with her. But Mrs. Blatchford, who works at Niven's, has confided to Norris that it is Vida's program to instill something of the "thrill of independence" in Manford now, by coaxing him to walk part of the way home by himself when his work is finished.

Since his infatuation with Vida began, Norris has watched very carefully as Mr. Niven escorts Manford across the Romsey Road, the baker's white apron flapping, his dusty flour cloth waving Manford along.

Stopping in the bakery for a loaf of bread late one afternoon, Norris paused at the door to watch Mr. Niven and Manford waiting at the curb. Mrs. Blatchford stepped outside at that moment and began pinching the brown leaves from the geraniums in the window boxes.

"Having his lesson," she said, following Norris's gaze to the two figures waiting patiently before the stream of traffic. "Vida's depending on us, you know." She lowered her voice, though there wasn't anyone else there to hear. "I do believe she's worrying about what will happen to him when she—*you know*. She wants to lengthen the reins a bit now, to prepare him."

Norris turned away from the cars on the Romsey Road and Mr. Niven and Manford waiting at the curb. He stared at Mrs. Blatchford, stricken. "When she *what?*" he managed finally. "What do you mean by 'you know,' said in that way?"

He felt himself growing fuzzy around the edges, the beginning of a faint—he was familiar with the symptoms. He'd fainted often when he was younger and doing most of his growing. Something to do with his blood pressure, Dr. Faber had said. "When she *dies?*" he asked finally, appalled.

Mrs. Blatchford glanced over at him. "Oh, *tsk!* Norris Lamb!" she said. "Every time someone mentions dying, all you men grow faint in the head! What a pack of ninnies you are! Vida's not going to die—at least, not before her time, we may hope," she said primly. She crumbled the dry leaves of the geranium, put them in her apron pocket. "She's just *worrying* about the day, whenever it may come. That's what we women do. We *must* worry. We're the designated worriers, if you will." She leaned over the window box.

Norris felt his heart begin beating again. He licked his lips. His mouth had gone dry.

"Of course, no one's asking me," Mrs. Blatchford went on blithely, "but I think his father might have done a bit more for him over the years. He's left him entirely in Vida's hands, you know. And he's plenty of money, I should think. He might have found a good institution for him! Left Vida to get on with her life."

Norris turned away from Mrs. Blatchford to watch Manford step down from the curb at Mr. Niven's urging, pausing in what Norris thought was a perilous manner to wave back at him. He felt distracted by the danger of their undertaking and wasn't able to pay full attention to Mrs. Blatchford. "He's not very attentive to traffic, is he?" he observed.

"What? Oh, no," Mrs. Blatchford said. "Not *yet*."

They watched Mr. Niven shoo Manford across. It seemed to Norris, who had little faith or understanding of Manford's dependability, a risky enterprise.

And then he turned around and looked at Mrs. Blatchford again. "An *institution*, did you say?" he asked abruptly, as if he'd just heard her. "Surely he doesn't need—all that? Restraints—and so forth? Aren't they rather—grim?"

"Oh, we're not in the Victorian age anymore, you know, Mr. Lamb. I think some of them are very modern, like individual flats and so forth. Atriums and lifts and craft circles and whatnot. Latest techniques, you know." Mrs. Blatchford leaned toward the geraniums again and wrenched at a brown stalk. "It's not that he's a bother. I like having him about. Makes one feel—quite homey, actually. I would have suggested it myself long ago, if I'd thought of it. But it's a shame for Vida, I say. Wild horses couldn't tear him from her now. Attached like a leech, he is."

"But she—cares for him." Norris felt squirmy at the mention of leeches.

Mrs. Blatchford dusted her hands on her apron. "Why, she *loves* him. I should say she does. Anyone would," she said defiantly, as if Norris had just contradicted her. "Why, you've only to spend a day with him and you'd see it," she went on. "So eager to please. That's just it."

"Well—that's not a *bad* thing then, is it?"

Mrs. Blatchford sighed and looked out across the Romsey Road. "No, not bad. Just—rather difficult. For *her,* I mean."

Norris turned and watched Manford disappear round the corner. Mr. Niven came back into the courtyard, stood in the doorway of the bakery, and lifted his face to the weak afternoon sun. His cheeks were bruised looking, crosshatched with dozens of broken capillaries.

"Bunch of lunatics they hire to drive those lorries," he said. He squinted at Mrs. Blatchford and Norris. "You know, I was born here—1901, it was"—at this remark Mrs. Blatchford rolled her eyes toward Norris; Mr. Niven was famous for hating change of any sort in Hursley—"and I never thought that one day I'd see the Romsey Road turned into a motor speedway. I'd have said you were mad! But there it is. Those idiots will make a puddle of Manford one day, mark my words."

Norris glanced at the street, the blur of traffic. He thought unpleasantly of Manford reduced to a vague shape splayed across the tarmac.

"We should have a sign installed," Mrs. Blatchford offered. "They have them for blind children, I think."

"That's deaf, you twit." Mr. Niven snorted. "What would a blind child be doing crossing the road?"

"You know what I meant!" Mrs. Blatchford looked offended. "It's the notion of it."

"Yes, but what would it say? Idiot crossing? With a little silhouette of Manford on it?"

"Oh. Really." Mrs. Blatchford shook her apron at him. "What a thought."

Mr. Niven shrugged. "Well, I can't be seeing to him every minute, can I?"

NORRIS WAS UNSETTLED by this conversation but grasped quickly the opportunity it presented. He now closes the post office just before four and walks down the road to see Manford (as unobtrusively as he can—he doesn't wish to excite scrutiny) safely to the entrance to the lane.

It is fortunate that he has done so, for twice now he has saved Manford from some possibly terrible fate, favors of which Vida is unaware.

Once, having safely crossed the Romsey Road, Manford became distracted by a rare commotion at the blacksmith's, which stands almost directly across the street from Niven's Bakery. The two institutions—along with the church and the pub and a few of the older houses—fall into the category Mr. Niven refers to as Hursley's historic jewels. It is true that few English villages still have a working blacksmith in 1969, though Norris sometimes thinks people continue to bring their horses and broken tools to Fergus simply because they are afraid not to, so foul is Fergus's temper. On the first occasion of Norris's acting as Manford's anonymous protector, Fergus had been busy shoeing a difficult mare, and sparks flew from the fire. Manford ambled slowly toward the flame. Fergus, busy with the struggling horse, his own implements, and the glowing shoe, which had fallen with a clatter to the floor, failed to notice Manford sidling toward the fire; but Norris, loitering a ways down the pavement and trying not to appear unduly attentive, suddenly realized the danger. Who knew whether Manford understood fire at all?

Though Norris hurried forward, he felt unsure about how to approach Manford, how to divert him. But as soon as Norris cried his name in alarm, Manford turned toward him. Thinking quickly—he was proud of himself later, for this—Norris fished a butterscotch from his pocket. Holding Manford's eyes in his own with what he hoped was a conjurer's hypnotic trance, he stepped slowly backward, proffering the butterscotch and urging Manford along with his beckoning hand. "Come," he said slowly, in a low, commanding tone. "Come this way, Manford." And Manford followed Norris obediently out the door of the blacksmith's. He took, when Norris jiggled it in his palm, the sticky sweet. And then, apparently recalling what he was about, he trotted off in the right direction.

Norris, who is not really a religious man despite his weekly employment at St. Alphage, closed his eyes briefly and made the sign of the cross over his heart. Then he went back to the post office, only to find several annoyed customers there in a queue outside, trying to look under the black shade pulled down at the window.

The second occasion when he managed to make himself useful to Manford and therefore to Vida, Norris again had to move just in time—more swiftly than a man of his years, and with such a bad back, might be expected to move—to take Manford's strong arm and yank him up from the gutter where he had stepped down into the street to retrieve a sixpence. A lorry sped by, spraying them with gravel, honking madly.

"Go along, Manford," Norris said then, as quietly as he could, trying to smile reassuringly. He didn't wish to alarm Manford, though he was shaking all over at their near escape. "Don't keep Vida—Miss Stephen—waiting." He resettled his glasses on his nose.

Manford, who didn't appear much perturbed by the incident, moved as if to leave, but as he turned away, Norris reached out and caught his sleeve. It was the first time he'd ever looked closely into Manford's face, though he had seen him hundreds of times. But suddenly Norris wanted to have a better look at Manford, wanted to understand what resided there, what intelligence struggled up from within him. Norris took his handkerchief, with which he had already mopped his own sopping brow, and wiped Manford's fingers clean.

"Put the sixpence in your pocket now," he said, but had to help him with it.

It was a strange feeling to touch Manford, to address this tall man as though he were a child. But Manford smiled pleasantly enough, a great wide smile so much like his handsome father's.

"Here," Norris said, fishing in his pocket. "Do you fancy these?" He put a peppermint in Manford's hand and turned him gently then to face down the road and the entrance to the lane. "Go on," he said. "There's the way home. Hurry along now." And Manford did.

At that moment, Norris was struck by what he might feel if Manford were his son—were *their* son. He noticed that Manford's shirt had come untucked. Such untidiness looked odd in a grown man. If Manford were his son, he thought, he could just trot up behind him now and fix him up. Instead, of course, he had to let him go.

IN GENERAL, NORRIS tries not to be too obvious about his interest in Manford's safety. He wants it to be a surprise, for Vida and for everyone, the realization of his tender care, how he's helped protect Manford. To that end he has purchased more than his share of doughnuts from Niven's lately, just to have the opportunity to say a kind word to Manford. He believes he knows how much such gestures would mean to Vida.

"Lovely doughnut, Manford," Norris often calls out to him at Niven's, craning round to catch sight of him where he sits at his high stool in the bakery's annex. Norris then gives Manford a wave, too, showing him the doughnut clearly in his hand and smiling encouragingly.

But he cannot resist tempting curiosity a little bit. Part of him, he knows, desperately wants to confide his secret to someone.

"I've a terrible sweet tooth of late, Mrs. Blatchford," he says impulsively one day, leaning over the glass counter and giving a great sigh.

She glances up at him. "Well, that explains the number of doughnuts I've sold you lately, Norris Lamb," she says. "You ought to have your sugar checked." She studies him from under her queer set of eyebrows, thatched gray and running right across her forehead in a straight line, with hardly any gap in between. Norris finds her rather marvelous looking, like a circus performer. Mrs. Blatchford looks away to replace the tray of iced buns on its shelf. She wipes her hands on a cloth. "It's not *natural,* a sudden appetite for jam doughnuts," she adds. "And the sugar *can* be a problem for those of us getting on, you know."

Those of *you,* you mean, Norris thinks gaily. But not much can insult him anymore. He just feeds the doughnuts to the sparrows, anyway, a bit at a time crumbled off between his fingers as he walks back to the post office, the birds hopping along beside him. (He brings an empty envelope for the jam; you wouldn't want *that* under your heel!)

He worries that the birds draw attention to him, though perhaps no more so than the shades pulled down now over the windows at the post office rather more frequently and at odd times, in order for him to conduct what he refers to as his mysterious errands of love. Though so far, he has to admit, he hasn't actually executed any of these errands, other than saving Manford's life on those two occasions, of course. He's still in what he thinks of as the planning stages.

He knows Vida would die should anything happen to Manford.

He does what he can.

EVERY DAY NOW, since Manford started at Niven's, Vida comes out the gates of Southend House and walks down the lane and seats herself on the bench in the alcove of boxwoods, the bench with the pair of broody doves carved into the backrest. If he is quick, Norris can see Manford safely to the corner of the lane before hurrying down the path that winds through the cowslips and nettles and over the cattle guards and by Mrs. Patrick's well and round all the cow paddies to his spot behind the horse chestnut tree. From there he can catch Vida emerging from Southend House and, a moment later, Manford's shambling progress toward her down the lane.

Often as not she has a hat on her head—a small gray hat, with a black ribbon around the brim and forking over the back like a duck's tail. She's lovely, Norris thinks, so lovely he wonders again that he never saw it before, her pale face like a cameo, and her long hands, and her chestnut hair. It perplexes Norris that he went so many years apparently insensitive to Vida's charms. It seems to him that until he fell in love with her he must have been trapped in ice, like a mastodon.

He made sure to mention to Mrs. Billy when she stopped in the post office last week what a lovely job she's been doing with Vida's hair. It's a pleasure for Norris to hear Vida's name spoken aloud, to feel it pass from between his own lips as though it—she—were something with which he was intimately familiar.

"Doesn't Vida Stephen look smashing lately," he'd said casually as he wrapped up Mrs. Billy's chocolates, took her parcel, and weighed it on the scales. "I caught sight of her just the other day and thought to myself—well, Millicent Billy's not lost her touch, has she? You're a wonder, you are, Mrs. Billy. You've a true talent for hairstyling, indeed."

"Oh, she's got lovely hair," Mrs. Billy confided. (Privately, Norris calls her the Milly-Billy, or the Silly-Billy, or just the Billy. She has long, comical ears, with a chip of some dull stone affixed to the lobes, a turned-up nose, eyes a bit red at the rims, a kindly demeanor. Her husband is Mr. William Billy—to Norris, the Billy-Billy, or the Willy-Billy. With his bloodstained apron, as he peers out from between the skinned carcasses of pigs twirling dreamily on their meat hooks, Mr. Billy looks like a fox, Norris thinks, with a long brown flank and toothsome expression.)

Mrs. Billy leaned toward Norris, the chocolates he'd just sold her melting already in her damp hands.

"So thick, Mr. Lamb," she said. She was wide eyed, Norris saw with satisfaction.

"And all that natural wave to it," Mrs. Billy went on. "Of course, I've been dying to give her a stylish cut, but she never would let me. And then, right out of the blue she says to me the other day, 'Not just the usual today, I think, Mrs. Billy. Time for—' And then, don't you know, she just stopped! Well, we exchanged our looks between us then, you know, Moira and myself. 'Is it a man then, Vida?' I teased her, taking up her hair in my hands, all that lovely hair. 'Have you a boyfriend now?' But she wouldn't say a word more, and I gave her the same cut as usual. Such a pity."

Mrs. Billy shook her head and sighed. "All those years, trapped with that poor dear boy in that empty house. She's needed a husband, that's what, but never had a moment to look and find one." She leaned forward, regarded Norris carefully, as if to assess how he might respond to her next admission. "But do you know, Mr. Lamb? She's a bit of a treat in store. We've invited her to join our book circle. We're newly formed," she went on, straightening her back and jutting out her chin. "We were saying amongst ourselves just the other day how we'd been neglecting the life of the mind. And then it came to us that we might do a book circle at the vicarage of an evening. I'm quite a reader myself, you know. And we've our first novel already chosen. Oh, don't let's start small, I said, with *Pride and Prejudice* or *Emma*. I'm so *sick* of *Emma*. Just because Miss Austen's buried at Winchester cathedral, everyone thinks we must always read her and nothing else, just to be loyal! Let's begin with a challenge, shall we, I said. Boldly forth, I said, into the avenues of learning. And Moira's daughter has recommended us *Lady Chatterley's Lover,* instead." She lowered her voice. "It's a bit *racy* in parts."

But Norris was not listening. He had closed his eyes a moment against the imagined feel of Vida's head in his hands, the rich and violent fall of her brown hair. "Yes, a scorcher," he said dreamily.

"Oooo! No! Not *that* bad, Mr. Lamb. We're not quite ready

for that in Hursley, I think!" Mrs. Billy clasped her handbag, twitched at the wrists of her cardigan. "But we've asked her to join and she's said yes. So that will be something for her, won't it? And—well, you never know what may happen. A little change in our appearance, a little social activity, a little loitering amongst the great works of literature . . . Why, I've a feeling our Vida may be in for a bit of a wake-up. Hold on to your hat, I say, Mr. Lamb. I believe our Vida may be on the mark."

She paused then. "Haven't you ever thought, Mr. Lamb," she said slowly, "that it would be the most romantic thing if they fell in love after all this time? She's a bit young for him, I know. But wouldn't it be just like—oh, like Jane Eyre! Mr. Rochester and the governess? And he is so *very handsome*." This last she uttered sotto voce, peculiarly husky.

Norris stared at her. "What? Who?"

Mrs. Billy then gave him a great wink.

Norris continued staring at her a moment longer until her meaning became clear to him. Oh! How awful! "Mr. *Perry?*" he sputtered. He had to restrain himself from reaching across the counter and shaking Mrs. Billy, wringing the abominable notion from her. He'd never had *any* such thought, indeed. Given the circumstances, it seemed positively—*heinous*. "No, Mrs. Billy," he managed at last, with as much force as he could muster. "I think that would be most—improper!"

"Oh, you *men*." Mrs. Billy leaned over and patted his hand comfortingly. "You've no imagination," she said airily. "None at all. I recommend a dose of literature for you as well, Mr. Lamb."

"I think literature has nothing to do with it. I think—"

"Do you know?" She interrupted him. "I wanted to give her a rinse, as well. She's more than a bit of gray. You take a close look next time you spy her. Tell me what you think. I've just the shade.

Venus, it's called. One of the new natural products. Lovely red highlights. You might say something to her in its favor."

"*Venus?*"

"It'd take years off her, too," Mrs. Billy said confidently. And then, putting the chocolates in her string bag, she gave Norris a coy look. "But aren't you one to notice now, Mr. Lamb?"

Norris attempted to recover himself, drew himself upright. "Women are the flowers of the universe, Mrs. Billy." He stopped. He liked the way it sounded. "It would be a crime not to stop and smell the roses now and again, wouldn't it?"

Mrs. Billy opened her eyes wide then, as though all of a sudden, after years of doing business with Norris Lamb, passing him air letters for the daughter gone to Australia, watching him parcel up a package for the grandchild she's never seen, she'd never noticed this romantic streak in him.

"*Well* then. I suppose we are," she said, smiling. She gave him a little wave and a wink. "Flowers of the universe—I fancy myself a rose. What do you think?" She tittered. "And you, Norris Lamb. You're nothing but an old bee now, aren't you?" And then she left, twittering, the bell jangling behind her.

A bee? Perhaps, he thought. Something that alights for just an instant, gathers a lick of sweetness upon its tongue, moves on to the next flower. Though he shall never move on. Not now. Not now that it's come to him, in this surprising and wonderful way, a veil drawn away from his eyes. Not now, he thinks, that he's seen the light.

Two

Manford is habitually a late sleeper. This morning, opening his door a crack and peering in at him before going downstairs, Vida observes that he sleeps the way a giant would, laid down as if felled over a patchwork of fields, his body cradled by a valley, fir trees bent like rushes beneath his cheek. Manford's dark, heavy head rests on a thick forearm. One calloused foot protrudes from the end of the bedclothes. Vida leans in and picks up his trousers and shirt from the floor, folds them over her arm. She retreats and goes quietly downstairs. Dim morning light, wavering with rain, lies across the floor in fluid stripes.

Since Manford started at Niven's, Vida has had more time than she knows what to do with. Still, she's uncomfortable with nothing to do—it makes her nervous—and so this morning she fixes herself a cup of tea and then sits down at her little desk in the sitting room off the kitchen to write a letter. Behind her, light rain falls against the window glass with the soft sound of fingertips striking a tabletop.

"Dear Uncle Laurence," she begins.

"I'm ashamed it has taken me so long to write and thank you for the card and the lovely little painting you sent for my birthday. (Forty-one years old! Can you believe it?) You'd think that with only Manford to look after I'd have heaps of time, but somehow—actually, I don't really know how to account for it—the time seems to go by so quickly. In fact, I've more time than ever these days because—you'll never guess—I have got Manford a job! Yes! Mr. Perry doesn't know yet; he's off in Amsterdam, I think it is, this week. Or perhaps that's next. In any case, Manford's working at Niven's now. You remember Mr. Niven? And Mrs. Blatchford? They've been so kind, really, and I think it will do Manford a world of good, being a useful member of society. And now that he's working and gone most of the day, I have all this time to myself. So much time! Perhaps too much, really. I don't exactly know what I shall do with myself.

"But I do want to catch up on all my correspondence, and you are first on my list. It is a *lovely* painting, really. I do thank you. I think one of your earlier letters (I have them *all,* you know, saved in a box!) mentioned the pensione where you first stayed when you went to Corfu. Do you remember? Is this painting the view from the terrace there? I thought it might be. Something about it—perhaps that funny group of big rocks out in the water—made me think of that letter. Oh! And the *Palinurus elephas* you ate for dinner each evening; that was in the letter, too, and now I see them here on the table—a still life, isn't it?—right in your painting! (You see, I've nearly memorized your letters!) Spiny lobster just brought up from the sea! I like the sound of *that!* It's quite a grand thing, you know, having a relative in such an exotic place as Corfu. I think it makes me quite the celebrity here, though Mrs. Billy's got a daughter in Australia now.

"And what news have I to tell you? Well, very little has changed here in Hursley (ha ha. What would you expect?) except that St. Alphage has a new organ since this spring. Some people say Mr. Lamb has been inspired ever since. Do you remember Mr. Lamb? He hasn't changed at all since you've gone away. It's funny, actually, now that I think about it—in fact, he looks probably very much the same as when you left! Still very tall and thin. So, he's the same, except that he seems a bit more, oh, impulsive, I find him lately. In conversation, that is. In any case, I do think I detect a change in his playing since the new organ arrived—it seems a trifle ferocious, if you ask me. But perhaps it is just the instrument. It is very grand. Mr. Perry helped pay for it, of course.

"I've planted a pot of lavender at Mum's stone in the cemetery at St. Alphage. It looks very nice. The vicar says it's the lime in the stone that makes the lavender flourish so.

"Well, I'll sign off now. Thank you so much again for remembering my birthday. Forty-one years old! Think of it! My life's half over, isn't it?

"Your loving niece, Vida Stephen."

When she finishes writing, Vida looks up at the clock on the mantel and sees that it's nearly half past eight, time to wake Manford if he's to be at Niven's on time. He likes an egg for his breakfast, too, and she likes to have him well fortified for the day, especially now that he's a working man, as she tells him. Perhaps he'd like a bit of ham to go with his egg, she thinks. He so loves salty things.

For a moment she wonders what her uncle Laurence, her romantic uncle Laurence, gone to Corfu now nearly twenty years ago, would be having for *his* breakfast. She turns her head slightly, as if to encompass a different view, and the pictures fly up easily, habitually, before her eyes, the way one encounters photographs in a long-familiar scrapbook: She imagines banquets laid upon tables at a cliff side, imagines herds of bright white goats sending stones scuttling down the mountain face, imagines silver fish twisting free of the sea, imagines a bell ringing. She has thought of Corfu so often over the years, bringing it up to comfort herself if she's worried about something, or going over the island in her mind if she's having trouble falling asleep. Of course, it isn't the real island—only the one she knows from Laurence or from what she's made up. It's her imaginary place.

But Manford will have to settle for an egg and ham and no view at all, she thinks then, closing her eyes briefly, and reaching up to shut the lid of her desk. An egg and ham and a pot of tea.

WHEN THEY REACH the Romsey Road an hour or so later, Vida takes her hand from Manford's and turns his attention to her. "Run along now, Manford," she says, affecting an air of casualness. "They're waiting on you at Niven's."

Manford does not acknowledge that she has spoken to him but bends over and inspects an insect at his feet.

"Manford!" Vida says pleadingly, all pretense dropping away.

He raises his head guiltily.

"Go on," she says, now that she has his attention. She waves her hand. "Go on now, while there's a lull."

Manford turns and steps off the curb. When he pauses and looks back over his shoulder, Vida taps her wristwatch. "You'll be late," she says warningly.

But Manford fails to move, standing there in the road as if something important has just occurred to him. Vida makes an impatient noise and steps into the road to take Manford by the arm, escorting him briskly across the street. At the courtyard to Niven's Bakery, she leaves go his arm, brushes at a smudge on his lapel, gives him a kiss on the cheek and then a little nudge. A bus speeds past behind them in a cloud of sour exhaust.

"Now *hurry,*" she says, and turns her face away deliberately.

Manford hesitates a moment and then disappears obediently into the courtyard. Vida remains with her back turned until she's sure he's gone inside. Then she leans round the corner of the wall and checks, just to be certain he isn't lurking outside the door, suddenly shy. But no, she can see Mrs. Blatchford coming out from behind the counter with Manford's apron on her arm, so it's all right. She thinks she can see Mrs. Blatchford smiling, but it's difficult to tell.

Vida straightens her skirt. She regards Niven's courtyard, the geraniums at the window. Perhaps another day, she thinks. Perhaps another day and he'll do it himself. Still, she mustn't be in a rush. It has gone so well, this matter of finding Manford independent occupation. She thinks of him on the high stool in the annex, surrounded by the sweet smell of baking bread. She thinks of the close, high walls of the courtyard before the bakery door, the safety of the small enclosure. She thinks of the small view from the windows: the whitewashed walls, the geraniums, the verbena. She travels over it in her mind like a list, every hazard accounted for.

It is part of her training to have Manford walk a bit of the route to Niven's by himself each day. A little more each week, she'd thought, until he could do the whole job himself, from Southend House all the way to the bakery, and back home again at the end of the day. But he won't leave hold of her hand except for the last bit, when they are right at the courtyard. She doesn't know what to do about this. Lately, and for the first time—she cannot say why, though perhaps it is just having Manford be even this slightest bit independent now—it has occurred to her that something might happen to her, something fatal. She is grateful that she has—God knows why—been prevented from entertaining this thought before, for she finds it so painful as to be almost intolerable. And now she feels an awful urgency to teach Manford so many things. There are so many important things she has neglected to teach him, she sees now. Why, at any moment she might be—oh, struck by a bus, she thinks, turning away from Niven's courtyard and facing the Romsey Road. Struck by a bus!

And then what would happen to Manford! She feels a real pain in her heart.

Oh, don't be such a worrywart, Vida Stephen, she tells herself helplessly. No one likes a worrywart.

MRS. BLATCHFORD SETS Manford up each morning with a cup of tea on the high stool in the old dairy, where she can keep an eye on him from the bakery by stepping into the hyphen, calling to him until he turns around slowly, his great smile taking over his whole face.

"Every morning! And always with a big smile! It's like he hasn't seen you for an age!" Mrs. Blatchford tells Vida in an undertone, when Vida stops in around midday later that same day on her way to the post office. She often stops in, just to check on Manford.

"I know," Vida says. "It's like that every time."

As if to demonstrate his happiness, Mrs. Blatchford leans over the counter and calls to him. "All right, Manford? Are you coming on?" He waves and smiles and goes back to his work.

"He's been no trouble at all," Mrs. Blatchford says, returning her attention to Vida. "Not in the least. Really—" She seems to want to say something grand now, something about how wonderful it is to have him there, something to make all of them—Vida, Manford, and herself—part of a fortunate group. "I can't think how we ever got on without him," she says at last. And Vida sees surprise suddenly flutter up into Mrs. Blatchford's face. She really does mean it, Vida discovers. She really can't imagine what it was like before Manford.

Vida thinks of how Manford sits there all morning, slowly filling the doughnuts with jam from the canvas bag, setting them out on their paper-covered trays. At eleven, when the sun arrives at the windowsill and lights up the cool, whitewashed walls in the dairy, the geraniums glowing in the window box, she knows that Mrs. Blatchford will come and fetch Manford for tea and a bite to eat. Mrs. Blatchford tells her that he holds her hand when she comes to lead him to the table, but only for a moment. He seems a little wary still, she says. He puts his hands over his face when she speaks to him if he's feeling too shy for conversation.

IN THE EVENINGS, during their supper, Vida has been working on his manners. She's ashamed that she hasn't spent more time on this—she believes that it pains him to be so awkward. But it isn't easy, and sometimes she thinks it's better just to let him eat in peace, without always nudging him about where his elbow is or leaning over to wipe his chin for him.

During their practice sessions, which she has begun since he started at Niven's—as he takes both lunch and his tea there now—she holds the cup to his lips, touches his mouth with her finger, speaks softly to him. His eyes watch her face. He tries.

"Gently, Manford," she says. "As though kissing a flower."

She spills a bit of tea into the saucer and he practices holding it, watching the tea lap the edge.

"Little bites," she says, passing him a triangle of toast spread with jam. He tries.

"Your napkin goes here," she says, spreading it on his lap where he pats it. She doesn't like it tied around his neck anymore. Makes him look the baby.

AT NIVEN'S THEY have elevenses and lunch and tea, and after each meal Manford goes back to the dairy to work. Now they have him icing the cakes as well. This he does surprisingly well, Mr. Niven says to Vida, the tiny garlands and miniature roses each set in their place, sometimes a fantastically shaped leaf or cluster of petals that the others come gradually to recognize as a likeness—a good likeness, in fact—of some native plant, nettle or cowslip.

Mr. Niven, who isn't usually one to appear surprised by much of anything, likes to stop his work and look over Manford's efforts from time to time. "It's quite remarkable," he tells Vida. "It's as if he's—memorized things. The way they look."

"He does have a talent for it, doesn't he?" Mrs. Blatchford agrees. She cocks her head and looks over a tray of cakes. "Though they're not what you would call traditional looking, are they?"

Mr. Niven frowns at a particular cake, iced with a tapestry of rampant, though lovely, green weeds. "Shall we have trouble selling it, do you think?"

"Well, we mustn't discourage him," Mrs. Blatchford says with conviction. "No one wants it, we'll just give it to the vicarage. They slice all their cakes aforehand."

THE IDEA OF the job at Niven's came to Vida so suddenly one day that she couldn't quite believe it hadn't ever occurred to her before. It wasn't that she hadn't wanted to see him feeling useful. One time, in fact, she'd explored the possibility of the Spastic Society's workshop, where people like Manford could have a job. She and Manford had gone on the bus one day into Winchester, and they'd had a look at the place.

The workshop was in an old garage, converted into a hall so brightly lit that Vida found herself squinting as she introduced herself to the woman who bustled over to greet them and introduced herself as *Matron,* of all things! As if Dickens or Trollope or someone might have invented her, Vida thought.

The employees—the clients, as Matron referred to them—some of them tied up in wheelchairs with twisted sheets so they wouldn't slump over, sat at long tables, nodding off over their work. As far as Vida was able to tell—Matron was Indian and had such a pronounced accent, full of wobbles, that Vida could hardly make out her trebled inflections—the employees were assembling luncheon trays for prison inmates. A plastic cup, plastic cutlery (no knife) wrapped in cellophane, and a paper serviette were put on each tray, and then the whole thing was sealed in more sticky cellophane by three young, overweight chaps stationed at the end of the table.

Occasionally clients would look up at Vida and Manford as they passed with Matron. Their expressions—desperate and defeated, as though their tongues had been cut out—had made Vida feel frantic with sympathy. On a table by the door, an urn for hot water sputtered steam; a collection of mossy mugs and tea things were arranged on a tray on an old desk under the one window, its glass still greased over with streaks of whitewash. A box with half a tired-looking cake in it sat nearby on a folding chair. Someone had rather inexpertly painted a rainbow and several disproportionately large flowers on the wall near a hand-lettered sign that read: WE WORK QUIETLY. WE KEEP OUR HANDS TO OURSELVES. WE NEVER, NEVER BITE OURSELVES OR ANYONE ELSE.

Manford had been positively ashen when they'd left, as if he'd been breathing in tiny, shallow breaths the whole while.

Riding home on the bus that afternoon, after a comfortingly large lunch in a cheerful, busy tearoom, Vida had held Manford's hand between her own and squeezed it often. He'd seemed subdued, and she had worried that she'd done the wrong thing by bringing him with her, though she didn't know who else she would have left him with.

That evening, Mr. Perry, who had been in London, had come home unexpectedly. Knocking at the door of his study that night, she had entered at the sound of his voice and stood before his desk, rigid with determination, to relate the events of the morning.

"And under no circumstances," she had said, finishing up, "will I remain in your employment any longer if you will be recommending that Manford attend such a facility."

Mr. Perry had looked up at her, surprised and faintly amused. "Why, Vida," he said. "I never said *I* was in favor of it."

She had stopped. "No," she said, hesitating. "No, I know you didn't. I'm just saying—it was *awful*. I just thought you should—know that."

"Well, thanks." Mr. Perry had smiled up at her. "Thanks for letting me know."

And after that, she'd put the matter of Manford's occupation out of her mind—until just this summer, passing the bakery with Manford, the thought of it suddenly came to her again. She had stopped and stared in through the window at the glass cases with the cakes and buns, the loaves of bread stacked like bricks. She'd heard the bell jangle, heard Mrs. Blatchford laugh. A customer, leaving, tipped his hat to Vida and Manford, looked over Manford the way people who don't know him do, taking a secretive second look as if they might have been mistaken about what they'd seen and were fearful of being rude. Manford looked back and then up at the sky, squinting. Vida patted his arm and then opened the door.

"Well, good morning to you, Vida," Mrs. Blatchford had said.

"Good morning, Mrs. Blatchford," Vida replied. Vida saw Manford look the buns over hungrily, though he'd just had egg-in-a-hole at home. He *is* a bottomless pit, Vida thought, always after something to eat.

She asked Mrs. Blatchford for a loaf of wheat bread and looked around with what she imagined to be casual interest. "It's a busy job you have here, Mrs. Blatchford," she said. "Do you still do all the baking yourself?"

"Oh, yes. Myself and Mr. Niven," Mrs. Blatchford said, sighing. "We can hardly keep up with it some days."

"You've enough help, though, I suppose?" Vida asked.

"Oh, we've never enough help. Can't keep them, you know. They're all off to London, the young nowadays. Don't want to stay in the village."

"Manford, here—he loves the bakery," Vida said then.

"Well, we'll have to give him something special then, today," Mrs. Blatchford said. "A jam doughnut in the bag for you, Manford." And she turned, a bit of tissue in her hand, to lift one from a tray, put it in the paper sack.

"Oh, Manford," Vida said. "Look at what Mrs. Blatchford's given you. Such a kind thing. A jam doughnut. You know," she went on after a moment, "Manford is a steady soul. Completely tireless, in fact. Not like myself. I'm getting on now, Mrs. Blatchford. I can hardly keep up with him anymore." She laughed a little.

"Oh, Vida. Now, how old are you?" Mrs. Blatchford looked her up and down. "What is it? Thirty-five? Thirty-six?"

"Oh, no! Forty-one, Mrs. Blatchford! I'm forty-one now!" Vida said. And then she brightened, deliberately. "But isn't it fortunate," she said, "our having this conversation this morning?" She waited a moment, allowing her gaze to travel over the place, its sweet smell of bread rising, the sugared buns, the iced cakes. "For I've been looking for a place of employment for Manford, Mrs. Blatchford. Something useful for him to do during the day. We all need to feel useful in the world."

"We do," Mrs. Blatchford said, standing still, staring at Manford.

"He could be most useful to you," Vida said.

"Could he," Mrs. Blatchford said slowly.

And it was done.

He started the next Monday. And once they saw that he could take care of himself all right, spend a penny on his own, come out buttoned up properly, not bother anyone, they took him in as if they'd been waiting for an opportunity like this all along. Vida could have told them this, if they'd asked, how he would make them feel happy.

But once he'd begun at Niven's, in that first week, when the days without him seemed so long and empty, she had time on her hands, time in great quantity.

During one of those empty mornings, she'd set about going through her mother's things. She'd been putting it off for a long time. It made her feel sad to look at the boxes; she missed her mother, whose last months had been painful and unhappy. Nursing her own mother, along with looking after Manford, had been a strain on her. While it was going on, she stopped by Dr. Faber's one day to have him look at a funny toenail of Manford's for her. But Dr. Faber had instead looked *her* over with studious concern, noting the tired shadows on her face. He'd wanted to give her something to help her relax, sleep better at night. But she'd worried about not being wholly alert—one might be needed at any moment, she'd pointed out to him—and so had declined.

She had, though, decided she could wait to go through her mother's things until she felt recovered. So three days into Manford's first week at Niven's, after doing as much housecleaning as she could contrive for herself, she carried the boxes with her mother's belongings from a spare room into the sitting room off the kitchen, where she and Manford spent most of their time.

And among the papers and mementos, she found her uncle Laurence's letters to the family from over the years.

Vida had been nineteen when Laurence left, just after the end of the war. Over time, he'd become in her mind a figure so improved in stature that she could scarcely feel her relation to him. She'd seen him only three or four times since his move to Corfu, most recently at her mother's funeral, but he had always written regularly, and he was good about remembering important occasions such as her birthday. Vida's parents, who'd run the small grocery in Hursley now managed by the Spooners, thought he'd felt guilty, abandoning them. He'd always been different, though, Vida remembered, wanting nothing more than to wander around the downs, painting pictures. One day he'd abruptly sold them his share in the grocery, and a week later he had left for Corfu, surprising them all. He was a bit mysterious about his life on Corfu, but he'd never asked for money, and his letters were always happy.

He'd written almost weekly in the first years he was gone, describing Corfu and his days there, how he spent them painting landscapes or arrangements on tables; he always employed the Greek words for what he saw: the bottles of *kokkino,* the spiny mauve heads of *anginares* and tempting shapes of *kolokithia,* the salads of dandelion leaves. Sometimes he sent a painting by parcel post, a dense little landscape carved out with a palette knife on a block of wood with canvas stretched across it. Once he'd sent a lovely figure of a young man, nude, bent over the rocks by the sea. Vida's mother had hung the paintings on the wall behind the counter at the grocery and would point them out to customers.

"Laurence is coming along splendidly over there in Greece," she'd say. "He's sent us another canvas. Isn't it grand?"

To Vida, who imagined Laurence's life in brilliant, cinematic detail, the presence of this relation in her life felt sometimes like its most important, most precious aspect.

VIDA IS IN the habit of saying to Manford every little thing that comes into her head, though he can't say a word in return. But she runs on, asking a question and answering it herself, amusing them both. She knows that people have a laugh at her, seeing her walking along with Manford, chattering away to him. The other day she saw deaf old Patrick Farley, sitting on the wall by the blacksmith's, point her out to Fergus. Patrick always spoke much louder than was necessary. "There they are," she heard him shout, ducking his head and spitting a caramel-colored wad into the street. "*Two* Daffy Ducks."

But Vida *likes* to talk, loves the whole *idea* of conversation—people pushing what she sees as a little boat of goodwill back and forth across a pond; she watches people in tearooms, at church, studying the way their mouths work, their expressions as they talk. So she talks to Manford, talks to the violent-tempered green budgerigar in his cage in the kitchen, talks to herself.

One evening, Vida read aloud to Manford a bit of one of Laurence's earliest aerogrammes, the paper fine as tissue between her fingers. Laurence's script was massive and gorgeous, the ascendant strokes like mountain peaks.

"This week I have been painting the olive orchards," she read to Manford, settling herself in her chair. "The trees are monumental, fifty feet tall some of them, and as old as five hundred years. The Greeks rig up white netting beneath them to catch the fruit when it falls and spare them the tedious job of picking. It looks like a shroud drifting among the trees, or a mist. It is very beautiful, and very green, here. Much like the countryside round Hampshire, in an odd way."

"Oh, think of it, Manford," Vida said, sinking back against the pillows of her chair, looking out the window into the darkening gardens at Southend House. Manford lay on the rug before her, pushing his toy lorries back and forth over the carpet, his head resting on his arm, his heels showing through the holes in his socks. "Old Uncle Laurence," Vida went on, "sitting at the base of Mount Pantokrator, watching the schools of dolphins, painting the olive orchards. Wouldn't you like to see that for yourself?"

She reached over and touched Manford's hair, smoothing it away from his forehead. He took her hand, pressed it to his cheek, and then turned it over in his own and with his finger traced its lines and creases. He brought her hand up close to his face and sniffed.

"What do you think, Manford?" she said, smiling down at him. "Shall we see the world one day after all?"

She looked up and saw herself reflected in the window glass. Her face, from the small distance across the room, seemed tiny and insignificant—like the head on an old coin, she thought, someone long gone and unrecoverable, rubbed away beneath the thumb. She stared at herself a moment longer, the tiny, white, frightened triangle of her own face glowing in the window across the room.

When Manford clambered to his feet and crossed the room to turn on the television, the image of her reflected face was swallowed instantly in a square of brilliant blue, a blue, she thought, as bright and miragelike as the waters of the Ionian Sea.

Three

Sometimes Norris feels as if he has been stopped up short by Cupid himself, stepping out from behind the corner of the pub and placing his small hand upon Norris's chest.

Steady now, Norris Anthony Lamb, Cupid says. I'm taking aim at your heart.

My old heart? Norris asks. After all this time? I've not the slightest idea how to do this, how to fall in love. I've come too late to this.

And the voice speaks to him again, saying, Norris, love is not ever wasted. Not even if it comes late in life. Especially if it comes late in life. Don't knock yourself down, Norris Lamb. You're as capable as the next man—more capable even, for waiting so long.

But whose is that voice, really? His own!

For after all, he has discovered he has a gift for it, a gift for being in love. He feels like a man who has at long last discovered his natural state. When he mounts the steps to the organ now on Sundays, when he takes his place before the pipes, he plays as never before.

"My dear *Norris,*" the vicar said to him after a recent service, stopping him on the walk, his balding head shining in the weak light. "That was truly—" Norris watched him appear to search for the word; actually, he'd probably found the music a trifle loud. "You were *inspired* this morning." The vicar put his hand to his heart. "You quite moved me. I am *surprised.*"

"Vicar," Norris said, "it's all due to the instrument. I am just—

an instrument of the instrument." How true, he thought, thinking of Vida, thinking of love.

"And faith is *indeed* the most marvelous instrument," the vicar replied, misunderstanding Norris completely but nevertheless pleased and moving away then with a nod toward the vicarage, where his lunch of salad and cream and potted shrimp awaited him.

NORRIS LIKES TO quote Honoré de Balzac on such matters, when he says that the new organ is "the grandest, the most daring, the most magnificent, of all instruments invented by human genius."

Norris believes that the organ procured for St. Alphage must be very nearly as perfect as anything can be. Norris quotes his "old friend Honoré" to anyone who'll listen, and indeed some are sorry to be in the post office at all these days, for Norris Lamb has turned into a babbling brook.

"As Honoré says, 'Surely it is in some sort a pedestal on which the soul poises for a flight forth into space, essaying on her course to draw picture after picture in an endless series'—oh, how does it go?" Norris has to consult his notebook here, the notebook in which he keeps memorable sayings. "Oh, yes, here it is—'to paint human life, to cross the Infinite that separates heaven from earth.'"

St. Alphage's organ committee, upon approaching Mr. Perry on one of his infrequent visits home, had been admitted to a sitting room at Southend House to explain its business. It had been thought that his career as a church architect would influence his contribution to the committee, though he was not a religious man, for he was rarely seen at church. And indeed it took him just a few moments to assess the nature of the committee's errand and to wave away, in a manner Norris saw as wonderfully American, all polite preliminaries. He took out his checkbook immediately.

"How much do you want?" he asked.

There was some hesitation at this point. The members of the committee were unprepared for such directness. But finally Dr. Faber, who as Hursley's physician occupies a rank of some stature in the village, spoke up and said, quite firmly, "We're told that Renatus Harris—no doubt you are familiar with his work, Mr. Perry?—will himself come to St. Alphage for sixteen thousand pounds."

Norris heard that Mr. Perry is said to have raised his eyebrows only fractionally at this point. "An instrument sui generis, I take it."

"Nothing less," averred Dr. Faber.

And that was all there was to it.

The organ at St. Alphage comprises four divisional organs, Norris likes to explain to anyone who will listen, one more than is generally appointed for a small church. The presence of the swell organ, however, in addition to the great, choir, and (of course) pedal organs, gives it an ability to occasionally outperform the choir on certain selections. (Norris has taken a wicked delight in this, especially when Lamartine Ramsey is the solo. Such a voice. Like a bombshell nearing its target.) In any case, the fourth makes it more of a concert organ than such a small church might be expected to need, but Norris believes Mr. Harris was right in persuading them of its virtue. With its splendid new organ, Hursley should be able to attract secular performers for the occasional weekend evening performance, and that would be a boon indeed. And, as Mr. Harris pointed out, it would have been a crime not to take advantage of the unique acoustical properties of St. Alphage.

And so Norris plays now as if he has his whole life to live over. That's it, isn't it? he thinks. It's made him a young man again, this love for Vida Stephen. No, better than young. Entirely reinvented, and with more sensibility this time. Staring at the glass in the mornings now as he passes the razor carefully over his cheeks, he trembles at the possibility of affront that rises in his breast, the boldness he feels stirring within him. Sometimes his hand shakes so dreadfully that he cuts himself, and he has to open the shades at the post office in the morning with bits of plaster stuck to his face to stanch the flow of blood.

"Sweet Jesus! What's happened to you, Lamb?" Fergus barked out the other morning, come in for his tobacco. "Had a quarrel with your razor?"

And Norris was self-conscious all morning after that, terrified lest Vida should drop in for something or other and see him that way, patched up like an old dog who's been in a fight.

So he looks himself in the eyes now of a morning and says aloud, "Steady on, Lamb. There's nothing to be frightened of. You can do it. Just pace yourself, my boy, and think it all through."

In the evenings now when he takes his walk, he tries to consider his campaign, how it should progress, what special thing he might contrive for her. He might leave flowers on the bench in the lane, he thinks. Or a box of chocolates on her pillow—if he could figure out how to get to her pillow. He wants to astonish her with how wonderful it is to be alive, to have her wake one morning and discover the world marvelously altered.

You've been awakened, Norris Lamb, he says to himself, after a long sleep, as it were, a sleep that might have, save for Providence's intervention, gone on forever.

This is it, he says. Carpe diem.

ONE AFTERNOON NORRIS takes a chance—he wouldn't wish to frighten her, have her think he's *lurking*—and peers out directly at Vida from behind the horse chestnut. He does admire her hair, her face, her profile. As she waits on the bench, he thinks, as he has so often, that she would make a lovely picture, just like this. *Woman Waits, Wearing Hat.*

In a moment Manford will appear from around the corner, his head with its untidy hair twisted into sticky cowlicks, his hands outstretched as if resting on the backs of great unseen lions who pace beside him. And when Manford sees Vida, he will begin to run, with his lumbering gait. She will rise, Norris knows, as she always does, take a step away from the bench, and prepare herself for his collision with her shirtfront, the embrace he delivers. She will stagger backward a moment, catch at her hat, smile, touch his face. And then, turning, they will clasp hands and carry on, back down the lane, back through the gates of Southend House, which will close slowly behind them.

And then Norris will step out from behind the horse chestnut, take up his blackthorn stick and tap it on the ground, peer up into the sky, eggshell white and fragile. This will be his only glimpse of her today, unless this evening, restless in his own house at night, he penetrates by means of a sweet stealth the garden at Southend House. There he might linger by the fountain. He might happen to see her hourglass form against a window.

SINCE IT ALL began, he has gone over in his mind a thousand times the instant of his transformation, the blinding instant in which Vida appeared—oh, not as a stranger, nor even as a neighbor whom he might meet from time to time and to whom he might raise his hand in greeting, taking note, meanwhile, in a desultory way, of some slight change in her appearance, some gradual change in her fashion or manner that suddenly makes itself apparent.

Certainly he has known her for a long time, his entire life—or her entire life, at least, as he's fifteen years ahead of her at least, he thinks. And there was, he is now certain, no warning, not even the merest suggestion, of their linked fates in all the years they have lived nearly side by side in Hursley.

Norris has tried to remember being a child, tried to see how far back he can go and still find her there. He remembers her as one in a string of girls in their straw boaters and blue plaid jumpers, each holding a jar containing a water hyacinth, the long, pallid roots waving in the water, the flowers cresting the top of the glass. The girls were on their way back to the classroom from a science walk, Norris knew, in which they had traversed Hursley's streets to the banks of the Tyre. He imagined each girl wading into the water through the tangled cress, socks and sandals removed, dresses carefully tucked inside knickers.

But which was Vida? Which among the pairs of girls was she? And why is Norris, on an errand for his mother—sent home from the post office, perhaps, to fetch their luncheon—so struck, suddenly, by this procession of solemn acolytes, the girls passing before him, the water hyacinths sloshing in their jars, Miss Newman at their head with her great, bound bust and brave forehead?

He is sure that he is right—Vida is the last of the lot, walking alone, their total being an odd number. She does not look up as they pass Norris, but he is struck by her profound attention to her task, her certainty that should one little drop of water spill she will be devastated. And he thinks it odd that no one has ever explained to her that the trick to carrying a full glass of water is never once to look at it.

Now she is alone, the last of the girls ahead of her having disappeared around the corner. Vida stops, squats upon the pavement. And then, as if some long buried, feral instinct has just returned to her, she plucks the flower from the glass and takes it carefully, root first, within her own moist and watery mouth, the blossom protruding from between her lips. This accomplished, she raises the glass again and with her free hand covers the top of it like a lid. And then she begins to run, to catch up with the others, and is gone in an instant.

He thinks now, considering this memory, what an artful and womanly solution that was. How generous. How clever. How, he now sees, like a woman.

But what did he think at the time? For he merely continued on his way, home to his family's cottage, where his grandmother had prepared their luncheon, moving blindly about the small kitchen, diverted by this task from her customary place before the organ. He said not a word to her about this strange moment he had witnessed, a girl crouching in the road and taking a flower into her mouth.

THIS BEING IN love—it's all very well, he thinks, but what about the technical difficulties? For instance, there's the challenge (he won't use the word *problem*) of how to make his feelings known. He doesn't want to do something dull, such as engage her in friendly conversation or ask her to dinner. No! This sort of love, he tells himself—like Antony's for Cleopatra, or Troilus's for Criseyde, or Romeo's for Juliet—requires something very grand. Something imaginative.

Such as—what?

Sometimes, after Vida and Manford have disappeared into the gates at Southend House, Norris paces up and down the lane, his hands behind his back, his blackthorn stick trailing behind him, and tries to think.

Skywriting? Could he hire some bloke with a little plane to write a message of some kind in the sky over Southend? He read in the paper once about someone who did that. But what if she didn't happen to be looking up at just the right moment? And what exactly would such a message say?

Could he sing under her window? Well, he has a passable tenor, but frankly the notion embarrasses him.

Could he ring at the door and, when she opened it, give her a box with a ring in it?

No.

He paces up and down, shaking his head. All these sorts of approaches seem too bold, too declarative, too insistent—too unlike him, he realizes sadly. And it's been days now, days and days, since he found himself falling so precipitously in love. Days, and he's yet to do a single thing except spy on her.

He sits down at last on the bench, puts his chin in his hand. The light of late afternoon closes in gently around him. He looks up, squints a little, attending to the light music in the leaves overhead, the squirrels, the sparrows.

There should be someone to help, it seems to him, and he feels suddenly aggrieved at the loneliness of his position. Why is there no one to help him? Why is there no one to consult? Why didn't his father tell him about such things? All those years, when his father might have helped him, he said nothing at all. There was just that once, when his mother had that scare with the lump in her breast. Norris had been—what? Sixteen? Seventeen? He tries to remember. He and his father had sat in the hospital waiting room together. Terry Lamb had looked at his hands, turning them over and over before him, his nails bitten to the quick.

"Norrie," he'd said at last, but so quietly that Norris could barely hear him. "Don't think," he said, "don't think that though you see me so sick at heart here now, today, that it hasn't all been worth it. Your mum . . ." And then he'd stopped, and his face had taken on a surprised expression, as if the feeling that pressed up out of his heart at that moment was transforming him into a different man. "Why don't . . ." He tried to go on, but he never did finish, and Norris, who had been terrified by the circumstance of his mother's illness, had hoped in a way that he wouldn't. It was all too much, too important to speak of.

But now—he jumps up from the bench in sudden frustration, begins to pace again. Oh, why is it all so difficult? Because his feelings—why, they're so simple, clear as day.

I love you, he wants to say to her.

Marry me, he wants to say.

He wants to jump out from behind his horse chestnut tree one day, drop to his knees before her. I'd do anything for you, he'd say. Anything to make you happy.

Oh, say yes, he thinks, stopping his pacing and staring at the bench now as though she might materialize there before him. And then, experimentally, he closes his eyes. After a moment he sinks slowly and painfully to one knee, puts out his hand to take her imagined fingers, cool and weightless as a breeze, between his own. Kneeling there, the stones of the lane beneath his kneecaps, he smiles at her astonishment.

Ah, Vida, he whispers, and leans forward.

There is a sharp report, and Norris lurches forward, his eyes flying open. He prods with his stick, scrambles to his feet, whirls around, breathing hard.

But there is nobody there.

High above, a raven flaps off heavily through the wood. The bird's hunched, miserable shape reminds Norris for one terrible moment of his father, going down the path to the end of the garden with a spade under one arm and the body of the Lambs' old fox terrier wrapped in a blanket under the other. Norris hadn't wanted to go with his father to bury the dog; he had been afraid of the stiff little body, found under the kitchen sink that morning. He had stood inside at the window, watching his father work the spade into the dark earth beneath the hawthorn tree, his father's back rounded as an old man's, a light rain beginning.

How horribly easy it is, he thinks now, breathing hard, watching the light retreat down the lane, to go from good to bad, from the dream to the memory, from what we want to all we've ever had.

Four

Vida feels dismay that Southend House has been let go so over the years, the gardens and the house both. When she started with Mr. Perry so long ago, Southend House was the pride of the village. The lawns were smooth, the orchards bore fruit, the stables and greenhouses were in perfect repair. A corporation, Standard Oil, she thinks it was, had bought the property, and for several years maintained the estate in absentia for visiting executives, continuing to host the annual Guy Fawkes Day celebration and other village events on the generous striped lawns. Vida remembers her spring dancing pageants held there, remembers the effigies of Guy Fawkes falling year after year into the bonfires, remembers sausages and potatoes hot from the coals.

Then, in 1949, Mr. Perry was hired as part of the international team planning a restoration of Winchester cathedral, and Vida's life changed overnight.

Thomas Perry had been a junior member of an American firm specializing in sacred architectures when he attracted the attention of the firm's principal partners. They'd admired his interpretation of the vernacular elements in an addition to a nineteenth-century monastery in the Hudson River valley. (Vida has seen his drawings for this monastery, a set of solemnly beautiful watercolors, and thinks them lovely, like the illustrations of a sorcerer's castle in a children's picture book.) Mr. Perry's mentors, sympathetic to the tragic circumstances of his wife's sudden death in childbirth earlier that year, had thought to distract him from his grief with the assignment in Winchester. He had leaped at the opportunity. "I always was a secret Anglophile," he told Vida later.

Leaving Manford, then just three months old, in the care of a nurse, he had come immediately to England, bought Southend House, and in a matter of days hired a full staff to run the place.

At the post office on one of his whirlwind mornings through the village, he had asked Norris Lamb about local girls who might help with his baby son. Norris had been completely unhelpful, but Vida's mother had been in the post office that morning and had volunteered her daughter to the handsome young American. That afternoon, in the huge, empty kitchen at Southend House, in an interview so brief and strangely elliptical that Vida walked around for days afterward feeling as though she might have been mistaken about the whole matter, she was hired as Manford's nanny.

One overcast morning two months later, Mr. Perry arrived at the port in Southampton with his personal effects and his infant son. His sister had made the passage with them and had been seasick the entire voyage, and she'd handed Manford over to Vida almost as soon as they alighted from the car in front of Southend. "Thank God you're here," she'd said. "I need a bath."

Vida, dressed carefully for the occasion in a white blouse and serge skirt, had been waiting nervously in the front hall for the sound of the approaching car. At Mr. Perry's instructions, she had seen that the furniture shipped three weeks before was in place. That afternoon, she carried Manford to his new nursery, changed his nappy, and laid him down to rest in the Perrys' heirloom cradle with its intricately turned spindles. Manford turned his heavy head gently from side to side, quietly restless. After a moment, regarding him solemnly, Vida took him in her arms again and carried him to the window. She held him up to see the view, and he blinked his eyes against the light, turning his face aside to nuzzle into her neck. As she held the warm, sweet weight of him against her, she contemplated the things that were his—the silver brush and comb engraved with his initials, the beautiful gardens below, the splendid house, the handsome father. And yet no mother, she thought, looking down at Manford in her arms. Rich as a lord, this baby, but yet so poor.

"Come see," she whispered. And she held him then to face the mirrored glass of the wardrobe doors. "I'm Vida," she said to his sleepy face. "We say it this way: Vee-da. You must just sing right out whenever you need me."

Later, when they were certain he would never speak, she remembered with hot shame having given him that particular instruction. For Manford would never sing out—never sing, nor shout, nor even whisper.

VIDA KEPT A photograph of Manford's mother in a silver frame on the dresser in Manford's room. Eleanor Perry had been blond and lovely, and as the years went by, Vida could see that Manford's good looks came from his mother as much as from his father. But sometimes, in the beginning, looking at herself in the mirror, she thought she saw a likeness between her and the grave and silent child now under her charge and pretended he was her own. It was easy enough to do, really, with no *real* mother to confront her. She would hold Manford's pudgy hands to the looking glass next to hers, where they left a moist and ghostly imprint. "Now you see it, now you don't," she said, and was rewarded one day by Manford's first smile.

Sometimes Vida turned around to catch sight of Thomas Perry standing silently in the door of the nursery, watching them. She would duck her head shyly—he was *so* handsome, his hair black as a crow's back, his nose so straight, his eyes so blue. But he always turned away after a moment. Before long he had begun to travel. Soon he was hardly ever at home.

For the first few years, Southend House was maintained in perfect repair. Mr. Perry kept a horse in the stable and, for Manford, though he was too young to ride him, a shaggy Shetland pony (of whom Vida was secretly afraid). Water flowed in the fountains. The roses bloomed with magical profusion, their intricate, blameless faces opening wide and then falling away silently, petal by petal, onto the emerald grass.

On her way to work in the mornings, when she still lived in her mother and father's house, Vida would come up through the wood. At the big horse chestnut tree on the lane, she would stop and take her compact from her purse, powder her nose, and ready herself, gazing up at the house. She considered herself a fortunate girl to have found work at Southend House. So many of her friends had left for London, for dull jobs as secretaries or clerks. But Vida loved the known confines of the village, and she was deeply attached to her mother. She enjoyed wandering the house with Manford, imagining herself lady of the manor. And her affection for Manford grew each day as the child, though he never uttered a sound, came to know her, welcome her, his eyes changing expression as she came into view before him, smiling and repeating his name—Manford Arthur Perry, Manford Arthur Perry—waiting for him to one day say the words back to her. From time to time she thought of Manford's mother and how different it might have been if Mrs. Perry had lived, how different her own life would have been. She was ashamed, sometimes, to realize that there would have been no place for her in Manford's world, or the world of Southend House, had Manford's mother survived; the knowledge of her own good fortune coming at such a high cost to another made her feel fierce and hopeless, all at once. She felt indebted to a ghost and under constant surveillance.

Once Manford's condition was known, Mr. Perry appeared to have more and more opportunities to leave home, and Vida noticed that some necessary repairs to the house and grounds began to be postponed, that two of the three gardeners were let go, that the horse and pony were, quietly one weekend, sold and taken away. Mr. Perry traveled widely. Sometimes he intimated that he had work abroad. Sometimes, Vida suspected, he traveled simply for pleasure or to forget about his son. And Southend House began to unravel, as if ghostly hands were pulling loose one thread at a time.

Standing at the window of her bedroom, Vida saw the lawns below ravaged by the tunneling paths of moles, saw the trees tangled with their own broken limbs. She wondered what it would take to bring Mr. Perry home again.

IN THE BEGINNING it had been so lovely. She would take Manford out in his pram to the lawns and stroll him back and forth by the stone pool, the fountain's music lulling him to sleep, the birds tossing water from their wings.

How soon had they realized that something was not right with Manford? It was slow, a slow dawning. He didn't speak, of course; even his crying was soundless, though there was no mistaking misery or pain from the look on his face. He'd wind his hands above his head, turning and turning them as if they were strange birds hovering above, twisting in a channel of air. But sweet, he was, Vida remembers—his heavy head falling to your shoulder, his eyes looking off into the distance, never a moment of nastiness, not in his whole life.

Manford was diagnosed as retarded, a mute, and permanently handicapped with some generalized motor impairments as well. One morning at church, shortly after news of this diagnosis had had sufficient time to spread round the village, Vida found herself saying hotly, in response to the vicar's wife's innocent inquiry about their health, that Manford was *perfectly lovely,* thank you. In fact, she went on hysterically, he was a kind of saint-child, really. He'd never been disobedient or unpleasant even for a moment. There wasn't another child in the whole village as sweet as Manford, in the whole of *England* probably. . . . She'd gone on and on and then burst into tears and had to be led away to the washroom in the vicarage to comb her hair and collect herself. The women exchanged looks of pity among themselves as the vicar's wife walked Vida down the garden path, her hand on her back.

"She's too attached, poor thing," they said. "Too attached. And he's not even her *own*."

VIDA REMEMBERS THE evening they first spoke of it, she and Mr. Perry. It had become her habit to stay awhile after Manford had fallen asleep, tidying up the kitchen and checking to see if there was anything Mr. Perry wanted before she left for the evening. She had put the bell in Manford's crib, looked to see that he could reach it if he was distressed. Vida slept in a cot in Manford's room when she stayed overnight, as she was terrified of his needing her but not being able to wake her in the usual fashion of children—by calling for her or crying. But when she slept at her own home, she had to content herself with the presence of the bell, which would jangle if Manford woke thrashing from a nightmare or pulled himself to stand at the bars of the crib. On those occasions, Mr. Perry would see to his boy himself. But more than once, while staying the night at Southend, Vida had woken with a start in an utterly silent room to see Manford sitting up in his crib, his big head soaked in nightmare sweat, his mouth open in an O of terror, tears running down his face. As the years went on, she slept at home less and less and gradually moved in to her own room at Southend House. This arrangement, though she and Mr. Perry never spoke of it formally, seemed to suit everyone best.

Manford was still an infant, however, the particular evening she paused in the door of the library, on her way home to her parents' house. "Will you be needing anything before I go, Mr. Perry?" she said to his back, for he was bent at the long table under the windows where he drew, the sound of tracing paper rustling beneath his hands.

He turned. "Thanks, no," he said. "You've been very kind."

"It's my pleasure, Mr. Perry," she said, and it was, though she didn't know if he would believe that.

He smiled at her. "Come in," he said, and then bent over his drawing again for a moment, adding something to the paper. She had stolen a look or two at his work from time to time while tidying the rooms. His drawings were marvelous things, the blue pencil lines so fine, views of Winchester Cathedral swelling up from the page in surprising feats of perspective, as though you were suspended midair up in the nave itself, she thought, each detail on the page looking as though it were composed of fine hairs. It always perplexed her, looking at those drawings, that he made the cathedral—such a vast and heavy place, she thought, built of enormous stone upon stone—appear so light, as if of spun sugar. At Christmas, when she went alone for the midnight service to hear the choir, she would raise her eyes and see Mr. Perry's lines in the vaulting roof, the empty space there scored by the invisible shapes of his geometry.

That evening he stared at his drawing a moment longer and then, without looking up at her, he said, "How would you like to go to London next week, Vida? For a trip."

"London?" Vida found herself looking vaguely around the room, as if someone might step forward from the shadows with a suitcase for her.

Mr. Perry continued to stare down at his drawing. He frowned and put his finger on the paper, stroking the surface lightly. "You've noticed, Vida, I'm sure," he said then, "that Manford's not—not like other children." He paused. "You remember Dr. Bernstein, the gentleman who stayed with us last month? My American friend?"

Vida had felt her pulse begin to race, as though she were being drawn blindfolded to what she sensed was the edge of a cliff. "Dr. Bernstein," she said faintly. "Very kind."

"Ted's a good friend," Mr. Perry said, and Vida thought wildly that perhaps that would be it, that the conversation had ended, disaster had been averted. But after a moment he went on. "I asked him here for a particular reason, Vida. I wanted him to see Manford." He stopped, searching for the words. "He believes—Dr. Bernstein believes—that Manford is—damaged. That there was some brain damage, probably at birth, when we lost Manford's mother. Manford is—" And here Mr. Perry wiped his hand over his eyes as if to clear away something that had fallen there. "He doesn't believe Manford will ever be like you or me, Vida," he said, and Vida heard the terrible fatigue in his voice, a sound that sent a cold breath over her skin.

"No," she said, very low. Because of course she had noticed. You couldn't help noticing.

And so they took him to London.

• • •

DR. FABER, HURSLEY'S local doctor as was his father before him, met them there.

"Thanks for making the trip, Faber," Mr. Perry said, jumping up from a chair in the London doctor's hospital office to shake Dr. Faber's hand when he came in on a breath of gritty fresh air. Vida was happy to see Dr. Faber herself. His long red sideburns and funny old jacket were familiar, reminding her with a rush of relief of home. The hospital was huge—the biggest building she'd ever been in except for the cathedral, and she jumped every time one of the lift doors opened or someone passed by with a patient on a gurney.

The morning of their appointment, they were shown into an office with red leather armchairs and a heavy desk. Vida held Manford tightly on her lap. He was heavy already, the size of most four-year-olds, though he was only two. And still in a nappy, Vida thought regretfully, for just at that moment she wanted Manford to show himself to his absolutely best advantage.

"Happy to oblige, Thomas," Dr. Faber said cheerfully, perching himself on the edge of the desk. "Change of pace from the country." He winked at Vida. "Enjoying your taste of the cosmopolitan life, Vida? Don't know as you've ever been to London before, have you?"

But she wasn't enjoying it, she wanted to tell him, dear Dr. Faber, who'd taken care of her ever since she'd been a thin little girl in a camisole. She couldn't concentrate on London, she was so worried about Manford. Mr. Perry hadn't been particular about what would happen, and she hadn't liked to ask, thinking that perhaps she was expected to know already. The night before, they had stayed in a hotel, she and Manford in one room with a crib set up specially for him, and Mr. Perry in the adjoining. She'd drawn a bath that night after seeing Manford to sleep and had marveled at the size of the tub, a huge thing you could sit in up to your neck. But it had made Vida feel as if she were drowning.

It seemed foolish to her later, but at the time she thought they might actually physically examine Manford's brain—cut open his poor head and reach in and touch his brain somehow, wiggle it under their thumbs, see what it did, see if they could make it jump. She'd felt sure they would hurt him. Thinking back on it, she realized that Mr. Perry must have been as nervous as she was. He probably hadn't known what would happen, either, and even capable people like Mr. Perry, she thought, could become hopeless and childlike around hospitals.

The worst point was when they met Dr. Tallent, the doctor who was to look Manford over. He'd stepped into his office that morning, surprising them while they were sitting there with Dr. Faber. Vida noticed unhappily that he gave her an odd once-over.

"Mr. and Mrs. Perry," Dr. Tallent said, sticking out his hand, and Mr. Perry turned horribly red in the face.

"No, no. This is Manford's *nanny,* Archie," Dr. Faber said comfortably, standing up. "Vida Stephen, Archie Tallent."

"Oh, quite," Dr. Tallent said, turning away from Vida after a moment to face Mr. Perry. "Sorry about that. Yes, I recall now, your wife, the circumstances—condolences, sir."

Dr. Faber and Dr. Tallent and Mr. Perry began to talk, but Vida sat still as a statue, her ears ringing, unable to concentrate on what they were saying. Manford rested quietly on her lap, sucking on his bottle.

"Right, then," Dr. Tallent said after a few minutes, standing up. "Let's see what we've got, shall we?" And he turned to Vida.

She stood up quickly, hoisting Manford along with her, still holding his bottle. Dr. Tallent stared at her and then, as if deciding something, came around from behind his desk and, smiling at a spot just past Vida's ear, reached over to chuck Manford on the chin with a finger. He came closer, bent over to look into Manford's face. Manford followed him with his eyes. Vida's knuckles grew white. Dr. Tallent lifted up one of Manford's eyelids with an antiseptic-smelling thumb, exposing Manford's eyeball. Manford rolled his eye. Dr. Tallent frowned.

"Right," he said again, standing upright.

Vida gave a long exhalation of relief. So that was it. She'd been silly to—

"Someone'll be in to fetch him," Dr. Tallent said then. And the tails of his white coat forked and vanished.

The walls around her seemed to bulge. Vida looked over at Dr. Faber, stunned. Was she that stupid? To think that was all—Dr. Tallent looking at Manford's *eyeball?*

Dr. Faber came across the room to her and put his hand on her shoulder. "They won't hurt him, Vida," he said kindly. "They're only going to have a look at his head, through an X ray, and do some tests. I'll be right there with him. We'll bring him straight back." He waited, smiling kindly. "Come on," he said then, and held out his hands.

But when Vida failed to move, staring up at Dr. Faber's face with a look so anguished that later he told her that he'd never felt like quite such a sod in his whole life, he had to reach and take Manford from her, hoisting him into one arm and bending to retrieve the dropped bottle. Vida felt Manford's body leave her. She put her hands up over her face.

But when she heard Dr. Faber open the door, she took her hands away and looked. Manford was gazing back at her with a look of puzzlement, and Vida felt herself leaning toward him.

Now, Manford, she thought. Now. Make a sound. Protest. Show them you can. Do it now.

And she'd wanted that for him then, as fiercely as she'd ever wanted anything. Though it had hardly yet begun, she had wanted it all to stop right then, all the prodding and the poking and the speculation and the misunderstanding and the confusion and the terror. After that visit to London, she would never again leave his side at the doctor's—though it was mostly Dr. Faber who saw him after that, and then just for colds and flus and the usual sorts of things. For there was nothing to be done about any of it, he explained to her later. He worried some about the stiffness in Manford's hips, the spasticity, he called it, but Manford had learned to walk all right, though awkwardly—with his hands held out in that funny way, for balance. "After this," Dr. Faber told Vida, "it's just a question of us all understanding each other."

But the doctors in London determined that Manford was indeed retarded, his brain injured in a permanent and significant way. Damaged is what they called it, Vida thought in disgust, as if Manford wasn't twice over—even as a baby—a better person than all of them put together. Over the next few weeks, as her fury over the London trip abated, her anger became localized within her, something hard and immovable. Some lively part of Manford's brain—an important part, Dr. Faber explained—lay hushed in silence, gray like moss. She'd put her hands to Manford's head, felt all over the slight lumps and bumps of it, the way she imagined the moon might feel in your hands. She'd wondered if she could feel with her fingers the places where the brain had died, as if there might be a special coolness there, like the cold, black caverns of the moon.

And sometimes she wonders if something *didn't* happen to him that day in the hospital in London when they took him away.

Dr. Faber had brought him back at last to where they had been told to sit in the waiting room. There'd been a fish tank there, and Vida had watched it the whole while he'd been gone, mad red fish circling round and round, following one another. Or not following, she reconsidered with a shock; chasing. Manford had been sound asleep against Dr. Faber's shoulder.

"Wore him out a bit, I think," Dr. Faber said, settling him in Vida's arms apologetically, and she'd thought Dr. Faber smelled strongly then, of sweat. He smiled at her, though. "He's quite all right, Vida. Just needs a sleep, I should think."

Manford had slept for ages that afternoon in the hotel. They missed their train while he slept, for Vida wouldn't wake him. Mr. Perry would stop in the room, and she'd put her finger to her lips and shake her head severely. Now, remembering it, she thinks it's funny that he took her word for what should be done. What on earth did *she* know?

When Manford woke at last, he'd opened his eyes and looked at her, and she thought for one, long, terrible moment then that he would turn his head away, that he would know she had deserted him. But he smiled at her, and she lifted him in her arms and thought there wasn't anything so worthy of gratitude as forgiveness. And she wouldn't ever let it happen again; the next time, she would go and stand by him.

But there never was a next time. That was it.

Five

NORRIS IS A postmaster, but he does not read other people's letters.

He reads picture postcards from time to time but feels he can say with confidence that so does every other postmaster. The regrettable truth, he's had to admit to himself, is that most picture postcards are very dull. But in any case, usually he doesn't have time to read everybody else's dreary mail, anyway, and in addition, people's handwriting is as a rule so poor that it would be impossible to make out much of them.

It's sort of a joke within the profession.

Moreover it is one thing, it seems to him, to glance casually over a postcard as one sorts the letters of the day, and another to hold an envelope to the light or secretly steam it apart in a back room. The one could be characterized as entirely innocent, the desultory—even unavoidable—perusal of life's traffic as it passes your doorstep. The other, it seems to him, reflects a certain deviance of character.

He reads postcards, when he does, less out of curiosity than habit, you might say.

He does take note of correspondence, though it's not something he does deliberately. He can't seem to help it. His mind has a propensity for keeping tallies. He knows exactly how many times Mrs. Billy has written her daughter gone to Australia. He knows how many times the daughter has written back. They are not equal, he can assure you.

He counts things, it seems, by instinct. Standing alone in the post office, watching the rain streak the window, thinking of Vida, he counts his heartbeats. The bricks beneath his feet as he walks between the post office and St. Alphage number 1,472. The number of panes in the windows in Dr. Faber's surgery—forty-eight. The number of dewdrops on the chandelier in the dining room at the vicarage—eighty-eight crystal tears exactly. He counts washing on the line, eggs in the fridge, horse chestnuts on the ground. Sometimes he finds it a distracting habit, almost an affliction. He has been asked a question and for a moment found himself literally unable to answer—as if his jaw were wired shut—while he helplessly counts away inside his head.

So he does not read other people's letters.

He has not been tempted, and he likes to think he would certainly resist such temptation, were it ever to come before him.

NORRIS HAS NOTICED that Vida very rarely receives what might be considered a personal letter, unless you count things from her uncle Laurence. Occasionally she'll have an aerogramme from her old friend Charlotte Patrick, now living in Switzerland. Vida always writes back very promptly. There was quite a lot of to-and-fro around the time of her father's death, and then later her mother's, from solicitors and so forth. Otherwise, nothing.

But along with his fervent belief in the privacy of the mails, Norris also believes that postmasters should refrain from inquiring *about* a person's letters. It would be impudent, he thinks, upon weighing a parcel or affixing a stamp, to stop up short and make some comment or another: "Writing about a Vietnamese bride this time, I see, Mr. MacKenzie? No luck with the Indonesians?" Or "Pursuing a new remedy for the hemorrhoids, Mrs. Larkin? Sea kelp from that Irish outfit stopped you up, did it? I've heard it can do that." These are things Norris knows he *could* say—any idiot can read addresses, after all, and come to his own sensible conclusions about another person's business.

So he knows he could say them. But he wouldn't.

It would amount, he believes, to a terrible invasion of privacy, a violation of trust. He simply takes his customers' parcels and letters—he *receives* them, as it were—and allows no expression to cross his face. Whatsoever. This is as it should be. People have great faith in the mail service, sending off their most intimate inquiries, their most passionate requests, via the hands of perfect strangers. After all, when you think how far the mail service has progressed—from dak runners, letters held high in a forked stick, a second rider bearing a burning log to ward off wild animals; or brave young men, strong and hairless, slipping into shark-infested waters to bear a letter to the shores of Cephalonia; or the dim islanders who sealed their mail in inflated sheep's bladders and floated them off hopefully on a boat of driftwood—when you think of all that, the mail service is really the most wonderful example of cooperation among peoples. Norris likes to imagine all the postmasters engaged in moving letters from one waiting hand to the next as not unlike a team of skilled surgeons—brave, astute, tender. Men of heart. The mails represent a marvelous system of common trust, he feels, a belief in government at its best. And it is so hard these days, he thinks with sorrow, to find something worth believing in.

Norris keeps his postal scales highly polished, and he employs a new rubber thumb frequently so as to avoid smudges. He believes people are entitled to cleanliness in their post office, a sense of perfect order, nothing that might suggest carelessness, or the possibility that someone's words might be mislaid in a slovenly environment, or that one letter might be more important than another. They are all important. And as a special courtesy, he uses his familiarity with the postal services of the world to acquire stamps for those who are interested. Manford has been a particularly devoted collector, though it is only recently, of course, that Norris has tried especially hard to please.

He has a long-running correspondence with gentlemen in post offices throughout the world, gentlemen who regularly send specimen stamps his way. They write to one another about the weather and natural disasters, occasionally about politics—so much more interesting elsewhere than in England. Sometimes he thinks of those men—bearded men in white turbans working in high, tiled rooms, ceiling fans rotating slowly above their heads, or Russians in thick coats, dragging mail sacks over mosaic floors. He has never seen such places, but he can imagine them. Mr. Nesser in Cairo has been one especially loyal correspondent over the years. Egypt produces the most marvelous stamps, often oversize, with the images appearing burned to the paper. Mr. Nesser is kind enough to send, free of charge, many of Egypt's commemorative stamps and always a sheet of the new permanent issue. Egypt puts out a new permanent issue practically every year. Living in Great Britain, where the authorities satisfy themselves with a new stamp only every other decade or so, Norris appreciates this. It is his country's stodgy habit of clinging to the past, awash in old concerns or still heroically marking the same old jubilees, that prevents it from enjoying a more varied family of stamps, a more heterogeneous community. Arnold Machin's sculpture of the queen in profile has been staring past citizens for aeons, it seems, and will, Norris supposes, until she dies. Oh, there have been some very nice butterflies and so forth. But stamps from the Channel Islands have been, in general, much more imaginative, no doubt thanks to the colorful influence of local habit and custom. Norris has a favorite, a lovely one from Jersey, of Mont Orgueil Castle in Gorey, in which the castle itself, its reflection streaming in the water below, appears lit from within by a phosphorescent vapor. And the French, of course, with their superior sense of style, have recently introduced those stunning stamps depicting French art, miniature Mirós or Matisses. England has no such artists, he fears. Just people in the habit of draping old buildings in London with cellophane or burlap, or constructing giant boxes with an icon of the queen buried up to her neck in Styrofoam. Why they do this, he cannot imagine. Such things do not translate to a stamp face. Perhaps they do not translate at all.

Egypt, though. Now there's a country so comfortable with—indeed, so rightfully proud of, Norris considers admiringly—the long and rich taproot of its history that it has mastered magnificently the habit of aging, adding to its lifeline a million leaves on the branches of the family tree. Old Egypt glories in itself, he thinks, not England, with its upsetting history of colonialism. It never did seem quite right to Norris, the British being so utterly British no matter where they were. One ought to adapt, he believes. One ought to accommodate. Change, after all, is the great elixir of life. He himself has often thought that he should like to adopt, for instance, some new manner of dress—Mr. Nesser's white pantaloons, perhaps, and flowing top garment.

"Lamb! Greetings!" Mr. Nesser's notes begin, and then affixed to them will be sheets of stamps of the most remarkable pigment, as though colored with that country's burning sun, or the slow-moving, silted waters of the Nile, or juice from the betel nut, the color of a live heart, colors as ancient as if they had been discovered dried to a powder in a king's tomb and then revived with a drop of twentieth-century spittle. Mr. Nesser's English is marvelously ornate. Colonial English, Norris supposes. He tends to refer to himself as "we."

"We send you warmest personal felicitations on your anniversary," he wrote at the start of Norris's thirtieth year in the post office. "May we continue to bind the world together, letter by letter by letter!"

And Norris liked that, the notion of each holding the globe together by the variously swift or plodding habits of the letter carrier. He thinks of letters in the bellies of airplanes, in baskets on the backs of donkeys, in satchels tied to bicycles, in one man's proffered hand. How eternally hopeful they seem to him, the letter carriers of the world.

He likes to imagine the thin, dapper men murmuring behind the fabulous and ornate grilles of post offices in Venice or Rome, their heels soundless upon crimson carpets, letters weightless in their fingertips, fading frescoes overhead. Now *that's* a fitting environment for the glorious career of postmaster, he thinks.

He likes all that. What he hates is to be the bearer of bad news.

Norris himself was surprised, when he first began at the post office, at how many people actually read their mail *in the post office itself.* They rip open envelopes or aerogrammes right in front of him, their eyes rushing back and forth across the lines, searching and searching. And then they smile or sigh or laugh out loud. And sometimes they look up at him and *actually read him a bit of their letter!* And then they make a comment about it, saying, "Well, I never. He says he's to have a new hip." Or "Oh, Sylvia's left Roger again. Could've predicted it. Oh, *splendid.* Now he'll be coming to stay." As if you had any idea what they were talking about, Norris thinks; as if you *knew.* It's as if, he realizes, he is somehow included in this correspondence, like a loyal friend standing by—eternally generous, eternally kind, eternally hopeful on his patrons' behalf.

He can always tell if it's bad news. People look up from their letters and stare at him a moment, as if they can't recollect quite who he is. And in their eyes is the dull bruise of disappointment or grief, the burden of unbearable news. Norris's own mother spent the whole of the war weeping, her own grief over her husband's fatal accident compounded by the death notices she had to deliver, the women's fainting to the floor, the men's falling onto her ample breast, the stricken children's grasping the banister. Telegram service was very spotty in Hursley during the war. They couldn't spare individual carriers, and they trusted Rosemary Lamb. Norris remembers her peddling off on her bicycle all hours of the day or night, the telegram pinned to her postal service blouse, tears streaming down her face.

And the recipients of sad letters? Well, people will have nothing, after that, Norris knows, except the one last letter, which they will slip into a drawer and withdraw from time to time. Sometimes, in their first moments of shock, as they reel with the insupportable consequences of it all, their eyes leave the page and find his face, lingering there as if he might correct them or reassure them. And then at last they glance down again at the paper, and after a minute they fold up the sheets again very quietly, very carefully. "Well," they say, very softly. Or "I see now." And then, worst of all to Norris, they look up at him again, and do you know what most of them say?

They say, "Thank you, Mr. Lamb." As if to offer him comfort! As if to show that they do not blame him! As if to reassure him that they will be all right.

He hates that.

• • •

IS HE OBSESSED? He is obsessive by temperament, perhaps, and therefore inclined, late in life, to one grand obsession, one in which all his ardor, all his vague and disturbing impatience, all his abbreviated thoughts, might be caught up in a single explosive shell, an athlete's last perfect reflex. A bomb.

How did it happen, this falling in love with Vida Stephen? Norris Anthony Lamb is not a man inclined to abrupt deviations, sudden and persuasive desires, clearly defined lusts. And yet now he feels himself transformed by love, forged in steel by this wondrous passion.

Norris has not been exactly content over the years. His life has been almost continually interrupted by the exhausting and time-consuming business of dying and all its observances—first his grandfather, then his father during the war, then his aged grandmother, and at last his own mother. The years between these passings have been spent anticipating the next one, as though the business of living were only a sort of insignificant prelude to death, a series of years spent in sparsely furnished and harshly lit waiting rooms where one passes the time as if it were completely without consequence. The women in his life were in the habit of making resigned and repeated reference to what little time remained left to them. "When I'm gone," they would say, and Norris heard the disguised petulance, even anger, in their voices. "Why, then you'll be able to get on with things, Norrie. Won't be long now."

He feels, in some way, that they were making excuses for him, excuses that neatly served their own purposes. How could he find a wife, produce progeny, how could he carry on, when those closest to him were marking their own time in such minute and interminable quantities? He excused his grandmother's morbidity as the lingering sorrow over her husband's and then her son's death. His mother's grief he saw as a result of the peculiarity of her wartime duties, a few years condensed into a lifetime of delivering death notices. As a consequence he too came to believe that furnishing his own life with the normal attributes of hope—such as a family—was, in some ways, entirely pointless.

And yet he has been restless, given to fantasies that seem to have no toehold in reality, faceless women or the women of his stamps stepping forth and disrobing for him, a sultan weighing his wives for an evening's diversion. His fantasies have been peopled by the women of history—Joan of Arc, Carry Nation, Eleanor Roosevelt—unlikely figures all, but women, nonetheless, who are familiar to him, their faces in his stamps like dear friends, tolerant and loyal.

His restlessness, for never being assuaged by gratification, has been inclined to manifest itself as a state of unnatural torpor. He might spend an hour in his chair in his darkened sitting room, watching the last light of the day squeeze into a single purple column between his drapes, a book unopened at his fingertips. He appears nearly asleep, but his mind at those moments is in a state of anticipation so acute that he could swear, were you to rouse him suddenly by shaking his arm with your hand, that something was just about to happen, had just been about to happen. What? He could not say. Something.

Also, he is a walker, a perambulator, banging out his back door through the damp pantry at odd hours of the evening, setting out over the fields with his stick. He walks in haste with his head forward, his eyes to the ground. Many in the village are familiar with his distant form, his coat flapping behind him, eclipsing a hillside or disappearing down a lane.

He is a haunter of ruined places. He investigates ruined cottages, the sky visible in shards through disintegrating thatch, a bit of cutlery or pottery unearthed by Norris's blackthorn stick, rubbed free of soil with his fingers, and pocketed. He has stood inside such places, erect and alert, listening, the sound of raining seed drifting from the roof, his tread soundless on the damp earth, the infinitesimal progress of earwigs resuming their interrupted path at his feet.

He has lain down in the wood, his eyes open. And when he leaves, there is a declivity in the tall weeds, as though an animal had curled there, matting the grass into the shape of its body.

He has found the bomb shelter deep in the wood beyond Southend House, in a clearing devoid of trees, a place so strange and frightening that village children (who also know of its whereabouts) avoid it. Or else terrify themselves by threatening to tie one unfortunate member of their unruly band to a nearby stump and leave him there. Norris has stood atop the shelter's heavy earthen roof and imagined a gunner crouched below, a man who does not know the war is over, the world changed, less reckless now. A soldier, he thinks, who has been living off the stores of tins, oiling his rifle, muttering in the dark, growing pale, the color of moonlight or mushrooms.

Norris stamps his foot on the sod, listens.

He has come across the occasional misdeed—a poacher on the prowl, who, waiting for censure and receiving none, shares a cigarette with him as they sit down on a stile, a rabbit limp and warm within the bag. Norris does not inquire about the man's business, does not appear surprised to encounter another solitary traveler.

"Lovely evening," he says.

He has, standing in the lane with its high blackthorn walls, been surprised by someone's husband, tying up his trousers, sprinting from the back door of someone's wife's kitchen. Or a woman in her blouse, rinsing her face in the trough at the door, soaping under her arms before she retires for the night, weeping all the while.

He takes in all such sights without judgment, as if his own mind were too occupied with another, more pressing problem to consider the implications of what he sees. Nothing may shake loose the formula in his head, the arranging and rearranging patterns of it.

So what can it be that awakens him so suddenly in his fifty-fifth year, that accosts him so roughly and yet with such unbearable sweetness, that travels a finger up his bony leg and touches the cleft and root of his manhood, awakening it at last?

Vida.

It is Vida.

He doesn't know how even to begin.

Six

So THEY KNEW after the trip to London that Manford would never be right. Arrested in his development, Mr. Perry said. Perhaps he would grow to have the mind of a five-year-old, but not likely more. Nor would he likely ever speak. He'd always be clumsy, childlike. Occasionally, they were told, he might exhibit some more mature talent, but it would be without significance—not indicative of anything. More like a stray bit of intelligence, random and unconnected, cropping up out of the fog of his mind. There would be nothing to attach itself to, though; no order.

"Like a lily in a patch of weeds, Vida," Dr. Faber said, trying to explain it to her. "A daylily. Lasts just a day, no more, and then it's gone."

In the beginning she didn't quite believe it. She thought they were wrong, for she could see that in some ways he was intelligent, lively in his mind, crawling round patiently after an ant on the terrace, letting it walk up on his finger. He was learning something there, down at eye level with the ground. She knew he was. And he was always so gentle with things, even when he was a baby. She imagined he would, slowly, over time, defy all their predictions, grow up into a man—maybe even a doctor himself, she thought wildly, like Dr. Faber.

And he *has* grown up, in his way, she acknowledges, though not ever as she'd hoped, of course. She has to say that now.

She used to read to him, page after page, Shakespeare and the Bible and Henry James and Chekhov, books she found in Mr. Perry's library. And from the back, as he stands on the terrace looking out over the ruined gardens at Southend House, Manford looks grown enough, fully developed, broad shoulders and straight back. But when he turns, you see the belly slack like an old man's, the wandering face, the untidy hair. And it gives you a start, Vida knows.

Still, there are things that do excite him. Flowers, for example, the scented variety in particular. Any sweet scent, for that matter. She remembers buttoning his shirt collar one day when he was a boy. He caught at her hand, raised it to his face, breathed in deeply. She was wearing on her wrists the scent Mr. Perry had given her for Christmas—Joy. She wears it every day now, has for years. She likes the way it makes her feel, a bit sophisticated. She knows it costs a lot of money.

Manford held her wrist the way a small child holds a bear to himself, hugging it. He dipped his nose to her hand, turned it over between his own, round and round as if he couldn't fully catch the scent. She thought to put a dab of it on his own wrists and ran up to her room to fetch the bottle. But later she regretted it, as he kept his hands crossed up against his face all day, his eyes closed, breathing it in. Now she just wears it herself, lets him hold her arm if he likes. They sit like that sometimes, Manford holding her arm, looking at the gardens, just sitting and looking.

Sometimes, though, she would try to rouse Manford. She was just bored or impatient. She was young when she started with him, of course, and she can remember wanting to run, wanting to set up a clatter in the halls. On weekend nights, when she'd go to the pub with a friend, she'd be amazed at the commotion of it all, after the quiet of Southend House—the punching laughter in the warm room, the bristled darts flying toward the target hung on the wall, someone's arm around her waist, teasing, tugging.

But she hated the way people spoke of Mr. Perry and Manford sometimes, the way they poked fun at him.

"Feed me, Nanny Stephen," said a big, ugly lad named Simon one night, leaning heavily on her arm, showing her his open mouth, flooding her with his beery breath. "Feed me, Vida, like you do your idiot."

She stepped back, revolted. And before she knew what she was doing, she slapped him hard across the face.

For a second he looked shocked, put his hand to his mouth. "Temper, temper," he said then, softly, meanly, and turned away.

"He didn't mean anything by it, Vida," her friend Charlotte said, turning around on her stool as Vida gathered her things to leave. "Come on. Don't be in a huff."

But she couldn't stay there in the pub then, not after that. Walking home alone to her parents' house, she thought of Manford asleep in his bed, the moonlight falling into his room, his heavy head, his curled hands.

SHE'D HOPED HE could learn to catch a ball, and she played with him outside by the fountain. She'd work her arms around—"Watch my fantastic windup, Manford!" she'd call, in an American accent—and toss the ball at him. But unless it sailed right up into his face, he wouldn't catch it. He couldn't seem to follow it unless it was right in front of him. She would climb up on the fountain's edge, play that she was going to fall in. "Help! Help!" she'd cry, to make him laugh.

And Manford would stand there and laugh, that choked and silent laugh, bent over with his hands planted on his thighs like an old man. The joke never seemed to get old for him, the funny idea of her falling in and getting all wet.

To help improve his balance, his coordination, she would play the phonograph for him—"Try a mazurka, or a rondo," Dr. Faber suggested thoughtfully, when she explained her idea to him. "Anything with a strong rhythm. And let me know how you progress. I'd be interested."

She started by trying to teach him to clap his hands, kneeling before him, bringing his palms together.

"Come on, Manford," she'd say, staring at his face, trying to communicate what she meant with her enthusiasm, her smile, her eyebrows lifted high. But he couldn't seem to catch the rhythm, couldn't seem to catch on, watching her with a worried look, as she brought his hands together over and over again.

The night she tried to teach him to dance, he was nearly grown, eighteen or nineteen, with a heaviness to his limbs that came of overeating. She felt guilty about his size; but she hated to deny him anything, and he'd point to the cake tin so pathetically. She'd give him a despairing look. "Oh, only a little piece," she'd say, laughing when he tried to hug her. "Think of your belly!"

She tried only once to teach him to dance; even today she doesn't like to recall the occasion.

That night, Mr. Perry had been out to dinner in London; he'd said not to expect him until late. The house had felt especially big and quiet to Vida, one whole wing of it unused, unfurnished, the chandeliers hooded with sheets. Vida had laid a fire in the library, where Mr. Perry kept his phonograph. Though she and Manford usually occupied the sitting room off the kitchen, she felt it was a shame to have the whole lovely house going to waste, and Manford liked to watch the reflection of his face in the globes of the brass andirons in the library's fireplace, his features there stretching like elastic as he veered in and out before them.

That night she drew aside the drapes for the view out onto the terrace, the row of moonlit statues there, their faces the color of quicksilver.

Manford sat with his stamp books while she cleaned up their supper things. But when she joined him by the fire, she found she couldn't keep still. It seemed to her that something was happening out there in the world—something. Dawn was breaking over Corfu, where her uncle Laurence lay asleep in his white house at the edge of the surf. Fishermen were wading out into the sea, breaking the surface of the water, stars fading overhead.

They were missing it, she thought suddenly, desperate. She and Manford. They were missing it all.

She tried to read but kept looking up from the page, unnerved, as if something were about to happen—as if the door might blow open or a handful of stones clatter against the window.

At last she stood up and put a record on the phonograph, some of Mr. Perry's American jazz—Benny Goodman. A friend had sent Mr. Perry the record. "Strut, Miss Lizzie." That was the song she liked.

She swayed back and forth on the carpet before the windows, looking out into the dark garden.

When she turned around, she saw that Manford was watching her.

She smiled at him, lifted her arms, took a turn with an imaginary partner around the furniture, around the chair he was sitting in, so that he had to swivel his head to keep her in view.

"I'm dancing, Manford," she called to him as she sailed away to the far side of the room. "This is how it's done."

And then she came back and stood before him, hopping up and down, smiling. "Come on," she said, breathing hard now, holding out her hands, happy. "Come on up and have a dance with us."

But he shook his head, put his face down on his forearm.

She leaned down, caught his hands in her own, pulled him up.

He stood woodenly before her, his face serious, and allowed her to hold his hands. She tried to swing them back and forth, smiling and nodding at him. "That's it," she said, as his arms began to loosen up, as she felt him begin to take up the rhythm.

She began to feel excited; perhaps this *was* what he'd needed, she thought—to learn to dance! And then he mightn't be so clumsy; he wouldn't fall so much. It was always shocking to see him fall, a grown man falling down like a child, like a little boy. She hated it, hated watching him pick himself up.

"Well done, Manford!" she said warmly. "That's it!"

Manford had grown into a big man. That night she felt for the first time how big he had become. He wasn't a boy anymore. Six feet two, and nearly fourteen stone. He swung his hands harder and harder, concentrating, his mouth open, his big head bobbing up and down. He began to stamp his feet.

"Well done," she said, gently now, quieter. "Lovely dancing, Manford."

And then she began to resist him a little, to try to calm him, slow him down. He was, she realized, so much stronger than she.

"Manford," she said at last, breathless. "You're hurting my hands."

She stopped dancing and stood still, tried to stand still.

She held fast to his hands to stop him from swinging. She pulled on his arms, but he only looked at her with a kind of desperation, stamping more wildly now, opening his mouth wider, as if he were being pulled apart somehow, as if there were a feeling inside of him that couldn't get out, something he wanted to be rid of, wanted expelled from his body.

She shook her head at him, frowned, tried again to wrest her hands away.

"No," she said. "That's enough now," she said.

And then, when he failed to stop, she had to speak sharply to him and heard, unmistakably, the little flicker of fear in her voice.

"No, Manford!" she said.

And then again, louder, "No! Manford!" she cried. "No! Stop it now."

And then finally she broke one hand free.

He was frightened, terrified, she saw, as his face came up close to hers. He'd seen that she wanted to get away from him, that she was angry, fearful, and so he tried to hug her to him—she understood it even as it was happening, with a kind of slow-moving clairvoyance. He was trying to prevent her from leaving him, trying to climb into her arms like a baby.

The weight of him as he jumped against her, still bobbing wildly up and down, was enough to knock her over.

She fell, striking her head against the claw foot of the table.

Manford dropped to his knees and crawled away fast across the rug, scurrying like a rabbit. She saw him trying to fit himself into the knee space beneath his father's desk, but he was too big. Only his head and shoulders were hidden.

Vida sat up, reeling, and touched her head. A little smear of blood, shockingly bright, came away on her hand. "Manford," she managed, to the twinkling air before her eyes. "It's all right."

Her head hurt terribly, and she felt sick to her stomach. "It's all right," she said. "Come out. Come on." She looked around for him, her vision clearing. There he was, still under the desk. "Manford," she said again. "Come on." But he wouldn't move, wouldn't turn round and look at her.

She got carefully to her feet, walked unsteadily across the room to where his backside protruded from beneath the desk. She could see how he shook. She knelt down, put her hand on his back, crooning his name. He flinched away from her. "It's all right," she said. "It was my fault. Come on out now."

She saw him contract his shoulders, as if trying to fit more of himself inside the well space of the desk. She sat down heavily beside him, put her head in her hands. The last notes of the record fell away. All over the world, she thought, things were passing from view, never to be seen again. Shooting stars. Ships disappearing over the horizon.

She reached over and put her hand on his back, began to rub gently between his shoulder blades.

"I'm sorry," she said. "I'm so sorry. It was all my fault."

THE VERY MORNING she writes her thank-you letter to her uncle Laurence for the painting for her birthday, she decides, as she's walking down the road after leaving Manford at Niven's, that she will pick up a cellophane envelope of stamps for Manford for his collection. Mr. Lamb has been very helpful about this in the past, and Vida has encouraged the hobby. It seems so normal. Manford has several bound volumes of stamps, from all over the world. He pastes them in place very neatly and can sit for hours turning the pages, looking at the tiny pictures.

She enters the post office that morning, the bell jingling overhead. Mr. Lamb is nowhere in sight.

"Hallo? Mr. Lamb?" she calls out.

He appears a moment later, bursting through the black curtain hung before the door to the rooms in back like a musketeer drawing his sword, making her jump.

"Oh! Good morning!" she says. He looks possessed, she

thinks, glancing away from him awkwardly. She hands him her letter to post. He takes it and sets it down on the countertop. He puts his hands to his hair and smooths it back nervously.

"I thought I'd see if you have any stamps for Manford," she says after a minute, looking away again. Mr. Lamb has been so odd lately, she thinks, so—disorganized. Perhaps he's going senile!

"Of course, of course," he says very heartily. He stares at her a moment longer and then bends over to shuffle madly through the drawers under his countertop. At last he stands up and extends toward her a sheet of eight stamps, all sailing vessels. He is red in the face.

Vida glances at him, dismayed. "Oh," she says, "he already has these."

But she is unprepared for the violence of Mr. Lamb's apology. He looks undone. "Oh! Has he? I'd forgotten, I'm so sorry, I—" He rushes over his words.

Vida stands there, frowning at him. He's been *so* queer lately, she thinks.

"I've written my friend at the Hellenic Post Office in Athens," he goes on desperately, "but I'm afraid they've misunderstood. This is all they would send." He holds his hands up helplessly.

Vida looks down at the stamps and then back at Mr. Lamb. His eyes are watering. She notices that he has a bit of sticking plaster on his chin and finds herself distracted by this. "Well, I *am* sorry," she says at last, finally dragging her eyes away from his chin. "It isn't your fault, Mr. Lamb." She closes her purse; suddenly she wants to be on her way.

But Mr. Lamb has disappeared from view. He has bent over and is rummaging beneath his counter again. Vida can hear his heavy breathing.

"I have these," he says, popping up suddenly and startling her. "From the Commonwealth of Dominica?"

He spreads the stamps before her on the counter. His hands are shaking slightly. She is dismayed by this.

She inspects the stamps. They feature American cartoon characters. Minnie. Huey, Dewey, and Louie. Goofy. They are all playing musical instruments.

"Will these do?" Mr. Lamb asks, wiping his forehead with his handkerchief. He puts a finger on one. "They're very bright." He touches his mouth with the handkerchief. "I thought, as they were very bright, he might—"

"Yes, well, thank you, Mr. Lamb." Vida finds herself strangely breathless, too, as though she has been breathing for Mr. Lamb as well as for herself. She's feels almost light-headed, in fact, and fumbles for her handbag to pay Mr. Lamb for the stamps.

"Shall I post this for you?"

She looks up.

Mr. Lamb is holding her aerogramme aloft. "Writing to your uncle Laurence?" he says.

But it doesn't sound like a question, she thinks. More like a comment about the weather. Poor *thing,* she thinks hopelessly. And then, surprised, she thinks, poor *us!* Poor us, to be standing here like this!

"Yes. To Laurence," she says unnecessarily. "You're very kind," she says quickly then, desperate but wishing to be kind herself. And she turns to go.

"And how is he? Painting coming on?"

Vida pauses, turns back again to face Mr. Lamb. His eyes are full of a strange pleading.

"Very nicely," she says weakly. "Nice of you to remember, Mr. Lamb." She looks around her vaguely, as though the post office is somewhere she's never been before. "He'd be pleased you remembered his painting."

"Oh, yes!" Mr. Lamb says emphatically, giving her a brilliant smile then. "Oh, yes. Marvelous painter, Laurence was. Is." He opens his mouth but nothing more comes out.

Vida tries to manage another little smile, as friendly as she can make it, but her face feels stiff, as if she's been cold. When Mr. Lamb says nothing more, she turns again to leave. He has fallen silent, staring down at his feet, apparently lost in thought. Then he lifts his head, looks out the window of the post office. "Ah! There goes the double-decker," he says brightly. He takes a deep breath. "Do you ever," he says, as she turns back to him again, confused about whether he is speaking to her or just to himself, "do you ever think about just hopping on a bus? Going someplace? Wherever it might take you?"

Vida looks at him. "That bus always goes into Winchester," she says at last.

"Yes." Mr. Lamb looks worried. "But some other bus, perhaps?"

"Perhaps." She smiles. He's *funny,* Mr. Lamb; what a notion! Jumping on a bus when you don't know where it will go! A vague relief, like the sun coming out, comes over her. She actually feels warmer.

"Seems as though we'll have fine weather for our Sadie Hawkins Day," he goes on. He looks calmer now, she sees. He's smiling, too. And he's stopped perspiring quite so much.

Vida pauses. "Oh, yes," she says. "I'd forgotten."

"Such good fun, Sadie Hawkins Day."

Vida doesn't know how to reply to this, exactly. She doesn't really like Hursley's Sadie Hawkins Day. It's an embarrassing business, she thinks, girls chasing after the boys, a custom imported to Hursley by an American woman who was briefly headmistress at Prince's Mead.

"The women having *their* go at things, for once." Mr. Lamb raises his eyebrows, smiling and leaning over the counter. He winks at her and then backs up, looking vaguely appalled at himself. He collects himself. "So you *will*—you *will* be going?"

"Well, I hadn't thought of it." Nearly everyone in the village *did* go, she considers. If the weather was fine, it could be a jolly enough afternoon, a chance for Manford to be out and about. "I might take Manford round," she concedes finally.

"Oh, *fine* idea," Mr. Lamb says enthusiastically. "He'll *enjoy* that. All those girls racing round."

Vida gives him a tight smile. Honestly, she thinks, what *do* they understand about Manford? Absolutely nothing!

But Mr. Lamb doesn't appear to notice. "I was quite a sprinter in my day, you know," he says.

Vida looks him over. It is true that he's quite tall, she thinks in surprise. And long legged as well. And she has a sudden memory then, as if it were a photograph held up before her eyes, of races day at Prince's Mead. She was young then, just twelve or so, and assigned late in the day, after her own events, to the spoon races for the younger set. Norris, she remembers, was one of the older ones, ten or more years ahead of her, most of them already done with school and working in the village or at nearby farms or in Winchester. But they all came back home for the games that day, the schoolgirls swooning over the older chaps, who were sporting soft new beards. She is surprised to find herself remembering Norris, tall and spindly in cricket whites, doing the pole vault, his limbs spread against the blue sky. She had looked up that afternoon from a gaggle of children at her knees to see Norris close by. "Well done, Lamb," she'd heard someone say, but Norris had brushed past, his long, narrow face flushed. He'd turned an ankle or something, hadn't he? She thinks she remembers him sitting down alone on a bench, nursing his foot, rolling back his sock, and probing tentatively at his shin, a worried look on his face. She had watched him, had noticed his white leg extending like a root, like something peeled, from within his trouser leg. After a while he'd stood up and hobbled away. Someone had veered into him, clapped him on the back, but she'd seen him wince, make fluttering gestures with his hands, say something inaudible.

"I remember—" She pauses and looks up to find Mr. Lamb surprisingly near, as though he has veered up into close focus. "You had an accident," she says vaguely. "You—" She stops.

"An accident?" Mr. Lamb looks alarmed. "I don't recall—"

"Yes." Vida pauses. "I remember you—up there. In the sky. Doing the pole vault."

Suddenly Mr. Lamb looks thrilled. "Yes, yes!" he cries. "The pole vault. I remember!" He spreads his arms up high. "Like this!" He throws his arms wide, a gesture of tossing something overboard.

Vida smiles at him. "Only, you fell. You hurt your ankle or something."

The excitement leaves Norris's face, replaced by something else. "It's so—remarkable," he says, looking at her, quieting, "that you should remember that."

"Yes," she says slowly. "Isn't it?"

There is a silence between them. They are both surprised to find themselves staring at each other.

"We've known one another such a long time," he says then, strangely tender, and as Vida looks at him, she suffers a surprising rush of feeling for them as young people again. She herself had been shy, but with passionate, speechless crushes on the boys around her. She'd been too young for real affairs, and by the time she was old enough, well, there was Manford. But she remembers watching the older boys and girls, wishing she were older, as well—old enough. Had she ever had feelings for Norris?

The notion surprises her and she finds herself staring at him. No, she thinks. Not a crush. And yet there had been a kind of curious recognition she'd felt for him as she'd watched him sitting on the bench that afternoon, nursing his ankle. At the end of that day, she'd stood by herself under the spreading arms of the cedars at the edge of the school grounds, watching couples disappearing arm in arm into the shade of evening, the boys in their whites stained green at the seat and on the knees, the girls changed hurriedly from their gymnasts' uniforms into spring skirts and blouses. Beneath her foot she had pushed at the fallen needles, a blanket of spongy turf, and had wondered how they would feel against her bare back, the relief of a boy's unnatural weight spread over her.

She starts from her reverie to see Mr. Lamb before her still. She feels, as she stands there, that he is witnessing that moment again with her. That she can travel back into her own life and he will be there, too, standing to the side, watching. They had missed each other then though, hadn't they, the fragile young man on the bench, wounded in some insignificant way, and she in the speechless torment of those adolescent years, her hair wild and coming unloosed, her expression pained. She looks up at him.

"I seem to remember—so many things," she says, feeling faintly stunned, as though she'd been hit over the head and were just coming round.

"Yes. Yes, I do as well," he says urgently. "So many—moments."

"Of course, we're still here. So we would. I mean, there are so many reminders." Vida glances around vaguely.

"Yes." Mr. Lamb looks down at his blotter. "I remember—how very pretty you were." He speaks so quietly that Vida feels the words brush against her ear. She looks up at him. She feels her grasp tighten round her purse.

"You had this—hair. It's such a lovely color." He gestures round his head in circles, as though wrapping a turban. "And you were so—" He glances away. "You always seemed so *inspired*."

The room has gone suddenly very bright. Vida feels she might need to close her eyes but manages to keep them open.

"I think your hair now—the way you've done it—" He points a trembling finger in her direction. "It's very—attractive."

She meets his eyes, reaches up her hand, touches her hair gently.

"You're happy—here in the village?" His voice is low, as if inviting a confidence.

"It's what I know," she says at last, dazed as a bird that has collided with a windowpane, its own reflection.

"That is how I feel," he says, letting out a long breath. "All of it."

They both jump as the bell above the door clatters. Fergus comes in on a draft of animal odor. Horse fear, Vida senses, recoiling.

"Yes?" Mr. Lamb straightens up, glares at Fergus impatiently.

"Box of matches," Fergus says shortly.

And Vida takes the opportunity then, with relief, to back away from the counter.

"Thank you," she calls. "For the stamps."

Mr. Lamb tosses a box of matches at Fergus. "I'll write them again!" he calls after her. "I'll tell them they must send some other stamps! A commemorative issue! The liberation perhaps?"

She waves, nods, passing quickly away down the pavement.

He waits a moment, placing both his hands flat on the counter's varnished surface, and closes his eyes. When he opens them, Fergus is emptying his pipe into his cupped palm, looking shrewdly at Norris.

"Well? Don't be making a nasty mess on my floor," Norris says.

"Ah, no." Fergus laughs. Then he jerks his head after Vida. "Done herself up lately," he says.

Norris stares him down. "Will there be anything else?" he inquires coldly.

"Not at all. Not a thing," Fergus says blithely. "Must be getting back. To *work*." He opens the door to leave. "Haven't got a cushy spot like you, Lamb. I've no time for chatting up the ladies. Good morning."

Well, he's done it. He's spoken to her. He'd thought he'd open with something better, but in the end, perhaps this was just right.

He is so excited. Almost too excited, he thinks. It can't be good for him, such excitement. But, oh, she remembers him! From their childhood! This must be significant.

He wants to do *something* now, anything, but he can't even think straight. He hops around the post office like a child unable to contain himself.

And then he catches sight of Mrs. Billy passing down the pavement outside. She has stopped and is staring in the post office window at him, bobbing up and down on the tiled floor of the post office. Well of *course* she thinks he's gone bonkers! He stops jumping and stands perfectly still, frozen in position; perhaps she'll think she imagined it.

Still, he doesn't really mind. And at the end of the day, when he goes home, Norris jogs round and round in the rooms of his house. Finally, just as evening begins to fall, he runs out his door, down the lane, past the pub, and along the Romsey Road to St. Alphage.

He passes the vicar, sitting on a moss-covered bench in the graveyard reading a letter, and gives him a wave.

Once inside, he takes his place at the organ and plays the "Triumphal March" from *Aida,* over and over again. It's one of the first pieces he committed to memory.

The vicar will wonder, he knows, what he is doing there, bent over the organ as if weeping on a Wednesday evening. But perhaps he will just be grateful, Norris thinks fiercely. Grateful for love. Grateful for everything. Grateful for anything at all.

Seven

NORRIS HAS SEEN nude women. He saw his mother in her white drawers and his grandmother in her narrow gray woolens. Before they had indoor plumbing, it was his job to fill the bath Saturday evenings, to carry the kettle back and forth. "Mind the heater, Norris," his mother would say from the tub, where she crouched, folded in upon herself like an old white mattress. "Don't slip now with the kettle."

He has seen, despite himself, the disturbing photographs in the magazine to which Mr. Blevins subscribes.

"Have a look, Lamb," Blevins said one day with a leer, leaning over Norris's clean counter and spreading the pages wide. "Look at those titties!"

"My!" Norris said. And they certainly were large.

"And look at this," Blevins said, showing Norris another picture, most distressing, of a young woman bound by the hands and feet to a tree.

"What will they think of next, Mr. Blevins," Norris said. "My, my."

People frequently show him things from their periodicals, Mrs. Billy with her *Afghan Bee,* Nigel Spooner with his motorbike journal. They flip through the pages as they stand there, commenting on this or that. He affects an interest, to be polite.

So he is not entirely naive about women, despite his lack of practical experience. But until that night in the garden at Southend House, he had never seen anything quite so beautiful as

Vida. It's not often that one sees something like that, something that must, in the end, be interpreted as a sign.

But who had turned on the fountain again?

MR. PERRY HAD turned on the fountain—or, more correctly, he'd seen to it that the fountain was turned on. He had returned to Southend House in June after a long absence. His first morning home, he'd gone round to have a chat with Dr. Faber, who had prescribed sleeping tablets for him some months before. Perry's spirits were better than usual, Dr. Faber thought—he spoke of doing some entertaining, issuing an invitation, perhaps, to a young Italian woman with whom, he intimated, he'd had a pleasant dalliance in Rome. Perhaps he'd even reunite some of his oldest friends from the States for a holiday, he said—a hunting holiday.

"I'd like to see the house and grounds as they were in the beginning," Mr. Perry told Dr. Faber, suddenly serious. And something about his face at that moment made Dr. Faber recall his first glimpse of Thomas Perry, some twenty years before. He'd thought then that no one so young should have cause to look so eaten away by grief already. "I'd like to see it all as it used to be," Mr. Perry went on, "when the place looked like paradise." He smiled, rather sadly, Dr. Faber thought. "When I thought it would soothe me to be somewhere so beautiful."

A week or so later, Mr. Perry hired a gardener, a young man named Jeremy Martin. He offered him an exorbitant wage and told him simply, "Clean it up. Clean it all up. There's an apartment above the stables. I think it's all right. Let me know if you need anything. Vida will cook for you."

• • •

JEREMY MARTIN UNDERSTOOD that Mr. Perry did not want to be consulted much, after a first look-round. He did not want to be bothered.

They toured the property together one Saturday in late June, before business called Mr. Perry abroad again. Jeremy explained that he would need a fortnight to let go his previous commitment, asked various questions about original drawings for the garden, water pipes and conduits, glass for the greenhouse, sprays for the orchards, and so forth. He appeared knowledgeable. He asked, too, about an account with Lauder and Lauder, a nearby nursery.

Mr. Perry waved his hand. "Whatever," he said shortly. "Whatever it takes."

Jeremy pursed his lips but felt he would not react to this largesse. "Priorities, sir?" he asked.

Frowning at the tennis courts, which were choked with weeds, Mr. Perry seemed to be considering. Then he looked up toward the big house, the heavy, silent shape of the fountains. "I'd like the fountains turned on again," he said impulsively. "I don't know what's the matter with them. Something with the plumbing, I guess. Rust? Do that first."

"Might be moles in the pipes," Jeremy said, his feet planted. "Or tree roots. Terra-cotta, I imagine they are. Could be prohibitive, sir."

"Whatever it takes," Mr. Perry repeated stubbornly.

That evening he mentioned briefly to Vida that he had hired someone to do something about the gardens.

"What?" But she didn't mean to sound so surprised.

"To fix them up," he said, a little defensive, and looked away from her. "I've been meaning . . ." He put his hand over his eyes, that gesture Vida recognized so well. "You won't mind feeding him, will you?" he asked.

Vida, turning to stare out the window at the littered lawns, the overgrown and crumbling balustrades, the blackened roses, said, "Of course not. How lovely."

FOR YEARS, LONG before discovering himself in love with Vida, Norris had walked through the grounds of Southend House from time to time for his nightly walk, drawn to the overgrown gardens there and the circus antics of bats that swerved sharply like tiny, dark kites against the fading sky. He'd been dismayed to see the property deteriorate over the years, understanding that he knew nothing of the reasons, but that there could be a hundred explanations for allowing something so beautiful to fall apart. He'd stolen a plant or two, taken it home in a leather sack, and planted it in his own garden. He did not consider this theft, exactly, but more a form of mercy.

And then, the night of his fifty-fifth birthday, that evening of the moon landing, Norris set out again. The air was soft, ambient; he sniffed—something fragrant was in bloom. The moon hung overhead, buoyant as a breath. He'd looked up, trying to imagine what it must be like to be up there so high, looking down at the earth. The sky had deepened from blue to rose to the silver gray of twilight to the lush velvet black of midnight. Norris felt peaceful, benevolent, charmed by the knowledge of the astronauts treading the moon so far above his head. It felt companionable, in a way, knowing they were out there, too.

He walked through the village, down the Romsey Road, and into the fields, crossing onto the estate of Southend from the low pasture. He hadn't been by there in a few weeks, having discovered some swans on the Tyre and, being fond of swans, deciding to walk down to the river every night instead. But the swans had flown off the previous evening, and so this night—still full of the miracle taking place so high above his head—he passed into the woods around Southend and through the pavilions of oaks. He passed the tennis courts, thick with Queen Anne's lace and nettles, the rose garden with its crumbling walls. He registered methodically the estate's familiar disrepair, statuary tumbled from their pedestals, gardens overgrown with weeds.

But parting the yews that surrounded the highest lawn at Southend, he stepped onto the still-warm grass surrounding the grotto and the fountain and stopped up short, for it appeared an army had been at work. Even in the darkness he could see that the beds had been hacked clean. The black earth overturned within them was rich as chocolate. Bowers of vine and branch had been pruned back sharply and bore a new froth of delicate white-and-yellow blossoms. Tools and implements lay scattered on the grass.

Norris gazed about him in surprise. Finally his eyes came to rest at the fountain, its tall plume of water breathing a fine mist into the evening air. It had been so long since he'd seen water in the fountain that for a moment he was transported back in time to the summer performances of the girls from Prince's Mead. Their annual pageants had been held on the lawns at Southend House, the fountain playing a joyous accompaniment to the assemblies of young ladies in pretty costume dancing figure eights across the grass. He remembered the music teacher, Miss Ferry, with her deep bodice and the silver serpent with ruby eyes that coiled round the loose flesh of her upper arm.

HE THOUGHT VIDA was a nymph at first, some trick of memory occasioned by the sudden blossoming of the fountain. And then he realized, no, not a nymph, not a figment nor a phantasm, but a real live woman, dancing there on the edge of the fountain in her dressing gown, the marvelous moon high overhead, the arcs of water raining onto the grass from a pyramid of arcing swans, their necks twisting with joy.

Norris's own heart twisted then. He came to his knees on the grass. On the terrace above him, at the thick stone lip of the fountain's edge, with the moon above her head inside a gauzy penumbra, Vida stood balanced on her toes, the silhouette of her body revealed inside her loosened dressing gown, facing the spray of the fountain. Norris withdrew on his knees into the lap of shadow thrown by a yew, his stick dropping soundlessly beside him.

At first she walked the way a child walks along a wall, balancing with her arms outspread. But she gained speed as she went, and at last she was running, around and around on the edge of the fountain, joyous and quick. Norris saw the high arch of her foot and her agile toes, her rounded calves and tiny waist, her throbbing neck and outflung hair and private, private pleasure.

He felt his limbs grow cold and then hot, as if brushed by cotton dipped in alcohol and drawn slowly across the skin. A tentative breeze touched his face. He watched her, his breath held high and light in his chest.

Then suddenly she froze, crumpled from her prancing pose, and fell to a crouch, glancing over her shoulder. After a moment, she climbed quickly to the ground, pulled her robe close around her, and ran from the grotto up toward Southend House, the white soles of her feet flickering. The house, its balanced wings of smooth stone, its terrace lined with statuary, swallowed her.

It was her leaving, the heartbreak of seeing her shame, her dancing interrupted, that struck Norris so hard. That, and the wild desire he experienced after she had gone. Not just desire for her, though there was that, but on her behalf. As if he should, from that moment on, stand sentinel at the garden of Southend House, see that it suffered no infiltrators, no sudden sounds or alarming rustles, nothing that might arrest Vida in her pursuit of such complete and glorious and utter abandon. He raised his blackthorn stick, spun round to strike whomever, whatever, had been responsible for Vida's fright. But there was no one there.

Who had turned on the fountains again? What was happening at Southend House?

He glanced up at the house, one light burning high in a bedroom, another far away in the deep interior of a sitting room. All was still. He turned to survey the garden, its checkerboard of shadows, his breath held. There was not a sound, but his mind raced like something darting through the darkness, checking everywhere for danger. Was there someone there? Someone who could spoil it all? Not an innocent voyeur like him, but someone who might dare to step forth into that scene, arrest the figures there, change the tableau, the unfolding, the ending?

A terrible fierceness gripped him. One should never be denied one's heart's desire. Dear God, he thought, putting his face in his hands.

BUT WEEKS AFTER this miraculous event, Norris still cannot settle on a plan of action.

Vida comes and goes, in and out of the post office. Sometimes he can speak to her, but more often he has a long queue of chatty customers and can do nothing except gaze significantly and mournfully at her as he hands over her mail.

And then one day, late in August, he receives an official inquiry from the Hellenic Post Office in Athens, noting the issue of a new set of commemoratives sponsored by the World Wildlife Fund. The stamps depict native animal species on the Ionian archipelago: the dolphin; the jackal, *Canis aureus;* seals colonizing beneath the Erimitis cliffs.

And the same day there is an envelope from his old friend Mr. Calfo on Corfu, enclosing a complimentary set of the new issue and accompanied by a brief note asking after his general health and spirits.

Norris stares at these two letters for some time.

And then he sits down, his pen in hand, and writes several letters, two to Vida—these come to him more easily than he might have imagined, flights of poetic fancy—one to his dear friend Petros Calfo, and another to old Nesser.

TO MR. CALFO, at the Corfu post office on Alexandras Avenue, he writes, "Dear Petros. I have received your kind gift of the new stamps from your islands. They are very handsome. Thank you. I have a customer who will appreciate them particularly.

"I have a rather odd request to make of you. Would you please attach a stamp to the enclosed letter and mail it off for me? I have in mind a stamp with love as its subject, should you have one lying about. (Not mother and child, however; I should prefer something *romantic.*) I enclose some stamps of the equivalent value for your trouble, a very nice set of Huey, Dewey, and Louie, from America.

"I know you are wondering what funny business I am up to! I assure you it is nothing that should disturb your conscience. It is just that I am engaged in a bit of a romp, you might say, and the foreign postmark is part of the plan, you see. I hope it gives you, as a member of the world's most romantic citizenry, some pleasure to have had a hand in my own little English love story! I do thank you.

"Cordially, Norris Lamb."

This he fits inside an envelope, along with his first letter to Vida.

Then he takes out another sheet of paper. This letter he addresses to Mr. Nesser at the Philatelic Office, Postal Organization, Cairo, United Arab Republic.

"My dear Nesser," he writes.

"Greetings! Do forgive the unorthodox nature of this request, old chap, but would you be so kind as to affix a stamp—theme of love, if you will—to the enclosed envelope and mail it off for me? There is nothing untoward here, I assure you. Only a little manner of *amour* I am engaged in. You can imagine how exciting this is.

"I inquire about your gout. Is it any better?

"Gratefully, Norris Lamb."

He seals this up, after enclosing his second letter to Vida.

Now he feels inordinately pleased with himself. This business of writing—it's really so easy, once you get the hang of it.

Eight

VIDA STANDS AT the deep sink in the kitchen of Southend House, washing up the morning's dishes. From time to time she looks out the window at the figure of the new gardener, spade in hand, digging in the beds that curl in interlocking shapes around the fountain. A scrim of fine mist floats in the air; a flock of ravens briefly divides the sky.

At one point she sees the gardener look up. Leaning on his spade handle, he draws a cloth from his pocket and wipes it across his face. He gazes up toward the house, resting.

Vida turns back abruptly to the washing, plunging her arms deep in water.

Behind her, at the long table set on the uneven flagstones of the floor, Manford sits with his book of stamps open before him, his finger touching each tiny image: a series of the dun-colored, sun-backed humps of the Ascension volcanoes; a collection of the spiny pink protea from South Africa; a collection of birds and their eggs from the Grenadines of St. Vincent—the purple gallinule with its mauve-spotted egg, the gray kingbird beside its ink-splattered egg.

Norris Lamb, passing these over the counter to Manford and Vida the week before, had explained in excited tones the history of South Africa's early postal system, how letters home to Holland or England from the colonists would be left under large stones at the coast and picked up by sea captains visiting Cape Town.

"Quite romantic, don't you think?" Mr. Lamb had said, wiping his mouth with a white handkerchief, his eyes watery, looking at Vida.

They'd been interrupted by the vicar, who'd come in with a great many mysterious parcels in very many extraordinary shapes and sizes, bound up with long lengths of a hairy-looking twine—the vicar did not offer to explain what the parcels were, and Vida noticed that Mr. Lamb didn't ask. She thought *she* would have asked, if she'd been in his place. The vicar also wanted to know how long Mr. Lamb thought it would be before there was a moon-landing stamp. He had a nephew in South Africa "excessively interested in all things having to do with the galaxy."

Vida had startled at the mention of the moon landing and blushed—it had been a moment of uncharacteristic abandon on her part, that business of dancing around the fountain. But she had been even more startled at Mr. Lamb's reaction to the vicar's comment. He had turned a violent shade of purple, as though filling up with India ink, and had failed to answer at all.

"The *Apollo* moon landing," the vicar had said helpfully after a moment, as if there might be another moon landing to confuse it with, and at last Mr. Lamb had appeared to recover slightly and said quickly that he was sure someone would do a stamp very soon. He'd been suddenly shy after that, and Vida and Manford had gone away soon afterward.

Manford lies on the rug now, his mouth making shapes as his finger travels over the pictures, his expression liquid and flowing. He turns the pages carefully, licking his thumb. He places his index finger squarely upon the faces staring out from the stamps, the explorers from the British Antarctic Territory—Lincoln Ellsworth smiling bravely out from within his white fur ruff, or Jean-Baptiste Charcot with his yellowed goatee and heavily shadowed eyes. Manford presses the soft ball of his finger flat upon the images as if taking the imprint of the men's features, lifting their expressions from the page. His feet are hooked over the rung of the chair, his back bent low over the tabletop.

Drying her hands on a towel, Vida leaves the room and returns a moment later with her coat and Manford's cap. Her coat folded over her arm, she tugs the cap down over Manford's head, bending over to look into his face and push his hair up close beneath the brim, tugging down one lock in a gallant fashion and pinching it into place. She licks her finger and rubs it across a smudge on his forehead. He takes no apparent notice of her fussing. She puts on her raincoat and buttons it.

Manford glances up at her and smiles when she says his name, but returns almost immediately to his page, his mouth working.

"Time to go now," Vida says, and reaches down to touch his elbow. He rises at her touch, although with apparent reluctance, and stands before her. She notices his soft belly, how it blossoms over his trousers. She gives it a poke. "Look at you," she says. "Oh, dear. You're getting quite *fat*, Manford."

He doubles over, then stands back upright and attempts to poke Vida at the waist.

"No, no," she says, twisting out of reach. "Not me. I mind my figure. Not like some I know," she says meaningfully. "Too many jam doughnuts is your trouble. Come on. They'll be waiting on you at Niven's."

Manford follows her out of the kitchen, down the long, tiled passageway whose whitewashed walls are punctuated by doors that open onto small pantries, the shelves there neatly stocked with cups and glassware and plates, fading labels in Vida's handwriting pasted to the woodwork: WHITE WINE, RED WINE, CHAMPAGNE, SPIRITS, APERITIF, DIGESTIVE, TEACUPS, DEMITASSE, DINNER, DESSERT, EVERYDAY, CONSOMMÉ, SOUP.

As they step outside into the small courtyard containing the coal and the wood sheds, the overgrown espaliers there woven through and choked with dead wood, Vida glances behind her through the passageway to the rear lawns. She sees the gardener crouched on the grass, his hands busy in the earth. He's been around for several weeks now, but she's never sure when he's working and when he's not. He hasn't come by the house at all. Mr. Perry has been away, though. Perhaps that's why.

Behind her, Manford stretches out his hands and bounces his palms gently on an invisible current.

Descending the steps to the gravel drive, shaking her coat hem free of coal dust, Vida hurries along briskly. This morning, she has decided, she will walk Manford only as far as the bench on the lane. Not a wink farther.

Mr. Niven has assured her that he thinks Manford has become very canny about the traffic on the Romsey Road, and so between them they have agreed to allow Manford to try crossing on his own. Mr. Niven has taught him to look in both directions for oncoming cars before stepping down from the curb. As an added inspiration, Mr. Niven has also instructed him to raise his hand like a bobby stopping traffic. In this way, Manford now walks home across the street by himself in the afternoons, his hands solemnly held high, palms outward to the invisible traffic. Mr. Niven has told Vida he watches from the entryway to the courtyard in front of the bakery, just to be safe.

"Well done, Manford," he calls when Manford is safely across and headed for home.

"Poor *chap,*" he confessed to Vida one afternoon, uncharacteristically emotional. "Nearly breaks my heart sometimes, watching him."

But Vida knows that for Manford, leaving Mr. Niven, who has

never once taken his hand, is not the same thing as being parted from her. She still allows Manford to twine his fingers with hers as they walk down the lane.

At the bench this morning she stops, disengages her hand, and folds her arms. Manford stares straight ahead of him, not moving a muscle.

Now we're going to have a moment, Vida thinks. She looks upward into the trees, at the still tent of leaves. "I want you to do the rest yourself now," she says firmly after a minute. "Go on. You know the way. It's right down the end of the lane."

Manford sidles a bit closer to her, reaches with one hand toward her folded arms.

"No," she says, twitching away. "I will not hold your hand any longer. You must do it yourself."

Manford licks his lips, reaches up, and with his fingers curled close together pushes his hair slowly under the brim of his cap. Vida has attempted to teach him this, to tidy his appearance. Now she sighs impatiently.

"*Thank* you, Manford. Very well done," she says. "Your hair looks lovely. Very handsome. Now, go *on*."

But Manford turns suddenly and starts to move at a lumbering trot, not quite an out-and-out run but still deliberate, back down the lane toward the gates of Southend House.

"Oh, Manford," Vida cries, and stamps her foot. "Please! *Why* won't you do this?"

She stares reproachfully at him. Perhaps she shouldn't hold his hand at all anymore, if this is what comes of it—such obstinacy. Why, she's spoiled him! But that doesn't feel quite right. His hand in hers is comforting to them both, she feels. In fact, she knows Manford's body almost as well as she knows her own, she thinks, his hands and face and the shape of his toenails and the curve of his back. Sometimes, if he is agitated, she will lie down on the bed beside him when he goes to sleep at night, the two of them staring at the circling figures of pretty colored fish thrown by the night-light Mr. Perry brought back from Italy for Manford many years ago. Vida admires its cleverness—it's just a box, fitted all around with onionskin. But inside is a cylinder of stiff paper, with the shapes of fish and seaweed and a tilting galleon cut out of it and pasted over with different-colored cellophanes. The cylinder revolves round a tiny lightbulb and throws the colored shapes onto the ceiling, very large, like the shadows you can make with your hands. Sometimes Manford leans over and laces his fingers together over the light. And then Vida thinks it is as if a net has been tossed over the sea, a net that would catch everything, even the stars in the sky. It's clever, the way he figured that out, she thinks. He does a bird with his hands, too, a diving pelican, its knuckled beak snapping, and a vaulting gazelle or a springbok—or perhaps it's a prehistoric horse. Sometimes she thinks he's made up the creatures he does with his shadow hands, as she calls them. And then every now and then she'll come across him looking at one of his picture books, and she'll realize that, no, he hasn't made anything up. It's all right there. It's real.

She herself couldn't have dreamed up the things he seems to know about the world. But between knowing and imagining, she thinks maybe knowing things is better, in the end.

You can count on it.

"WELL, HE WOULDN'T do it," she says in exasperation a few minutes later, ushering Manford in the door at Niven's with an impatient shooing motion. Manford heads quickly for the pantry, where his stool awaits, sits down immediately, and begins filling the doughnuts with the pastry cone. Vida and Mrs. Blatchford crane round and stare at him.

"What a busy bee," Mrs. Blatchford says. "Well, I *am* sorry. Still won't leave go your hand, will he?"

"He turned right around and ran home! I had to fetch him back! I don't know what to do." Vida hears the uncharacteristic despair in her own voice and is a little ashamed of herself. But since Manford has started at Niven's, she has enjoyed, more than she ever expected, their interest in him, their growing understanding of his ways. They've all taken to him, no question, Mrs. Blatchford fixing the buttons on his cardigan for him, Mr. Niven clapping him on the back. And who wouldn't love him, after all, so gentle and so quiet? And yet full of surprises, in his own way. Vida thinks what intelligence Manford has is sly and wondrous—creatures springing to life on his bedroom walls at night. Now, feeling herself among friends, among *Manford's* friends, she allows herself an instant of confession.

"It is so worrying!" she exclaims. "Mrs. Blatchford—think of it! What if something should, should"—she lowers her voice, as if to prevent him from hearing—"should *happen* to me? *Then* where would he be? Oh, I felt *sure* he could learn this."

Mrs. Blatchford gives her a correcting glance. "Now, Vida," she says, as if speaking to a small child. "Nothing whatsoever is going to happen to you. Let's not have any such nonsense." She hands Vida a doughnut, which Vida takes but only holds, as if she's forgotten that they are things to be eaten.

"Not that I think it would be a bad thing," Mrs. Blatchford goes on, "his being able to do it on his own. He's come so far really, hasn't he? But I can understand your wanting him to be as independent as possible. After all, what if"—she appears to search for a reason—"what if you should want to, oh, go on holiday, for instance? Had you ever thought of that, Vida? Having a holiday?" She stops wiping the glass counter and looks straight at Vida. "Have you ever *had* a holiday?"

Vida stares at her. "A holiday," she repeats. "No, I—not as you would call it, I suppose. No. I've—" But she can't finish. For suddenly it strikes her as so odd, that she hasn't ever had a holiday, that the idea has never even occurred to her. Or maybe it had once, a long time ago. But, of course, what she does—it no longer feels like work to her. It feels like her life. It *is* her life. And then she thinks of her uncle Laurence, what he'd written about going to Corfu in one of his earliest letters: "Where else but on an island," he'd asked, with undisguised enthusiasm, "can one reinvent oneself so entirely? The only thing to fear is that one day one's old identity will wash up on shore like a shipwreck."

"Well, I do see what he means, but would that be such a dreadful thing?" Vida's mother had asked at the time, looking up at Vida from Laurence's aerogramme. Her eyes had held a wounded look. "His old self?"

"*Well,*" Mrs. Blatchford says smartly now, "I think a holiday is most certainly in order. Perhaps his father will look after him for you when you go," she adds irrationally, as if it were a fait accompli.

"But where would I go?" Vida asks, baffled. "And besides, Mr. Perry's rarely there! He's hardly ever at home."

Though he had been home more of late, she thinks now. He'd hired the gardener, for instance. Mr. Perry had told her the fellow would be taking his meals at the house, but he'd never yet come inside, at least not when she'd been around. She hoped Mr. Perry didn't want an accounting from her of how the man spent his time. Oh well. It wasn't any of her business what the gardener, whoever he was, did with himself. Perhaps he was eating in the village. Or perhaps he had a home somewhere nearby. She'd set a place for him at the table one afternoon when she'd glimpsed him puttering around the greenhouses, but he'd never come up to the house. She and Manford had eaten their supper with the third place empty, as if for a ghost. It hadn't been a special supper anyway, just beans on toast.

She hadn't really been surprised much by the gardener's mercurial comings and goings, though. They confirmed a rather vague idea she had of the rest of the world's being always engaged in urgent business; she frequently worried that she was interrupting people. She remembered calling Dr. Faber late one night, when Manford was still a young child. It had seemed to Vida at the time, passing her hand over his forehead, that he was running an unnaturally high fever. Mr. Perry had been abroad, as usual. She'd been terrified, alone in the enormous house with the silent, feverish boy. She'd rung her mother at home and woken her. Her mother, sleepy but understanding, had said she'd try to reach Dr. Faber for her. But hours had gone by, and still there was no sign of him.

At last, about two o'clock in the morning, Dr. Faber had rung the bell. Vida, who'd been nearly hysterical with anxiety at that point, had hurried him upstairs to Manford's bedroom.

"Well, we might open the windows for starters," he'd said, preceding her into the room and blowing out a noise of annoyance. "It's hot as blazes in here, Vida!"

Advancing to the window, he had pushed the drapes aside and struggled with the latch on the casement, grunting with effort. "Damn," he'd muttered under his breath. And then it had given way at last, an envelope of cool, wet air sliding into the room, the moon floating full and white.

Dr. Faber had peered into Manford's eyes with a little light, listened carefully to his chest.

"He'll be all right," he'd said at last, straightening up. "Nothing but a cold. You can bring him by in the morning if you like, though. I'll have another look at him then." He glanced down at the boy, whose eyes followed the physician's face. "I think you'll live to see morning, Manford. All right?"

He had turned to Vida, who was standing at the foot of the bed and winding her hands anxiously. She saw a quick sympathy rise into his eyes. "I'm sorry it took me so long to come, Vida," he said. "I had another case to attend to."

She waved her hands. "I quite understand," she started to say, but suddenly found herself very near tears.

Dr. Faber took off his glasses, folded them, and put them into his pocket. He picked up his bag and came around the bed to her, where he stopped and put a hand on her shoulder. "You've done a fine job here, Vida," he said then kindly. He looked down at Manford again and then back to Vida. "Not many have the patience for it, you know," he said after a minute. "They make a lot of mistakes along the way. Some can be quite cruel. But you seem—" He paused. "Well, I admire you, is all. . . . You've stuck with it. Manford's a lucky chap." He unwound the stethoscope from around his neck, held it in his fist. "Of course, he could be a great deal more difficult," he added. "It's a blessing he's not. Some of them aren't, you know, and then we can all be grateful, but many of them can be quite trying in their own ways." He glanced back at Manford curled in the bed, his bright eyes watching them. "Still doesn't speak?"

Vida shook her head. It was true that Manford had never uttered a word, not even a sound that might approximate a word, an infant's blundering attempt at precise speech. Still, she felt she understood him. Sometimes, it seemed to her, Manford could speak if he wished. His expression was often so—complicit. As if he agreed with everything you said, a sort of silent witness to your own conscience.

Dr. Faber shook his head. "Strange," he said. "I might have thought—" But he said nothing else.

Vida had closed the door after him, had stood in the front hall with its cavernous, empty fireplace, the two small, velvet-covered chairs with their twisted legs standing by either side of it, their faded and unraveling tassels stirring slightly in the draft from the closing door. She thought of the strange, mute child above her, his twisted bedsheets and dull expression. She had wanted, at that moment, to run from the house and had hated herself for that feeling. At last, her hand on the banister, she had climbed the stairs slowly and had taken her place at Manford's bedside, where she passed the night sleeping fitfully in a chair, her hand upon the coverlet, Manford curled beside her palm.

Now, with Mrs. Blatchford gazing at her sympathetically, it seems to her that the idea of a holiday is the silliest thing she's ever heard of.

She couldn't ever leave Manford. He would never love anyone as much as he loved her.

And yet—she looks down at her hands now, perturbed; for how strange it is, she thinks. Because what she is feeling, really, is not how much *he* loves *her*, but how much *she* loves *him*, how much she depends on it. And for a moment she sees herself in the lane, waiting and waiting, a dark, wet wind whistling away over the fields, Manford never coming, never again coming home from Niven's, the moon rising slowly overhead, herself turning to stone.

"I expect his father wouldn't know how to look after him properly anyway," Mrs. Blatchford says then.

Vida looks up, startled. "Oh," she says, and the sun comes up again; the world floods with the plain, unremarkable light of morning. "Yes," she says, blinking. "Well, he hasn't ever had to."

"No, I suppose not. *Men,*" Mrs. Blatchford says then, and gives a low snort.

Vida leans over the counter for a last look at Manford. He seems to be avoiding her eye. She sighs, touches the collar of her coat. "Well, I'm off," she says then. "Going round to pick up the post."

There seems nothing else to say.

Outside, she stops to adjust her hat and have a final look at Manford through the window.

"What does she do with herself all day?" she hears Mrs. Blatchford say to Mr. Niven, who's just come through the door with a tray of bread in his arms.

He shrugs. "Can't imagine."

"Isn't it a shame about her holiday, though," she hears Mrs. Blatchford say to him.

"What holiday?" he says. "Is our Vida going somewhere?"

And then Vida can't hear them anymore, because they've turned away.

After a minute she walks down the side of the building and peeps carefully in the window at Manford, his shaggy head bent over his work. His cap has fallen to the floor, where it is pinned under one of the legs of the stool, acquiring a snowfall of dusty sugar. One foot is planted on the brim, crumpling it. But he looks exactly, she thinks, like a statue. A Greek statue.

IN THE POST office she has to ring the bell for Mr. Lamb, who comes out immediately, as if he's been waiting for someone behind his curtain. He is wearing a suit—a rather old suit, with narrow lapels and a greenish cast to it. A white rosebud is pinned to his lapel, and his hair has been freshly dampened and combed.

Perhaps he's going to a funeral, she thinks.

"Good morning, Mr. Lamb—" She stops, for she finds herself suddenly shy in the presence of his unusually formal appearance.

He utters not a word but turns around to get her mail for her.

Perhaps it's the grief, she thinks, disconcerted, looking away. Perhaps it's a sort of observation of respect, not to speak. She notices, however, despite herself, a thin, glistening line of sweat running from his temple down into his shirt collar and thinks that, after all, he must be rather hot in his suit. She sniffs, detecting an odd odor. It's Mr. Lamb himself, she realizes, smelling of something old-fashioned and medicinal, though she can't exactly place it.

He turns back around and hands her her mail. His expression is strange, she thinks, glancing up briefly into his face and then away again. He appears to be—*holding something in his mouth!* Oh! She reconsiders, trying to think, trying not to look at him. He *can't* be. Why would he have something in his mouth? No, no. Perhaps he is trying not to cry? She steals another glance at him and then looks away in horror. For it is not grief he is suppressing, she sees now. It is mirth! He isn't trying not to *cry*. He is trying not to *laugh!*

Well! *Not* very suitable for a funeral, she thinks, her forehead creasing.

She turns away from him and begins to sift through the envelopes. But as she does so, she thinks to ask Mr. Lamb whether he's got any more stamps for Manford.

She looks up, her mouth open. But he has disappeared. The black curtain to his rear rooms billows slightly. Not a sound comes from the corridor.

"Mr. Lamb?" she says hesitantly after a moment to the empty room. But her voice seems to echo queerly in the silence.

She frowns, shrugs a little, returns to her letters.

A weak light falls across the floor, threading through the window's many tiny panes between mullions thick and ridged with years of paint. She does not see the sunlight advancing toward her but feels the unexpected heat across the back of her neck, like a warm, possessive hand resting there.

Among the usual sorts of things in the daily post is an overseas envelope addressed to her in an unfamiliar handwriting, postmarked from Corfu. She frowns again. It doesn't look like Laurence's script.

She fits the other letters and catalogs under her elbow, lifts the flaps of the air letter with her fingernail, tearing the paper slightly and biting her lip. She unfolds the sheet and begins to read.

And then she feels her face grow bright red. She almost drops her bundle of mail. She folds over the sheet again quickly, looks up hastily as though whoever has sent her this must be standing right there, watching her. And postmarked from Corfu? Who did she know in Corfu except Laurence? No one!

And no one, no one has *ever* said such things to her.

She couldn't even have imagined them, not if she tried for days and days and days.

She peeks at the letter again.

Vida Stephen. The sun may rise and fall, but nothing shall ever eclipse your beauty. You are the moon and the stars and everything in the world to me. You are a beacon in the dark night, an eternal flame. I crawl along the rays of the sun and they lead a path to your feet. I am your servant, your knight. One day you will know me.

The black curtain twitches, but Mr. Lamb does not emerge.

Her face scarlet with embarrassment, Vida gathers up her things hurriedly and rushes out of the post office, the bell clanging loudly behind her. She walks quickly along the Romsey Road back toward home, the letter held tightly in her sweating hand, her heart beating so wildly that she feels deafened by the sound of her own racing pulse.

Turning onto the lane on shaking legs, she thinks that she must calm herself. She actually finds that she wants a nip of something for her nerves! And she never wants a drink.

At the bench in the lane she feels so weak she has to sit down. She takes out the letter again, opening it with shaking fingers. *Moon and stars, eternal flame, beacon in the dark, beauty* . . . My! she thinks. My, my!

Tears have begun to fall mysteriously down her cheeks.

But she is smiling.

Oh, such a mystery! Such excitement! Such strangeness!

But then—oh, why is she to be forever embarrassed by this! It almost makes her angry!—she finds herself remembering the night of the moon landing, the night of her escapade on the fountain.

She jumps up from the bench, crumpling the letter into her pocket, gathers up the other letters and her handbag, and hurries down the lane toward Southend House.

In the silent, shadowy library she pours herself a small amount of brandy from one of the crystal decanters in Mr. Perry's bar, takes the glass to a chair, and sits down heavily in it. She puts her hand over her heart a moment.

It was the fountain itself, she thinks now. It was hearing it again after so many years. It was only the fountain that was to blame. But why should this letter—she leans down and picks it up from the floor near her feet, where she had dumped her belongings, and unfolds it more calmly now—*why should this letter make her think of that night?*

She takes another sip of brandy.

It was that she'd heard something, she thinks now. She'd remembered suddenly the new gardener in his apartment above the stables; she had fled in shame.

And this letter—it too exposes her somehow, in exactly the same way she'd felt exposed that night in the garden. *One day you will know me*—that was what made her think of it.

She leans her head back against the chair. She does not understand it at all. It is wonderful and awful and disturbing and exciting, all mixed together. She cannot exactly separate the feelings it produces in her, a sort of twin column of fear and desire at once.

Who would love *her,* Vida Stephen?

She takes another tiny sip of the brandy, holds it in her cheeks, grimaces as she swallows, and then wipes the back of her hand across her mouth. Setting the glass on the table beside her, she stands and moves to the window.

She is surprised to find the gardener there, dragging the large dead limb of a tree toward a bonfire he has built down near the greenhouses, a greasy smoke issuing from it in a thin curl. She watches him a moment as he wrestles with the wood, levering it into the pile. When it falls, an explosion of sparks flies up into the air.

Stepping outside through the French doors onto the terrace, she takes in the sharp scent of the smoke, the raked and emptied condition of the beds. It didn't look very pretty, she considers, but you could see how it was the right thing to do, clearing it all out, how the spines and arms of the garden had begun to stand out again what with all the rubbish being pruned away. You couldn't really tell what the garden had once been like, whether it had ever been grand, so overgrown had it become after years of neglect. But now, now you could see how fine it was, how fine it could be again. She admires the sweeping terraces, the graceful stone walls and balustrades now released from their burden of overgrowth.

You could see that it only wanted some attention to be beautiful again.

THE FIRST THING she says to him is, "It looks much better."

He turns round, holds his arm up before his face as a billow of smoke engulfs him in black.

Vida takes a step back, away from the smoke.

He coughs as the smoke swerves in a sudden breeze, sweeping toward him. He glances at her, his eyes red, then grinds a handkerchief to his face with his fist, rubbing. He coughs.

Vida waits a moment and then gestures behind her uncertainly.

"You've made tremendous progress," she says, starting again. "I'd almost forgotten—" She indicates the garden beds.

He stuffs the cloth back into his pocket, regards her. "You must have been here awhile then, for this to seem an improvement." He turns his head and spits to the side.

Vida jumps. "Oh, yes." She laughs uncomfortably. She looks around. "Well, it used to be very grand."

"It shouldn't have been let go like this," the man says. "It'll take years to clear it out."

"Oh, but I think you've made wonderful progress," she repeats stubbornly. It seems important to her suddenly that the garden be nearly restored, that this gardener feel utterly committed to it, that the era of its flowering be near at hand again. She feels strangely defensive about it.

"You're the cook?" he asks, squinting at her through the smoke.

Vida is taken aback a moment. She does cook, she considers,

of course she does. They have to eat, don't they? But that isn't how she thinks of herself. She thinks to say she is the nanny, but it occurs to her, as if for the first time, that for a twenty-year-old man, a nanny seems a strange necessity. She hardly ever has to explain things to people. Everyone knows her, knows Manford.

"I look after the son," she says, carefully choosing her words from the small store of appropriate phrases. "Mr. Perry's son. Manford."

The man coughs again and then turns to throw more brush on the bonfire. Sparks fly and collide.

"That's the idiot?" he asks over his shoulder.

Vida flares. No one ever says such a thing! She is sorry now that she came down here to speak to him. How stupid he is! "Why do you call him that?" she says angrily.

He shrugs. "Someone told me. He's the big one? I've seen him wandering about."

Vida waits, though she's not sure for what. She thinks of Manford sitting on the edge of the fountain, birds pecking at his feet. "He's not an *idiot,*" she says finally, though less forcefully, she discovers, than she intends. "He's handicapped."

The man kicks the fire with his boot, jabs a pitchfork into the fragile tent of branches. "Like a golfer?" he says, laughing. "Is that it?"

But Vida withdraws as if she has been slapped. For the second time that day, a fierce blush rises to her cheeks. She stares at the man's grimy shirt a moment, then turns to walk away. She will just go home, she thinks. He's awful!

"Hey!" he calls after her, laughing. "I didn't mean anything."

Vida stops, spins toward him, and takes a deep breath. "You don't know what you're talking about," she says furiously. "You haven't any idea what it's like to be Manford."

"No, I suppose not," he says affably, and flashes his teeth at her in a smile. Vida looks back at him stonily. He kicks the fire again. "Look, I'm sorry," he says. "I didn't mean anything."

Vida waits, staring at the fire. She takes a step toward it, holds out her hands as if to warm them, though it is hot enough already, a surprising late-summer heat, muggy and still. "He's very sweet," she says at last. "He wouldn't harm a single living creature."

"He's a big oaf, though, isn't he?" the man says then. "I should put him to work around here, give me a hand. Twenty men couldn't put this place to rights in a year. Don't tell his lordship I said so, though," he adds, jerking his thumb toward the house. "I need the job." He steps back and surveys the garden. "It's a crime, really, isn't it?" he goes on, shaking his head. "It'll cost him a small fortune. He's got pots though, I suppose?"

Vida feels faintly affronted by this question. "I wouldn't know," she says delicately. "I suppose there's enough."

"Well, there'd better be, or I'll be off for greener pastures, as they say." The man laughs again. He looks at Vida. "I'm Jeremy Martin," he says, sticking out his hand.

"Vida Stephen," she says, and for a moment their hands touch, but not before Vida sees how filthy his are.

SHE STAYS WITH him that morning, though she's not sure why. After all, he's so unpleasant at first. But then he asks her to give him a hand with a broken window in the greenhouse, holding the frame while he putties in the new pane.

"You need three hands for this job," he says, and she thinks it's charming the way he says it, so friendly.

And then he asks if she would have a look at the roses with him, advise him about the shapes and all. She tells him she doesn't know the first thing about it, but they go up there, and then suddenly Vida finds herself feeling exhilarated by the fresh air, feels that she wants to work, to "really put my back into it," she says, looking up eagerly at Jeremy. "Don't you have another spade?" she asks, looking around.

He laughs but fetches one for her, and they dig awhile together. Vida thinks she has never seen such big worms as those they discover in the rose beds. Jeremy holds one out on his palm for her to see, a giant one with a bulbous gray ring around its middle. And then suddenly, brutally, he splits it in half with his knife.

"That's it," he says, dropping the pieces on the ground. "Like Christ dividing the endless loaf. You can chop them into a hundred pieces, and each one will grow a whole new worm. Did you know that?"

She doesn't think this is exactly right, but she doesn't say anything. The worm's divided selves disappear into the grass. A queer chill runs over her arms.

He's nice, though, she thinks.

He has pretty eyes.

AT NOON, VIDA makes tomato sandwiches, brings them out to the garden on a tray with a jelly roll and some iced tea and some figs.

"That hit the spot," Jeremy says afterward. He shifts from his elbows and lies back down on the grass, hooking his arms beneath his head.

"What do you do with yourself all day, now he's got a job?" he asks idly after a minute. "Tidy the house?" He laughs.

Vida laughs, too, the thought of the huge, empty house with its innumerable unused rooms cloaked in dust and sheets. "Oh, yes," she says. "I clean the whole house, top to bottom." Yet a twinge of some feeling, disloyalty perhaps, sweeps through her as soon as she's said this.

"It's quite sad, really," she says soberly after a moment, wanting vaguely to make amends. "It's a lovely house, and Mr. Perry's rarely home. No one to enjoy it."

"You enjoy it, though." Jeremy turns to look at her and winks.

Vida feels uncomfortable. She can't catch the meaning behind this conspiratorial wink. She thinks of herself and Manford, sitting in the small sitting room off the kitchen in the evenings, working on his stamp books. Sometimes she has him help her polish the silver. He seems to like that.

She decides to change the subject.

"And what about you?" she asks, taking the warm, round weight of a fig in her hand. "The stable apartment's all right for you?"

"I'm not there much," Jeremy says lazily. "It's all right."

"You live nearby then?"

"Well, I've a friend," he says. He closes his eyes.

Vida looks him over shyly. He's not a big man. Not half as big as Manford, for instance. But he's good looking, she thinks, the strong color of youth in his cheeks and lovely long eyelashes. Dark hair, curly. She realizes suddenly, blushing, that *friend* means a woman. "I see," she says, turning away.

Jeremy opens his eyes, hoists himself to a sitting position. "Back to work," he says. He leans over, claps Vida once on the back. "Thanks for the grub," he says, and his hand touches her shoulder blade and rests there a moment. Vida jumps.

"I won't bite you!" he says, laughing, getting to his feet. "Thanks for the company, too. See you."

And he walks off toward the greenhouses, whistling, pausing once to fetch the barrow and trundle it along in front of him.

"Good-bye!" she calls. But he doesn't seem to hear her.

Inside, Vida washes up their lunch things, and then she rinses out some underwear for herself in the laundry sink, and then she does a cardigan of Manford's, laying it out on a towel in a spreading parallelogram of sun that falls in the French doors of the library. Kneeling on the carpet, the sun on her back, she feels a sleepy languor come over her.

And then she sees the letter, the mysterious love letter, fallen on the floor by the armchair, along with her overturned sherry glass.

She sits up. How could she have forgotten!

Someone is in love with her!

Fetching the letter from under the chair, she sits down and smooths the paper on her thigh. Bringing the envelope closer to her face, she examines the stamp. She sees that it is in fact a tiny photograph of some ruins, reduced to minute proportions and hand-painted in palest turquoise, rose, and yellow, as though the sun were setting behind the empty arches. A man and a woman, their arms entwined, stand beneath the capstone of the arch. Vida holds up the letter and reads the words again. Such short, declarative sentences, such fierce ardor. Like a man who speaks through clenched teeth.

But who would be in love with *her*?

She leans back against the seat of the armchair. Sunlight falls like an anvil, hard and hot, on the part in her hair. The letter is unfathomable, really. It makes such little sense that she can hardly connect it with herself. She cannot imagine anyone who might have sent it.

She runs over in her head the men she knows. The parade of unlikely suspects leaves her aghast. Why, who are the men she sees regularly? She decides to go through them one by one. Mr. Niven? He's only interested in *golfing*. She knows that from his wife. Oh, Lord, she thinks with a shock—not nasty old *Fergus?* Well, he might be an old lecher, that wouldn't surprise her. But he'd never send a letter like this. Why, she didn't even think he could write properly! There was the vicar—well, he was completely above suspicion. He was the *vicar,* for heaven's sake. Dr. *Faber?* No, no, no. And she *trusted* him.

She looks down at the letter again. What about Tony, at the Dolphin? He pours out the pints, she thinks now, and is friendly to everyone. Has a soft spot for poetry, too. Bartenders seem to, she thinks. But she hardly ever goes in there anymore. It's been years, fifteen years anyway, since she went regularly with her old friend Charlotte. And the young men of her youth—only a few of them are still about, and those she can name are all married, with a brood of children.

And then she goes quite cold. Another idea has struck her.

Perhaps it's a joke. A very cruel joke.

A terrific headache suddenly announces itself to her, as though the sun has succeeded finally in breaking open her skull with its riveting insistence.

Who would do such a thing to her? It's nearly as unthinkable as the notion of some sincere lover, some waiting suitor. Oh, the cruelty of it, if it were a joke! But it can't be. It *can't* be.

One day you will know me. But does that mean she doesn't know him now? Well, then, how could he know her?

She reads the sentences again. She admires them. Someone sophisticated must have written them. It wasn't the work of a boy. These are a man's words, she thinks. And then, quite by surprise, a picture of Mr. Perry's face flashes into her head. There it is—the sadness, and the elegance, the educated hand.

She stills inside.

Yes, she had thought of it once, thought of being in love with him. Actually, it was Charlotte who'd suggested it. "Perhaps he'll marry *you*," she'd said in an offhand way one evening—oh, it was years ago, now—when she and Vida had been sitting on the wall outside the Dolphin.

Vida had been sharing with Charlotte her opinion of Mr. Perry's summer houseguests that year, an American couple and a woman Vida took to be a divorcée—a friend of the family, Mr. Perry had said. But Vida hadn't liked her, hadn't approved of the way she draped herself on the arm of Mr. Perry's chair when they sat in the garden. She'd been *sickening* with Manford, too, she'd told Charlotte, talking baby talk to him, patting him on the head. And she'd overheard her talking with the other woman, the wife, when the ladies had come in before dinner to wash up.

Having settled Manford in front of the telly with his supper—he was only six or seven then—Vida had come back through the hall with a tray for the glasses from the garden. The two women had been lounging in the library, drinks in hand, their shoes kicked off. When Vida heard their voices, she had paused in the hall.

"Well, he's depressed, Sally, for God's sake," she heard one of the women say.

"Oh, I know, I know." Sally sighed. "But it's so *boring*. You'd think he'd be over it by now."

There had been no reply from her companion.

"And it's not *good* for him to be holed up here away from all his *friends*," Sally went on petulantly. "And that child—you have to feel sorry for him. But wouldn't he be better off someplace where he could be taken care of? And that nurse—she treats him as if there weren't a thing wrong with him! But of course you can *see* it—all over his face." Vida heard a pause. "God, poor Eleanor. She would have just died."

Vida heard ice clatter in a glass. Her own fingers and face had turned to stone.

"You're cruel." The other voice was reproachful.

"Oh, I don't mean it like that. You *know* I don't. What I say is, just put it all behind him! Get the poor boy in some place where they're all just like him, where he won't feel—you know. And then let Thomas get on with his life."

"You mean, get on with *your* life." The other woman laughed.

Sally laughed, too. "*I* wouldn't mind."

Vida heard the soft sound of a pillow thrown across the room, landing with a thick thud. She jumped. The women laughed again.

"I could use some fun. I admit it. Divorce makes one so—disgustingly celibate."

Vida had turned then sharply and gone back to the kitchen. Manford had looked up at her as she'd come into the room and dropped to her knees beside him. She put her arms around him. Manford craned round her shoulder to see *The Magic Roundabout*. Egg on his face smeared onto her collar.

"I love you," she said fiercely into his neck. "Such a good boy, my Manford."

He had patted her shoulder kindly.

But conveying her outrage to Charlotte later that night had left Vida feeling not more comforted, but less. Mr. Perry didn't need to *forget* about Manford—she'd understood that from the beginning. He needed to take him in. To recognize him. And her, too, she'd thought once. He needed to recognize her. We could be a family, she'd thought fiercely.

But it had lasted only a moment, this thought. Because almost at the same moment, she had realized the absurdity of the notion.

It was true she thought Mr. Perry handsome. She still did. But more than just their stations separated them. It wasn't just that she was the nanny to the retarded son, he her distant employer. Though they'd known each other nearly twenty-one years now and had developed the habit of familiarity between them, something stood between them, had always stood between them. Though they both loved Manford—for she believed that Mr. Perry did love his son—only she took any pleasure from that. Mr. Perry was, despite his wealth, his talent, his worldliness, small in her eyes.

She could never forgive him, in a way, for being such a coward.

She looks down at the letter in her hand now. Would Mr. Perry have written this to her? After all these years? Was he trying to find his way back? Mailing love letters to her from distant lands, still unable to stand in the same place as she and look at what lay between them, the daft boy with his terrible innocence? Could it be? After all this time? She closes her eyes. She knows she wanted it once, her own expectations so much larger, richer, finer, than what might have been possible. They'd been a child's expectations. She had thought, a moment here and moment there, that he might have touched her. In gratitude or for comfort, a touch that might have led to something. But on the whole, she thought, her love for Mr. Perry—if you could even call it that—was so much less than for his son, this boy she had raised as her own.

If he loved her now, if Mr. Perry had fallen in love with her—oh, would she even want it?

She thinks of him coming home, loosening his tie, throwing it across the room toward the back of a chair. She had stood there so many times for this ritual, holding Manford's hand, the two of them watching him, the event of his homecoming. The tie would sail lightly, endlessly. "Any gin in the house, Vida?"

But he would not look directly at them.

She had watched Mr. Perry's tie flying through the air and had thought, as she stood there with Manford's hot hand held in her own, of her own shedded clothing lifting, billowing in air, leaving the body behind, warm and expectant.

"I'll be out for dinner tonight, Vida," he would say.

"But you've only just come home!"

She had been surprised, expecting once, twice, a hundred times, that he would stop before Manford, bring some gift from his pocket, touch him gently, lovingly. But Mr. Perry had turned away from her reproach, embarrassed. She had been so angry.

Now she hardly ever thinks of him.

A chill travels up her breast and to her face. The sun has moved on now, lingering on the fire irons, the empty grate, a lonely china shepherdess on the mantel, her gilded crook glowing.

It couldn't be Mr. Perry, she thinks. It wasn't then, and it isn't now.

But if not him, then who?

Returning to the kitchen, she folds the letter neatly and puts it in a drawer. Then she turns to regard her face in the small mirror over the old sideboard. She touches her hair, its springy weight bouncing around her face and neck. She pushes her fingers through it tentatively. What was it Mrs. Billy had said about that hair color? Venus, did she call it?

She looks at her watch. She has just time, she thinks, for a rinse before Manford is done at Niven's. She goes and fetches her coat.

But on her way down the lane toward the village and Mrs. Billy's, her eyes, caught by a flash of color, fly sideways to the bench, the bench where she waits for Manford in the afternoons. There, resting on its seat as though left behind, is a bouquet of flowers, tied with a ribbon.

Vida stops, frozen. Then she spins round as if to catch some departing figure, the owner, or the conveyor, of the bouquet. There is no one there. She takes a step closer. A small card is fitted into the ribbon. Gingerly she lifts it free, brings it close to her face.

For you.

Nine

NORRIS AWAKENS SO early Saturday morning that it is still dark. His sheets are hot and disheveled; he knows he has been dreaming.

But yesterday was no dream. He emerges into full wakefulness with the rising joy of one who has won a victory and is now realizing the full extent of the splendid consequences.

Vida has read his first letter. He has sent her flowers. She knows someone—a mysterious someone—loves her.

Norris rolls over in his narrow bed. A thin crease of gray light shows beyond the sill.

Mr. Calfo was wonderfully prompt about returning his letter, Norris thinks, and with a very pretty stamp, too. He must send him something by way of thanks—perhaps Mr. Calfo would like one of his stamps from those tiny little Faeroe Islands? A friend had put Norris onto these stamps—they were pretty, sunsets over the Baltic and so forth, and might one day be valuable. Norris had bought two at the time and thinks now that he might be willing to give one to Mr. Calfo for his expediency and cooperation.

But what could have happened to old Nesser, he ponders, rolling over again with restless happiness. Well, he supposes it will be along.

And the flowers, too—wasn't that a bit of luck?

"Won't you come along and dig up some of my lavender, Mr. Lamb?" Dr. Faber's wife had said, stopping in the post office Friday morning shortly after Vida had left with his letter. "Or at least come and cut yourself a bunch. It's a profusion!" And then she had stopped and sniffed, looking round the post office as if she couldn't quite locate the source of some scent that had suddenly filled her nose.

So he'd gone round to the Fabers' when he'd run home for lunch. Hermione Faber had been out in the garden herself—she was a spirited, handsome woman, with red cheeks and a high forehead and a cultivated accent, generally thought to do Dr. Faber credit, though he was well liked on his own. And she had the prettiest garden in Hursley, thought Norris, who prided himself on the performance of his own modest borders round the side of his cottage. Along with the lavender—she'd kindly put up three big pots for him; "Making room for these infernal hollyhocks," she'd said—she'd also pressed on him an armload of pink roses. "Simplicity, this one's called," she'd said, laying the bundle in his arms, "but I told Dr. Faber they ought to call it Multiplicity! Have you ever seen so many flowers? Mind the thorns."

But now, he thinks, rolling over to face the window again, pulling the sheet up over his shoulder—now he wants to do something more, something really clever. Nesser will send along his other letter, and won't she be surprised when that one comes? But Norris must think of something else for the meanwhile.

He wants to buy her a gift. He stares out the window, where the slice of light has thickened to a slab. He can hear birds now. There's no place in Hursley to go shopping, he knows, and everything will be closed if he waits until tomorrow. And this afternoon is the Sadie Hawkins races; he doesn't want to miss those, as he might see Vida there.

Well, there's no hope for it. He'll have to close up shop.

It is still very early when he steps out onto the Romsey Road. The wide white paper shades are rolled down at the butcher's, and the blacksmith's is quiet as death, Fergus upstairs in his foul bedchamber sleeping off his habitual Friday night affair with gin. Norris hurries down the Romsey Road and lets himself furtively into the dark, damp-smelling post office, where he writes out a sign, which he props in the window with a box of Crunchie bars.

CLOSED FOR THE MORNING. SORRY.

Locking the door again behind him, he walks down the road and stands anxiously in front of the shuttered windows of the Dolphin, looking up and down the street, breathing in the cloudy odor of the stale bitters and ale spilled on the flagstones beneath his feet and examining his watch until the bus comes into view, like a large prehistoric animal insinuating itself through the old houses tilting close by the road. A historian who'd once done a study of Hursley dated parts of the village—based on various ornamented stones, including one that now formed part of the wall of Mrs. Patrick's sheep pen—to 1138, when Henry of Blois, bishop of Winchester, built a castle whose vast ruins stood inside an Iron Age fort two miles north of the village. The vicar himself, though an acknowledged amateur in such matters, believed that St. Alphage, particularly its tower, had undeniable roots in the fourteenth century. But in any case, it seemed to Norris that regardless of exactly how old Hursley was—Saxon, Norman, whatever—the modern contrivances of buses and autos would always seem out of place there. He would have liked to have seen the village when there was nothing but horse traffic on the Romsey Road, when Fergus, whose business was now mostly given over to repairing tools and the occasional length of wrought iron fence, still shod twenty horses a day right at his forge. Now only the occasional mare was brought in, usually one of Winstead-Harris's. He rode them down into the village himself. Just like a lord, Norris thought. He'd always rather admired the man's doomed and anachronistic flair.

Excited by the sense of freedom from his own life (and its novel undercurrent of disobedience, for he always opens the post office Saturday mornings), he climbs aboard the bus, when it grinds to a halt before him, and heads immediately for the upper deck, the last seat in the rear, where he can turn and watch the village disappear as the bus rocks round the last of the Romsey Road's serpentine curves and gathers speed down the long slope through yellow and mint-colored fields toward Winchester. He blinks as the warm air of the compartment and the gritty stink of exhaust from the bus are replaced in a moment with the slightly sour, damp smell of a summer morning, riding the breeze through the windows.

He is pleased to have his seat. There are usually children who claim it, a row of squirming little boys in caps and high socks, and who appreciate the exaggerated bounce to be had at the back of the bus. But Norris, too, secretly likes the faintly thrilling quality of the ride in the last seat and the unobstructed view of what he is leaving behind, the trees swallowing the village behind him. In a shocking instant, Hursley is gone as completely as if it never existed, even the tower of St. Alphage and the silvery roof of Southend, and Norris experiences again the strange, empowering sensation of one feeling's canceling out the other, of being able instantly to ameliorate his grief at seeing his place on earth disappear—for of course Hursley couldn't just vanish. It will be there when he returns, rising up as they round the corner as magically as it has just now disappeared from view.

In Winchester a half hour later, the bus stops by the cathedral to let off a few passengers. Norris had gone by once to have a look-round after the archeological dig started there. But he had been vaguely disturbed by the sight of the underground civilization breaking through the terra firma beneath his feet, as if the ground he stood upon were not wholly stable. It had made him feel sad to imagine that his world, too, with all its lively industry, might one day be nothing but a layer of pottery shards and crude tools baked in the hot and dusty oven of the underground, the familiar rites of his own civilization rendered strange and somehow pathetic—for being lost and buried—by the passage of time.

Now, though, with his errand to consider, his mission firmly in his mind, he puts his cap on his lap and gazes quietly out the window at the inviting caverns of shade under awnings, the mysterious and interesting passages between buildings, the reassuring traffic of pedestrians going about their Saturday morning errands.

HE CONSIDERS WHETHER underthings might be appropriate. That's a romantic gift, isn't it? A catalog had come for Sam Saxon at the post office the other day, and Norris had taken the opportunity to glance over it. Saxon must have ordered something once for his wife, for Christmas perhaps. But, of course, she's left him now, gone to London, Norris had heard, with a second cousin. So perhaps it had been a last-ditch thing that had failed, he thinks now, Sam's ordering something from the catalog. How sad. Still, Saxon is rather an unappealing sort. Very bad teeth, Norris thinks.

But they'd had some lovely things in that catalog, nighties and so forth. He had admired one called the Hollywood, all in red, with a little jacket to it. But he had thought that red was not exactly Vida's color; he'd only admired the Hollywood and its blond occupant objectively. Actually, he thinks he has in mind something trimmed with fur—he doesn't know why, exactly. He likes the thought of little ermine cuffs. Or maybe something with feathers—pink feathers, such as an American woman might wear.

But Vida's not a schoolgirl, after all, and should have something that suits her level of maturity. No Little Bo-Peep bows and so on, he decides. No peekaboo.

HE PASSES THE women's lingerie shop, which is just off the close, once, twice, three times, without being able exactly to walk in through the door; there always seem to be a great many customers inside. And then he thinks that he will just go and have a cup of tea in the lobby of the Wessex first. He feels in need of refreshment.

At the Wessex he is brought a pot of tea and some rather charred toast in a rack, and he sits by a window, almost hidden by the long gold-colored drapes. Outside, across the lawn stretching up to the cathedral, the young workers with their colorful head scarves and striped jerseys begin to arrive at the dig. The sky is cloudy; Norris stares up into its utterly flat surface. When a single raindrop slaps against the glass before him, he jumps as if a plate has been dropped.

On his way out of the hotel, he pauses by the fountain in the lobby and fishes in his pocket for a penny.

He stands there for some time, the penny in his hand, thinking, and while he is standing there, a little boy comes and stands beside him. The child glances up at Norris through spectacles so thick that Norris cannot see the child's eyes, but only a rapid, blurring motion, like a hand waving from behind streaked glass.

"What will you wish for?" the boy asks.

Norris, who has been almost submerged by a wave of generalized, inchoate longing as he stands watching the water splash into the fountain, is speechless for a moment. The child waits and then glances away. "I always throw two, in any case," he offers generously, as if letting Norris in on a trick.

Norris looks over at him. "Two?" he says. "In case of what?"

"In case I've made a bad wish," the child says.

Norris considers this. "What's a bad wish?"

The boy glances at Norris, as if to see whether he's to be trusted. "Something I shouldn't wish for," he answers at last. He appears to be thinking. "Like—all the chocolate in the world," he says finally.

"Oh!" Norris is vaguely relieved. "Well, that doesn't seem *such* a bad wish," he says jovially, as if to cheer up this serious little fellow.

The boy shrugs. "It's never come true, anyway," he says. "They don't ever, do they?"

And now he is looking up at Norris, his eyes a blue, watery blur. Norris is stricken. He feels as if he had thrown the boy a life ring, but the child had missed it and was now vanishing under the waves.

"I think," Norris says quickly, more heatedly than he intends, "that perhaps we only get one wish. One in the whole of our lifetime. But you never know when it's going to be granted, you see. It might be anytime. So you might as well just keep on wishing. In fact, you'd better wish every chance you get, because if you don't"—he looks down at the boy standing beside him—"if you don't keep wishing, you might just miss your chance."

THE SALESWOMAN IN the boutique is young. Norris is relieved by this. Addressing his needs to a woman more his age would be somehow embarrassing, he thinks.

There are three mannequins clustered near the door to the shop, and Norris negotiates their delicately dressed, immobile selves carefully, making his way to the center of the room. The carpet under his feet is a weary green; the walls, by contrast, are a fresh white, and the various gowns and nightdresses stand out like the occupants of a crowded and colorful aviary. The salesgirl, a plain young woman—with her pale blue shirt misbuttoned, giving her a somewhat lopsided appearance, Norris notes immediately—has looked up at him inquiringly.

"I'm looking—" He pauses, glancing around and feeling distracted by the fluttering racks of gauzy material. "I'm looking for a—gift."

"For yourself?" The young woman smiles a tiny, almost sorrowful smile, revealing two long front teeth, slightly crossed one over the other.

Norris stares at her teeth in confusion. "No," he says. "Not for myself. For someone *else*. I should like to buy something—for a female," he adds, hoping to clarify matters. "But—I'll be the one paying, if that's what you mean."

The girl smiles again. She has quite a pretty smile, Norris thinks, despite her teeth. He wishes she had got her shirt right. She stands there very patiently, as if she feels Norris is trying to remember something and she doesn't want to interrupt his train of thought.

Norris feels frozen to the spot. This has been a bad idea, he thinks.

At last, somewhat shyly, the girl raises her eyelashes and asks, "Your age, is she?"

"A bit younger," he manages to reply.

"Robe and nightie, or undergarments?"

Norris cannot completely believe that the word *undergarments* has come out of this nice young woman's mouth. He manages to say, "Robe."

Slow as a sleepwalker, the girl begins to move out from behind the counter. Norris closes his eyes, as if she might come out with no skirt on.

"We've several lovely matching sets." He hears her voice and opens his eyes quickly to avoid being ambushed. But the girl is on the other side of the room, indicating a rack. She has on a thickly woven tweed skirt, knee-length.

She turns to him with a swirl, surprisingly graceful, and holds up a floor-length gown in Oriental silk, printed with pale blue waterfalls, peacocks, and yellow-and-red butterflies against a trelliswork of Chinese Chippendale in soft chestnut. A swarm of birds the color of indigo buntings flies across the cream-colored breast. The lapels are of brushed green silk, fringed with golden tassels. The girl shakes it slightly, and it rises and falls, a woman swaying, the world tilting. "This is for underneath," she says quietly, and slips a cord to reveal a black silk nightdress, cut deeply across the shoulders in a ballerina neckline, smaller versions of the same butterflies and birds twinkling against the black.

"Isn't it pretty?" she asks. "I thought we should put it in the window, all by itself. Just like a princess standing there. You wouldn't need anything else, if you had this."

And Norris is reminded then of his stamps of eighteenth-century costumes. They're oversize, printed on the occasion of an exhibit of ladies' dress mounted at the British Museum in Cairo. Norris had thought the stamps were curious, the elaborate gowns standing out in solemn relief against black backgrounds as if, as soon as the photographer aimed his camera, the women themselves had vanished, leaving only their clothing behind. He had thought there was something tragic about the empty dresses, like fallen film idols, or princesses taken hostage in a coup.

Norris feels it best just to stay where is he is, but he gestures toward the robe. "It's very—" He pauses. "How much—"

The girl inspects the tags. "Fifty pounds. For the set."

"Fifty pounds!" Norris reaches for his handkerchief, dabs at his neck.

"We've got them cheaper." But she looks disappointed, begins to turn away with the gown folded over her arm, a discarded partner.

"No, no!" Norris's heart contracts with shame. "No, I'll take it."

She brightens, like a child. "Oh! You *do* love her, don't you?"

Norris stares at her, her thin neck inside the crooked collar of her blouse like the stem of a flower held in a rough hand. She's used rather too much eyeliner, he notices. Her eyes, rimmed heavily in kohl, look like a baby owl's.

"I can tell you do," she goes on happily. "It's in your face."

She smiles again, her lips coming together over her teeth like a stage curtain, and moves back to the counter, where she begins to fold the robe and nightgown into elaborate pleats. "I knew you were the right sort," she goes on shyly. "Not like the others. I saw it the moment you came in. You're the real thing, aren't you?"

She stops her folding for a moment and gazes up at Norris with eyes full of tears. "God," she says, blinking up at him. "I wish *I* were old."

THAT AFTERNOON, NORRIS sets his umbrella, rug, and hamper down on a weathered gray bench at the edge of the cemetery, looks through the trees to the lawns sloping down to the Tyre. The bridge over the gray water is woven with streamers and flowers, unnaturally bright in the greenish light that filters through the clouds. In a few minutes the young men will gather on the bridge, laughing and jostling one another. And then at a signal the girls will race down the grass and across the bridge, streaming over it in pursuit of the boys, who will take off over the far bank.

Norris sits down on the bench. He's packed a lunch—hard-boiled eggs, meat sandwiches, a jelly roll—but he doesn't think he will get to eat it here now, much less with Vida. He feels vaguely depressed after his morning of shopping, lonely and deflated. A few people have spread rugs across the grass, but a great many more stand by the road near their cars, where they can keep their luncheons safely dry should the rain begin.

This evening a dance will be held at Prince's Mead. Norris's grandmother used to play the piano for village dances, but over time, with the influence of the young, who prefer a different sort of music, real musicians had yielded to a phonograph and records. Norris could remember standing at his grandmother's shoulder turning pages for her before she lost her sight, the couples spinning past him. "Go on and ask someone, Norrie," his mother had whispered, coming up close behind him. "Go and ask Lucinda Horsey there. She's sitting all by herself. Go on."

But no one had caught Norris at the races earlier in the day, and he was grateful for the duty of organizing the sheet music, of appearing busily occupied. He'd said nothing to his mother, had nodded vaguely and failed to move. He didn't know why he had not been pursued by anybody at the race. He had tried not to run too fast, glancing over his shoulder. But the girls had flown past him, almost veering away deliberately, he'd thought in shame and agony. And he would have been so tender with any one of them, plaiting flowers for a crown, or kissing the sweet-smelling napes of their necks! He had stopped still at last, hopeless and stiff in his new shirt, and looked down at his feet. But that had been his fatal move, he'd thought. You mustn't look as though you wanted to be caught. He had glanced around, seen that a few other young men had drifted away as if they were bored with the game, when it was plain to Norris that they, too, were among the unselected. He had understood suddenly the cruelty of the contest. Why do such rites exist? he'd thought. And also, It doesn't matter what I think. I've no power to stop it.

Now, sitting on the bench watching the crowds assemble in a hesitant fashion on the lawns below, he hesitates. If it rains, Vida certainly won't come. He had taken out the nightdress for her when he'd arrived home from Winchester, spread it across his bed, and stared at it a long while. The way it lay there, empty and lifeless, had left him feeling peculiarly sad and hopeless, like a man who has been abandoned by his wife. Like Sam Saxon, he'd thought in distaste.

"Oh, there you are, Mr. Lamb. Where've you been all morning? What little mystery are you up to?"

Norris startles at the voice of Mrs. Billy, who is approaching through the cemetery, a brightly patterned shawl round her shoulders. Mr. Billy walks placidly behind her, toting a large hamper. "Come and have a sausage pie with us, won't you?" she invites Norris. "I've just made them."

He looks up at her glumly. "Don't you think they'll cancel?"

"Oh, pish, I shouldn't think so. The young don't mind a bit of rain. Don't tip the hamper, Mr. Billy. The cake will slide." She directs her attention back to Norris. "You're such a worrier, Mr. Lamb! Stay here under the trees like this and it will surely rain. You'll be bad luck!"

But Norris shakes his head.

Mrs. Billy puts her hands on her hips. "Now Mr. Lamb. You're a bachelor. You ought to be down there on the bridge, some pretty girl chasing you. You might find you enjoy it! You don't think you're too old now, do you?"

"It's not a question of age," he replies stiffly, looking away.

"Well, I've plenty of pies. Suit yourself," she calls.

He's offended her now. Mr. Billy marches past, nods impassively to Norris, his pipe clenched between his teeth.

Norris stares out through the trees. After a while, with a kind of grim relief, he hears the first of several large drops of rain smack the leaves overhead. The organizers of the festivities are running about under their umbrellas. Now they'll just move things inside, Norris thinks, though he can see a group of young men, their white shirts already plastered to their backs with rain, still idling by the bridge. He stands up and turns to lift his hamper from the bench. And then he hears her voice, thin and high and sourceless among the tall monuments of the cemetery.

"Come on, Manford," she is calling. "Hurry."

HE LIFTS HIS head and sees her, in a white dress, running awkwardly with her basket, Manford lumbering along behind her, through the vicarage garden toward the west end of St. Alphage.

When he pulls open the door behind them a moment later, panting and drenched, Vida has set her basket down inside and is wiping her face, lifting her wet hair away from her cheeks strand by strand, her fingers delicately extended as though operated by an invisible puppeteer.

"Oh! Mr. Lamb! You were caught as well." She turns to him, and her face glows in the dimness of the church, her white dress a sanctuary of shadows. "It came on very suddenly, didn't it? We're sopped."

Manford crosses his arms in front of him and shivers, slaps at his chest, making a bright, hard smacking sound. Norris sees Vida glance at Manford and then vaguely around the vestibule.

"Have they got a towel somewhere, do you think?" She holds out her arms hopelessly, her sleeves clinging.

Norris sets his hamper down. A violent shiver of fear and excitement runs through him. "There's the choir robes. I'll fetch them."

He comes back into the shadowy vestibule with three robes over his arm. He hands one to Vida. "Would *he* like one?" he asks, gesturing with his head in Manford's direction.

She helps Manford into the crimson robe. He looks heartbreaking in it, Norris thinks, the solemn and dignified cloth exaggerating his idiocy in a painful way. Manford lifts his arms experimentally and the sleeves billow. Vida smiles at him. "You look like an angel," she says fondly.

She steps away from them to the door, the hem of the robe dragging on the floor. "It's really raining hard now," she says, speaking into the vicar's garden through the open doors. "It's a shame. It's not nearly so much sport for them indoors."

Norris watches her, framed in the doorway. She looks both important and childlike. Gusts of rain blow across the cemetery like the sails of phantom ships.

"Did you ever go to one indoors?" he asks. "The races?"

"I didn't go to one *ever*," she says lightly. "I thought they were awful."

She turns around, apparently in search of Manford, who has moved off down the aisle, his arms wrapped round himself so that he appears, from behind, to be straitjacketed. He is looking up at the stained-glass windows. The light falls, faded and streaked, into the dim church. Manford stops below the repentance window, St. Peter with his keys and a cockerel.

Norris looks down at his feet, back up at her. "You never went to the races? I thought—"

"Oh, I went," she says. "I just didn't *run*." She hesitates. "There weren't enough girls. Didn't you ever notice that? And it was all prearranged."

"Prearranged?" Norris is baffled.

"Everyone knew who everyone else was going for. It was all set already." She glances over at him and gives a small laugh. "But you ran. I remember." Then she cocks her head. "Didn't you know how it would be? Didn't you know if someone was all set for you?"

"No. I—" Norris puts his hand to the back of his neck, drops of water trickling from his hair into his collar. "I only did it once. I wasn't caught."

"Oh. Well, that's what I mean." She speaks quietly. "Some were left out. I couldn't bear that."

"You're so kind!" The words rush from him, and he has to stop himself from throwing open his arms. He is filled even more with admiration for her. So young, he thinks irrationally, and yet she had understood.

She laughs, surprised. "I don't know. I think I was afraid of it, actually. Isn't that silly? Now, I—" She pauses. "I think perhaps I was afraid to chase the one I wanted."

The one she wanted? Norris can feel his face seize. Did she still harbor feelings for someone? Some chap now grown and married perhaps? Was that why she'd never married?

"Was there one?" His voice is very small.

"Oh, yes." She laughs lightly. "There was always one or another, wasn't there?"

Norris is stricken. Yet he senses something—some bravado—in her words.

She turns away from him, puts her hands to her face, brushes the wet hair away again. The wind pants just outside the door. The sky darkens purposefully. "I can't think why I didn't bring an umbrella," she says. "I knew it would rain."

Manford is standing now on the south side of the sanctuary beneath St. Stephen, his death by stoning. His own head thrown back and his mouth gaping open, Manford stares at the picture, St. Stephen's broken and anguished form, the staff he'd held to protect himself. Norris glances around the church and then back to Vida, feeling that he has something more to say. How amazing, he thinks, to be having this conversation with her. He wants to say something important, about what those years had been like for him.

"I didn't like it either," he offers suddenly, "but I always wanted to dance, you know. I felt rather shy, I suppose. It's funny—" He considers, and then looks up as if surprised. "I always thought I'd be quite a good dancer."

She turns round from the door to look at him. "Didn't you ever dance? Never once?"

He shakes his head. "You did, though?"

She looks at him. Norris is suddenly aware of how his hair must look, wet and disarranged oddly over the top of his head. He begins to raise his hand but stops when she starts to speak again.

"I loved to dance." She pauses. "Sometimes I still think about it. But there isn't any occasion for older people, is there? To dance, I mean." She looks at him; it's as if she has held out her hand.

"Are we older?" He smiles, grateful.

"Yes!" She laughs. "*I* am. And you certainly are, Mr. Lamb. You're older than me!"

He takes a step toward her. "I am," he says. "I *am* old, perhaps.

But we're not too old, are we? It's not too late?" It seems to him that she will steer them away. "I believe," he says, taking a deep breath, "I believe I would dance—like a gazelle!"

"A gazelle!" Her eyes are round.

"And you—" He takes another step, almost involuntarily, toward her. "And you'd be a—a—oh, what is it called?" He laughs. "One of those birds that leaps up from the ground, twisting and turning? A woodcock! That's what it is! It's their mating dance. Haven't you ever seen it?"

She stares back at him. "A *woodcock?*"

"Yes!" He has caught up her hands, is wringing them. "It's the most amazing thing. I've seen them, up near Winstead-Harris's house, in a spinney there. They start low to the ground"—Norris crouches slightly, and Vida must crouch along with him, for he has hold of her hands—"and then the female bird, she spins straight up in the air! Like a corkscrew! Really! It's fantastic!"

"Whatever for?" But she is laughing.

"Why, it's all part of the ritual, I suppose. It's how they do it." But he hears his own words then, and drops her hands in embarrassment. A *woodcock.* Good lord.

"It's a dance, you see," he says helplessly. "It's an art. A talent."

She smiles, and then he can see recollection pass over her features. "Did you ever go to Miss Ferry's pageants?" she asks him. "Do you remember them? The ones at Southend? I don't know whether they do them anymore. They've never asked Mr. Perry about using the house. But we had to wear Gypsy skirts and bangles. We liked the way we looked, all made up, with mascara and eyeliner and lipstick. We thought we looked quite exotic. We used to kiss one another before we went out, for luck."

Norris feels so happy. "Yes, yes, I remember," he says. "Of course you would like that, wouldn't you? Anyone would—like being somebody else. Someone with a more interesting life. More exotic, as you say." He appraises her shyly, appreciatively. "I should think you'd be a wonderful Gypsy. I like costumes, myself. I—admire the change they can effect. I think I—long for it, really, in a way."

"Being somebody else." Vida repeats his words. "You long for that?"

Norris feels disconcerted. He can't exactly judge her tone. Does she disapprove? "I used to think that I might have done so well, if only I'd had the chance," he says, trying to explain, and the words and the time are getting all mixed up for him. "If things had been different, I might have been—"

"Somebody else? You might have been different, too?" She is eager now, almost straining inside her robe. Her wet hair is slicked back from her face. Norris can see the slight protrusion of her brow above her temples, the fine bone there curved like a shell. He wants to put his finger to it, touch her pulse, the steady, astonishing measure of her existence.

"I thought, in a way," he begins awkwardly, touching his fist to his heart, the words coming slowly, carefully, for he has never said such things before, never to anyone; he is surprising himself, what he knows. "I thought once I might be capable of anything, really. Just that I walked and breathed—that seemed miraculous in and of itself! That I was one of the—the marvelous contrivances of the world, all so cleverly put together—" He wiggles his fingers like a man counting money. "The tympanic membrane of the ear, the great wings of the skull, and tissue and blood and ligament and bone. It all seems so fantastic, in a way, that it works!"

Vida looks baffled, almost agonized.

Norris tries to think. What is it he wants to say? He runs on desperately, despite himself. "But then, I don't know—one day I realized that I wasn't really so miraculous after all." He thrusts out his hand. "I've got a wart on my finger. You see? And I've got terrible eyesight. And a bad back. Kept me out of the war!" He says this last as if accusing himself, accusing his own back of having prevented him from being heroic. "But still, I've got to hope, don't I? Don't I? Don't we all?"

"Yes, of course," Vida says, but the baffled look hasn't left her face. Norris feels as though he will burst. He is so stupid! Why can't he just tell her?

A sudden, dull crash causes them to turn away. Manford flounders in a pile of hymnals down near the last pew. The tower he's built of them lies scattered.

Vida hurries down the aisle. She helps Manford to his feet, picks up the books, and arranges them neatly. She returns to Norris, holding Manford tightly by the hand. Manford's skin looks gray in the poor light.

She takes off her robe, hands it gravely to Norris without exactly looking at him. He reaches for it, holding it tightly, as if holding the robe will cause her to stay.

"It's let up a bit," she says. She helps Manford out of his robe, hands it to Norris, too.

She will leave now. Norris feels as though he were being buried in sand, that soon even his mouth and eyes will be buried.

She turns after ushering Manford outside.

"It was lovely seeing you," she says suddenly, warmly.

"Yes. Thank you," he replies.

WHEN HE STEPS outside, he finds Mr. Niven and his wife sitting under the dormer, a rug over their laps, and a thermos between them.

Mrs. Niven looks up in surprise. "*Another* refugee?" she says. "But it doesn't look as though you made it quite in time, Mr. Lamb."

"No," Norris says, feeling vaguely guilty, as though he's been caught at something. Had they seen Vida and Manford as well?

"Did you see Miss Stephen inside?" Mrs. Niven asks.

"Ah—yes. I did." He pauses. "She was wet as well," he adds.

Mr. Niven glances up at him. "Tea?" He extends a mug.

"Yes, thank you," Norris says, for he feels unnatural and light-headed, as though he has run a hard race.

"We've our book circle tonight, Mr. Lamb," Mrs. Niven says, leaning round her husband. "And, do you know, Charles has said he'll mind Manford for Miss Stephen while she joins us. Don't you think that will be lovely for her?"

"I'm going to practice with my putter is all," Mr. Niven says gruffly. "She said he'd be asleep."

But Norris is hardly hearing them, for suddenly an idea has come into his head. "So," he says, bringing the steaming tea to his lips. "Your book circle is tonight, is it? An hour of intellectual adventure on the high seas of literature?"

"Oh, not just an hour, Mr. Lamb. We shall be going on late into the evening," Mrs. Niven says. "We're having wine, as well," she adds. "A rosé. I expect I'll have to wake Charles, we'll go on so long. We're all terribly excited."

"I'm sure you are. It sounds fascinating," Norris says. Now he feels much better. All his botched efforts this afternoon, babbling on at Vida like an idiot—showing her his warts, for God's sake! But he can redeem himself now. Could he, really, get past Niven? Get the robe to her bedroom? He feels infinitely revived.

He takes a mouthful of tea. "Pity about the race, isn't it?" he says casually.

"Oh, they're *so* disappointed," Mrs. Niven says.

Norris hands his cup back to her. "That was just the thing, Mrs. Niven," he says. "Now I'll just run home and change into some dry clothes."

Mr. Niven looks up at him. "Are you opening up later?"

Norris is perplexed. "Sorry?"

"The *post office?*" Mr. Niven says, as if reminding him. "You weren't there this morning. I've something to post."

"Oh! Yes. Of course. Sorry for the inconvenience." He gives them a brilliant smile, touches two fingers to his forehead in a salute, and moves off. But he has no intention of spending his afternoon at the post office. He has far too much thinking to do.

THAT EVENING, NORRIS folds the nightgown and robe carefully in tissue and then in a length of torn sheet taken from the linen chest. When he opens the cupboard, a bundle of curled, dry roots tied with string falls out on the floor. Norris picks it up and puts it to his nose—vetiver, the smell of his bedsheets. He replaces it on the shelf and then puts the wrapped nightdress in a haversack. He senses that he might need both hands free for this mission, though if he had stopped to examine that thought he might have been embarrassed. What, did he expect to scale the brick and stone of Southend's facade, a patch over one eye and ivy tickling his chin, and enter through a window?

But he will not allow reason to interfere with the anticipation of adventure, even danger, that accompanies the matter of delivering his gift. He has in mind to lay it across her bed so that she might, stepping into her room later that night—possibly *naked*—from the bath, find it there waiting, as if someone watching had followed her. He has in mind something magical, impossible. He has in mind to surprise her. Everybody loves to be surprised, he thinks.

When he steps from his back door into the darkness, the pair of doves that nestle in the wisteria are disturbed and blow a long, warbling cry into the night, like the imitative whistle of a young boy meeting a cohort for a secret assignation. Then all is quiet.

He lets himself in at the post office as quietly as he can. He doesn't want to turn on a light and excite the suspicion of the drunken patrons at the Dolphin, lounging about on the corner at the two oak tables there, and so instead takes a torch from his haversack and trains it on the supply of letters and parcels that had come Friday afternoon. He had expected to sort the post Saturday morning, and then the notion of traveling to Winchester had seized him instead. But he hopes now that his second letter to Vida will have arrived, courtesy of old Nesser. He wants to deliver it along with the robe.

And there it is, an envelope of pale blue paper, a stamp on its face so lovely he feels instantly grateful to Nesser for his good judgment and excellent taste. It must have been from his own collection, Norris thinks, from a series he remembered that represented the civil virtues, issued by the independent Republic of San Marino some years back. Each stamp is a sketch, loosely drawn like a Matisse, showing a woman's body in various attitudes, heroic or modest. This stamp, depicting love, is of a beautiful woman seen in profile, her neck inclined backward in a faintly ecstatic pose, her gaze half-lidded and erotic. The faintest suggestion of her naked breasts can be seen, rising mounds beneath her collarbones. Norris is reminded of his own secret collection of breast-feeding stamps. He has several Madonnas, of course, and one stamp from Laos showing a pert young mother in an opened blouse with a high Oriental collar, her infant at her nipple. Another, from Tanzania, in celebration of the Year of the Child, features a dark-skinned woman, her enormous teat stretched by her hungry child. A Bostwanian stamp shows a woman tilting her large nipple playfully toward a cartoonish crocodile, its jaws stretched into a smile. Norris's favorite, though, is from Transkei, one of the South African homelands with its own postal service. In this stamp an older woman, a wet nurse, perhaps, naked from the waist up except for a massive necklace of rough white shells, offers her breast to a tiny starveling. Norris likes this stamp for the woman's patient service, her grave and heavy features, and the supposed life-giving magic of her milk.

Oh, Nesser is a marvel, he thinks now. How perfect this is.

He puts the envelope in the haversack, flicks off his torch beam, and steals quietly back outside.

HE DOES NOT expect to find the doors at Southend locked. No one in Hursley ever locks a door. He walks soundlessly through the high-pruned white oaks; a wide, leafless blackness, serene as a museum chamber, lies beneath the massive branches. Through a ragged passage in a towering boxwood already strung with the moist netting of spiders' webs, he steps into the garden and looks up at the house. A broad flight of steps, the capitals of the columns at its base carved with stone fruit borne lightly on a frozen froth of waves, leads to the terrace. And he imagines then that he can rise to her room like a hero, his heels sprouting wings.

But naturally he must walk like any ordinary mortal, and so he ascends the steps to the house, advances quietly along the terrace until he reaches the lighted frame of a set of French doors. He peeps round the frame.

Mr. Niven is there with his back to Norris, his putter gripped between two hands, his shoulders rounded, his gaze fixed on the golf ball and, fifteen feet away across the infinitely varied terrain of an Oriental rug, an overturned sherry glass that serves as the hole. The chandelier above him spreads light into the vast room with its coved ceiling; the dangling prisms issue a confetti of blue-white snowflakes the color of evening moths. Mr. Niven rocks slightly on his feet. He strikes the ball. Norris, crouched by a parapet, watches it roll soundlessly across the carpet and glance off the edge of the faceted glass with a single, perfect chime.

Oh, too bad, he thinks.

Mr. Niven walks across the room, fetches his ball, and returns again to his original position. Through the window, Norris follows the second shot, sees it roll clear of the glass altogether.

Tucking the club under his arm like a shotgun, Mr. Niven advances on the glass and touches it gingerly with his foot, adjusting its angle slightly, and then aligns himself over the ball again, somewhat nearer this time. Norris sees the ball describe a gentle arc and sink, with the sound of ice hitting the bottom of a tumbler, into the glass.

But he cannot stay and watch, though something in Mr. Niven's patient endeavor, something in his complete ignorance of Norris's presence outside the French doors, makes Norris feel somnolent and contented, like a sleepy child watching his mother's hands form dumplings or knit and purl an afghan. The danger of his errand, its preposterousness, licks at the back of his mind the way a forgotten caution rises into the conscience of a child—there is something he is supposed to remember, though he only wants to watch Mr. Niven and his ball traverse the carpet, back and forth, all night, the little white ball rolling.

But when Mr. Niven turns his back and bends over his putter again, Norris rouses himself and walks softly the length of the terrace to the short flight of steps that leads down to the kitchen garden by the back door. The beds there are a tangle of overgrown herbs, the long, spiny stalks of lavender waving like sea grass, the rue perfuming the air with its sour, volatile fragrance. At the kitchen door he stops and unlaces his shoes, tucking them beneath the dank boxwood, releasing a tiny shower of drops from the leaves cupped like tiny bowls.

The door moves inward lightly, soundlessly, swinging wide like doors in dreams.

He feels his breath quicken now, for he has never been inside Southend before. At last he is in the presence of so many things she has touched, the fraying cloth hung over the handle of the stove, the slick, pearly oval of white soap in the dish by the sink —it might have slid into the bend of her wrist, up her white arm!—the teacups draining on the board, an apple, partly eaten, browning on a plate with a scalloped edge. Norris wants to put the bitten slice to his own lips, to run his tongue over the clean edge, like a shelf of coral, made by her teeth. He steps close to the sink, to the windowsill, where an assortment of objects lies perfectly arranged as if by a painter: a tangle of hairpins; a small jar of hand lotion, pink gel crusted round its rim; two knobbed horse chestnuts from some previous autumn, their luster dim; the spindly dried flower of a tulip poplar like a medieval crown of thorns; one broken and lifeless monarch butterfly, its scales turning to dust. What did it say about her that she had chosen to collect these things? he wonders. He reaches his hand to touch them, sends the chestnuts wobbling, stirs the pins.

He moves soundlessly through the room, his gaze caressing each surface her hand might have trailed across, might have rested upon.

When he stands at last in the central hall, he feels frightened for the first time. He does not know exactly where Mr. Niven is; the house is so large. It occurs to him that explaining his presence here to him would be almost worse than explaining it to Vida herself. So when he hears the distant sound of a door opening and a set of approaching footsteps, he turns and runs wildly up the staircase, reaching the landing just as Mr. Niven, putter under his arm, and a bottle of sherry in one hand, passes through the hall, whistling tunelessly under his breath.

On his knees on the landing, Norris touches his forehead gently to the carpet as Mr. Niven's steps recede.

And then he raises his eyes to find that he is in a nightmare, faces with distorted Teutonic features growing like burls out of the lintels over the doors, strange creatures—half wyvern, half stag—emerging from the scrollwork, feathery-tailed dolphins diving from the wall brackets, all of it rococo and queer, the gold paint faded and glowing morosely.

Standing shakily, moving down the hall, he looks into several rooms and then arrives at what must be Vida's. He finds her bed, where the coverlet has been disarranged as though she had lain down briefly before going out, her hair, her cheek, against the pillowcase. He puts his face to it, and a wild feeling comes over him, as though he has lost her, as though she has died.

It is the room of a penitent, the small white bed pushed beneath the window, where the sleeper would have a view of the moon at night.

DOWNSTAIRS, MR. NIVEN returns through the hall with his glass of sherry and his putter. At the foot of the stairs he stops. Putting on her hat earlier that evening at the door, while thanking him profusely, Vida had said nervously that Manford would be asleep, that Mr. Niven needn't go check on him.

"Of course, he does sleepwalk from time to time," she'd added, turning round as he began to close the door after her. "But he hasn't done it for some time now, so I wouldn't worry. But if he does, you should just steer him back to bed. Don't, though," she said earnestly, as Mr. Niven again tried to close the door, "attempt to wake him. That can have—consequences."

Mr. Niven takes a sip of his sherry, glances up the darkened stair. Perhaps he will just go up and have a look in on him. He'd done that with his own children when he was left to mind them while his wife went off for some evening's entertainment. Of course, Manford isn't a child. But he *is* helpless, Mr. Niven thinks. And he begins to ascend the stairs, but as he does so, he looks up and meets the heavy-lidded eyes of one of the carvings, a great ho-ho bird standing atop the newel post at the landing. Mr. Niven stops uncomfortably at the sight of the coiled creature, its head thrown back over its bristling shoulder. He takes one more step, keeping his eyes fixed on the thing, and then turns round abruptly and heads back toward the kitchen and the small sitting room there. I think I'll just have a look at the telly, he thinks. And, How does she stand this place all by herself?

NORRIS UNPACKS THE nightdress, lays it across the bed, and pulls and pinches its folds until it looks just right to him. Then he fetches the letter Nesser had forwarded and places it carefully atop the gown. At last he steps back and looks around. The nightdress makes the room seem even shabbier, in a way, like the queen visiting a prisoner in his cell. He picks up a piece of the tissue that has fallen to the floor and is about to put it back in the haversack when he hears Vida's voice from the stairs.

"Good night!" she calls. "Thanks ever so much!"

Norris, frozen with terror, hears Mr. Niven's muffled, unintelligible reply. He looks around wildly and then steps quickly into the closet and closes the door after him, sinking to his knees inside as if his limbs have turned to water. He cannot see or hear anything. He feels the floor with his hands, places his palms flat against it, and tries to breathe deeply. But as he moves, as quietly as he can on his trembling hands and knees, toward what he supposes is the back of the closet, where he might hope to remain undetected if Vida has to open the door, he is surprised to fail to encounter a rear wall. In fact, the closet seems unnaturally deep. He ducks his head beneath the slips of hanging dresses, their intimate odor, and crawls slowly until the cloth brushing his forehead no longer has the light, hesitant brush of a woman's hemline but has become heavier, like a hand pressed to his shoulder. He reaches up in the darkness and feels velvety nap and rough wools, realizes that they are overcoats, that it must be a shared closet, that he has crawled from Vida's chamber into the closet used by Mr. Perry for his winter storage. And suddenly the thought of their garments intermingling in that single space, that tunnel—the thought of the insignificant weight of her dresses beneath the masculine heft of Mr. Perry's topcoats—makes Norris practically ill. He closes his eyes.

He falls asleep in the closet eventually, drowning in shame. Or perhaps he faints; he is not sure which. Sometime late in the night, he wakes and crawls out quietly into an unused bedroom. He feels as though he has been ill for a long time. The house is so dark and still that as he passes down the stairs in his socks he wonders what spell has overtaken them all, Vida and Manford and Mr. Niven and perhaps even the whole village fallen asleep, shafts of moonlight laid over their faces like veils. He is cold and exhausted.

By the back door he finds his shoes, full of water, and walks home. But as he walks, he looks up and sees that the moon has come out and bobs along behind him cheerfully like a toy on a string. As he turns the corner from the lane onto the Romsey Road, the moon swings round his shoulder as if to light the way, and when Norris reaches the street, he has to gasp, for there she has laid down a trail of silver for him to follow, a carpet rolled out for a king.

And now he can hold his head up again as he steps onto this river of light, the windows behind which his neighbors sleep filled with the blinding reflection of wonder, the moondust sparkling and twinkling around his forehead in a crown of a thousand brilliant stars.

Ten

VIDA USUALLY FINDS the services at St. Alphage restful, and so when she comes to her knees at the pew Sunday morning, Manford kneeling heavily beside her, his hands folded in a pious fashion, she closes her eyes, hoping for relief.

Coming home last night from the book circle to find the robe laid out on her bed had been one of the most unsettling experiences of her life. That, and the accompanying letter, postmarked this time from Cairo:

I am the man with the world at his fingertips. I am the gateway to adventure. I am your personal ticket to paradise. I fall at your knees in worship.

As beautiful as the robe was—and it *was* beautiful—and as mysterious as the letter was, the charm of both had almost been destroyed for her by something very unexpected and unpleasant indeed—fear. Someone had been in her bedroom. Someone she did not know, or the emissary of someone she did not know, had put his hands where she lay down to sleep. Perhaps he had watched her enter the house, wave good night to Mr. and Mrs. Niven, had seen her light come on in her window. This was too much, she felt. It was too—near.

She had been looking forward to her hour in church this morning. She had hoped that it would calm her, the tedium and the music both immersing the congregation in a soothing bath of piety and fellowship. She had hoped it would remind her of the ordinariness of everything. But now she finds that she will not be soothed by the morning's service in the least. The new organ is very loud, and there is a ferociousness to Mr. Lamb's playing.

She rises from her knees, putting a hand on Manford's arm, and stares dully at Mr. Lamb's back as he sits at the organ, his head shaking wildly on his neck like a flower on a long stem, his hands darting over the keys, his knees pumping as though he were running a race. He seems to have gone mad, playing with a fervor that strikes her as profane, a profane gaiety. But it is not as if she can sit still herself. She wriggles and shifts on the pew; her shoulders feel tight and uncomfortable.

In the absence of any other evidence, it now seems likely to her that *Mr. Niven* might be her mysterious admirer, the deliverer of the robe, the writer of the letters. After all, he was the only one at the house last night. And now she can't rid herself of the feeling that he must be sitting somewhere behind her, a notion that fills her with dismay. It isn't at all pleasant to have to think of him in this new way. And, worse yet, something about it doesn't seem exactly right. Still, she knows so little of the world, really, so little of human character; and though she doesn't really like to be reminded of it, if she can dance about on the fountain like a fairy, then perhaps Mr. Niven, too, is capable of surprises.

Manford, as if sensing her discomfort, is as restless as she is. He tries repeatedly to stand up from the pew. She frequently has to prevent him from standing during church services, as if the music reaches him at some instinctive level, prompting from him a soldier's salute. This morning he seems to require particular restraint, however. She turns and glares deliberately at him, her most reproving face, after several instances in which she has to clamp a hand on his knee. "Do be still, Manford," she hisses at him.

But Manford, beaming and ignoring her reprimand, turns

around in his seat and—to Vida's horror, as she follows his gaze—catches sight of Mr. and Mrs. Niven a few pews behind them. Manford grins broadly and gives them a wave. Mr. Niven raises his hand and flutters his fingers in reply, meanwhile putting a finger to his lips. Mrs. Niven smiles indulgently. Vida freezes, an ugly flush creeping up the back of her neck. She snatches at Manford's hand and squeezes it, harder than she intends. Manford, going limp next to her, looks down at his lap, takes back his injured hand, and nurses it carefully in the other, testing his fingers and giving her baleful looks.

Vida hates herself immediately. And an image of Manford from the night before, disheveled and forlorn in his nightshirt, arrives in front of her eyes. She shudders, puts her own hand apologetically on Manford's fingers to still them, and wishes fiercely that he had not started sleepwalking again.

THE WHOLE NIGHT had been wrong, had gotten off to the wrong start, she thinks, beginning with the robe.

She hadn't even noticed it right away. She'd seen the Nivens out and had gone straight up to bed, tired by the interminable chat of the book circle. She'd gone to wash up and had come back into the room, her hair in a towel—and then she had literally jumped. It was lying there on her bed like a royal visitor.

She had come forward, one hand holding the towel to her head, and had leaned down to touch the robe in disbelief, as if it might not be real. But it was real, cool and silky, and she had run her hands over the waterfalls and birds like peacocks, with long, trailing plumage, the butterflies like sapphires, the golden tassels. It had smelled extraordinarily sweet as well, like vetiver, she realized. She hadn't smelled vetiver in years; her mother had always kept a bit tied up with the sheets. As she lifted the sleeve of the robe to her nose, though, it struck her that she'd smelled vetiver somewhere else, more recently. Where had it been?

And then she'd noticed the letter. She sat down on her bed to open it—and that's when all the lovely wonder turned to fear. *I am the man with the world at his fingertips.*

She didn't like the sound of it. It implied a kind of dark magic, she thought, a promise that couldn't be kept and was therefore no sort of promise at all but only a taunt. She wound her hands together and tried to breathe deeply, her yoga breathing—she'd learned some yoga from a show on the telly once—but it didn't really help. It occurred to her that she would be unable to scream, for her heart had rolled into a high, tight place, lodged against her windpipe like a stone before a cave.

Now think, Vida, she'd admonished herself. Think carefully. Calm yourself. For it *must* be Mr. Perry—no one else could have got into the house—and there's nothing to be frightened of there. She'd thought he was in Venice, but of course she really had no way of knowing exactly where he was, and perhaps he'd been called to Cairo suddenly? He could be anywhere. Or everywhere —and at that, the fear began ticking away again inside of her. He could be in Cairo, and Corfu, and on the bench in the lane . . . *and in her bedroom!*

He must have come home, she thought wildly. He'd come home unannounced, while she'd been out. He'd done such things before.

But wouldn't Mr. Niven have said so?

She stood up and went down the hallway to his bedroom. After a hesitation, she knocked. There wasn't any answer, of course, and she wouldn't open the door; she knew he wasn't there. She stood in the hall, the robe in her arms, her heart beating very quickly, like a moth trapped inside the cup of her hand. She had not wanted to turn around. But at last she had mastered herself and had gone back to her own room.

It couldn't be Mr. Perry, she'd thought. It must be Mr. Niven himself.

But how funny: she was *disappointed.*

She had wanted something else, hadn't she?

It was sad, just imagining it. Poor, red-faced Mr. Niven, with his hair always smudged with flour and his silly old putter—could he have fallen in *love* with her? And written those letters? It wasn't what she might have imagined, not at *all*. And poor *Mrs*. Niven! She was really a very sweet person, even if she did monopolize the book circle, she and Mrs. Billy going on and on about homosexuality.

She folded up the robe inside some paper and stowed it away in a drawer. Her hands trembled, so she shut off the light and lay down. But she couldn't rid herself of the feeling that whoever had brought her the robe, whoever had written her the letters, whoever *loved* her—as menacing an emotion as that now seemed—whoever he was, was watching her, she thought, watching her at that very moment. She lay there, staring up at the ceiling. She thought she might never sleep again.

But she did sleep, for she was woken sometime later in the night by a crash coming from somewhere below her in the house. She recognized the sound: a chair toppling as Manford plowed mindlessly through the rooms, stepping through the furniture as though chairs and tables were nothing more than tall grasses bending before his weight.

She sat upright in bed. Pulling on a cardigan, she looked in the door to Manford's room. His bed was empty in a square of moonlight; the coverlet pooled on the floor. Fear blossomed up in Vida's heart.

Though she had no medical evidence for it, she had read somewhere—in a magazine, she thought it was—that it was very dangerous to wake a sleepwalker; the article had been somewhat unclear, suggesting profound mental alteration, even coma, as a consequence. And so her efforts to locate Manford during one of his spells were always prolonged in an agonizing way by her unwillingness to call for him, searching instead through the cold and dark house until she came upon him at last, often standing sentinel in the middle of a room or pressed up near the draperies by a window, nearly hidden by their long and dusty folds, his eyes staring strangely into the darkness.

Sometimes it was easy. He was so unaware of his own movements at such times that he could be found simply by the noise he made jostling through the rooms, knocking aside vases or clocks, catching tassels and the edges of carpets. But sometimes his path seemed eerily stealthy. He wound silently then, like a cat, narrowly missing things, his hands riding the invisible waves of air beside him.

Once she had been tempted to mention this habit to Dr. Faber, but she was sure he would recommend a lock on Manford's door. She did not like to invite this suggestion, as she was terrified of fire. She could not bear the thought of Manford's being contained in an inferno, vainly wrestling with the door latch applied against this mysterious habit of sleepwalking. And so she had trained herself to sleep lightly over the years. More often than not, she woke to the sound of Manford's rising from bed in the next room and could steer him back even before he reached the door.

But this night, no longer in the habit of waking, perhaps—Manford had been sleeping peacefully now for quite a long stretch—she did not wake until the noise of the toppling chair, or whatever it was, reached her. He must have been abroad now for some time, she thought in alarm, hurrying down the hall.

Though she raised a prayer against it, as she reached the landing, the old feeling of terror came over her. Oh, you've seen too many films, Vida Stephen, she thought, to comfort herself. But there it was, all the same, this unreasonable but certain fear, as if the house itself were animated by demons and stalkers, bad men with no business being there, its expressionless gargoyles and fading frescoes suddenly transformed into leering monsters. And the presence of the robe laid upon her bed, which she remembered now as she descended the stairs, seemed to confirm her sense that the house itself was not trustworthy, that she was not safe there. Mr. Perry thought Southend a lark; he called its strange carvings and paintings a bit of Italian import. But sometimes, at times like this, she thought they made the house seem possessed.

But it wasn't just the house, its endless rooms and hallways, its hidden staircases and warren of damp basement chambers, ganglions of iron hardware for storing smoked meats and draining fowl hanging from the beams. The worst was that she was afraid, could be made afraid, of Manford himself. It was as if the parts of him that were unknown to her, and even to him, perhaps, were not just absent—missing faculties, as she sometimes thought of them, like the dead air of so many unused rooms—but hidden away and subject to possession by evil forces. She did not know why she thought this. Manford had never exhibited even the faintest tendency in this direction. In fact, he was just a baby, lying down on the floor by the fire in the evenings and pushing a little lorry back and forth or dreamily stroking the threadbare mane of a stuffed lion.

Still, it was the mystery of him, the impossible idea of there being nothing there. She was sure that, at some level, Manford had an appreciation of the ways of the world that he could not express but that remained trapped within him, a glittering hoard in the silt of his damaged mind, the crushed and lopsided cells of his brain. Sometimes she was so proud of him, his odd ability to render what he saw in the tendrils of icing he drew over Niven's cakes, the curious botanical likenesses he could fashion, or the play of his hands against the slanting light of late afternoon, shadow shapes leaping from his fingers. That he was sympathetic by nature, stroking her arm or touching her face gently with his fingertips—this only increased her admiration of him. The world could be full of meanness. In its midst, Manford was a sort of artist, she thought, a genius in his own way, too good for the world. A saint.

But at night, when he rose from his bed and wandered through the house, she was sometimes seized by this unreasonable terror of him. Coming upon him, she would think he seemed larger than she remembered, the muscles twitching beneath the soft skin of his arms. She would touch him tentatively then, as though he might lash out at her.

"Is he—frustrated—do you think?" she had asked Dr. Faber anxiously once when Manford was fourteen or fifteen and had suffered a spell of upsetting attention to his own body, his hands straying to the buttons of his trousers time and again, a pained look on his face.

Dr. Faber had shaken his head. "It's just adolescence, I would say," he said. "Though, of course, it's hard to tell."

"No, I mean—" Vida had paused, embarrassed, turning her head aside carefully as she helped Manford do himself up. She did think he needed his privacy, like anyone else, but it was awkward tending to him in front of other people. She stared at a black vein in one of the cracked green tiles on the floor of Dr. Faber's examining room. Really, sometimes she simply had to look at him. You can't do buttons with your eyes closed, she thought, and Manford was most uncooperative.

She tried to think how to ask Dr. Faber what she meant. Though perturbed by it in public, she was not really worried about the business of Manford's manliness exactly, or rather his awakening interest in it. It seemed natural enough to her, though sometimes she was surprised at how he had grown up to be so big. If she had to tussle with him over something—putting aside his stamp albums at night or bringing him in from the garden—she found herself struck by how strong he had become. But she did worry, in a general way, that Manford was coming to understand his own limitations more and more. It seemed to her he was fretting about something. That he was embarrassed. When they rode the bus or went for a walk in the village, he had taken to hiding behind her shoulder and averting his face from people they knew when they spoke to him. Sometimes he even waved them off. And, of course, hiding behind her was useless, even when he was just thirteen or fourteen. He was already nearly a foot taller than she by then.

She had finished with Manford's shirt, knelt to help stuff his feet into his shoes.

"Does he," she'd said slowly at last, "—do you think he knows how he is?"

Dr. Faber had patted her shoulder, turned to rinse his hands in the sink of his examining room. "Not any more than a dog knows he's a dog," he'd replied. "Don't play with yourself now, Manford," he'd added sternly, turning round and drying his hands on a rough bit of paper toweling. "It's not polite company."

Though it was unlike Vida to question anybody, least of all Dr. Faber, whose learning she admired, she had been unsatisfied at these remarks. No, more than unsatisfied. She had been angry. She'd never had a dog, but she felt sure that it was inappropriate to compare Manford to one.

SHE HAD PAUSED at the bottom of the stairs, listening. Though she knew the sound that had woken her had come from below, she couldn't help sweeping her eyes over the gallery that ran round three walls of the great hall, the closed doors there each with their carved lintels and brooding faces. She half expected a door to creak open as she glanced anxiously over them.

She stood lightly on her feet. Perhaps Manford had hurt himself, was lying in a pool of blood somewhere! Her heart wrenched at the thought, but she gathered herself together and walked resolutely across the hall. I shall just go room by room, she said to herself, and I shall certainly find him.

At the door to the drawing room, she paused again. White light from the uncurtained French doors fell in leaning parallelograms across the floor, pebbling the carpet like a stony beach. She had been to the seaside only once, to Brighton with her mother and father on a holiday. They had stayed in a little hotel with a damp kitchenette and sand in the pots. She still recalled the feel of the stones beneath her feet at the edge of the water, how they had shifted alarmingly under her tread. Now, stepping noiselessly across the carpet, she recalled the sensation of it. Manford was nowhere to be seen.

She passed through the whole house, arriving at last at Mr. Perry's library. The door, which she kept closed in Mr. Perry's absences, was ajar. Inside, one of his drawing tables had been overturned. There were three such tables, arranged corner to corner in the center of the room so that Mr. Perry could spin on his chair and easily reach one or the other, shifting his focus from drawing to drawing, the perspectives differing one to the next. Vida had tried it once and it had made her dizzy, gazing now up or down or from some impossible perspective right *into* a particular building, as though she were hanging upside down from one foot. Now, though, the table nearest the door had fallen over. The roll of white tissue hinged cleverly to the back of it lay unfurled across the floor, a ghostly path.

Yet Manford was not there.

Now Vida's alarm spread beyond her control. She knew she would start to cry. It was too much, too much. She was so afraid of the house at night as it was, and now to come upon this scene—it was so disturbing, as if something dreadful had happened—and not find Manford anywhere. She tried to calm herself. I mustn't call for him, she thought, a near hysteria sweeping her. I mustn't frighten him.

And she saw what she had not seen before: the hidden door at the rear corner of the room, a door that led by a narrow passage into a small and ornate greenhouse erected on a high terrace, was open. This door, cleverly paneled so as to seem part of the wall itself, had not been opened for years.

Vida and Mr. Perry had inspected the greenhouse once, shortly after she had begun working at Southend House, when Mr. Perry was busy furnishing the estate to his own tastes. What they found there had shocked them both.

"I guess no one wanted these," Mr. Perry had said after a moment, when the two of them had emerged blinking into the bright and arid space of the greenhouse and stopped up short at the sight that greeted them, the shelves of the high, curving étagères crowded with enormous Japanese porcelain pots, each sprouting a dead and brittle miniature tree, its twisted limbs and writhing roots curling over the vases' rims. There were perhaps fifty of the little bonsai trees, a dead legion. The air in the greenhouse had felt to Vida like the air of a tomb, as if it had acquired a deathly weight of its own that supplanted the characteristic liveliness of light.

Mr. Perry had stepped toward the shelves, reached out to touch one of the little trees. A tiny branch broke away in his hand. He regarded it a moment before dropping it to the floor. Then he looked around and sighed impatiently.

"You need a particular sort of mind for this, don't you?" he asked.

Vida, unsure of her place with Mr. Perry then and feeling herself unsophisticated beside him, had said nothing. But she had felt moved to sadness by the forest of dead trees, each bound in its beautiful urn. "They're very old, aren't they?" she'd said at last. "Hundreds of years perhaps?"

Mr. Perry had not addressed her remark directly. "Maybe *these* are worth something," he'd said, stooping and tracing his finger over the scene of a waterfall painted on one of the sloping vases. "I'll call Sotheby's, I guess. Get someone to come and take a look at them. But I guess they wouldn't have left them if they'd been worth anything. Still, you'd think—I mean, some of these must have been around a couple of centuries ago. Or something like that." He squinted, frowned. "It's kind of criminal, just leaving them here like this. Who was it, do you think? It's strange—they've been untouched all these years?"

He had put his hands on his hips, squinted again at the dusty panes overhead, the litter of broken branches from the oak trees lying black against the glass. And Vida had gazed at the little bonsai trees, gray and withered, and had felt a sort of guilty conspiracy, as if by coming across this scene, so terrible and sad, like unearthing old bones in a potter's field, she bore some responsibility for what had happened.

Mr. Perry had turned after a moment and ushered her out. "Let's just leave it for now," he'd said. "I'll make a couple of calls about it." But he never had. Vida didn't even know whether he'd ever gone back in there. She herself had been back only once, when it was discovered that squirrels were nesting in the house. She had let a pair of old men with traps back there, stopping, herself, at the door.

"There's this," she'd said, wrenching the door open for them. "But I don't suppose they'd be in *there*."

And later, when the men were leaving, one of them had said to her, "That's a queer little place, that greenhouse. What do you call those things?"

Vida had startled. She'd forgotten the trees. "Bonsai," she'd said, and had felt guilty all over again.

"Well, they're all dead, you know," the man had said implacably. "Oh," he'd added. "I took care of a pair of blackbirds in there for you. No charge for that. They were dead, too." He laughed. "I don't charge for the dead ones. Tell him he needs to have the roof mended, though." He tipped his hat. "I'll be back for the traps."

Now the image of the silent, tortured trees reared up in Vida's mind; she shrank before the memory of them. Oh, he *can't* be in there. *Please*.

But he was.

He was seated on the lowest of the étagères, wedged between two vases like an unmoving shelf of rock. His hands were folded carefully in his lap; his eyes were wide open. His hair stood on end, tufted and torn looking. His nightshirt was wrenched about him, as if he'd tried to free himself from it. He was gray in the moonlight, as gray as the landscape of tiny gray trees, the faded porcelains, the shelves' chalky paint chipped upon the floor.

Vida fought the impulse to wretch at the sight of him, a boy grown suddenly old, a man aged before his time, changed overnight into a ghost, colorless and ancient and webbed with dust. As she knelt before him and took his hands gently into her own, she felt her own tears fall on her hands like something sharp, diamonds or crystals.

He rose without protest, allowed her to take his hand. She led him upstairs. They left behind them as they passed through the house a trail of white footprints, growing fainter as the dust and paint chips wore off onto the carpets. At his bedside, her hands trembling, she stripped him of his soaked nightshirt, exchanged it for a fresh one hung inside his wardrobe, fitted the buttons carefully, her lips moving soundlessly, a soundless comfort. When she pressed him to the pillows, he closed his eyes at last, reached for her, and caught a measure of her dressing gown in his hand. She lay down beside him, fitted her knees up against his own. She wept into his back.

She dreamed that night of Corfu, of her uncle Laurence standing on the sand by the sea, waving a red handkerchief toward her, his mouth moving. She was on a rock, and in the wake of a passing boat spread the extravagant silken robe, waterfalls and peacocks, sunset and sunrise both. She had leaned down to disturb the surface of the water, and then, in her dream, Manford had become a dolphin, a porpoise with Manford's aggrieved expression, his swollen brow. She had knelt at the shore, but he could not come to land to meet her.

Now, in church this morning, holding Manford's fingers between her own, she regrets her sharp tone. "Listen to the music," she whispers, stroking his hand. He quiets, sits heavily against her, his eyelids drooping. She must dispatch this business with Mr. Niven, she thinks resolutely, if in fact it *is* him. One firm word from her—uttered privately, of course—and it will be over.

Yet she feels, instead of relief, a thick fury. Something has come and gone, leaving her the same as before.

Well, what had she hoped for? Stupid woman, she thinks with vehemence. Stupid woman.

When they rise for the final hymn, Manford pulls his hand away from hers and begins to clap, not quite in time with the music. Vida stops him. He has been a nuisance this morning; she hopes no one has minded. She does like to bring him to church, believing at some level that God notices Manford particularly, is especially tender with this damaged lamb, that He likes having him under His roof.

On the way out, though, Manford crouches suddenly like a baboon and makes a face at a small girl in a pretty blue dress, her yellow hair done up fussily with ribbon. Though Vida understands Manford's gesture is playful, the child shrinks from him, pressing back against her father's knee. The man grimaces at Vida, who catches Manford hurriedly under the arm and pushes him forward. "Sorry," she says, but cannot spare more this morning.

When they arrive at the door, the vicar takes her hand gently in his, reaching for Manford with the other. Vida looks with relief at the square of light from the opened door, the disappearing heads of people as they pass down the path ahead of her. The vicar is kind, but all she wants, right then, is to be out in the air, away from people, away from the Nivens, and walking home with Manford.

The vicar detains her, however. "God bless you both," he says, smiling. Vida smiles back, but she is busy keeping a wary eye out for Mr. Niven. And meanwhile she sees that Manford's attention has been caught at that moment by Mr. Lamb, who is standing a few feet away energetically pumping Dr. Faber's hand and saying something in an excited tone about the organ. Vida sees Manford withdraw from the vicar's grasp and go to stand up close beside Mr. Lamb. She attempts to disengage herself from the vicar as well, but he is asking about the book circle. He murmurs inquiries; she glances away from Manford, tries to attend to the conversation. And then, out of the corner of her eye, she sees in horror that Manford has thrust his hand inside Mr. Lamb's coat pocket.

The smile fades from Mr. Lamb's face and he stands frozen, stiff as a rake, Manford fishing in his pocket. Dr. Faber has turned around, recalled to someone by a tap on his shoulder, and as Vida breaks away from the vicar at last and hurries up to disengage Manford's arm, Mr. Lamb flushes a deep, mortifying shade of red.

"He thinks—" he says to her, low and urgent, worried, "he thinks I've a sweet in my pocket. I haven't any—*today,*" he adds incomprehensibly.

"Manford!" Vida says, tugging on his arm. "Do leave go Mr. Lamb's pocket!" She looks up at Norris. "I'm terribly sorry," she says, struggling with Manford and feeling horribly flustered. "I can't think why he would do such a thing!"

Norris clears his throat with difficulty, glancing down at Manford's hand as if it were a small animal with a sharp bite. "Well, perhaps—" he says, trying delicately to twist his jacket away from Manford's grasp, "perhaps he's hungry? It was rather a long—or rather, it *is* nearly time for lunch!" He says this last quite brightly, as if glad to have an explanation.

Vida succeeds in removing Manford's hand, but they have moved down the path by now, jostled together, carried along by the press of people behind them.

"I am so terribly sorry," she begins again, reaching up to adjust her hat, a small, deep purple cloche that belonged to her mother and that has fallen forward on her forehead. She can feel a trickle of sweat proceed down between her breasts. She is forced to take another step closer to Mr. Lamb as a group of people come up behind her, laughing and chattering.

"Pardon me," she says.

And then she looks up into Mr. Lamb's face.

It is quite close to her, for though she has stepped toward him, he has not moved away so as to make room for her and Manford. She can smell some odor on him, tooth powder, mixed with the strong tannin of tea, she thinks, and—how odd—vetiver! She'd smelled it in the post office the other day, too, she realizes, when he was so dressed up for that funeral. And now his eyes—she notices how they look down into her own at that moment—how blue they are.

"I can't think—" she begins faintly, but a wild feeling has come over her; she wants to run away!

He interrupts her. "I have given him a peppermint, once before," he says quickly, staring into her face, his tone apologetic and serious, as for a confession. "And a lozenge. Orange, I think it was. Or, no. Butterscotch." He pauses. "My God. I hope I didn't do wrong."

Vida stares at him. They are in such close proximity that she can detect a tiny, crescent-shaped scar above one of his eyebrows. Gave Manford a sweet? When? "No," she begins, "but when—"

But Mr. Lamb smiles at her then, blinding. "Oh! I'm so *glad!*" he says, and puts a hand over his heart.

And then she gasps as he reaches for her, grasps her hand. "Would you—" He is so eager, so eager! And his words come in a rush, come so fast that a bit of white spittle gathers at the corner of his mouth. Vida stares, astonished. He leans toward her, holding her hand, his face inclined down toward her mouth, so close that she can feel the brush of his jacket against her breast. "Would you care to have lunch with me?" Mr. Lamb is asking, and at first all she hears is a row of unintelligible sounds, as if she were underwater. She comes up for air—"Seeing as *he's* peckish already," Mr. Lamb is saying, and now she can understand him, "and of course I have quite an appetite myself after that, and, I thought, perhaps, it might be nice to have *fish*. I so rarely have fish, unless there's an occasion. And this *is* an occasion, I think. I—"

Fish? Vida thinks.

"I haven't a car, but we could take the bus?" Mr. Lamb stops, his hand still holding her own. "He does ride the bus?" he asks, worried.

"Yes, of course," Vida says. Why wouldn't he ride the bus? Of course he rides the bus. But—is he asking us to lunch? And then she thinks of the last time she ate a meal out, as if somehow this thought will help her understand what is happening now, at this moment.

Mr. Perry had been home at the time and had said jovially to her at breakfast that she ought to have a day out, an outing for herself. He'd even said he'd mind Manford; he was going round to have a word with Peter Shields about the cows and would take Manford along. Manford likes the cows but he won't walk over the cattle guard, Vida had told Mr. Perry; he's dreadfully afraid of the cattle guard. You'll have to go round the other way, drive up to the house. Yes, yes, he had said. Stop worrying!

So she'd had a hamburger at a pub in Winchester, had looked in the shops. She'd gone by the cathedral, too, to see about the dig. A young, round-faced woman there had shown her a bit of a pot she'd found—it had a fragment of a drawing on it, faint and pink, like a fossil. "Isn't it grand?" the young woman had asked Vida, and Vida had found herself swelling with a near sob of appreciation for that chip of pottery, for the young woman, for the cathedral, for the whole sacred enterprise of the dig. She had had to look away from the girl, in fact, almost overcome.

The young woman had helped Vida step down a little ladder into the tiny, boxlike chamber in which she was working. It had been a kitchen, she'd said. Vida had stood there, breathing the ground, breathing the old, cold air. A chill of unmistakable, suffocating familiarity had risen up around her. She'd thought of the women who had worked in that place so many centuries before, how they might have looked, thick, olive-colored foreheads like Neanderthals, or tall and pale like Norse goddesses, and then she had known, as if the great book of her own life had opened and shown her, that she had been there before, had been someone with a different life, a heart engaged with things she could no longer imagine, though they had once been her own feelings.

She had looked back as she was leaving and had seen the city emerging in the shade of the cathedral wall, a lost, buried civilization, lines of string running every which way, little steps carved out of the dirt, deep down inside the pits. The young woman had raised a hand to her, waving good-bye, and Vida had reeled at the sense of her former self bidding her a hopeless farewell.

That was the last time she'd had lunch out.

"I'VE A ROAST in the oven," she says at last to Mr. Lamb, because she cannot think what else to say, and because it is true.

"A roast—"

"I always put a roast in on Sunday. Before church."

"Oh. Well, then—" He glances away, devastated.

"Perhaps—" She thinks of Mr. Lamb in the kitchen at Southend House, his shoes off, perhaps, his hair mussed. "Perhaps you would join us?" she says, surprising herself. "It's not *fish,*" she apologizes hurriedly.

He is so close to her. She thinks she sees his shirtfront move over his heart, thudding and thudding, as though he's run a race. She stops before she puts a hand there, to quiet it.

"I do *love*—" he says then, the breath leaving him, "I do *love* a good roast. How very kind. Yes, I should. Yes." And he releases her hand.

For a moment she thinks he will offer her his arm. But he reaches instead for his handkerchief. He touches it to his eyes and turns away, showing her for a moment only the green field of his shoulder.

SHE HAD ALWAYS thought that someday she would be in love with someone.

Her friend Charlotte had told her that before she and Tommy were married he would try to coax her round back to the shed behind his parent's house. He had a sofa there and his phonograph, and some posters and whatnot on the walls. "Very dark and *cozy,*" Charlotte had confided to Vida. "We've come this close," she'd say, squeezing the air between her fingers. "Go on!" she'd squeal, when Vida would look at her skeptically. "Tell me *you* don't want it too, Vida Stephen."

But it wasn't what Vida had ever imagined for herself—not some nasty old shed with dirt for a floor and a smelly old sofa. Not some small, familiar space with the sounds of the kitchen nearby. She couldn't explain it, exactly—not to Charlotte, certainly, and not even really to herself. It was all because of Uncle Laurence, she thought, his letters about Corfu. She'd listen to her mother reading them aloud, about the sea and the olive orchards and the little wayside shrines in the middle of nowhere—like lamps in the night, Laurence had written. Wandering the hills once in search of subjects to paint, he had come upon and tasted the water from the Kardaki Spring, a trickle that flowed from the mouth of an ancient Venetian lion, its features nearly worn away by the centuries. The water, he'd written, was said to transform one.

How? she had wondered. How?

And he was eating well, he'd said, better than ever, damsons and wild strawberries for breakfast, and kumquats, a very Corfiote fruit.

He'd told them about swimming through the eel grass at Agios Gordis at night, and the schools of tiny phosphorescent fish there like sparks in the dark.

He'd written about a *panagiros,* when they all walked up to the summit of Mount Pantokrator and danced and danced round the crumbling walls until the sky was thick, blistered with stars. He fell asleep that night, dead drunk on *aspro,* he wrote exultantly, beside a young boy in one of the cells in the monastery there. And when he woke in the morning in his bed of straw, he and the boy were both wearing crowns of flowers, valerian and the narcotic pheasant's-eye, grass of Parnassus and early sternbergia.

Vida had thought then—or not exactly thought; it was as though she could see it, as though a picture had been placed before her eyes while she slept—that one day something like that would happen to her. One day, she thought, she would fall asleep and would be wakened wearing a crown of orchids and the tiny woven bodies of *Orchis italica,* its pink blossoms like the human form itself. And she thought that she would like to live someplace beautiful. That when she awoke one morning in that beautiful place, she would be beautiful. That she would know how things happened, why they happened.

That it would happen like that.

"AH," MR. LAMB says, arriving at the door to her little sitting room. He had kept up, the whole walk home, a baffling stream of conversation so circular and incongruous, with references to stamps and the complexities of the new organ, that she could scarcely follow it, much less offer a reply. At one point, when they had passed the Hughes-Onslow's lawn, five mean peacocks had come racing out from round the corner of the low whitewashed house and rushed over the grass, hissing, their fabulous tails fanned out behind them.

"I *so* admire peacocks," Mr. Lamb had said, completely ignoring the nasty spirit of aggression with which they seemed to be pursuing one another. "Peacocks and butterflies are among the world's loveliest creations. Don't you agree?" He had turned to her, fixed his eyes on her, and Vida had nodded vaguely; a picture of her robe, its Oriental birds and flashing monarchs, had flown up before her, as though two invisible hands held it aloft and invited her to step within the circle of its golden cord.

"So *this* is where you live. I can tell," Mr. Lamb says now, turning to her, light in his eyes. "This is the room you like best. Isn't it?

"Miss Stephen," he says. "Vida, if I may? What a very cozy room indeed. I can see exactly why you like it here.

"Ah!" He spies Manford's stamp albums on the table and hurries over to them. "May I?"

He pulls out a chair, sits down, and opens the first book. Then he spins round. "Oh," he says, dismayed. "Perhaps I am delaying the meal? Forgive me."

He stands up again, wipes his hands pointlessly on his trousers.

He's so nervous, Vida thinks. Perhaps he's shy. Perhaps, like me, he hasn't much occasion for company. This is all new to him, as it is to me. I must help us along. Friendship is such a rare thing. "No," she says. "Not at all. Please. Be comfortable, Mr. Lamb."

Mr. Lamb turns to look out the window but stiffens suddenly. "There's someone—" He points out the glass, accusing. "There's someone in your garden."

Vida takes a step forward, follows his finger. "Oh!" A little tremor of excitement has found its way into her voice, surprising her. "That's—Jerome," she says. "Or—" How can I not remember his name? she thinks desperately. Jason? Jonathan? Justin? "No, no—it's Jeremy," she says at last in relief. She remembers the curling eyelashes, the spiny rake in his hand, his body laid upon the grass.

Mr. Lamb turns slowly to look at her, and for some reason she cannot bring herself to meet his eyes.

"Jeremy's the new gardener," she says. There is an awkward pause. And after a moment she adds, although she isn't sure exactly what she means, "He's changing everything."

Eleven

Vida comes to stand beside Norris, and they look together out the window at the figure of the gardener below. After a moment she turns away. "I'll just check the roast," she says.

Norris, his hand idling along the soft drape of the curtain, turns and blinks at the empty door frame, the place where she had been a moment before. After a second, though, she reappears, her hat still in her hand. "Please, do make yourself at home." She nods toward one of the yellow silk chairs near the fire. "I'll just see to the potatoes, and then we'll eat," she says. "Manford, come along and wash up."

Norris watches Manford rise from the table where he has been working a large puzzle and leave the room. A lump has risen unexpectedly in Norris's throat. An ocean presses behind his eyelids. Why is this so very hard? he thinks. And then, surprising himself: I wish I were home.

Blinking rapidly to clear his eyes of the foolish tears that hover there, he turns back to the window. The gardener is bent over in a Herculean fashion, squatting, his arms around a stone urn on the lower terrace. As Norris watches, the young man stands, the massive urn lifted in his embrace. Even from his distance at the window, Norris can see the man's neck swell perceptibly with effort. He sees his shoulders grow broad and flat, sees the muscles in his thighs flex like rabbits trapped in a bag, sees the black hair, dampened with sweat, curling over the temple, a coiled lash. The man's entire body, concentrated on arriving at the delicate balance between the urn's bulk and his own elastic strength, seems to Norris a sort of beau ideal, polished and perfect. It occurs to him, not for the first time, that the instrument of the body, especially when it is as young and beautiful as this gardener's, is indeed worthy of idolatry. Norris leans closer to the pane; the young man staggers once, twice, his jaw jutted forward as if to confront an enemy, and moves the urn a foot to one side. Norris feels his own breath leave him in a sympathetic burst.

When the gardener stands upright at last, Norris realizes that he is not a large man, despite his ambitious efforts with the urn. He sees the man's hand come up to clasp his opposing shoulder, as if to discourage some pain there. Norris feels his own head incline sympathetically toward his shoulder.

He jumps when Vida speaks from behind him, for he has been so absorbed in watching the gardener that he has not noticed that she has returned to the sitting room, has come to stand just behind him.

"He's done a great deal of work," she says quietly, craning round Norris and looking out the window with him. "He says he'll never get it all to rights, not in years. But I think he's made an enormous difference already." She cocks her head; they both watch as the gardener strolls away. "He's young, anyway," she says. "He's got years to finish."

The gardener disappears down the steps by the fountain toward the greenhouses, a rake poised in his hand like a javelin. He vanishes as if he were actually descending into the earth, down a set of endless stairs; it's an odd, disturbing effect. Norris frowns. Yes, a *young* man, he thinks. Young and handsome. But he wants to change the subject now, for something about the young gardener's body, its display of strength, makes him aware of his own extreme and awkward height, the thinness of his shins and arms, the pale color of the skin on his shoulders.

Vida rescues him. "Shall we have wine, Mr. Lamb?" she says, and he looks down to see that she has laid her hand gently on his arm a moment. She withdraws it when she sees him looking at her hand and glances away. "I think there's half a bottle of quite a nice red somewhere," she says. "Would you care for a glass?"

"Yes, thank you," Norris says gratefully, and turns to face her fully.

Who cares about a *gardener,* he thinks. Not him.

"Please—Vida," he says, smiling at her. "Do let me set the table or *something*. This is so kind of you."

NORRIS SMILES DETERMINEDLY at Manford, who sits across from him at the far end of the long kitchen table. Manford rests his large head on his folded arms, his eyes fixed on Norris.

Striving to maintain a pleasant expression, and forcing himself to keep his eyes on Manford's face in what he hopes is a friendly manner, Norris directs a question at Vida. He's afraid of being a Nosy Parker, but he would rather talk than have silence between them. Silence feels like failure, and there is so much he wants to know.

Her back is to them as she bends into the oven and pulls out a heavy roasting pan, the juices from the roast crackling.

"He can hear all right, can't he?" Norris asks at last, clearing his throat and smiling broadly at Manford.

"Who? Manford?" She glances over her shoulder as she sets the pan down on the counter. "Yes, he hears you perfectly well."

"But—" Norris scrapes his feet over the tile floor's sandy surface. He glances at Vida. Her blouse has puckered prettily over the strings of her apron.

Norris closes his eyes briefly and struggles with the confusing notion of Manford's faculties: If he can hear, why can't he understand? Or perhaps he does understand? Norris wasn't sure.

"But—he can't speak." This isn't exactly a question, he realizes. It's obvious that Manford doesn't speak.

"He's never said a single word," Vida replies, still with her back to him, sharpening a knife. "Not once."

Norris looks down at his hands and frowns. He tries to think how he might rephrase his question. Vida's tone suggests that matters should be clear now: He never speaks; can't; won't; though he appears to understand what you say. But Norris, though trying hard, still feels confused. Then he realizes, alighting happily upon the idea, that perhaps it is like being in the presence of a dog—an intelligent and kindly dog, no doubt—who catches the tone of what you are saying but not the actual meaning.

"Well!" He looks up, brightening. "He's rather like a *dog* then, isn't he? I mean, he attends to you as a dog might, but he can't actually participate in the conversation. A very nice dog," he adds hastily, the word *dog* suddenly conjuring up images of teeth and slobber and hair. Norris nods helpfully at Manford, as if Manford himself has just advanced this theory.

But when Vida says nothing, ceasing her business with the roast, standing still with her back to them, Norris feels sure he has misspoken in some way. It wasn't what he meant exactly, Manford's being like a dog. He tries to think.

"Or perhaps," he says, and he can hear the suffocated tone that has crept into his voice, "perhaps it's more like a foreigner. You know, someone who doesn't speak the language, and yet it all seems familiar somehow, the hand gestures and whatnot. Have you ever noticed," he goes on bravely, his voice rising, despite himself, "how one tends to speak more loudly in the presence of a foreigner? How one tries to enunciate a bit more clearly? As if it would help? It's silly, I know, but—"

He rises abruptly to his feet. Vida's back has begun to quiver, as if she were crying. Or laughing! Oh, which is it? Which would be worse?

He stands helplessly behind her, his hands dangling. Manford lifts his head from the table, looks at Vida, alert.

Oh, Lord! She's crying. Another one, crying! He feels wild with despair and confusion. Why did they *always* have to be crying? What was it that he did to them?

"Vida," he says, his voice low and ashamed. "Miss Stephen. I am so sorry. I didn't mean—I'm only trying to understand. I so want to understand. Please, I know I'm very stupid, that it must seem very stupid, my asking such questions and saying it all so badly. But I do—"

I do what? he thinks.

I do love her so much.

HE WANTS TO know everything about her life, everything about how it is with Manford. He feels that he has never experienced anything so difficult in his whole life as this, this wanting to know about them. He had once thought that it was simple, he realizes now, how people come to know one another. He'd thought it was a simple accumulation of evidence. His grandmother would touch his face, hold it in her hands. "Norrie," she'd say, "you're getting the big nose like your father. Be a good boy, Norrie. Be so very good now, won't you?" And then she'd release him. But he would notice that his mother had begun to cry, ever so quietly. And though she couldn't see a thing, his grandmother knew her daughter-in-law was weeping away in her corner.

"Don't be sniffling now, Rosemary," she'd say sharply. "It does no harm to tell him that he looks like his father."

And Norris knew that it would never go away, that his being there was no replacement, really, for his father's absence. And yet no one had to say so for him to understand that! And so he thought that was how it was done, how people came to know one another. *With no words.*

People came to understand one another not by words but by what had happened between them. It couldn't be said, in so many words.

And yet it's all he's got now, he feels—nothing but questions, nothing but words.

He's watched her. He's seen her come and go about the village. Everyone seems to know her, or they're used to seeing her, at least. But since spying her that night on the fountain, he believes that he understands her in some essential way. At that moment, standing in the garden at Southend, he had realized that he simply hadn't been *looking;* that it was all a question of looking. If he'd looked before, surely he would have seen it, how lovely she is.

He knows something about her, and now he wants to know everything, for it's as if he's had a glimpse of something hiding behind the curtain, as if a drape has been pulled aside to show just a corner of a beautiful painting. He has something small now—like a postage stamp, he realizes happily—that small image of her upon the fountain, or waiting on the bench in the lane. But now he wants to pull the drape aside, wants to see the whole thing, wants something so large it fills the room, the universe!

He's not satisfied, anymore, with something small.

And he's afraid that he will never be able to tell her how he feels, never be able to show her what a help he could be. Because he knows that he is good at helping, an expert, you might say. He knows how women are. His mother and grandmother would sit beside him on the bed at night after his father had been killed. "Is there anything you want, Norrie?" they'd say. "Is there anything we can get you?" And they'd argue between themselves. "Leave the boy alone," one would say to the other. "Just let him sleep," the other would reply, all the while both of them smoothing the coverlet, tucking in the sheet corner.

But he'd understood that they wanted him to stay awake for them.

"Should I play for you, Norrie, whilst you go to sleep?" his grandmother would ask.

Oh, yes, please. For that was what they wanted. And before he closed his eyes, he would see them, his mother winding her hands at the door frame in the square of light, his grandmother at the organ. He knew how to make a gift, then. He knew how to please.

He'd love to please Manford, too, if he knew how. He knows he likes stamps, and it frustrates him that he can't simply give him stamps in quantity, lovely ones, as many as he'd like. He'd even give Manford one of his own collections, if he would enjoy it, Christmas all over the world—Renaissance religious paintings from the smaller islands of the British Commonwealth, and a jolly lot of colorful stamps from the United States, with happy snowmen and reindeer and so forth, and some charming ones from Ireland, the nativity in gold leaf.

He's bought jam doughnuts, masses of them by now, enough to make a man sick.

He's tried to be attentive.

But he doesn't know what Manford wants; he doesn't understand him.

What does he want? Norris thinks, staring at Manford across the table. How will I ever know?

He watches Vida carefully put aside the towels with which she lifted the roasting pan. Her shoulders have quieted. She runs her hands down the front of her apron, touches her palms to her cheeks. But when she turns around, her face is gentle, kind; she smiles at him. Why, she wasn't crying! Not a bit of it! She's been—*laughing!*

But before she can speak, the kitchen door opens. The young man from the garden, black hair tousled over his forehead, his cheeks pale as milk, appears in the doorway, grasping one wrist with his hand. Blood spills on the floor.

"Hallo," he says weakly. "Could I get a bandage?"

Norris backs away as Vida sweeps past him. "Oh, what have you done?" she cries.

The young man smiles. "Sorry to interrupt the *party,*" he says. He looks around the room.

Norris thinks he smirks at them, but perhaps he is only grimacing.

The young man indicates a chair with his elbow, smiles as if both Vida and Norris were idiots not to have offered it to him already, a man dripping blood on the floor. "Mind if I have a seat?" he asks, and his lip curls.

"No, no, of course!" Vida pulls out the chair for him; Norris sees that the young man has embarrassed her, made her feel guilty. Norris frowns.

She leans over the gardener's hands, her back to Norris. "What *happened,* Jeremy?"

"Putting in another window in the greenhouse," he says. "One of the sloping ones for the roof." He lifts his hand slightly, experimentally, releasing the pressure on his wrist. Blood fountains up. "Should have waited for *you,*" he adds, and glances up at Vida, winking heavily. "Came right down on my wrist, just like a guillotine." He makes a noise with his mouth, like something bitten off neatly.

Norris shivers.

Jeremy closes his eyes.

"I think you need stitching up!" Vida says. "Let me see it."

The young man draws his hand away again. Blood bubbles up as his fingers release.

Vida gasps. "You must see Dr. Faber straightaway." She reaches down and begins to lift him at the elbow. "I'll take you in the car. Oh—let me get a towel first." She turns as if to find one on the cluttered countertop beside the sinking roast and the scattered plates. Then she spins back to face Norris, as if she has just remembered something.

"Manford—" she begins. A high hot color has risen into her cheeks. "Mr. Lamb—do you, would you—could you mind him while I take Jeremy to Dr. Faber's?" She says this, Norris thinks, as though he has not been here the whole while, listening to matters develop. "I'd rather not take him to Dr. Faber's with me," she goes on, lowering her voice. "He's so squeamish about blood. Do you think you could stay here with him? He'll be no trouble. I'd *so* appreciate it, Mr. Lamb."

Her face is pleading; he glances down at her skirt, sees she has got some of Jeremy's blood on her apron. Or perhaps it is from the roast?

"Here," she says, turning quickly again and opening a drawer, withdrawing a stack of cellophane stamp envelopes. "There's these you could do together, in his album? We haven't got to them." She holds them out to Norris. "They're your recent ones. We haven't had the time," she adds apologetically.

Norris takes them from her hands. "No, of course," he says faintly. He feels as if it were he who had lost a lot of blood, not this young gardener with the black hair and milk white cheeks.

"Oh." Vida stops again as she lifts her coat from the stand in the corner. "Jeremy Martin," she says, "Mr. Norris Lamb. I'm so sorry."

She seems very young to Norris at this moment. The excitement has brought a high color into her lips as well as her cheeks, as if she has been pinched. He steps toward her, for it has come into his mind that he might kiss her now as if they were an old married pair, as if he were simply sending her on her way, on an errand of kindness.

But she is bending protectively over Jeremy. "Are you all right to stand?" Norris hears her say.

The gardener rises slowly to his feet. "Nice meeting you," he says to Norris, and Norris feels ashamed of himself then, for Jeremy looks very young as well at this moment, and quite pale and sickly. There's not a trace of the—what was it?—superiority he'd shown a few minutes ago.

Vida holds the towel toward Jeremy but then appears to realize that he can't wrap it himself. Her eyebrows lift inquiringly. "Should I?"

"That would help," he says.

She inclines toward him then, leaning necessarily close to him, wrapping the towel gingerly around his arm.

Is that her breast, brushing his shoulder?

His dark eyelashes come to rest slowly against his cheeks. His head, lolling, is inches from her.

Norris looks away, hard, at the floor, at the tiles there set in even rows, stretching away across the floor one after the other.

AND THEN THEY are gone.

Norris hears the car start somewhere far below, far away, hears its motor recede. He stares at the door through which Vida and Jeremy exited, as if they might reappear at any moment. He sniffs the air, the damp smell of the meat's pooling pan juices. It is, he realizes suddenly, very quiet. When he turns around with a start, he sees that Manford has disappeared.

Norris looks round wildly. "Hallo?" he calls to the empty kitchen.

He steps to the door of the small sitting room: empty. And then, furtively, as if he might be ambushed at any moment, feeling vaguely as though Manford might pop out at him, he sets off down the hall toward the interior of the house, calling loudly, "Hallo! Hallo?" He raps repeatedly on the wall with his knuckles as he passes, as if the sound, with its steady reverberations, might reach Manford more easily than a voice and with clearer purpose.

He senses that the afternoon has closed in as he steps into the front hall. Now day has passed the noon mark, with its spreading lap of possibility, that hour that seems to last from morning to night in an endless lull of time. He stands in the mingling shadows of the hall with its empty hearth, its walls of tapestries. The balcony runs high above, balanced, it seems, now that he sees it in daylight, upon the arched backs of what appear to be winged lions. He tries to calculate how late it is. There'd been the walk home from St. Alphage, all his pointless chatter, the bloody gardener—is it three? Or even four now? In the dim and silent hall, its stone walls ringing his footsteps back to him, he can't be sure.

He hurries onward then, struggling to contain the feeling that Manford, too, is moving, can move so much quicker than he. He could be miles away by now, roving away down some distant lane, stroking the air in that odd way he has, as if feeling it billow past him like green waves around the trunk of a giant, a giant striding through the teeming leagues of an ocean, birds wheeling above his bowed head.

Norris scurries from room to room. The house is extravagant, baffling, hallways turning at invisible corners, double doors bracketed by carved wood panels opening here and there in the walls, the odd piece of furniture—an enormous chest, its brass fittings gleaming in the gloom, a chair forked with antlers—placed as if to trip him up. As he hurries from door to door, he sees that many rooms are almost entirely unfurnished, sheets webbing the chandeliers. In one—he judges it to be a ballroom, perhaps, the silvered pier mirrors streaked with gray—the tent of sheeting has come loose and dangles from the arms of the fixture high above, a sculpture of flowing marble, suspended stone.

Manford is nowhere to be found.

At last Norris enters a room that is, he senses, in use. The long gallery is hung floor to ceiling with dark paintings. An arrangement of settees and end tables are gathered in the center, newspapers and books lie scattered on the floor, and pillows and footstools are tucked among the larger furnishings for apparent comfort. A carved plaster ceiling caps the tall walls, cupping the light from several French doors that give out onto the garden.

Norris hurries across the room, soundlessly crossing a carpet of spring flowers and grasses, endless repetitions of nodding bells in faded greens and silvers and blues and rose. It strikes him that he has seen a stamp of this pattern once, a brocade—from Austria? The Alps?

One of the French doors is ajar. Norris steps outside. Set at intervals on the broad terrace, poised as if to leap to the garden below, are several marble statues—of Mercury, Norris realizes now, though he has seen them before from afar.

He moves quietly among them now in the dove gray light of late afternoon, raising his hand to touch the pitted feet, the wings sprouting from heels, the arms raised in a delicate attitude of balance, the platonic ascent. The statues' hooded eyes stare past him; the genitals float, soft and obscure.

Norris has seen the figures from the garden below while wandering on his evening walks through the wilderness areas of orchard and stanchion oaks and passing through the bowed hedges of boxwood that circle the fountain and its surrounding Venetian grotto. But he has never been up to this side of the house, never been so close to the statues before, never felt, as he does now, the inevitability of their flight nor the heroism of their sacrificial pose. He rests his hand on the outflung calf of the nearest statue, follows the figure's ecstatic gaze.

And there he finds Manford.

Down below in the grotto, seated on the curving bowl of the fountain's rim, he looks exactly, Norris thinks, like a portrait of Melancholy.

And now that he can see him, now that the high pulse of his fear has begun to steady, Norris waits, staring at Manford. He feels a profound and painful surge of sympathy—how sad Manford must be, so alone in whatever world he lives in. For there can be no other like him in that place, Norris supposes, no other with exactly the same disarranged features and mind. How does it all arrange itself for Manford, Norris wonders, the complicated universe flattened out to suit his understanding of it? As he stands there, staring at Manford, an image of Manford's mind rises before Norris—he imagines it held aloft in some strange light, like an image from a dream. It revolves slowly, some torch's beam trained on it, its surface mottled like a planet, run through with the branching streams of capillaries, the dark lakes of desire, of yearning.

Norris shakes his head, puts out a hand against Mercury's calf as if to steady himself. What do we know of ourselves except as through a prism, he wonders, the endless refractions of our mind turning back on itself like a dog chasing its own tail? And Manford? What does he think when he thinks of himself? Does he think a word, or a picture that tells him who he is?

And what about the heart, the heart as the seat of the soul?

What about Manford's heart?

NORRIS DESCENDS THE steps from the terrace, advances across the newly clipped lawns. Shadows fall over the grass, the elongated shapes of the topiary urns spreading over the green. Norris's own shadow wavers and bleeds at the edges, shivering and contracting around him, spinning under his feet as he passes from west to north and at last enters the grotto through its twisting stair, the parapet around it bristling with the pruned canes of roses.

He steps out onto the flagstones at last, breathing hard. "Here you are!" he says, as if just discovering Manford. "Gave me quite a start when you disappeared like that." He tries to smile.

But Manford does not look up at him. It's as if he isn't interested, Norris thinks, his relief ceding briefly to annoyance at what seems like Manford's obstinate silence. He tries to check this feeling in himself—it doesn't seem right to be irritated. And then his own attention is diverted anyway by the fountain, the glassy surface in the basin pebbled with droplets of water, the rising obelisk in the center bearing, at its crest, a bronze froth of statuary, a bouquet of erect female forms, arrows threaded through their bows. They are all Dianas, Norris recognizes, marveling; their bows aimed into the darkening wood beyond. From the feet of the grave and slender figures, from the massed and tangled bodies of swans, their beaks open, crests of bright water rise into the sky. For a moment the image of Vida on the basin's rim flashes before Norris—her white feet, the dark patch.

"It's lovely, isn't it," Norris says quietly at last, "to have the fountain turned on again?"

He glances at Manford, sitting oddly on the rim of the fountain with his feet splayed wide apart, his arms outstretched, his hands held before him, his interlocking fingers twisting and writhing.

And then Norris sees what is happening, how the flagstones beneath their feet grow lively and tremble with the dancing shapes of Manford's hands, the shadows thrown from the descending sun through his webbed fingers. Norris draws a step closer.

Manford works his hands with a puppeteer's concentration, the imbroglio of his fingers spreading a pantomime across the stones, a lavish tapestry of animals melting one into the next: A delicate swan pedals through water, giving way to some hooked and horned beast, and then to an amusing crouched cat, its back lithe, its ears two pointed knuckles. They come so fast, a carnival of creatures both known and fantastic, that Norris cannot catch them all. He leans forward, his mouth gaping.

And then at last Manford stops. He drops his head. His hands, like the hands of a musician or a conductor—like his own hands fallen from the organ's keys, Norris recognizes—come to rest slowly in his lap.

"Oh! Don't stop!" Norris lurches forward in dismay, flutters his hands. "Don't stop! That's—marvelous! That's the most marvelous thing I've ever seen! How do you do it?"

He flickers his own long fingers. The shadows lengthen like flares and then contract, extinguished. He makes a fist, sees it bleed huge and menacing across the stones. He raises his arm, sees the tower of it loom. He snaps his ankles together, flattens his arms to his side, rocks like a penguin, and laughs to see his bouncing shape roll. He laughs again, flaps his arms, and sees the cloak of his shadow unfold, immense and piratelike, dashing and iconoclastic.

He turns to Manford, panting. *"How do you do it?"* He is beaming, breathing hard. "All those clever shapes! It's stunning, Manford! It's perfectly wonderful!"

But Manford makes no reply, looking away from Norris at the ground as if trying to divine himself how those shadow figures appeared, as if they might have struggled up from the earth itself, parting the flagstones with their mortar of ancient moss, raising the roof of the globe.

Norris feels vaguely rebuked, as though his own enthusiasm has been ridiculous beside the exact sophistication of Manford's creations—the turkey with its quivering wattle, the dog begging a bone, the alert rabbit, twin birds in flight. He pulls out his handkerchief and mops at his brow. And then he takes a seat beside Manford on the fountain's rim, turns his face toward the cooling spray, and closes his eyes.

"You don't want to talk about it. You don't want to do any more of it. That's all right. I understand," he says quietly, not opening his eyes. "I'm just glad to have found you. I was worried, you see. Vida's entrusted you to me for this little while, and when you wandered off, I thought I'd failed her in the blink of an eye. She cares terribly for you, you know. She—"

He opens his eyes, stares at the back of Manford's heavy head framed against the sky. "I wish," he says after a moment, "that you could tell me what I might do for her. How I might make her love me. I know—I know I'm a poor sort of suitor in some ways. Many ways, perhaps. I know *you* amuse her in all sorts of ways, that she's chosen you, after a fashion, chosen to live her life here with you. I must tell you—I wouldn't want to change any of that. I understand how it is. But—"

He stops then, for Manford has raised his hands.

A swirl like smoke floats at first over the flagstones, a face materializing from the darkness, a tantalizing flash of profiles like inkblots.

Norris stares, transfixed.

The image steadies, stills.

And Norris sees the face then—the clown's peaked hat, crumpled at the top, the white wink of an eye, Punch's great hooked nose and hinged jaw working slowly, up and down, the mirthless jester berating his audience.

They stare together, Manford and Norris, at the famous fool; the bent proboscis, the snapping jaw, the inaudible stream of exhortation. Silence is all around them.

FROM THAT MOMENT on, Norris feels he wants to stay near Manford. It is as if in Manford's presence something might happen—Norris might see something, he thinks, witness it as he witnessed those shadows that came out of nothing, out of nowhere, with the agility of air itself.

By the time Vida returns from having tended to Jeremy, Norris and Manford have come back up to the house. Norris had wept, surprising himself, though the tears had been threatening all day, he knew. He had taken Manford's arm in his own, walked back up to the house, no longer worried that he might try to run off. He knew he wouldn't, somehow; he understood that Manford had made him a gift, had linked the two of them together in that final shadow of Punch.

Manford sat quietly at the table, looking over his stamp books, while Norris sliced the roast and put the potatoes in a pan to warm. He set the table, too, noting with pleasure how everything in the pantry was labeled so neatly and clearly.

When Vida comes in and hangs up her coat, Norris doesn't say anything at first; he just feels happy to have her there, the three of them now together. He wants it to last, the moment to last, is happy to have the meal all ready for her. He wants her to see that, to have time to take it all in.

She looks from one to the other of them.

And then Norris steps forward and touches Manford's head with his palm, resting it there and smiling at her, the long spoon in his hand, her apron tied round his waist.

"Welcome home," he says. "We've been getting to know one another."

Twelve

WHEN VIDA COMES in the door to the kitchen, Jeremy's bloody shirt rolled in her arms, Mr. Lamb turns in surprise and then smiles at her beatifically, waving the wooden spoon vaguely in the air above his head—a sort of salute, she thinks, taken aback. And then he steps near to Manford to lay a hand on his head.

She knows something has happened between them.

But they appear so peaceful, it seems to her, that she thinks it must be nothing to worry about, their air of conspiracy; they've only hit it off. She smiles shyly at Mr. Lamb and then goes to put Jeremy's shirt to soak in a basin in the larder.

When she comes back into the kitchen, she allows Mr. Lamb to help her to the table and pull out her chair. He shakes out her napkin and lays it over her lap.

"Put your stamp books aside, Manford," she says, disconcerted by Mr. Lamb's attentions. "You don't want to spill on them."

But Mr. Lamb picks them up himself and then brings the plates to the table, the roast in its pool of ruby-colored juices. "Here we *are,*" he says, and smiles all around.

THERE'D BEEN A great deal of blood, Vida had noticed, and from a rather small gash, after all. Dr. Faber, working away over Jeremy's wrist, had said it was the placement, where the glass had caught the vein, that made it bleed so much.

After he was done sewing Jeremy up, Dr. Faber had taken them into his private office. Manford always liked Dr. Faber's office; there was so much to look at. He especially liked the skeleton lurking in the corner, each of its bones numbered with a tiny carved black numeral. Manford often went to stand in front of it, cocking his head. Vida has thought that it's as if he recognizes it in some way—as a person.

"That's old Percy there," Dr. Faber once said to him. "Say hello, Manford."

Dr. Faber's office was really horribly crowded, though. Vida always felt she'd better not touch anything for fear a stack of papers would topple onto her. There were cases of books, too, and boxes still in their brown paper wrapping. It was known that Dr. Faber was a great reader, and indeed he had books piled everywhere. The office and attached surgery had belonged to his father before him; Vida suspected he'd never cleared out a thing.

But he managed to sweep aside some papers and find a place for Jeremy to sit, motioning for him to relax. Vida lingered in the doorway behind Jeremy's chair while Dr. Faber fetched the decanter from the cupboard and poured brandies for the three of them.

"Bolster your blood," he said jovially, raising his glass to Jeremy.

Vida watched Jeremy's Adam's apple bob twice, and then the glass was empty.

"Well then," Dr. Faber said, smacking his lips and holding the glass critically up to the light. "All in a Sunday's work. I'll have a look at you in ten days. Come back then and we'll take the stitches out. Try to keep it clean, though. Got a long glove? That'll do, if you want to work meanwhile. Don't go lifting any circus elephants, though."

He winked and set his glass down on the papers on his desk, put his hand to Vida's back, and steered her toward the coatrack. He helped her into her coat, laid a broad palm briefly on Jeremy's shoulder, and saw them firmly to the door.

How nice, Vida thought, as they went away down the path, to be Dr. Faber. In they come bleeding to death, and you just sew them up and send them on their way and go home to your dinner.

SHE HAD HELPED Jeremy up the walk to Dr. Faber's, holding his arm in case he should feel faint, but it didn't seem right, their touching again when they left, he being all right then and sewn up. Still, she had turned a deep, mortifying red, first when she realized that she had been about to reach for his arm, and then realizing that she was disappointed to see how awkward it would be.

When Dr. Faber'd had him take off his shirt, she had opened her eyes wide at the perfect shape of the man beneath the bloody cloth. He was made of marble, she'd thought, marble run through with color—the blue veins of his neck, the flat, plum-colored nipples, the tiny curl of black hair like seaweed low on his belly. Her awareness of her own appreciation had embarrassed her. She had looked away helplessly; and there were Dr. Faber's surgical instruments, all lined up on the towel, including the thing she called privately to herself the duck's bill.

What does he need that for? she had thought, aghast.

"Sit down, Vida," Dr. Faber had said, glancing over at her, the needle flashing through his fingers. "Can't have you going over on me. Put your head down."

And then, to Jeremy, "Such a worrywart, our Vida! Always rushing Manford in here as though he were at death's door. That fellow will outlive us all, mark my words. He's a giant among men." But he had winked at Vida when she'd raised her head at last, everything swimming; it was the blood, she thought. All that blood.

"She's a good sort, Vida," she heard Dr. Faber say. "You could have a worse nursemaid than Vida here, my friend," he added to Jeremy. "She'll see you through."

Jeremy had raised his eyes then to meet hers with a look so direct she had put her hand to her throat in a kind of weak defense. And it went through her mind suddenly that perhaps *he* had written the letters; perhaps *he* had sent the robe and the flowers. Perhaps it wasn't Mr. Niven at all!

For though she hadn't really been thinking about it deliberately, the notion of her mysterious lover had been there in the back of her head all day. And though she'd made herself settle on Mr. Niven, she recognized that it was a conclusion reached only by default. She'd even had, for a flash, the unpleasant suspicion that it might be Mr. Spooner in love with her, for the way he was always trying to pinch her bottom. He'd come round after her in the store, down the dark aisle in his musty socks. "Can I *help* you?" he'd say, breathing hard behind her. But of course she understood he wasn't interested in helping her find *anything!* Once he'd put his hand right on her bottom, as though she were a loaf of bread. "Hallo, hallo," he'd said then softly, as if he were surprised to find her flesh beneath his palm. And she had never liked to say anything back, with Mrs. Spooner at the front of the store doing her sums with a little stub of a pencil, eating handfuls of bran from the sack on the floor, following Vida and the other women of the village with her worried eyes. Everybody knew Mr. Spooner was an affliction and a trial.

But she couldn't imagine Mr. Spooner would have such lovely things to say as were in the letters, anyway; "Hallo, hallo" was all he could manage, she thought, his hand on your bottom, as if his hand suddenly recognized you. And you just had to move away then quickly, Vida knew, as though it hadn't happened. You'd fetch whatever it was you'd come for and hurry out, wishing there were another grocery. Vida thought that her mother would be horrified, seeing him in their old grocery with his terrible socks and groping hands.

Glancing surreptitiously at Jeremy beside her as they left Dr. Faber's and walked down the path to her car, she thought *he* would have something more to say than "Hallo, hallo," anyway.

Something more like poetry, she supposed. It was something about him, she thought, the way he—well, the way he looked, she decided. He looked like a man who might write poetry.

"I'LL DRIVE, SHALL I?" she'd asked when they got to the car.

She'd expected to take him back to Southend House, but as they drove off, he said, "You can just drop me in the village, if you don't mind. I don't think I'll do any more today."

"No, of course not," she said quickly. "You shouldn't do another thing."

"It's round by the dairy," he said. "One of the bungalows back there."

Vida drove down the muddy lane toward the dairy. It was always muddy in the lane, with the cows going up and down for milking twice a day. Yet it was overgrown with hawthorn, as well, so the scents of sweet flowers and rank milk and lime warred in the air. Jeremy rolled down the window and stuck his head out. Vida glanced to her right. The houses were a poor, sad lot, one-story bungalows with brown tile roofs and a lot of mud for gardens, except where someone had a tiny plot, stitched over now with thick lines of green and a tangle of tomato plants. The bungalows were dreary, with sheets up at the windows for curtains and washing on the lines.

"Here," he said suddenly, and she was so surprised by the

sound of his voice that she stepped on the brake too hard, jolting them in their seats. Jeremy caught himself with his good hand. "Steady!"

She dropped her chin, a fierce blush rising into her cheeks again. She felt so stupid around him!

The house they had stopped before was dark and quiet. It looked as if no one lived there. Certainly no one was at home, she thought.

Jeremy put one leg out, as though he might be stiff. But then he seemed to think of something and turned back. And Vida saw his eyes close in on her own, felt his mouth come up against her cheek, felt the brush of his unshaven chin rough against her face.

"You're a love," he said. "Thanks for everything."

And then he was gone.

"YOU KNOW," MR. Lamb says at last, wiping his lips and pushing back from the table. "He's really astonishing, isn't he?"

He leans toward Vida and lowers his voice as if to prevent Manford from hearing, though he's sitting right there between them at the kitchen table. "You've seen that, I'm sure, what he does with his hands? The shadows?"

Vida looks up from her plate, the tired-looking purple beef and the shrunken potatoes. Dinner had sat too long in the oven.

"Pardon?" she says. And then, as if she were coming to after having been asleep, she manages, "Oh, yes. His shadow play?" She is surprised that there'd been an occasion for Manford to demonstrate this talent to Mr. Lamb while she'd been at Dr. Faber's. What could have caused it? She lifts her fork, hesitating a moment. "Did he do the birds?" She can't help feeling oddly disoriented—one moment she's with Jeremy, she thinks, and there's all that blood and Dr. Faber's needle, and the next she's here, with Mr. Lamb, who is still sawing away at his meat with vigor.

"Oh, yes," Mr. Lamb says, with the faintly superior air of an expert impatient with a novice. "Yes, he did the birds. *And* a lot of others as well!"

Vida puts down her fork and knife. Manford must like him, to have shown Mr. Lamb his shadows. She sees Mr. Lamb glance over at her plate and notice that she's left most of her roast. He looks away, and she feels guilty that she hasn't more of an appetite. It was lovely of him to have taken over with the dinner. She feels slightly ashamed that she doesn't seem able to manage a greater display of gratitude. And now he won't even look at her, she sees with regret, but busies himself with his meat.

When she stands to take her plate to the sink, Mr. Lamb leaps up, overturning a glass of water. "Please!" he cries. "Please! Let me do the washing up."

They collide in the front of the sink, both of them reaching for a cloth to mop up the spilled water, and for a moment, when she feels his shoulder against her own, Vida wants suddenly to wrap her arms around him, the two of them somehow shoring each other up the way two trees that have collapsed together will each prevent the other from falling to the ground. He's so desperately awkward. She feels she'd do anything to soothe him, to make him happy. She only wants to make him happy now!

"Thank you," she says, as earnestly as she can, so that he will believe her gratitude. "Thank you, Mr. Lamb. That would be lovely." She finds she is breathing hard; with an air of desperation she hands him a tea towel. "I'm afraid I asked you to supper and then I—"

He raises his hand to halt her. His confidence seems restored and his eyes have a grateful look.

"Not a bit of it," he says warningly. "None of that, now. I'm an expert washer-upper."

Manford has gone to stand by the door. Vida notices him there, waiting expectantly, and smiles. "It's getting on late," she says to him, handing Mr. Lamb a plate from the table and then going over to take Manford's napkin from under his chin. "You don't want to walk tonight, do you?" But Manford turns around and opens the door, then glances back at Vida.

"He wants to take a walk?"

Vida turns around again; she had forgotten Mr. Lamb for a moment.

"I like to walk as well," Mr. Lamb offers, and he looks amazed, as if it were such a coincidence. "I walk all the time."

"We go through the village sometimes in the evening," Vida says, smiling at him. "Manford likes that. He likes looking in the windows, I'm afraid," she adds, lowering her voice in mock seriousness, but Mr. Lamb laughs rather too loudly, and she suspects for a moment she has caught him at something.

"It's funny," he says after a moment, staring at her. "I've never seen you walking in the evenings."

And then—she doesn't know what prompts her to say such a thing—she tells him, "Well, that's because we're invisible, Manford and I."

She expects him to laugh, but his face has grown quiet, and she sees that he understands the truth of this, that people in a bright room at night can't see out the windows. In fact, what you see if you look out is only your own face staring back at you. It's not a fiction, not a fancy, she realizes. They *are* invisible, she and Manford, passing along the street in the darkness. No one ever sees them. It's as if they weren't there.

"Come on, Mr. Lamb," she says then, and reaches for his hand across the long space of the air between them. "Come along with us. Perhaps you'll be invisible, too."

THE IDEA STAYS with her, that they can't be seen.

Manford leads the way, walking fast, his arms riding the air. Vida sees Mr. Lamb glance at her, smile, raise his own arms in a pantomime of Manford, bouncing high on his feet. He dips around her like a long-legged insect, like that silly woodcock he'd told her about in church that time. She laughs.

She brushes the hair from her eyes as they descend to the dark tunnel of the lane, its soft air, the pretty lace of the shadows like a veil drawn behind them, obscuring them from the world. Glancing from side to side as they walk, she feels as though she has eyes like a bat, rays of light beaming, streaming into the dusk. Beneath her shoes, she feels the turf and cobble of the lane. A fine sweat rises on her upper lip. She loosens her collar; moisture prickles her temples.

They pass from the lane onto the Romsey Road, the high hedgerows and open fields of its passage through the countryside giving way to the stretch of buildings close upon its curbs, the butcher's and the blacksmith's, Niven's Bakery behind its high courtyard walls, the post office and Dr. Faber's brick house with its annexed office. They pass small houses with curtains drawn at the windows, St. Alphage with its ancient cemetery and gardens, the stones there bathed in green moss. They pass the playing field and Prince's Mead with its wide steps, the basin garden beside it with its sloping, slumbering border of high yews, its postage stamp of grass. They pass before Vida's parents' old grocery, now managed by the Spooners. Vida recalls the dark rooms tilting away within it, the low ceilings and freezers with their crusts of bitter frost, the smooth floorboards worn in gentle waves. Strange, breathless Nigel Spooner, when he is not pursuing ladies down the aisles, has smartened things up a bit, cleared the window of its dusty collection of tins and boxes with faded labels. His wife has built clever tiers of cans there instead, their labels turned carefully to the street. She's even hung a bit of curtain up high, white and lacy. Vida notices a new sign, propped in the window: SPOONER'S CONVENIENCE.

Mr. Lamb walks quietly at her side. How strange it is to be walking with someone she can talk with, who can answer her back, and yet to whom she suddenly has nothing to say. She wonders about him—she's never known him to be sociable, exactly. He takes her parcels and her letters at the post office, usually without remark except to say something about the weather perhaps, or some bit of news from the village. He's been very kind and helpful about stamps for Manford over the years, though appearing a bit surprised that he'd be interested in such things. He has always seemed to her to be lost in thought. She often feels, as the bell above her head rings when she opens the door to the post office, that she has interrupted him. And yet, he's rather sweet, she realizes. He's been rather sweet.

Now having him beside her, trudging along, she feels she ought to say something.

"I really must thank you, Mr. Lamb—"

"Norris," he says quickly. "Please."

"Norris—" Vida pauses. "Well, Norris, I do want to thank you—for watching Manford while I went with Jeremy." She takes a little breath and goes on. "He's going to be quite all right, Dr. Faber said. A nasty cut, but clean. There was quite a lot of blood, though. He took it very well, I thought. He was very brave . . . " She trails off, disappointed. It seems to her that Mr. Lamb hasn't heard her, for he makes no reply.

After a moment, though, he asks abruptly, "Does he always walk that way?"

Manford's dark shape wavers ahead of them. From time to time he raises his arms, billows them on air.

"Ever since he was little," Vida says, trying to adjust to this turn in the conversation. "I used to think it was for balance. He's clumsy, you know. Such children often are. It has to do with the brain damage. But now I think it's to—" She pauses, searching for the right words. "To feel the air. I think he feels it in a way we don't. I think he feels it around him, on his skin."

"Yes," Norris says quietly.

Vida's eyes follow Manford, his hands plying the invisible undulations of air. "It's as though something's beside him, walks beside him," she continues, and she realizes, as she speaks, that this really *is* what she believes—that in his mind Manford keeps company with, oh, not spirits of the air, but the air itself, its scaffolding and frescoes of light and shadow and moisture. He keeps company, she thinks, with the unseen.

As they near the end of the village, where the oak trees overshadow the road, Vida feels the shift into darkness, something cold and dead upon her arms. She shivers. The chill recalls for her the ominous hours of Manford's sleepwalking. And then she feels strangely angry at the presumption of that dark span of time—how frightened she becomes at night. She does not like having to be afraid. Her mind makes a little leap; that someone could enter her bedroom, for instance, could be always on the periphery of her life, unseen and yet all-seeing—this is equally horrifying, she thinks. A fierce righteousness grows in her. Suddenly she wants to tell someone that there is a secret in her life, a person who comes and goes without being seen. She wants to be rid of the secret of it. What is wrong with this man, whoever he is? she thinks now—

Mr. Niven or Mr. Perry or Mr. Spooner or Jeremy—what is wrong with him that he can't simply come to her, declare his love? There must be something wrong with him.

And now the whole weight of her day and the night before crashes down around her—finding Manford in the greenhouse, Jeremy's injury, worrying about Mr. Lamb. She is tired of this, so tired. She wants to be done with the weight of it. She wants whoever it is to show himself.

"Mr. Lamb," she says suddenly. "I haven't been hospitable. I haven't been friendly to you. I'm sorry for that." She stops, sets her mouth.

Why does she feel so angry at *him*? He's only been nice; he's lonely himself. Still, she *is* angry, she finds, especially at him just now, because he knows nothing about her, cannot be complicitous with her, cannot know all that has befallen her. She has had no one to talk to, she thinks. She has to tell someone.

"It's just that I've been—I'm being stalked, you see." She stops abruptly and turns to face Mr. Lamb. "I'm afraid that sounds melodramatic. But it's quite true." She looks aggressively at him, as if he has challenged her. "You wouldn't think such a thing could happen here in Hursley," she goes on in a high tone, and suddenly it really does seem too bad then, too cruel!

She keeps her eyes on Mr. Lamb's face. She wants him to say something, but he looks absolutely stricken, as though he's swallowed poison. She glances down the road impatiently and sighs. Manford is far ahead of them, almost disappearing into the darkness.

"We'll lose him," she says, and begins walking again, more swiftly.

"Miss Stephen. Vida," Mr. Lamb says, hurrying up behind her. "I cannot understand—I'm afraid I—"

"Oh, you mustn't bother yourself, Mr. Lamb," she says then, airily at first, and then her foolish anger abates and she is embarrassed. Oh, *he* isn't to blame. And what did it all matter, anyway? "It's just—" She sighs. "It's only that—you see, someone's been writing me letters. And leaving me things. On my *bed.*" She stops walking as if the ability has suddenly left her.

"On your bed—" his voice echoes faintly.

"Yes! Actually," she goes on, "it was beautiful, really—a lovely robe and nightgown. I never thought I'd have anything so fine. But I don't feel right taking them, you see. Keeping them or wearing them or even enjoying them." She stares off vaguely into the dark leaves of the trees around them. "I know it seems impossible to imagine, Mr. Lamb, but apparently I've got an admirer. Only, he's a very strange sort. You see, I haven't any idea who it is. And now I'm afraid that—well, there must be something wrong with him, that he can't declare himself."

Turning back to Mr. Lamb, she sees that he looks utterly undone. No doubt she has shocked him with such a confession. She sighs again. All the happiness of the mystery has drained away from her. It wasn't going to be wonderful. It wasn't anything at all. And to make it worse, she's been wretched company for Mr. Lamb. "Now, I've told you my secret," she says, and takes a deep breath, meaning to try to cheer him up. "And I've upset you. I didn't mean to do that. I only wanted to explain why I've been so—why I'm so—distracted." She pauses. "Actually, I know who it is, anyhow. Or, at least, I think I do. I—"

"You *do?*" He seems startled.

"Yes." She looks ahead into the darkness for Manford. He has stopped by a tree, has placed his hands on the bark and leans there as if he and the tree had engaged in a struggle but were resting now, forgiven, in each other's arms. She sighs.

"I'm afraid," she says, taking a deep breath, "that it's Mr. *Niven*—"

"Oh! Oh, I don't *think* so!" Mr. Lamb speaks quickly. "I think that's *completely* the wrong conclusion."

She turns to him, surprised.

"No, no indeed," he goes on, rather wildly. "Niven's not—not imaginative enough."

"Well, that's what I thought, at first," Vida says, surprised again. She feels a little better now, just talking about it. And Mr. Lamb is taking it so very seriously, not laughing at her at all. Some of the deliciousness of it, the sweetness of it, creeps back. "I thought so, too," she goes on, "but there couldn't be any other explanation for it. You see, the robe came just last night, while I was at the book circle. And he was there minding Manford for me. There wasn't anyone else there."

Mr. Lamb seems to be searching rapidly over his thoughts. She feels pleased, grateful for his interest. "But couldn't—" he says, "couldn't someone have *eluded* him? I mean, come into the house without his knowing? Someone very—clever?" He stops her, his hand on her arm. "And it must be someone—you say he's writing letters?"

"Yes." Vida looks up at him. "They're quite—they're wonderful, really. Poetic."

"But then—he couldn't mean any harm? If he writes letters? *Poetry*," he adds significantly.

She sees that he is trying to comfort her. And she does want to be comforted.

"No one who writes letters is—well, there couldn't be anything *so* wrong with him. He must just be shy. And very sincere, I should think. To write letters." Mr. Lamb stops. "Are they—all right? He hasn't done anything"—he lowers his voice—"*crude?*"

"Oh, no!" she says quickly, embarrassed. "It's all been—no, I—oh, Mr. Lamb, do you think someone could really be in *love*? With me?" She is almost whispering. "Do you believe that, Mr. Lamb?"

"Oh, yes. Yes," he says. "I do believe that, Miss Stephen. I do absolutely. He must be—terribly in love. Not to want to show himself. He thinks he isn't worthy. Worthy of you. I think he just wants to make you *happy*."

Vida glances at him, shy. "I see you understand him, man to man," she says thoughtfully. Perhaps, being a man himself, Mr. Lamb understands this better than she herself could hope to. There's no need for her to feel so—violated. She just has to be patient, perhaps, and then—"It's just that women," she bursts out, "—we always have to wait for something to happen to us."

Mr. Lamb looks up into the dark canopy of leaves overhead. His high forehead makes him seem so innocent, she thinks, and so vulnerable. He looks down after a minute, studying his shoes. "I think you are perfectly free, Miss Stephen," he says urgently. "You must feel that you can do anything you like. You will be perfectly safe."

"Yes," she says faintly, though not exactly taking his meaning. "I will."

She looks down the road behind them, the way they have come. The moon has vanished entirely, buried behind cloud, a marble rolled into the cup of a hand and concealed.

When they reach Manford, he is waiting impatiently for them, shaggy-headed, rocking from side to side.

"He wants to get on," she says to Mr. Lamb. "He hates to wait." She turns around. "We should be starting back anyway."

So she takes a step to go back, a neat step over the curb, and then she hears Mr. Lamb stumble behind her—rather, she just feels him brushing past her shoulder, then hears the sound of his voice, and when she spins around, he is on his knees in a puddle.

"Oh, God," she hears him say. "My God, how bloody *stupid*."

Vida claps her hand over her mouth but cannot contain the explosion of laughter that leaves her then. She tries to compose herself; she is horrified to find herself so inappropriately doubled over at the sight of Mr. Lamb in the puddle. She reaches down to help him up. "I'm so sorry!" she says through her laughter. "What *happened*? Are you all right?"

Mr. Lamb has his hands over his face. "Only my bloody nose," he says. She is relieved to hear that he is not crying. He is only sitting up now in the puddle, laughing. "Just my bloody nose," he repeats. "My stupid, ugly nose."

"Oh, do *get up*," Vida manages at last through tears of laughter, reaching for him again.

But Mr. Lamb laughs even harder. "I'm all *wet!*" he says, as if it were the greatest joke in the world. "I'm *completely* sopped!"

Vida makes a final effort to quiet herself, taking deep breaths. "Oh, you're a fright," she says as she helps him to stand and hands him a tissue from her coat pocket. "I *am* sorry—for laughing, Mr. Lamb. Completely uncalled for, I know—"

"No, no, it's all right. I—" He takes the tissue she hands him, applies it to his nose, which is bleeding slightly. He is covered with mud. He stands before her, brushing at himself hopelessly. She feels her heart expand with pity, expand to such a degree that for a moment she thinks she will lift from the earth itself. He looks into her eyes. She smiles back at him.

"I—" He puts out a hand toward her. "I'm a fool," he whispers.

But Vida catches him hard by both arms, shakes him a little, and then, embarrassed at having taken such a liberty, lets him go. But she is still smiling. "Mr. Lamb," she says. "I haven't laughed that hard in years."

VIDA AND MANFORD see him to his house. At the door he turns and gives her a little wave, holding his coat open in the unfortunate posture of a man exposing himself, Vida notices, but she understands that his gesture is meant to remind her of how wet he is, of how funny it all was, of how she laughed. "Good night!" she calls.

She takes Manford by the arm. "Let's hurry," she says, for now it seems she must be away from him, cannot bear to look at him so cheerful and filthy and hopeful. "Let's run home."

They run together all the way to Fergus's before Vida has to stop and catch her breath. Manford won't stop, though. "Up the lane, Manford," she calls to him as he pushes past her. "Time to go home." She sees him disappear round the corner to the lane.

And who had seen them, after all, she thinks. Who had seen Vida Stephen and Manford Perry, running hand in hand down the streets of Hursley in the night? No one. No one had seen Mr. Lamb trip and fall in the street. No one had seen the look on his face. No one had seen anything at all.

LATER THAT NIGHT, Vida stands at the door to Manford's room, listening to the steady sound of his breathing. Then, from down the hall, she fetches a chair and wedges it under the knob. It wouldn't exactly prevent him from getting out if he started to sleepwalk again, but it might dissuade him. Perhaps he would, rattling the knob and finding the door stuck, just turn round and get back into bed. Vida closes her eyes and tries to imagine Manford getting back into bed, getting safely back into bed. At least, she thinks, she'll hear the chair fall and can stop him before he gets to the stairs. She worries so about the stairs.

She finishes clearing up in the kitchen and then goes to the library to fetch her book. The moon bobs at the window, full and bright, and she is drawn to the French doors to look out upon the sight. It still seems unfathomable to her that American astronauts have now set their feet on the moon, though she is struck by how quickly something that was once considered impossible can pass over into the realm of the accomplished.

She steps out onto the terrace to walk behind the row of Mercuries, a shadow behind the solid figures. Staring out over the dark velvet of the lawns, she remembers dancing on those same lawns as a girl in Miss Ferry's pageants, Miss Ferry with her wobbling jowls and deeply hooded eyes and velvet waistcoat, the silver serpent with the ruby eye coiled around her upper arm. She remembers as if it were yesterday Miss Ferry clapping loudly in measure, tra-*la* tra-*la* tra-*la,* neatly smacking the girls' backsides as they flowed past her in their circling skirts out from between the wings of boxwood. Leaping and curtsying over the grass, bangles on her ankles, a scarf in her hair, Vida had felt then that she might have been anybody, anybody else, a wild girl with Gypsy blood, capable of a kind of ecstasy ordinary life seemed to dampen like a blanket thrown over a fire.

A small breeze flutters the leaves of the trees below her, moving like the surface of a lake. Vida wraps her arms around herself and shivers slightly. The Prince's Mead dance performances had always been preceded, for her, by such excitement that she was nearly sick from it, as though another body, another person, were struggling up from within her, *that* girl's exotic spirit rising up within her like a body from a grave, subduing her own nature by means of flashing looks and snapping castanets. She had loved those ritualized performances, yet afterward she had felt such grief, such disappointment that it was over, that she would not feel so inhabited again for another year.

Finished with their dancing, the girls would come back out on the lawn at Southend, receive their parents' embraces, take a glass of orangeade, and stand demurely and quietly amid the adults' chatter, smiling politely. And yet Vida would feel exhausted, ashamed, that other self within her scornful and proud, gradually parting from her as if in disgust, as if Vida herself had failed to seize some opportunity, had shown herself a traitor. She stands now motionless between two Mercuries, the dark garden before her full of the fading echoes of her past.

Where are all those other girls? she wonders. What has happened to them? Would their lives, held side by side, resemble her own in any way?

Once, she believed that she was only waiting for something to happen to her. And yet now it seems that something *has* begun around her. The thing she has been waiting for—though she cannot say what it is—has started making itself felt in the very air around her. She does not know how to behave, she realizes, nor what to expect.

She does not even know anymore what to hope for.

Thirteen

When Norris opens the door of the post office Monday morning, the room seems unfamiliar to him—smaller, somehow—as if he has been away on a long journey. Beneath his feet the linoleum, dark green and patterned with darker, ambiguous shapes suggesting the blurred hoofprints of animals, is worn and faded, buckling up along a filthy seam. When he raises the black shades at the window—just halfway, not enough to suggest he is open for business—a shaft of dull, pale light falls first across the high oak counter installed against the front wall beneath the window. There, his patrons address letters and packages, pause to gossip and chat. Pens attached to long beaded chains are riveted to the top of the counter, which is scarred and stained under its polished surface from many years of being borne down upon with damp palms and leaky pens. Small pink sponges swim in tiny bowls of filmy water.

Along another wall of the post office, Norris maintains a dual confectionery and stationers, selling tablets of onionskin and heavy, cream-colored stock, envelopes of all sizes, postal cards and gummed labels, all stacked on shelves alongside boxes of chocolates and sweets in tiny sachets, as well as sacks of tobacco and a few brands of cigarettes. Norris also keeps a contract with a company that manufactures greeting cards featuring pencil and watercolor drawings of baby animals, their faces and attitudes either fetching or pathetic, depending on the occasion. CHEER UP! reads the inside of one card featuring a small kitten with the large eyes of a malnourished creature. These cards are typically purchased by the older women of the village. Norris has kept this particular line in stock for so long that many ladies have received at least one and usually more from a neighbor over the years. Norris has been in enough of his neighbors' houses to see the cards, some of them quite faded, lined up on the mantels, and the sight pleases him, as though he has contributed something important to his neighbors' lives.

From time to time he has been approached by salesmen from other companies, who open their cases briskly on his counter and spread out their wares. But Norris hasn't cared for the rude cartoons they assured him were popular.

"These are simple people, people who are fond of animals," he protests. "I don't believe they would care for these at all."

Once, though, he agreed reluctantly to take a set of free samples from a pushy young woman selling cards of tarted-up old men and women apparently enjoying rather debauched birthday celebrations. "You're not as old as you look!" the cards read inside. It was insulting! Norris watched surreptitiously as a few people took them off the display rack that first week and looked at them without expression, returning them after a moment. Some days later, when the young woman came back to see about how her cards had done, Norris was able to return the entire lot triumphantly to her.

"I'm afraid," he said somewhat disingenuously, "I wasn't able to sell a single one. They don't know," he added, "your company, what people really like. They like animals," he repeated. "Small animals. Something dear."

On the empty wall across from the shelves of stationery supplies, Norris has hung several framed stamp displays, including one of his own favorites—stamp errors—which he assembled and mounted while still a young man. It includes stamps with simple printing mistakes—one issued by the Bahamas, for instance, featuring the face of Queen Elizabeth in the foreground gazing over an oddly empty silhouette of Government House, a ghostly outline where the printer's ink had run out. Another is a 1930 stamp from Germany, showing a portrait of the composer Robert Schumann against a background of sheet music—composed by Franz Schubert. And Norris is particularly proud of a 1903 stamp from St. Kitts-Nevis, depicting Christopher Columbus using a telescope—one hundred years before such an implement was invented. This stamp is especially rare and valuable now; Norris is proud of owning it and imagines that all of Hursley benefits from its presence among them.

Norris also framed, after his mother's death, part of her collection of stamps featuring famous women, including an oversize portrait of pioneer pilot Harriet Quimby, her aviatrix's goggles staring out darkly above a smile of brilliant white teeth. There is also a humble stamp depicting Clara Barton, and several of the Virgin Mary, of course. (His own private collection of breastfeeding stamps he keeps concealed at home in a box marked TROPHIES. It has occurred to him that someone might find these stamps pornographic at one level, but in fact he has an oddly reverent, almost paternal feeling for the scenes of domestic comfort they suggest; he keeps them shut away out of protectiveness rather than shame.)

This morning, staring around the post office, he walks irresolutely into the center of the room and pauses. He inspects the stamps on the wall; their effect, he senses suddenly, is to make him feel peculiarly tiny, as though he has shrunk uncomfortably to the size of a pencil and is passing through a gallery of paintings now scaled perfectly to his new stature. He frowns, shakes his head slightly against the sensation of diminishment, the dismaying sense that everything around him has grown either small or shabby or both.

At the back of the room runs Norris's postal counter; he has always wished for a grille for it, something that suggests that when you pass your letters over, they will acquire, in that moment, some worldly and important mission of their own—like a child sent off for the first time to perform an errand by himself—passing into the wondrous stream of mail traveling to distant corners of the globe. He has never found exactly what he wants, though, and so makes do instead with a large leather-trimmed blotter flanked by tall, unsteady cardboard stamp displays. And he tries to make his manner, when he takes a letter or parcel in his hands, both serious and mysterious at once, perhaps as compensation for the modest environment. He tries to maintain a cachet about the transactions.

Beneath the counter are shallow drawers containing stamps, aerogrammes, stamped postcards, and registered mail envelopes. Against the back wall are his scales, his cancellation machine (recently and reluctantly purchased to replace the failing hand-operated duplex cancel he had continued to use, despite vastly improved mechanical equipment), and the pigeonholed cabinet into which he sorts received mail. A black rubber mat that holds the indentations of his feet lies across the floor.

Norris slowly crosses the room and steps behind his counter. A small door, between the scales and the pigeonholed cabinet, opens to a narrow hallway with a buckled brown tile floor that slopes noticeably downhill. To one side is the lavatory; to the other is the tiny room Norris maintains as an office for himself, with a desk and a narrow chair, an electric kettle for tea on an unsteady rattan table, and on the wall a framed engraving of a *chasqui,* the helmeted runner employed in ancient Peru to deliver messages from *Sapa Inca,* the emperor.

Norris sits down at his desk, his head in his hands. Since parting from Vida last night he has hardly slept, lying awake on and off all night, aware of the sense of urgency their conversation has created in him. That he might have actually frightened her by leaving the robe on her bed—the thought is dreadful! He closes his eyes, shakes his head back and forth within the brace of his hands. He had managed to reassure her a little, it's true, but he also suspects that it will prove to be only a temporary comfort. Now, he fears, it is time to show himself to her, to declare himself. And yet he feels utterly unprepared for this. He had planned—what? *Weeks* of courtship, flowers left here and there in surprising places, gifts of dresses and jewels, more letters, each more enticing, more deliciously romantic than the last. By the end, he had supposed, there would be no question: He would have won her entirely. She would be in love already just with the idea of him.

But if he is done with that now, what is left? Nothing but himself, the poor excuse of himself. This is a terrible notion; and he finds that he has risen unconsciously to his feet behind his desk, as if to defend himself before a jury. He is not ready! He will never be ready!

And now, running his hands through his hair again, turning around and around in the oppressively close confines of this little, windowless room, he realizes as well that there is Manford to be considered. He had not counted on that, not counted on having to consider him at all, in fact. Oh, foolish man—what had he thought? That he would marry Vida Stephen, take her away, and someone else would step in to replace her at Southend House? The idea is preposterous! What would Manford do without Vida? They can no more be separated than—well, he can't exactly find a comparison. But there can be no question about it, he realizes now. And there is something special about the boy, Norris thinks, something that makes him want to take care what he does, take very great care.

He is startled at this moment by the distant sound of a fist pounding on the door outside. He hurries into the front room to open the door, where he nearly falls over the mail sacks slumped against the jamb.

"You're late opening up. Got anything to go out?" A young man Norris has never seen before, an annoyed look on his face, is climbing into the postal truck idling at the curb. He leans out when Norris does not answer immediately.

"The other fellow brings them inside," Norris says stiffly, ignoring the young man's obvious impatience and bending to lift the sacks himself to carry them.

"I'm going to be late! And your blinds weren't up!" the man retorts, blowing a gust of cigarette smoke out of his mouth. "Come on," he repeats after a moment, racing the engine. "I haven't got all day. Be a good chap and bring out what you've got, won't you?"

"I haven't anything," Norris says primly. "It all went Friday with Mr. Howard. Where *is* Mr. Howard, anyway?"

"Had an accident. Banged up a vehicle. I'm doing Hursley and Stoke Charity." The man grinds the gears of the truck. "See you at five, then," he calls as he drives off.

Norris surveys the still-empty street a moment and then hefts the canvas sacks himself and pulls them inside. Mr. Howard always carries them in himself and hands them to Norris over the counter; they exchange a word or two. It is a moment Norris enjoys, the two men remarking about the volume of mail that day, Mr. Howard offering some bit of news from the central post office in Winchester. He hopes now that Mr. Howard wasn't seriously injured in the accident. How like that young man not to have said; probably couldn't care less about Mr. Howard! Tugging the bags across the floor, Norris feels his distaste for the task; it's like trolling a dead body.

Behind the counter he begins the business of sorting the letters and magazines, church bulletins and advertisements. He has developed over the years the trick of catching a fistful of envelopes and splaying them quickly in his hand, like a card trick. Many he recognizes simply by color and shape, and he can fit them into their accustomed boxes almost without thinking. Each day he likes to time himself, glancing at the clock and promising himself a certain number of minutes to finish the task. He hardly ever stops to look at a letter for more than a fraction of a second, just long enough to see who it's for. Unless, of course, there is an interesting stamp on it.

He pauses now, in fact, distracted by the stamp on a long, slender, almost weightless envelope. It's a truly striking stamp, a careful engraving of an ancient building, its front studded with pillars, set against a midnight blue sky. Below the templelike building, a landscape of curling russet lines and the shadowy folds of chalky cliffs tumble toward a distant skyline rendered in inky black silhouette, the jumbled rooftops and spires of a foreign city. It's a copper photogravure, Norris thinks in surprise; one doesn't see many such stamps nowadays. Though offset printing produces stamps with sharper images, Norris thinks recess-printed stamps have a special quality. Like snowflakes, no two are alike.

And then his eyes drift, almost accidentally, from the stamp itself to the name on the envelope: MISS VIDA STEPHEN.

The shock of seeing her name gives him a jolt, an uncomfortable one.

Who has sent her this letter?

He finds himself staring vacantly across the post office now, the letter still held in his hand, as if someone might at that moment step forward in accusation: Oh, you're a bungler, Norris Lamb. Nothing but a bungler. Go on, step aside. Give it up. She won't look twice at you!

Dazed by the force of this imagined reproof, he looks down at the letter again. He had tried to persuade Vida that there was no one to fear, that the mystery of this campaign to woo her would end well, would end—happily. He had spoken with a confidence he does not really possess. He had spoken from sheer will. But he has never imagined that there might be some unexpected rival, some intervention from the world itself; it is as if his own ardor, abandoning him in disgust, has formed itself into someone against whom he can never hope to compete, some man who is everything Norris wishes himself to be. The postmark of the letter has been nearly obliterated by a damaging smudge; he can't make out where it might have been sent from. Norris brushes at it with his fingertip; there is no return address, either. There is only the handwriting to go by, a heavy, masculine, admirably formed hand, the letters of Vida's name executed with a triumphal flourish.

IF NORRIS HAD anyone to advise him, if he had a friend who could clap him on the back and give him courage, he might be rescued from what comes next. But he is so sure of his failure, so confident that despite all his longing—because of all his longing, perhaps—he will be humiliated, that he can't think clearly now. He thinks not what a reasonable man might suppose—that this is a letter about some business or legal affair, that this is a correspondence of some official capacity. It does not occur to him that this letter might be from a friend or even from her uncle Laurence, though he knows she has recently written to him; and the building in the stamp does look like the Parthenon, a stamp Laurence might easily have come by. Instead of such conclusions, his mind leaps ahead like a dog madly in pursuit of a phantom fox.

He is jealous, flagrantly jealous, wounded deep in his heart by what feels, already, like an infidelity, and so he reads the script on the front of the envelope as the haughty penmanship of some very well-to-do gentleman, a friend of Mr. Perry's perhaps, someone he has brought back to Southend House once or twice. And this gentleman, this friend of Perry's—well, he would have had occasion to meet Vida, wouldn't he? She might even have made up his bed for him in the morning, or hung up his shirts as a courtesy, or brought him a gin while he sat in the garden. And Mr. Perry would have had the most marvelous things to say about her, of course, about how she's like a mother to Manford. The gentleman friend, eyeing her retreating back as she walked away across the lawn with the pitcher of water and the plate of limes, would have noticed her beauty. "I see why you've kept her here in hiding, Thomas," he might have said, his eyes never leaving her back. And then he would have found opportunities to speak to her here and there, in the kitchen or the garden. They would have spoken about his business and his travels; she would have told him how she'd always wished to travel herself. He would have heard this remark, received it in thoughtful silence. And since then, he would have found that he cannot forget her. She seems to be everywhere, no matter where he goes, no matter what room with splendid views he unpacks his bag in, no matter what countess or rich American divorcée takes his hand across a table. He would not be able to forget Vida.

I could lose her, Norris thinks, gripping the envelope between his fingers. A surge of hate rises up in him, so vicious that he feels nearly suffocated by it. Who is this man, imposing himself on her in this insidious and disgusting way! He glares at the envelope as if it has emitted some foul odor, as if it contained the evidence of some monstrous, criminal urge.

He puts out a hand, finds the back of the tall chair he uses behind the counter, and lowers himself into it. He is shaking; the feeling terrifies him, sickens him. He is used to frustration, not rage, though he understands that sometimes, when matters seem too confounding, too intransigent, he experiences moments of an indifferencc so final that it seems permanent, as permanent as his own skin. He has felt his own eyes roll briefly to the back of his head as if he could will himself to faint in the middle of his own life, will himself to be absent from whatever troubles him. At his mother's funeral, he had felt himself hardly present, for instance; waves of a sliding unconsciousness folded over him again and again as he stood at the graveside, a clod of earth clenched in his hand. As he leaned forward and scattered the earth into the grave, prompted by a touch from the vicar at his elbow, he heard the sod smack hard upon the coffin, like a rock, and the sound frightened him. Afterward, returning alone to the empty house, he moved quietly through the dark rooms, sat down before his grandmother's organ. Yet he did not play; he felt the muscles in his arms seize—he understood that some part of him wished to smash the instrument with his fists. He forced himself, at last, to play a chorale, his hands trembling. And afterward he tasted blood, realized he had bitten himself. Stumbling to the lavatory, he pulled the chain for the light, fumbled vainly in the cupboard for something to help, felt the warm blood in his mouth, and spat into the basin. He fell to his knees on the cold tile floor and wept then, blood and spittle dribbling down his chin.

NOW HE STARES down at the envelope still in his hand. He lets the others fall from his grasp, scatter over the floor.

In his office he puts the letter carefully on his desk. He fills the kettle with water from the rusty sink in the lavatory, plugs it in. He sits heavily in his chair, as if drunk, waiting until steam rises from the kettle. When he holds the envelope to the vapor, trying to angle it in his hand so that the steam pries up the sealed edge, his fingers burn from the wet, sharp heat, and he sucks in his breath and retreats. Casting about, he spies a pair of scissors, fixes the letter gently between the blades, and then offers it to the chimney of steam again. After a minute the envelope begins to curl. He shakes the scissors, turning them like a long fork. The sealed seam of the envelope begins to buckle and part.

"My dear Vida," he reads.

"I'm so glad you liked the little painting. I've got boxes of them here, I have to tell you; you'll probably inherit them when I go, and have to sell them off for a shilling apiece to cover my funeral expenses! But no, now that I think of it, Ari has already said he'll have me burned at the stake and my ashes tossed into the Aegean! Have I written you about Ari? I hired him about a year ago to help me clean up around here; your old bachelor uncle has never been much good with the mop, I'm afraid. Ari arrived in answer to a few vague inquiries I'd placed in the village, perfectly gorgeous to look at and not a word of English, and now he claims he'll never leave me. What have I done to deserve such riches, I ask you!

"But I ramble, and there isn't any need of me going on and on about Ari (though I could go on and on, I assure you), because I want you to meet him in person. Your last letter made me think—your mother would never forgive me if I didn't see to it that we had you here in Corfu to visit, at least once. I know you've been the soul of conscientiousness with Manford, and I admire you for it; but your news that he's working at Niven's now (does Mr. Niven still wear that funny monocle?) made me think that this was just the right time for you to have a proper holiday. Or a permanent one, for that matter. What's holding you in Hursley, after all? Here I've got this gorgeous, rambling old place, with the most spectacular views on earth, and Ari brings me figs and olives and fresh fish every day, and I sell enough paintings (particularly in the summer, to the silly tourists) to provide for all three of us—you, me, and Ari. I remember you, Vida. I knew we really were blood relations because you were such a romantic. I remember how much you wanted to see the world once. Come along and join us, dear girl. It would do my selfish old heart good to think your mother would be proud of me. I think I need some real family around me at last, and Ari's too splendid a cook to waste on just me.

"Ari is painting your room, as we speak—sky blue. He can't imagine anyone not wanting to come to Corfu, in any case, and wants to know whether I think you'd prefer a rose-colored blanket on your bed or palest dove gray. Well? Which shall it be? We await you, my dear, with open arms.

"Fondly, fondly, fondly, your uncle Laurence."

Norris's hands are shaking. He tries to fold the paper, forces it back unevenly into the envelope, and then, quivering, tries to lick the edges to seal it again. The paper is wet, though, and comes away on his tongue, bits of weak blue paper, sweetish-tasting. He tries to press the folds closed with his trembling fingers, but the damp paper refuses to lie smoothly. He puts it down on the desk, presses his palms against it, leans down as though trying to stifle the breath from a man. The ink bleeds away under his hands. The letter is ruined.

She will go away.

Go on then, he thinks. Go on. Damn you. Damn you.

"HALLOO? MR. LAMB? Anyone at home?"

The voice holds a false, happy trill. The Billy.

Norris freezes, his hands still over the letter. He picks it up after a second, folds it hurriedly several times, and shoves it into his breast pocket. He touches his upper lip, feels the sweat there and a bit of paper, which he picks off with shaking fingers.

"Coming!" He buttons his cardigan and tries to take a deep breath, but his heart feels as if it has been shot full of holes; he will never stop up so many wounds.

"Ah, Mrs. Billy," he says, coming through the door at last. "What a pleasure. And how are you this morning?"

But he feels as mean as he has ever felt in his whole life.

HE PASSES THE day in a stupor. He hardly speaks to the villagers who stop in to collect their mail. He forgets to have anything to eat. He sits at his stool and stares ahead of him. He hears the sound of waves, far off, and sees, again and again, Vida's body on the fountain's rim, tiny and tempting like a ballerina on a music box.

At last, at four, he pulls down the blinds with a fierce clatter and locks the door and goes round to Niven's. The bakery is empty. Norris cranes round the door to look in the annex where Manford usually sits, but it's empty there as well, Manford's stool pushed beneath the high table. On the counter is a tray of iced buns. Norris stares at them, then reaches out and pushes his finger deliberately into the top of one, collapsing the pastry and grinding the icing. When he hears a sound from the back of the bakery, he grabs the bun and stuffs it in his pocket, smearing sugar on his coat.

"Oh! Mr. Lamb!" Mrs. Blatchford comes through the door with her arms full of boxed cakes, her face flushed red.

Norris stares at her impassively.

"Well? What have you got up your sleeve?" she asks impatiently when Norris fails to say anything. "Just standing here like a ghost? There's the bell, you know! You might have rung if you'd wanted something." She jerks her head toward the bell on the counter and sets down her boxes with a thud.

"Where is he?" Norris says.

"Who? Manford?" Mrs. Blatchford glares at him. "Well, aren't we pleasant today?" She bends over heavily, fitting the boxes into the glass shelves below. "A lovely day to you, too, Norris Lamb. Just the day for pleasantries. Mr. Niven gone off to his golfing and me here all alone, the vicar needing six cakes for the committee, and no one's thought to tell me until the last moment." She huffs, stands up again. "He's never come in today. Vida rang up, said they were both ill. What's it to you, anyhow?" she adds sharply.

But Norris doesn't answer her. He bangs out the door and sets off down the lane.

She laughed at me, he thinks. She laughed when I fell down in the mud.

At the front door to Southend House he reaches for the chain, pulls hard on it. After a long moment, Vida opens the door. She is wearing an old dressing gown—not his gift—a worn blue one with the satin collar faded away. Her face is very pale. She cranes round the door and stares up at Norris, puts her hand up to her mouth as if she might be sick. She seems very small, smaller than ever. He sees the declivity at her throat, her tiny wrist crossed before her chin.

"Mr. Lamb!" she says. "I thought you might be Dr. Faber."

"No," Norris says. "Sorry."

"Excuse me." She closes the door slightly and disappears behind it; he hears her cough. She opens it again and looks out at him.

Norris glances away as if something up in the trees has just caught his eye. "Manford?" he asks, not looking at her. "He's not well either?"

"He's in bed."

Norris waits. "Nothing serious, I hope," he says quietly after a moment.

She makes a gesture of slight fatigue. "Just a flu, I'm sure," she says, "but I like to have Dr. Faber see him, in any case."

"Of course." Norris looks down at his feet and then glances up only as far as her throat, stopping before he meets her eyes. He points to her dressing gown. "You'll catch cold, with that thin thing on," he says. He allows his eyes to linger on the fragile proportions of her neck. "Perhaps you need a fire," he says.

He looks up at last and meets her gaze. "And some tea," he says. "My mother used to make me a nettle tea. Very effective. Very—soothing."

Vida looks back at him; her eyes have filled surprisingly with tears. Her lips part but no sound comes from her.

He steps toward her then, takes her arm. "Come on," he says gently, and feels how his heart has suddenly sent forth a million branches, buds flinging themselves open to the rain. "I'll make you some tea," he says. "We'll see about Manford."

"ALL RIGHT THEN?" He tucks the rug around her knees, places the teacup on her lap. She steadies it with her fingertips, leans back against the chair, and closes her eyes. "Go on. Take a sip," he says, standing over her. Vida puts the cup to her lips, takes a swallow, grimaces.

Norris clucks his tongue. "It's very beneficial," he says. "You'll see."

Vida looks up at him. "You used to drink this?"

He nods firmly. "Got so's I didn't even mind the taste. I knew it would set me to rights."

She wrinkles her nose. "It smells awful, brewing."

"Yes." He turns toward the kitchen. "I think it smells worse than it tastes, though."

Vida makes another face, glances up at him skeptically.

He crosses the room and kneels at the hearth. He builds a careful fire from the basket of twigs, laying the sticks neatly to form a box, and then lights it with a long match from the box on the mantel. When he turns around, Vida's head has fallen gently to the side, the teacup tilted in her lap, a little tea spilled into the saucer. Her eyes have closed. Norris crosses the room and looks down at her pale face for a long while. And then he raises his eyes and stares out the window, a light, steady rain falling outside as the afternoon darkens into evening.

Woman waits, he thinks. In her dressing gown.

HE TRIES TO remember when he last thought seriously about a holiday. Once, he knew, he'd wanted to rent one of those brightly painted tinker's caravans in Ireland, take a month to do the coast, ending up at Dingle, perhaps, or the Aran Islands. And once, he'd investigated—thanks to Mr. Nesser, who'd first put the opportunity before him—renting a houseboat in India near Kashmir. Seems Nesser is related to someone there who has them. Teddy Roosevelt had let one several years in a row, Nesser had written Norris; he'd had a grand one, of course, all hung round with Indian tapestries and so forth and filled with heavy British colonial furnishings and silver service. Nesser's great-uncle, or something like that, had been Roosevelt's Himalayan guide, apparently. Norris had liked the notion of it—the locals would moor up to the houseboats in their little boats and sell you flowers or fruit, and at dawn you could hear the Moslem call to prayer drift out across the water. But it all proved too dear for Norris's salary. He still has the photos Nesser sent, though. He takes them out and looks at them from time to time. In his head he's woven quite a story about his houseboat, his adventures on it.

NORRIS'S GAZE LINGERS on Vida's face for another moment, and then he turns and leaves the room. He climbs the staircase quietly, reaches a door partly ajar, and then pauses as a sensation of unsteadiness arrives at his feet. The room has become unmoored; were he to step over the threshold, he would find himself lost in a strange land. A trembling light spills out from over the sill and around the edge of the door, the heavy light of late afternoon melted at last into evening. And something else.

He pushes slightly against the door. It swings inward, and Norris's eyes widen at the swimming, swirling shapes around him—orange and turquoise fish circling the walls and ceiling, diving and darting; a yellow sun spinning madly as if at the end of a tether; clumps of wavering water plants bobbing through blue waves. The shapes flow round the walls like ghosts, over the paintings, over the cavernous wardrobe, the long windows, the wide bed with its heavy headboard and the body beneath the sheets. Beside the bed, on a small nightstand, the night-light glows. The shadow shapes spiral out from it and into the falling dark.

Norris steps into the room, feels the light against his face, feels the bouncing fish and the sun sweep over him, feels the blue sea close in around him, feels the seaweed brush his hands. It is as exquisite as longing, like a face in a dream that inclines toward your own and then withdraws, hands poised lightly over your body, breath in your ear. He stands still, the sweet, pure colors thrown by the night-light, the whole world, flowing over him.

At the bed the body moves slightly, Manford's shoulders rising, hesitating, and then falling again. Norris steps closer. In his sleep, Manford's hair has slicked to his forehead and parted in waves over the heavy brow, damp from fever.

Norris raises his hand. A fish swims through it, capillaries and corpuscles and flesh and blood no obstacle for a moment. For a moment he holds the sun in his hand.

He touches him then, feels his forehead. It is moist, cool.

It's passed, Norris thinks.

He covers Manford's foot, heavy and white, shaken loose from the blankets. He raises the sheet gently to Manford's shoulders, smooths it lightly with his fingertips. How many times has *she* done this, he thinks, tiptoed in here, covered Manford again as though he were a baby. Through so many years. Years and years of vigilance over Manford's preposterous failure to grow, to speak, to walk away, to take matters into his own hands. All these years they have had this between them, this love. How lucky.

He backs away from the bed, from the body within it, the pretty rain of colored shapes falling over them both now, the universe spinning around them, infinity reduced in this room to a child's crudely shaped school of fish, a punched-out sun, the stiff grasses waving at heaven, and a milky blue light, far away. All of it, the whole world, here.

And not until he arrives home later that night, soaking wet from the rain but cleansed in a way he has not been, he thinks, for perhaps his whole life, does he remember Laurence's letter to Vida. The words, for having been in his pocket the whole while, are blurred but still, for anyone who might want to try to read them, faintly, barely legible.

Fourteen

"WELL, *YOU'VE* MADE a quick recovery, I must say," Vida says, helping Manford into his shirt Tuesday morning and turning him round to face her so that she can do his buttons. "Come on," she says, beckoning with her free hand as she kneels on the floor before him. "Give us your leg."

Manford obligingly inclines his foot, thick in its heavy sock. She loosens the laces of the shoe and opens it, its tongue bent backward. "You *could* learn to do this yourself, you know," she grumbles, struggling with his foot; but her tone is gentle.

She is unprepared when Manford leans over suddenly and ruffles her hair with his hands.

"Oh! No, Manford! You'll muss my hair!" She sits back on her heels and puts her hands to her hair defensively. Manford gives her a wild-eyed look, smiles hugely, and lunges at her again with both hands, fingers wiggling. She slaps at the air between them. "Manford! Leave go my hair, will you! What's come over you? You're a regular nuisance!"

He sits back, hands limp in his lap, a bored expression on his face.

"Now, that's it then," she says as she gives the laces a final tug. "You're ready to go." She sits back on her heels again to appraise him. "You're certainly lively this morning," she tells him. "I never saw someone turn around a fever so fast." She puts her hand up and feels his forehead, brushing his hair aside. "Cool as the driven snow." She smiles at him. "Dr. Faber says I'm a worrywart. Do you think I'm a worrywart?"

Manford winds his hands in his lap, glances at her face, and then stares off out the window. She follows his gaze. "It does look like rain, doesn't it? Well, we'll take an umbrella to Niven's. You're right enough to work, I think. Come on. The fresh air will do us both good."

Downstairs in the kitchen, she fixes Manford toast, sits beside him while he eats. She had woken late last night in her chair, the fire low and her teacup on the table beside her. Mr. Lamb had been nowhere in sight; she supposed he had gone home. She hoped he didn't think her rude to have fallen asleep. She had drifted up to bed at last feeling wonderfully restored, strangely content, and sleepy. When she'd woken this morning, she'd known that whatever it was that had made her feel so drippy the day before had passed. And though she'd been glad enough yesterday to wake feeling poorly, so as to postpone a meeting with Mr. Niven and whatever discomfort a meeting might cause them both, this morning the whole idea of Mr. Niven as her mysterious suitor seems positively absurd. What was it Mr. Lamb had said? That Mr. Niven hadn't enough—imagination? He was right; it *couldn't* be Mr. Niven. She feels a little thrill run through her. She stands up and takes Manford's plate to the sink. Perhaps it is all still to be discovered.

"Will you have an egg?" she asks Manford over her shoulder, turning to the fridge and rummaging around inside. "Oh, dear. We're out," she apologizes, standing upright again and surveying Manford. "Perhaps you'd like to have a doughnut at Niven's instead? I'll go round later today for eggs. I know you love an egg." Manford looks up from the tablecloth, where he has been pushing a little pile of crumbs to and fro. He smiles, puts his hands up, and wiggles his fingers at her.

She moves over beside him then, puts her hands on his head,

and leans down to put her lips to the shock of heavy hair that stands up from his cowlick. "I'm sorry about the eggs," she says. When he reaches up to clasp her hand, she holds his fingers tight in her own, rests her cheek against his hair. "It's been ages since you've seen your father, hasn't it?" she says quietly, her eyes closed. "Perhaps we'll have a card from him today. See how he's getting on in Amsterdam, or Italy—wherever he is. Isn't he lucky, getting to travel like that, anywhere he likes? I wish he'd take us with him sometime. You'd like that, wouldn't you? Travel with your father? Travel in the high style?"

Manford reaches up with his other hand, covers hers with his soft palm.

"Good boy," she says, and gives his hand a squeeze.

BUT AS SHE is washing up Manford's breakfast things, it occurs to her that Mr. Perry has never taken them anywhere, with the exception of that one trip to London to have Manford examined. They'd make an odd threesome, she supposes, though Manford is perfectly well behaved in public. Once, Mr. Perry had suggested he might take them to Paris; he'd seemed astonished that she'd never been. "It's so close!" he'd said in surprise when she confessed that she'd never been out of the country at all. "Well, we'll have to fix that," he'd said, and had appeared to be thinking of some arrangement he might make. "How would you like to see Notre-Dame?" he'd said.

She had wanted to go very much. She remembered that. But nothing had ever come of it. Mr. Perry had left again, alone, shortly thereafter, the name of a hotel or private party left with Vida should she need to reach him. And what sort of good-bye did he ever make to Manford? He would stop, sitting before him silently a moment, watching him. Vida has always thought it made Manford uncomfortable to bear his father's scrutiny in that way. But at last Mr. Perry would lean forward, put a hand briefly to Manford's head. And then he would leave.

She did once want to see Notre-Dame; and with Mr. Perry, too. There was a day when she would have thought it romantic, would have cherished a silly girl's hopes. But now the whole notion seems out of reach, impossible; and she wouldn't want to go with Mr. Perry anyway. Really, she realizes, she'd want to go somewhere by herself. She's never been anywhere by herself.

A few weeks ago, she was reading over her uncle Laurence's letters and found an early one in which he asked if they could locate for him Heinzel, Fitter, and Parslow's *Birds of Britain and Europe with North Africa and the Middle East*.

"It's the guide for bird-watching in these parts," he wrote. "And I've a mind to improve my education. In the holm oaks out behind the tavern where I'm staying lives a Scops owl who's become my charming nocturnal companion. I hear him at night when I'm closing up, shoving off the last of the inebriates. He has the most plaintive call. Just the other night, as I was mopping up the terrace, I found one of our oldest patrons—I think the fellow's a hundred years old at least, liver of steel—lying stretched out on the terrace wall. As I sloshed the bucket over the stones, he waved his arm at me in annoyance. And then I heard that owl call.

"'Yianni! Yianni!' the old man called back—it was perfectly heartbreaking! And then, raising himself on one elbow, he fixed me with his eye. 'She calls for her lover, but he is gone for good,' the old fellow told me. And then the owl sounded again, and the man pressed his hands to his eyes and wept, 'Yianni! Yianni!'

"Now I sit awhile at night after closing, listen for the owl, and offer my poor reply.

"Won't you see if you can't find the book?"

Vida had been struck by this letter, as she had by so many of them. She remembered having been dispatched by her mother to ask the vicar about the book. After searching his shelves for some time, he had indeed found the guide Laurence wished and had turned it over, though not before giving Vida a long tour through its well-thumbed pages.

Now, she thinks, wiping a damp cloth over the kitchen table, she should like to hear that owl for herself, that owl calling "Yianni! Yianni!" into the starry night. Once, when she was a girl, she had thought she should see all sorts of things. It surprises her, in a way, to realize that she has been nowhere at all, has seen nothing of the world.

She turns from the table and stops, for Manford has moved to the little sitting room and stands in front of the tiny mirror there, his face pressed up close to the glass. He stands so near the surface of the mirror, in fact, that he must not be able to see anything at all, she thinks in surprise—nothing but his nose pressed flat like a pugilist's, the distorted terrain of his own face, and a glimpse of the stranger who lives there behind his own eyes.

"AND WHAT WILL I do today whilst you're off at Niven's?" She tries to speak cheerfully, for she sees that Manford is now suddenly melancholic; left over from the fever, no doubt.

"Well, there's the eggs," she blathers on. "I'll go round and fetch us some eggs." She helps Manford into his mackintosh, shoos him out the back door ahead of her. "And, let's see. There's the sheets. We might as well have fresh sheets after both of us being ill. Do you know, Manford, I think that tea Mr. Lamb made me was quite the miracle cure. I feel entirely well this morning. We must ask him about it for the future."

They descend the steps, Manford moving ahead of her, riding the air, his feet disturbing the morning mist. Vida feels the damp on her face and throat. The sky seems lowered, a tent pitched overhead. At the gates to Southend House, Manford stops, turns, holds out his hand. Vida takes it this morning without argument, though she's been trying to break him of this habit, and tucks it under her arm. They pass out onto the lane, its long concourse braided with mist like a delicate, fraying twine. She pats his hand. "There," she says. "You see? The mist is lifting."

Manford smiles as they step into the mist, its gray wreaths circling the tree trunks; she sees some feeling she cannot fathom pass over his face. He blinks, opens his mouth, raises his free hand, and wobbles his fingers in the air. He purses his lips and blows the vaporous steam of his breath into the lightening morning.

When he stops up short, she is startled. "What is it?" she says, turning to look at his face. And then she follows his eyes.

The bench in the lane where they so often rest, where Vida waits for him in the afternoons, where a few days ago she had found the flowers, is now strung from armrest to armrest with an elaborate spider's web, each strand beaded with pearls of dew, like a hammock of silver chains strung across the seat. If she reaches out and plucks a strand, Vida thinks irrationally, it will chime a perfect note.

"Oh," she breathes. "Isn't that something, Manford? Like what a fairy would do. It's a fairy bench, Manford. Look!"

But he *is* looking; he is staring at the bench as though watching the web for some sudden movement—as though it might fly up and flit off into the mist, or fly toward them, the lightest of chain mail, an invisible encumbrance. When he shudders, drawing nearer to Vida, she looks at him, puzzled, and then laughs, nudging him in the ribs.

"Oh, it's just a *spider's* web! You're not afraid of it, are you?"

Manford takes a few steps to the side, giving the bench a wide berth, eyeing it like a shy horse.

"Look," she says again, tugging on his arm, anxious for him to see what a lovely thing it is. "You could do this on one of your cakes," she says. "Look how pretty it is, Manford." She drags him with her, approaching the bench with its stirring, glinting web. She puts out her hand as if to touch it, but he grabs at her arm, jerks her backward, hard.

"Manford!" She turns, surprised. "Why, you *are* afraid of it! Oh, that's silly! It's nothing but an old spider's web!"

But Manford lets go her hand then and pulls away from her, throwing up his arms and fluttering his hands around his head as though there were bats flying at his eyes. He ducks and swerves, running circles in the lane, his own hands pursuing him. He moves his mouth in odd ways, but no sound comes from his lips. He brushes his hands wildly about his hair, grimacing, his eyes squinted shut.

"Manford!" Vida cries. "Stop!" She raises her own hands to stay him, but he twitches away from her, his hands frantically slapping his hair, his head ducking.

Looking around in a panic, Vida catches sight of a piece of broken branch. She darts to it, catches it up, and runs toward the bench, waving it wildly. "Look!" she cries. "Look, Manford! I'll be rid of it!"

And she sweeps the stick through the web, its sticky warp collapsing, tangling. She bears the stick down upon the seat, crashing it against the rungs, the filaments of web flying upward, dissolving into nothing. She swings as hard as she can, Manford reeling behind her, his face tormented. The stick shatters in her hand, wormy wood, cottony and soft. She feels she is beating nothing, the air itself. At last she drops the stick to the ground, turns to Manford.

He is standing at the far side of the lane in the rut, crouched low, shaking.

"There," she says, and realizes she is trembling. "I've got rid of it. It's all right now. Come on to me, Manford. It's all gone. I've killed it, do you see?"

"WELL! UP AND about again, I see," Mrs. Blatchford says as Vida and Manford come in the door of Niven's. "Right as—" She stops abruptly as she takes in Vida's white face, Manford's disarray.

Vida puts her finger to her lips.

"Here you are, then," Vida says in a tone of forced cheerfulness, helping Manford off with his coat. "Now, right to work with you," she orders. Manford trots obediently into the dairy, sits down hard on his stool, and immediately begins filling the paper cone with jam and squirting it into the tray of doughnuts waiting for him.

Mrs. Blatchford glances at Vida, a question on her face, and then goes to fetch Manford's apron. Tying it round his waist, she speaks kindly to him. "One day away and you've forgotten already," she says. "You'll have jam all over without your apron."

Mrs. Blatchford raises her eyebrows at Vida when she comes back into the room.

"He had a terrible fright this morning," Vida whispers, leaning toward her, her voice low. "It was all over a *spider's* web! He went berserk!"

"A *spider's* web!" Mrs. Blatchford rears back. "Frightened by a spider?"

"No!" Vida whispers. "It wasn't anything like that. We didn't even *see* a spider! It was just the web, over the bench in the lane. It was very large—I've never seen one like it. But he was—he was terribly afraid of it. It was the strangest thing. I've never seen him like that before."

"No spider at all?"

"No." Vida glances at Manford. He still looks worried. In his haste he has crumpled the paper cone. Jam has spilled onto his hand and the table. "Perhaps I shouldn't have made him come on," she says. "Do you think he'll be all right?"

Mrs. Blatchford looks at Manford doubtfully. "He went *berserk,* you say?"

Vida stops. She hears something in Mrs. Blatchford's tone that suddenly raises all her alarms. As much as they might seem to love him, she knows, he is essentially beyond knowing for them; they could cast him out, would cast him out, at the first sign of—of anything they couldn't understand. But she would not have him turned out now! She would not! No one, no grown man, ought to spend all his days with a nanny, shut up in a big, empty house. He needs friends. He needs to be in the world.

She has to be very careful. Words like *berserk*—well, when used in conjunction with Manford—people might make the wrong assumption. She considers what she might say. "He was *frightened* by it," she offers at last, stressing the word.

"What did he *do?*" Mrs. Blatchford inquires, her eyes wide.

"Well, he just—" Vida pauses, for it *had* been alarming. He had behaved as if a net had been thrown over him, trapping him like a fish. She'd never seen him so wild. "He didn't want it touching him," she says finally.

"But it wasn't—touching him," Mrs. Blatchford repeats, watching her.

"No." Vida collects up her purse straps then, throws Manford another glance. He is sloppily filling the doughnuts, setting them unevenly on the tray. "I'm just going round to pick up eggs," she says. "I'll stop back on my way home and check on him. I'm quite sure he'll be all right." She gathers in a breath. "You mustn't worry," she says to Mrs. Blatchford, and her tone suggests she will have nothing more to say, that such things happen from time to time and signify nothing. "Just carry on as you usually do. I'm sure he'll calm down presently. Perhaps a cup of tea would soothe him."

"I haven't anyone with me today," Mrs. Blatchford calls after Vida as she leaves. "I'm all alone! Mr. Niven's taken Mary into Winchester—they're seeing about a new sofa!"

But Vida doesn't wait to answer her.

SHE IS HALFWAY down the dairy road, its close shoulder thick with the briery hawthorn, before she remembers Jeremy, the house with the drawn curtains and ringing silence. Thinking of Jeremy makes her think of her mystery lover—for hadn't she imagined it might be Jeremy himself writing to her?—and she grows suddenly awkward and watchful, wondering if whoever this suitor is could be observing her right at this moment. She realizes that she is looking about under hedges and up in the trees as if this man weren't actually real but were composed instead of magical elements—a talking frog, for instance, or hedgehog.

When she rounds the corner and sees the string of dreary bungalows, the stained white walls of the dairy on the far side of the road, she tries to keep her eyes away from the house. She ducks her head and averts her face and begins instead to peer interestedly at the hawthorn, its white flowers stirred by agitated bees storming the blossoms. The sky feels so heavy that it seems to rest directly upon her sleeve, the crown of her head. In the humid air, the astringent lime from the dairy pinches her nostrils. She wrinkles her face.

When she reaches the gate at the corner of the dairy yard, she pauses to find a path through the mud. She does not like stopping here; she is too aware of the house behind her, of Jeremy's possible presence there. Suddenly she is mortified at the thought of seeing him, though whether it is her own shame at having thought him responsible for her love letters or her memory of the odd admiration she'd felt, seeing him without his shirt in Dr. Faber's office, she does not want to consider.

But she is stepping to the side of the gate, preparing to execute a small leap over the worst of the mud, when he calls to her.

He is standing at the door of the bungalow in a gray jersey. Even from her distance across the road, she can see how pale he is.

He raises his arm. "I thought it was you," he calls. His voice sounds very far away, as though there were something wrong with her ears.

"Yes," she calls back, and hears her own echo. She waits a moment. "I've come for eggs."

He does not reply; he seems to be waiting for something else.

"Generally I have them delivered, you know, along with the milk," she calls desperately, her voice overly loud in the still air. "I've run out early, though, so I thought I'd come myself."

He seems to be thinking. Presently he says, "Half a sec," and disappears inside. A moment later he reappears, closing the door behind him, and walks across the road to her. When he reaches her, he holds up his hand, sheathed in a black glove. "Look like a murderer, don't I?" he says. "The strangler." He surveys the mud around the gate. "Stinking mess. Look," he says, gesturing with his good arm. "You can go on round the back."

She follows him to a green-tiled passageway, low and dim and shrouded thick with dusty cobwebs. He stops at the entryway, takes out a cigarette, and lights it. "You going back home after?"

She nods.

"I'll walk with you then," he says. And then he adds, as though needing to explain himself, "I want to have a look at some of the drawings for the garden. He said they were in the library. Can't do much else anyway like this." He raises his black hand, regards it with a frown. She stares at it. He returns his attention to her after a moment, dragging his eyes away from his hand. "You can take the eggs right from the fridge," he says.

In the small, cool room, Vida takes six brown eggs from the cardboard trays lined up on shelves in the refrigerator. A bit of straw clings to one; she pries it loose with her fingernail. She puts the cool egg to her cheek briefly, rolls it between her palm and the concave shell of her cheek; she thinks of Jeremy with his black glove, waiting. She leaves her coins on the enamel tray on the table under the window.

Outside, when she rejoins him, he stubs out his cigarette and sets off down the lane. Vida does not know what to say; she walks along carrying the eggs carefully, cradled in a paper sack close to her chest. At last she glances over at him. "How's your hand?"

"Actually, it's bloody painful," he says.

And then he does not say anything else. Vida, remembering his kiss, is a little offended by his silence. She thinks he might thank her again for taking him to Dr. Faber's, but he doesn't seem to have anything to say to her. They leave the lane for St. Andrew's Place, pass the few houses there off the Romsey Road. Tony Spooner, Nigel's son, mounts a bicycle leaning against a fence before one of the houses and pedals off down the road ahead of them, his tires issuing a spray of water as he sweeps through the puddles. These are among the smallest houses in the village; the grander residences front the Romsey Road. Vida's parents' old house is here, now occupied by a retired teacher from Prince's Mead, a swaybacked spinster who cultivates a large perennial border, working all the spring and summer folded like a praying mantis over her flowers and wearing a cotton hat. Vida tries to admire the roses sprayed over the walk to the front door, a bower of white and pink, but realizes she is having to work to be cheerful.

When they turn onto the Romsey Road, the silence between them feels as though it has acquired something noticeable, that by walking along side by side without speaking, they are calling attention to themselves. But Jeremy does not look at her; he seems in a black humor, his gloved hand hanging limply by his side, his face averted and closed as a stone. She hurries to keep pace with him, holding the eggs tightly.

When they pass the post office, Vida turns her head involuntarily and glances through the window. She sees Mr. Lamb, engaged in some transaction with a customer at the counter, look up and meet her eyes before she passes from view. She raises one hand to him, but he freezes as he catches sight of her, and suddenly she feels that she is engaged in something improper, even hurtful. She wants to speak to Mr. Lamb—she wants to thank him for the night before, the nettle tea. Where had he gone when she'd fallen asleep? When she'd woken, still in her chair, the house had been silent, still. How long had he stayed by her side?

But there seems no way to address these complicated questions. Jeremy is hurrying on.

At the courtyard to Niven's, it occurs to her that she wants to stop and check on Manford as she had said she would, but now she cannot imagine breaking the silence between them to explain her errand. And then they are turning onto the lane to Southend House, the sound of the Romsey Road receding behind them as they enter the long tunnel of green. They walk along, their tread soundless. As they draw near the bench, Vida glances surreptitiously to the side, sees that no trace of the web remains. The growing heat of the morning has evaporated it like the memory of a dream that gradually disintegrates as the day wears on. Remembering the bouquet of flowers, she tries to see whether Jeremy looks, too, whether the place holds any significance for him, but he stares straight ahead.

In the kitchen she puts the sack of eggs on the table and takes off her coat. Jeremy looks around the room, then steps to the door of the small sitting room and pokes his head in. "You eat in the kitchen?" he asks abruptly.

"Usually," Vida says, a bit surprised at the question. "Or sometimes in there." She indicates the sitting room. "In front of the telly, if there's something on."

Jeremy laughs. "He never has you eat in the dining room with him?"

"If there's houseguests." She feels confused by this line of questioning. "They eat in the dining room then."

"Ah, yes. Houseguests."

He moves to the pantry, stops, runs a finger over the labels on the shelves. She watches him a moment and then returns to the center of the room by the table, waiting and winding her hands together. After a pause she puts the eggs away and turns to fill the kettle. "Will you have a cup of tea?" she calls.

He does not answer. When he comes back into the room, he is carrying an enormous soup tureen, its fluted sides painted with minute pastorals, a formal Italian parterre seen in columns as though divided by a trick of light. "Every*day* china?" he says, holding it aloft oddly.

Vida draws in her breath sharply. "It's very old," she says quickly. "I've never used it."

"An antique," he says. She holds her breath. "He has nice things," he says calmly after a moment and returns with the tureen to the pantry.

The kettle shrieks and Vida jumps. In relief she fills the pot with the dry tea, pours in the water, and replaces the lid carefully, resting her hand over the faint halo of steam that escapes around the lid.

"Right, then. Let's have a look at the library," he says, returning to the room.

She is glad to see that he is empty handed this time. "I'll bring my tea, then," she says. She fills a cup. "Will you have one?"

"No. I drink too much tea," he says.

She leads the way down the passage, through the great hall with its dim balcony. In the center of the room, Jeremy stops and whistles, craning his head back. "How many bedrooms?"

"There's fourteen."

"Musical bedrooms," he says, and laughs again. "For the houseguests," he adds, and winks at her.

She walks on, but he wants to stop again and again, standing in the doorways, staring at the rooms. "You could put up the whole bloody village in here," he says quietly at one point, walking into one of the unused rooms, the few furnishings covered with dusty cloths. He stares around him. "He doesn't use much of it, does he?"

"During the war," Vida says slowly, "I believe many people stayed here."

"Refugees from London," Jeremy says, running a hand over the curved back of a settee. "Running from the bomb."

Vida thinks of that for a moment—the sitting room crowded with various people, the remnants of families, perhaps single ladies like her or early war widows, invited to stay at Southend for the long months of the bombing, when whole sections of London were falling under the rain of shelling, ruins toppling into ruins, heaps of ancient stone. She doesn't remember much from then, though she seems to recall that some people from London had come out to stay at Southend. It seems odd to imagine the house full, servants catering to the odd collection of people who must have taken shelter here. Since then, of course, the house has been mostly empty, unused, she and Manford and, less often, Mr. Perry, moving through its grand and deserted spaces like refugees themselves, alert, easily alarmed, nervous. As if someone were missing. Or in danger. As if they all were.

She jumps at the sound of the double doors across the hall being swung open, Jeremy wrenching the stiff hinges against disuse. The rich parquet floor of the ballroom spreads out before them, gleaming chestnut dulled under the glaze of dust, the cool morning light like frost, the mirrors full of silver. Vida sneezes, but Jeremy laughs and strides into the room, shattering the cool silence. "Aha!" he cries. "It's a party!" He takes a silent turn around the floor, upright and military, his black-gloved hand stiff as a raven tied to his wrist.

"Come on," he says, stopping before her, gesturing in a way that seems to her, for an instant, faintly crude.

"Oh, no," she says, cringing. But he comes at her, puts his good hand round her waist, a hard grip, and raises her other hand lightly in the fork of his black glove. With a wrenching movement he turns with her, executes another turn round the room. She feels the stiff hand holding hers, imagines she can feel the raised line of black stitches along his hand and wrist, the seam holding him together.

"Oh, be careful!" she cries out.

But he is laughing, galloping her around the room until she is dizzy. She catches her own reflection in the mirror, her white face, her dress hiked up in the back. He smells like stale tea. "Watch out!" he cries. "We'll take them all down!"

She feels the force of his thighs parting hers, the neat scissoring of their paired steps; and she remembers this about dancing, remembers her instinct for it. There'd been that boy, James, her partner at the dancing school held on Sunday evenings in the chilled dining hall at Prince's Mead, the boys and girls of the village scrubbed clean, the parents conscripted by the definite and regal Miss Ferry to bring their unruly youngsters, awkward and uncomfortable, for formal lessons. Being a gentleman. Being a lady. And James, at thirteen already the tallest boy in the village, a sapling, down on his upper lip, had agreeably taken her round the waist and whispered to her, "Let's get it right then." So they had learned it, James speaking to the air above her head, "That's it, that's the way. My mum and dad can dance, you know. They're grand together."

And she'd loved it, loved him. She'd loved that they seemed to dance so well together, just like his parents, whom Vida imagined in their own closed bedroom, twirling in front of the dark glass on an uneven floor, James's father loosening his wife's hair, the combs flying loose, his red neck bent over, obscuring her white face. Vida had imagined herself married to this James, this black-haired boy; she'd thought of herself as his partner in this familiar place, the various smells of the room—old bread and soup, wet wood—peeling away before the honorable smell of this boy, his clean sweat, his easy dancing, his parents in love. But she'd been only ten or eleven, too young even for possibility; they'd been paired randomly, Miss Ferry nudging couples together with her stick.

"I love you," she had whispered once into his chest, feeling as though she would have given up her life for him at that moment, there in the cleared dining hall with the black windows, the faraway smells, the evanescent music.

"What?" he'd said with his sweet breath, bending down his head. And, stepping on her foot, he'd said, "Oh, sorry."

"I'M SORRY," SHE says breathlessly now and pulls away from Jeremy, overcome by the memory the dancing has roused in her, by what she had felt back then.

"Tired you out?" Jeremy laughs. "Don't tell me you're getting too old for this."

But it isn't a question. Vida sees that. Perhaps he does consider her old, she thinks, feeling foolish; not the sun and the moon and stars.

Oh, what had ever happened to James?

"My teacup," she says faintly.

He looks at her, looks around as if annoyed that she would be worrying about her cup. "You could be a good dancer," he says then, and spying her cup, he picks it up and hands it to her. "You must have been good at it once."

"Yes. Once, perhaps," she says. She looks away.

"You should enjoy yourself more, Vida." He holds out his hands, the black glove. He glances around the empty room, the windows full of dust and light, no one there. "We could enjoy ourselves." He takes a step toward her. "It's all just going to waste, you know. You're wasting away here, Vida."

She feels him darken the light from the window.

Fifteen

Yes, it most certainly was Vida, going down the road with the gardener, and as soon as he can free himself from his customers, Norris hurries down the pavement toward Niven's in pursuit of her. He does not actually intend to speak to her, and he certainly does not want her to think he's following her. He tells himself that he just wants to see that she's all right.

Something must be amiss. Of course, it's fine that she's up and about. But to be walking about in this damp, with the gardener—what can she be thinking? Only last night, she was too weak even to finish her nettle tea, falling asleep with it only half gone!

Norris frowns into the thick, damp air before him as he passes the blacksmith's and turns the corner near Niven's; he does hope this fogginess will burn off. He feels positively suffocated.

There's something about the gardener he does not like, he thinks as he walks quickly down the pavement, trying to catch sight of Vida. He can't quite put his finger on it, but he would venture to guess that that young gardener is not a wholly reliable sort of person. It was very careless, Norris considers now, his dropping that glass pane on himself on Sunday. And what a bother, his appearing all bloodied up and Vida's having to take him off to Dr. Faber's! She was awfully kind, wasn't she? And now he's got her off on another errand, and she just over the flu!

How inconsiderate.

How thoughtless.

And how bold he is, dragging her through the village like that.

Last night, stepping into the black river of the lane on his way home from Southend House, he had felt himself disperse into the night air as effortlessly as the air itself. A sudden trill of alarm from a thrush disturbed upon its nest had risen in the wood near him, a wild, sharp cry from an unseen throat, and then nothing. Norris had raised his head at the sound and taken in the stars lining the road of the sky overhead, the narrow strip of black paving a path between the tops of the trees.

He had been grateful for the sensation of a steady walk. Out on his perambulations, he often lost all sense of purpose. He had no destination, no sense of time, only some compass within his body accustomed to steering him like a gentle hand at his back. At the end, near dawn, there would be the surprise of his own door, his bed, and sleep.

Norris knew that he seemed, probably to most of Hursley, a happy-enough man. He knew his duties; he talked to himself and others in a kindly and busy way, dispensing postage, admiring the stamps, asking after his neighbors. He was not insensitive, and he knew he could be charming if he chose to be. Week after week he would climb the steps to the organ; he understood its complexities, and he could play well enough to satisfy the congregation and the vicar. But it had now become too late for anything else, he feared. No one would ever really know him. He did not, perhaps, even know himself. The more time went by, the more he sensed that a gulf between him and the rest of the world was growing larger, a more dangerous crossing.

Yet walking through the darkness last night toward his own house, he had felt urgently that he needed to be successful now. He had been drawn to Vida—and to Manford, too, for Manford had become part of this cure Norris imagined for himself, this bringing together of the lost and the found, this one final effort he must make.

In the lane, doves called back and forth to one another in the soft summer-night air over his head. Norris saw the lights of the village ahead. He felt fiercely, as he passed the bench, how desirable another person's separateness could be, how hospitable, a sea in which to wade, another world unto itself.

Seeing Vida alone that night on the fountain's rim, he had recognized something, the wondrous, private theatrics of the unobserved self. Together, he'd imagined, he and Vida could step out onto the stage of their unknowing and enact the perfect event of creation, of creating themselves together. He believed he saw her, really saw her, and saw Manford, too. He believed he knew them, because he himself knew what it was to be lost.

Hadn't he been right to go slowly, to be a gentleman?

But now she thinks she's being stalked. That was the word she had used—*stalked*.

Dear *God*, he thought, turning on the light in his kitchen at last, blinking at the glare. It is not what I meant.

HE SAT IN his chair for an hour, but he had been unbearably restless, trying to sort out his feelings; he felt wretchedly guilty after steaming open and reading Laurence's letter to Vida. A hot shame—the same as a thousand needles, he told himself sorrowfully—prickled him all over his body whenever he thought about it. He had arrived at a wall through which there seemed to be no door in his campaign to win Vida's heart. She thought her admirer was—peculiar.

Peculiar!

Finally, though it was getting on toward midnight, he took up his stick and left the house again.

He walked in the darkness, up toward the farm where his grandmother's cottage, now falling into disrepair, still stood. After her son, Norris's father, had died and she had moved in with her daughter-in-law and young grandson, the three had gone back to the house occasionally—the summer cottage, they called it, as if giving it that romantic name changed its purpose in their lives, made it seem a luxurious second property, not the scene of his grandmother's eyesight's gradual failure, the shared grief over Norris's father's death, the beginning of his grandmother's end.

It was a lovely place, though, on a bend of the Tyre. They had brought picnics there from time to time. Norris's grandmother had liked to go back and poke around the place with her stick, rooting around in the jack-in-the-pulpits and the violets that grew down by the water, exclaiming over all its small delights, the things she could still see if they were brought up close before her eyes.

"You might like this for yourself one day, Norrie," she'd said. "It'd be a little retreat for you. A gentleman's retreat."

But instead of the usual comforting nothingness that swept over him when he walked, that he'd been so glad of, walking home from Southend just an hour before, his head was bristling. It was the guilt, he thought again. He'd broken a cardinal rule. He had read another person's mail. He had steamed open an envelope like a common criminal. He knew things he should not know.

He came upon the house in its little glade.

He unlatched the gate and walked down the path. Round the side of the cottage, by the water, was a small terrace where his grandparents had placed a round table and a bench. He sat at the bench, watched the moonlight fall in delicate sheets over the grass and the water. The darkness was comforting on his face and hands. He saw that the house needed a whitewash and the thatch needed mending. But the garden had gone to weeds that flower at night, white and fragrant. It was all lovely, he felt. And then he had a vision, a vision of Vida there on the terrace, her face lifted to the moon.

He leapt up, almost frightened by the clarity of this picture, how real and near she seemed.

He began poking around the house, and after a while he came to see that, really, there wasn't so much work to be done after all. He let himself in through the kitchen and stood in the empty first room. Vines came in through the casement, fingering the stone. But there was the good, deep sink and the old Aga.

And he allowed himself to think then that they could have a little holiday themselves, right there. It wasn't Corfu; of course it wasn't, he told himself. But it was away from the world in its own fashion. Perhaps they could come only at night, he thought, and he'd wash Vida's hair in the deep sink and dry it in his fingers on the terrace in the moonlight. He'd bring his phonograph. They'd have music, and they could dance on the deep moss.

He could have the whole place mended, restored.

He would come to her with roses. He would blindfold her. He would lead her by the hand to the cottage, unwrap her eyes, and all the darkness would fall away.

"AH, HERE IT is, just in time," the Billy said early the following morning in the post office, shaking out a small catalog and holding it up for Norris's inspection. "Morris's puzzlers. He's just yesterday finished the last of the previous month's."

She folded the catalog around her other mail, adjusted the lot beneath her arm, and painstakingly shook out her rain hat. "Looks like rain again, wouldn't you say, Mr. Lamb? The garden's very glad of it, I must say, but it's brought out the beetles something terrible. Why, they're all over the cabbages, and me out with my beetle jar in the mornings, picking them off." She sighed.

Norris rolled his eyes, and that was when he caught sight of Vida.

He struggled vainly to see around Mrs. Billy's billowing rain hat, its blue cellophane sheen obscuring his view through the window.

And it certainly *was* Vida, being towed along by the gardener.

"Matter with your neck, Mr. Lamb?" Mrs. Billy inquired. She nodded sympathetically. "It's the damp what does it. A terrible stiffness in the joints, this weather causes. I should have thought it might be fine this month, *last* month being so wet. But, that's it then. Can't do a thing about it. Think of them over in Saudi Arabia, Mr. Lamb. Now, aren't you glad you don't live there? Parching away in the desert like a lot of dried-up crisps?"

Norris glanced at her in annoyance and then back to the window.

"Oh, dear!" Mrs. Billy bent over suddenly, her mail slipping from beneath her arm, her hand to her face. "Oh! Something's in my eye, Mr. Lamb!" She dabbed at her eye, which was squeezed shut. "Oh! Something sharp!"

Norris gave a last, frantic look out the window. The Billy's envelopes had scattered at her feet. She held both hands to her face.

"Oh! Most annoying," she cried in agitation. "Whatever can it be?"

"Let me help you," Norris said, sighing, and he came round his counter. He put his hands out. "Let me have a look."

Mrs. Billy turned her face toward him, her features bunched up in discomfort, her eyes tearing from beneath short, clenched lashes.

Norris poked at her face. "You need to open your eye," he told her. "I can't see whether there's anything in it like that."

Mrs. Billy contorted her face, one eye gaping open hotly at him, pooling water. Norris peered at her. "Now, let me—" He reached with a finger, gently pulled down the skin beneath the eye. The eyeball rolled, a pickled egg. "Ooooh," Mrs. Billy moaned. "Quick, quick, it's there."

"Well, I can't *see* anything," Norris said in irritation. "Honestly, there's nothing there. It might just be a sty." He dropped his hands. "Or perhaps you've cried it out."

Mrs. Billy blinked madly, her hands fluttering before her. "Why, yes," she said at last. "I believe I have."

She smiled gratefully at him. "It's gone! Have you a hankie?"

Norris reached in his pocket, withdrew a handkerchief, and handed it to her. She patted her eye tenderly. "Now then—"

Norris stooped to the floor, collected her envelopes, and handed them to her.

"Thank you *ever* so much, Mr. Lamb," she said as Norris took her by the elbow and steered her toward the door.

"Not at all," he said hurriedly. "Not at all."

But as Mrs. Billy headed away down the street, waving her hand at him, Norris realized he was too late. Vida must have turned the corner by the blacksmith's already, was heading—where? Home, perhaps?

Another customer came in, Mr. Titus's grown and married daughter, wanting chocolates and cigarettes for herself. Norris tried to hurry her along. The ugly shape of jealousy was arranging itself in his heart.

NOW, NEARLY OUT of breath from hurrying down the pavement in pursuit of Vida along the Romsey Road, he turns in the door of the bakery.

Mrs. Blatchford looks up at him from behind the counter and

frowns. "I hope you're in a better humor than you were yesterday," she says tartly.

Norris tries to appear contrite but decides to forgo any apologies. It seems too complicated to explain his anxiety of yesterday. And now—now he feels such a mixture of things, both cheered, even emboldened, by his vague plan with his grandmother's cottage, his restoration of it, the gift of it to Vida, and perplexed and worried by Vida's appearance outside his window with the gardener. He will just check on Manford, he thinks. And then? He doesn't know exactly.

"All alone again today, are you?" he says sympathetically to Mrs. Blatchford instead. He leans round and sees Manford at his worktable, a two-tiered cake with dark icing before him. Manford holds a pastry cone in his hand, is bent over his work. "Except you have your helper back today," he adds. "Hallo, Manford!" he calls brightly.

But Manford makes no reply.

Mrs. Blatchford sighs. "Vida says he hears quite well," she says in a confiding tone to Norris, "but I've noticed that sometimes he doesn't seem to hear you at all. It's quite selective, I have noticed."

Norris regards Manford. "Mind if I have a word with him?" he asks. "I won't keep him. Just see how he's getting on?"

Mrs. Blatchford shrugs. "Oh, he's everybody's favorite now," she says. "You'd think it was he did all the work round here. No one minds old Mrs. Blatchford anymore. I'm just a fixture."

"Oh, you're necessary as the sun and the moon, Mrs. Blatchford," Norris says soothingly. "We all know that. And I've just got stamps for him," he adds, patting his empty pocket. "Won't be a minute."

WHEN HE STEPS into the hyphen, Norris pauses a moment. Manford is bent low over the cake, the arc of his back that of a defender or protector, his work concealed. One shoelace dangles limply; his ankles are crossed over the rung of the stool like a schoolboy's.

"Feeling better, Manford?" Norris inquires, and steps forward. But he stops, for though Manford has made no sound, nor even any apparent gesture, Norris sees the muscles across his back tighten, his posture over the cake grow rigid.

"Working on a cake today?" Norris says, and then the stupidity of the remark floods his face with embarrassment.

But as he takes a step forward, intending to pat Manford's shoulder in a jovial way, Manford's hand freezes and he turns his face slightly, not to look directly at Norris, but as if in allowance of Norris's presence, in acknowledgment of some helplessness to prevent what will happen.

For Norris stops then, astonished once again by Manford, by his hand, by whatever mechanism in his mind snaps and closes like a shutter, releasing the world in little pictures—shadow play, a replication of some tiny corner of the universe. The cake is iced with an elaborate spider's web, its white filaments fine as hairs, bowed in the center as if a drifting wind has caught it.

Norris steps away slowly and returns to Mrs. Blatchford.

"Well, it's rather odd, I must say." He searches for his handkerchief and then realizes in dismay that he lent it to the Billy.

"What?"

"Well, it's quite inventive. It's—" He pauses, glances at Manford, who has retrieved his pastry cone and is bent again over the cake. "Do you let him have free rein like that?" he whispers. "I mean, it's a bit gothic."

"What's he done?" Mrs. Blatchford looks at him suspiciously.

"Well, it's a—it's a—well, it's a spider's web, I'm afraid." Norris looks at her helplessly.

"A spider's web!"

"I shouldn't think many would find it *appetizing,*" he says, confession in his voice.

"Well, no!" Mrs. Blatchford looks undone. "It's nasty!"

"Perhaps, after being ill—perhaps his mind has taken a dark turn," Norris says. "Perhaps he's not quite well yet."

Mrs. Blatchford glances sidelong at Manford, appears to be thinking it over. "Mr. Lamb," she says sweetly, cajolingly, after a moment. "Do you think—would you mind just running him home? I don't want to hurt his feelings"—she lowers her voice—"but I can't have him doing spiders' webs and such on the cakes. There's three more to do, and if he's in that frame of mind, I'm afraid they'll all be ruined. Perhaps he'd be best off at home today, resting. Would you mind?"

"No bother at all, Mrs. Blatchford," he says, calculating the advantage of this proposal; now he'll have an excuse to pop in on Vida.

But he stops in the hyphen, struck by Manford's concentration on his labor. He knows what Mrs. Blatchford means about not wanting to hurt Manford's feelings. He seems so devoted to his work. Every time Norris has stopped in at Niven's and seen Manford there, he has been surprised at Manford's air of delighted occupation—just like Rumpelstiltskin, Norris thinks now, thrilled to have another pile of straw to weave into gold. He never seems to see it as straw, though, all those jam doughnuts. And how is he to know, anyway, that one doesn't put a sugar spider's web on a cake? That some might be put off by that? Suddenly Norris feels horrible, as if extracting Manford from the bakery is tantamount to kicking a dog, a good dog who only wants to be friendly.

Perhaps he should propose an outing, something that might be taken not as a rebuke but as a reward. After all, to take him straight home—well, that's like being in disgrace. And that won't do. That isn't what should be conveyed here. No, Manford is doing his very best, and he should never be discouraged. Vida would hate that.

So instead Norris makes a great show of being impressed by the cake. "Well done, Manford!" he says, clapping Manford strongly on the back. "You've certainly earned your shilling today!"

Too loud, he thinks nervously; he'll have to lower his voice. He leans forward and gently takes the sticky pastry cone from Manford's hands, lays it gingerly on the table. "Manford," he says, "I've an idea. How would you like to have a walk with your old friend Norris, here? You love a good walk, don't you?"

Manford looks up at Norris.

"Well, come on then!" Norris says, making an enthusiastic rising motion with his arms, like a conductor. "Up you go. Let's have our walk. You've done splendidly here," he adds hastily.

Manford stands. Norris looks him over, points to his shoes. "You've a lace undone." He shakes a finger in the direction of Manford's shoe. Manford cranes over and looks at his lace. When he sits back down heavily on his stool and inclines his foot, Norris looks at him and searches his face in confusion.

"Can't you do it yourself?" he asks in surprise.

But Manford continues to hold his foot out in the air. He raises his leg a little and looks off vacantly into the distance somewhere beyond Norris's right shoulder.

After a moment, Norris kneels awkwardly and laces Manford's shoe. "Fine," he says, standing back up, breathing hard.

But the tail of Manford's shirt hangs loose; his hair is flyaway, unkempt. Norris gestures awkwardly at him. "You might want to tidy yourself up a bit," he begins.

Manford licks his fingers slowly then, tucks his curled fingers under his fringe, and pushes the hair slowly to one side, his eyes rolling upward strangely, following the motion of his hand.

Norris regards him. Manford still looks as though he's had an encounter with a lot of bats, the creatures sweeping into him, tangling his hair in their sticky wings.

And so Norris reaches out with his own hands to smooth Manford's hair. Manford drops his head, submits to Norris like a small child. Under his fingers, Norris feels the solid bone of Manford's skull, the rigid substance of it. He keeps his hands there, smoothing and smoothing, and realizes then that he has never touched another person like this. And as Norris stands there holding Manford's head, Manford reaches forward suddenly to clasp Norris by the lapels, burying his face briefly against his shirtfront, inhaling. When Manford raises his face, it wears the sweetest smile.

Norris smiles back, a smile he knows isn't half so good as Manford's; he deserves so much more.

And when they pass together through the bakery hand in hand, Mrs. Blatchford raises her eyebrows at them. "Well, Mr. Lamb," she says. "Turns out you've quite a way with him, doesn't it?"

Sixteen

Vida twists away from Jeremy. "You haven't seen the library yet."

She hears the frightened battery of her own footsteps, the fussy clicking of her heels as she hurries out of the ballroom away from him, the dead air of the room cool against her flushed cheeks. For a moment she thinks she hears him laugh, but she is not certain of this. Certainly, as she pulls away, she hears his breath escape in an expression of—disgust, she thinks. But she won't wait for him now. It's better not to wait, she thinks. It's best just to go on, pretend nothing's happened. And perhaps nothing has.

"Close the doors after you?" She hurries ahead down the hall. Her own voice sounds to her high and alarmed. Oh, what is there to be so frightened of? She is annoyed at herself. But, "I like to keep them shut in case of birds," she hears herself call over her shoulder. "So many seem to find their way in."

He is close at her heels now, having followed her toward the library, and she feels a slick of perspiration break out over her skin.

"You know what they say about that, don't you?" he asks.

"What?" She does not turn to answer him but hurries away down the hall.

"Birds in the house," she hears him say. "It's a sign of bad luck. Evil omen."

She waits an instant at the door to the library, her back still to him, before replying. "Well, I don't believe in any of that," she says firmly. "They're just a nuisance."

But she does believe it. An aching feeling of dread comes over her whenever she discovers a bird trapped in one of Southend's airless rooms, the creature flapping away wildly and scaring her half to death when she opens the door. They come in through the chimneys, she believes. She has found several over the years, starlings usually; their oily black bodies leave smudges against the walls and on the heavy draperies at the windows. It is as if they became suddenly blind, as if they couldn't see the walls around them; they fly at the plaster or the mullioned panes, falling stunned to the floor in collision after pointless collision. It's the stupidity of it she hates. That they can't see where they are. That they can't see how they'd got in, such a simple thing, and so can't get out, either.

"All the same, it *is* a bad omen. Whether you believe in it or not," Jeremy says now from behind her. His tone is oddly companionable, agreeable; Vida finds herself annoyed by it. She turns to him. "You've certainly a morbid turn of mind today," she says sharply. He just shrugs. "After you," he says as she turns away again to open the door to the library.

She hears it then, no mistaking it—the sarcasm in his voice.

She had averted something, there in the ballroom. She understands that. And she had been frightened, she knows, recognizing it. He would have kissed her! When had she last been kissed? She'd been—she was—unprepared! Any other man—a *good* man, she thinks fiercely—would have seen that! He wouldn't have come at her so—suddenly! But thinking of Jeremy, of his dark good looks, she feels a tidal surge of embarrassment. What would this man want with *her,* anyway?

Something's wrong, she thinks. Or something's wrong with him to be frightening her in this way.

She crosses the shadowy library to pull aside the heavy drapes, but as the chalky light of midday falls into the room, she hears the words from the letter, the love letter, as if they had been spoken aloud. *I fall at your knees in worship,* the letter had said.

But who had almost fallen there in the ballroom? Not Jeremy, she realizes. Someone else. She herself.

She takes a deep breath and switches on the light by the drawing table. In one of the wide, shallow drawers Mr. Perry uses to store his work, she finds the garden drawings. Several of Mr. Perry's own sketches are laid on top of the yellowed sheets that detail the original diagrams, a complicated crosshatching of underground pipes and foundations for the fountain.

She stiffens as Jeremy leans in close over her shoulder.

"Did he do those?"

She nods.

He reaches past her for them. "Let's have a look."

He takes several sheets from her hand, walks to the window, and holds them to the light, where she can see black lines reversed through the transparent paper, Jeremy's glove a dark blossom against the white. She doesn't like the way he holds the drawings, as if he might damage them, crumple them suddenly in his hands.

"He's an architect, for churches. Someone told me," he says, still looking at the drawings.

"Yes."

Jeremy seems transfixed by the drawings, tilting them this way and that to the light. He holds one up for her. "Where's this?"

"Oh, that's St. Nevin's," she says after a moment, pleased to recognize the little church with its circular window over the front door, like a brilliant eye. She remembers driving there with Mr. Perry and Manford, when Manford was just a boy. Mr. Perry had taken them along when he went to sketch the church the first time, and she and Manford played in the tiny close, setting fragments of twigs afloat in the pencil-thin stream of water that ran down the cobbled gutter. There hadn't been anyone about except a char, a scarf knotted over her head and a pail and rag in her hand, who hurried through the gray courtyard, her glance pausing at Manford's awkward antics.

They had remained there in the high-walled enclosure for the whole afternoon, racing a flotilla of seeds and twigs, watching them vanish through the gutter's low aperture in the stone wall. Wondering what became of them, Vida had wandered to the gate, seen the gutter's stream empty into a brook that wound, low in its bed, through a field waving prettily with poppies and Queen Anne's lace. She would have liked to follow the stream, but Manford could not be persuaded away from the activity, tugging on her hand and drawing her to her knees on the hard stone, where they gathered more detritus to send down the quick channel. She had thought, in the end, that it was a penitent's work, that between them they had cleared the whole close of anything the wind might lift. Still, Manford had loved it, the sensation of excitement as their little craft sped away and vanished. I know where they go, she'd thought, but to him it is like a magic trick.

She had hoped they would stop somewhere for tea on the way home, as it was late in the day when Mr. Perry finally finished and came to fetch them. But he pulled up outside a shop in Southampton and brought fish-and-chips out to the car for them instead. She had understood, at the time, that he didn't want to bring Manford into a pub, where he could be closely observed, a silence falling among the patrons as the child's strange, silent animation excited notice. So the three of them had sat in the car in silence, licking their fingers over the rumple of newspaper, Vida and Manford in the backseat together so she could help him. It began to rain, she remembers, and she looked out the window, which was beaded and streaked with water, the world gradually disappearing into the rain and early dark, an occasional car driving by and sending a spray of dirty gray water up from its tires. She sat beside Manford, reaching over to wipe his chin gently as he ate, the sweet fish hot and delicious.

Once, feeling eyes upon her, she had looked up and seen Mr. Perry watching her through the mirror. But he had turned his gaze away quickly, and she had felt embarrassed. He is thinking about his wife, she had thought, how he wishes she were still alive. And she had felt ashamed then to be herself, to be who she was.

Now, though, she is happy to recognize the church. "See, there's the window," she says, pointing. "The round one. That's how I know it. It's quite unusual, apparently."

Jeremy nods his head. "It's a talent, isn't it?" he says. "To draw like this."

His tone is so serious that Vida finds suddenly that she feels sorry for him. He's young, after all. She softens, taking in his clear skin and shiny hair. He's too young to have any accomplishments of his own, perhaps, and being a gardener, while very fine work, well, it isn't nearly as grand as being a builder of churches, is it? It occurs to her that perhaps he envies Mr. Perry, and she thinks she understands that, that envy of *class*. Poor boy. She relents; why had she been afraid of him? Wasn't it silly? They were alike, both of them. Servants, in the end.

She feels a prick of disloyalty then but goes on, wanting him to feel better. "Well, we *all* have our talents," she says stoutly. "You've got your talent in the garden," she adds.

He laughs, and she feels puzzled by this—hurt, really.

"And what's yours?" he asks, looking over at her. "What's *your* talent, Vida?"

The question so startles her that she thinks for a minute she might have imagined it. But the words ring there in the air between them, an echoing accusation.

How is it that I have no answer? she thinks wildly. How is it I have no answer to that question?

She has a talent for Manford, she wants to shout then. That's not *nothing*. She has loved him.

She used to worry so, she thinks distractedly, over Manford's not having any friends. She'd wanted him to go to school, but Mr. Perry had discouraged it. "What's the point?" he'd asked, but not as if it were a discussion. "It'll just be hard for him."

He was wrong, she'd thought, but she hadn't had any choice. He was the father, and she was nothing but the nanny.

Instead, when Manford was a little boy, she'd have other boys over, organize games for them, cricket and so on. But they grew up, those boys, and Manford didn't. And that he couldn't speak to them—they didn't have the patience for him.

They had no imagination, she thinks now, staring over Jeremy's shoulder toward the window. Perhaps, she thinks, you have to have imagination to love anybody.

"COME ON," JEREMY repeats. "What's yours?"

Vida turns away from him, his teasing tone. "I don't know," she says quietly. "I—I'm very *dependable*," she finishes lamely.

He laughs.

Why is he always laughing? she thinks, unnerved. She realizes that the few times she's been with him, he seems to laugh all the time, but it isn't always a nice laugh, and sometimes she doesn't see anything funny. And then a picture flashes into her mind of Mr. Lamb on his knees in the muddy street, of herself laughing as she reached down to help him stand, Mr. Lamb laughing, too, his hands held awkwardly away from his dirty trousers.

What had the first letter said? *I crawl along the rays of the sun.*

"*I'm* dependable," Jeremy says then. "You'd never go unsatisfied with me."

She looks up, his tone having alerted her, but not quickly enough. He swerves and comes from behind her, reaches around and places his hands over her breasts. "I can promise you that," he says.

He squeezes, fitting in close behind her, his mouth on her ear, biting on the small lobe. "You're nice, Vida," he says. "You like me, don't you?"

She feels her heart thrash out against his hand, but her body will not move.

"You're all alone here, Vida. Aren't you lonely? Come on, dear. We could have us some fun. Wouldn't you like to have some fun?" His voice drops."Wouldn't you like that?" His hands find her nipples; he pinches them between his thumbs and forefingers. "Come on." He rocks against her, and she starts in real terror when he lifts his bad hand from her breast and holds it up close before her face.

"I'm wounded," he says. "Don't you want to help me?"

He holds her tightly with his good arm, reaches down, and she sees her dress come up, his hand beneath the hem, the cracked leather of the glove against her thighs and belly. He bends her over, forcing her down. The skirt of her dress comes up before her face, his one hand holding it there over her mouth, the other pressing down across her shoulders where she might wear a yoke if she were a cow.

"I can't see," she cries wildly at last, freeing her arms, struggling at the cloth before her face. "I can't see! Please!"

On her hands and knees she struggles to crawl away from him. "Get away from me," she says. "Get away!"

For a moment he clings to her, a parasite against her back. And then he rolls off. He lies on his back, breathing hard, holding his injured hand on the wrist below the glove. "I've hurt my hand," he says dully, like a child.

Vida closes her eyes and places her cheek carefully against a bell-shaped silver flower woven into the carpet, its stem knotted into a helix. She reaches, her eyes still closed, to adjust her skirt over her thighs, curls her knees to her chest. She licks her lips; her mouth feels so dry. Her breasts ache.

I am your servant, your knight.

When she opens her eyes and looks at him, after just a moment, he is still lying on his back, his hand held over his chest, his eyes shut. His hair is damp at his temples, his cheeks flushed. His mouth is open slightly. She watches him swallow, a delicate movement at his throat. Though she tries to veer away from the thought, she sees herself then, a middle-aged woman lying on the ground, her dress wrenched around her.

He is standing over her when she opens her eyes again. "Get up," he says. "You don't need to lie there. I didn't hurt you."

And she thinks when she hears his tone that it is exactly that of a frightened child, petulant and angry. It's funny, she thinks, that when you're with someone who *doesn't* speak, you learn a different way of understanding people. You don't even need to hear them to know exactly what they're feeling. She has stood a pace away from Manford and closed her eyes and tried to listen with her heart, and her heart has heard something, she knows, something absolutely unmistakable, though it has no words. Once, she tried asking Dr. Faber about it, whether he believed there was something—oh, something *electrical,* perhaps—that passed between two people in place of words.

"I know what he wants," she told Dr. Faber. "I can't tell you how I do, but I do."

And he laughed at her and rapped at Manford's head with his knuckles and then looked back to Vida significantly. "Who can say?" he said. "Who can say what miracles the human heart is capable of?"

"I'm *not* hurt," she says. She sits up and pushes her hands through her hair.

Jeremy turns away from her, walks over to the window, and picks up the drawings from the floor. He looks embarrassed. She assesses him, the cheap shoes on his feet, the pilled knees of his worn trousers. His profile, almost lordly from the nose up to the high brow, falls away at his mouth and chin, where some weakness, some failure of bearing, has made the lines selfish and small. He stares at the drawings in his hand as though nothing has happened, as though he has simply been considering them in a responsible fashion. For a moment she thinks she might laugh at him.

But the moment passes, and she lies back down again and stretches her arms over her head. Around her the carpet blooms with a hundred species of wildflowers, their vines and tendrils interlocked in an intricate pandemonium. She rubs the back of her hand lazily over the coarse nap of the weave.

"What are you doing?" he asks, annoyed.

"I'm looking," she says, "at the sky."

He gives a huff of surprise. "You're crazy."

She looks up at him seriously. "No," she says. And though she wouldn't say it aloud, she hears the letter again, that voice: *You are the moon and the stars.*

He snorts again and turns away.

When she says nothing, remaining silent like a felled statue on the meadow of carpet, he turns back to her. "Aren't you going to get up?"

"I suppose so." She stands at last and smooths her dress carefully. She does not look at him.

"Well, I'm sorry," he says after a moment. "I thought you wanted a bit of fun."

She turns her eyes on him then, and she knows her look holds only a suggestion of all she is feeling. "You have no idea what I want," she says. "None at all."

WHEN THE TELEPHONE rings a moment later, they both jump. Vida crosses the room to answer it after a delay in which she cannot, for a second, recall the meaning of the sound. Hardly anyone calls at Southend.

"Vida?" Mr. Perry's voice sounds as if he were shouting from far off, the volume whisked away by the wind, diverted and cupped into the bowl of a mountain or driven down into the sea. "How's everything?"

She glances at Jeremy, who stands frozen, the drawings in his hand. She touches her hand to her hair. "Everything's quite all right," she says after a moment.

Jeremy turns away and busies himself with the drawings. She can sense his relief.

"Manford's had a touch of a flu, but we're both over it now," she manages to say. "How are you coming on? In Florence, are you?"

"We've had some delays. Bad weather. They don't like to work on the frescoes when it's wet, and it's been raining here for two weeks," he says. "The fixative won't set when it's wet out. What's Manford been up to?"

Vida hesitates. She hadn't consulted Mr. Perry about the job at Niven's, not out of deceitfulness or even a suspicion that he might not like the idea, but mostly because it had come to her so suddenly. One day she'd had the notion of it, and the next he was there working. Now, though, it occurs to her that Mr. Perry might in fact disapprove in some way, though he's never had any complaint about her care of Manford. But it doesn't seem right to be dishonest about it.

"Well, you'll never guess," she says now, a false tone creeping into her voice. She sees that Jeremy has moved over to Mr. Perry's desk and is examining the pens and brushes. He lifts a pen and unscrews the cap, puts the nib delicately to his fingertip. Vida makes a sharp motion to him to put the pen down.

"I've got Manford a job!" she says brightly into the phone.

There is a pause at the other end. She isn't sure whether it is Mr. Perry's surprise or the delay of the long distance.

"A job?" His voice arrives in her ear at last.

"Yes, at Niven's," she says. "He's working at Niven's." She thinks how to add to that information, but the truth of it, that he stuffs the doughnuts with jam, suddenly sounds pathetic to her. "He's doing marvelously," she says instead. "They all love him."

"He's there without you?"

Now there's no mistaking it, she thinks—Mr. Perry's tone of uncertainty.

"He's done very well," she says. She draws a breath. "I think it's good for him. And to be away from me," she adds, though she hadn't meant that exactly.

"What do you mean?"

Now his voice sounds decidedly suspicious. Anger flares up in her.

"He's not a baby, you know," she says hotly. "He's a grown man. He's needed an *occupation.*" She is right about that; she knows she is. They couldn't have gone on, playing as though he were just the idle scion of an aristocrat. This was Manford's life, here in the village, even if his father behaved like a sort of distant lord. He needed to be able to step fully into it instead of remaining locked in his tower with her, the two of them roaming the perimeter of the garden like prisoners who do not know they are kept.

"Hold on." Mr. Perry's voice sounds rough, as if scratched over with a file.

She hears a crackling sound, the phone being shifted or some static interrupting the line. She takes a deep breath, stares down at her feet.

"I can't hear you very well." Mr. Perry's voice comes through again, but crinkled somehow, like crushed paper. Another pause. "What did you say he was doing?"

Vida closes her eyes. "He's filling the doughnuts."

And she could see Mr. Perry then: He would be in a chair by a window, she thinks, overlooking the scattered surface of a canal, its quick water like a black fault line through the earth. The window would be open, his jacket tossed across a bed. Several streets away, a small chapel would be harnessed within the delicate framework of a scaffolding, the crumbling white walls billowing against a web of wood and rope. She has seen photographs of this chapel, its listing wall scored in the picture with Mr. Perry's blue lines, the corrected angle. Mr. Perry had pointed to the damaged wall, explained how the frescoes inside had to be protected before they could tear off the side of the chapel and rebuild. "Just the sort of job I hate," he'd said, tossing the photographs on the desk. "Too many things can go wrong."

Still, she knew he had been pleased to have it, an excuse to leave again. His hair, which sprang back from his forehead, would be mussed now from the damp, she knows. She sees him place a hand before his eyes, the gesture he applies so often when talking to her of Manford, as if he could stand either to think of him or to see him, but not both at once. Both were too much, the awful truth of Manford's circumstances, his bouncing gait and fat belly, colliding with Mr. Perry's own horror. She has seen him kneel before the boy, take him in his arms once or twice. She was encouraged at those moments, hoping for some sustaining embrace between them. But Mr. Perry is afraid of his son, she thinks. Sickened by him. And because of her, he has been able to leave him. She thinks of Manford, the hopeful, concentrated way he lifts his hands to make his shadow play, the springing menagerie that tumbles like a row of circus acrobats across a wall, the intelligent agility of those creations. And she thinks, too, of the look of terror on his soft, surprised face when he saw the spider's web on the bench. Mr. Perry has missed so much.

"Vida, I can't hear you. Vida?"

"Yes. I'm here," she says faintly. A surge of static fills the receiver. She hears one word, "Damn," clearly.

"You mustn't worry," she says vaguely, though with feeling. And then, because she recognizes it suddenly herself, and because she thinks Mr. Perry will appreciate this at least, she adds, "Manford's made a sort of friend, too. A patron. Someone looking out for him."

She is not sure what Mr. Perry hears then, whether any of her words reach him or whether they drift apart like unraveling stitches, some warp disintegrating like that fading fresco. "It's Mr. Lamb," she says, surprised to hear herself say it. "They have stamps in common. And some other things."

And she sees Mr. Lamb then, his funny way of imitating Manford's walk, not in a mean way, she understands, but in delight at Manford's perfect manner of having his body express what his heart must feel. She sees Mr. Lamb again in the kitchen, his hand on Manford's head, the long spoon held in his other hand. "We've been getting to know one another," he'd said.

"Are you there?" she asks into the silence. There is no reply. "You mustn't worry," she says again, kindly.

His voice breaks free then. She startles at it in her ear, suddenly clear and close. "Vida, I can't hear you very well. Look, I'm delayed here. I'll be another month. We'll talk again. I'll call again." There is a pause. She thinks it best to say nothing.

"Vida?"

"All right," she says finally.

"Give him my love." Then she hears the receiver click off and the line go dead.

JEREMY IS STILL toying with the things on Mr. Perry's desk. Vida replaces the phone carefully on its cradle. She crosses the room and picks up the stack of drawings for the garden. "Do you want these?" she says, holding them out in her hands.

He shrugs.

And she feels, as she stands there waiting for him to cross the room to her, that something has shifted between them; some balance of power has now inclined itself delicately toward her, like a boat's cargo sliding slowly across a deck. Her heart beats quickly, aroused by her conversation with Mr. Perry and her sense that she needed to defend herself, defend this thing she had done, getting Manford a job. Mr. Perry might want to keep them shut up here, she thinks clearly, as if for the first time, but it is too late. They're out in the world now, she and Manford. And though she does not know how it will end, though she cannot say what might happen next, nor that they won't, in the end, be defeated, she feels as sure of her decision as she has ever felt about anything.

Jeremy takes the papers from her, shamefaced.

She waves him out of the room and follows him, shutting off the lights. She wants a wash, she thinks. She wants to wash every bit of him off her, and then she'll go and fetch Manford, and—take him out to dinner. They'll go to the pub and have fish-and-chips together. They've never done that.

They'll have a new thing, every day from now on, she thinks. Something new, every single day.

Seventeen

As THEY LEAVE Niven's courtyard and turn onto the pavement along the Romsey Road, Norris struggles with his feelings: He discovers he rather likes holding Manford's hand, so large and substantial; through the slight pressure against his fingers he can feel the rhythm of Manford's pace beside him, like the tugging rope of a buoy, something secure and friendly. But the intimacy of their attachment makes Norris uncomfortable, too, and though he is ashamed of his discomfort, he nonetheless looks about nervously to see whether anyone might be watching them.

After a few moments he dislodges Manford's fingers from his own and waves his arms backward and forward in an enthusiastic manner, like a soldier. "Ah, the air does one good," he says firmly, taking deep, military breaths and hoping to distract Manford from the gesture of separation. It seems to him that he has failed in some way, failed them both, but he simply cannot bring himself to walk down the Romsey Road holding hands with Manford Perry. "Come along," he says as brightly as he can. He hopes he sounds, at least, as though he had some definite purpose in mind.

But as they draw near the post office, he feels even less sure of his errand.

Fergus is lounging against the doorjamb, tamping his pipe. He looks up as Norris and Manford approach, and his eyebrows rise in his face.

Norris stops. Manford waits beside him, looking at Fergus with interest and sniffing.

There is an awkward silence. Norris notices a bit of sparkling rubbish, a foil chocolate wrapper, lying in the gutter.

Fergus gestures to Manford with his pipe. "Got someone with you," he says, as if Norris might not have noticed.

"Yes." Norris puts his hands in his pockets. He cranes round Fergus and looks in the window of the post office as if he, too, were waiting for the shade to be rolled up, for himself to come to the door murmuring apologies and ushering them inside.

"Well? Aren't you going to open up?"

"What?" Norris starts; it feels as though Fergus has pinched him somewhere!

"The post office," Fergus says slowly, as if to an idiot, removing his pipe. "It's your place, isn't it?"

"I—I have some other business to attend to this morning," Norris says finally, indicating Manford with a slight jerk of his head.

Fergus looks back and forth between the two of them, a doubtful expression on his face.

"Well, we're off," Norris says then, with as much resolve as he can summon, and moves around Fergus and down the pavement toward the Dolphin, Manford following behind him.

"Hallo!" Fergus calls after him. "I'm needing tobacco!"

Norris waves his hand behind his head in a vague gesture, as if to brush away a fly. "Yes, well," he calls faintly. "I'll be back."

But in truth he cannot imagine how he will ever come back. He seems to be marching off not on some errand with Manford, some pleasant ramble, but on a journey whose destination is yet unknown to him. He feels now that he must marshal his faculties, bring himself under strict control. I'm responsible for him now, he thinks. It's up to me to see that he doesn't come to any harm.

It occurs to him that it would be so helpful, at moments like this, if Manford could speak.

A DOOR IN the stone wall before St. Alphage opens, and the vicar backs out. Norris has to come to a sudden stop to avoid ploughing into him.

"Ah! Lamb!" the vicar says, turning round, his eyes widening. "I've just rung you." But he stops at the sight of Manford.

"We're having a walk," Norris says stonily, hoping to forestall any questions.

"A walk," the vicar repeats, his eyebrows permanently arrested, it seems, in an upside-down victory symbol over his nose. "Lovely morning for it." He stares at Norris and Manford a moment longer and then leans forward and reaches out his hand to Manford's arm, placing his palm over Manford's floury sleeve. "Good morning, Manford," he says slowly and loudly, nodding and smiling.

"You don't need to *shout*," Norris says. "He hears you perfectly well."

The vicar straightens up, embarrassed. "Yes, of course." He glances back and forth between Norris and Manford. "Are you—in charge of him?"

"Yes, I am," Norris says shortly, and folds his arms as if to suggest that he will not be answering any further questions.

"Well, that's *fine*," the vicar says with warmth. Norris thinks how the vicar can revert to enthusiasm at the drop of a hat, as though to be amiable were a sort of clerical duty. Usually he quite likes this about the Reverend Keble, his benign and sympathetic manner. Yet there is a certain air of the dead end about him, too; no matter what befalls you, the vicar always manages to convey a vast tolerance for life's injustices, as if your own fury and frustration were of no consequence when weighed in the enormous context of the hereafter.

As if deciding that it would be too complicated to inquire any more about how Norris and Manford have come to be in each other's company, the vicar smiles at Norris and resumes briskly. "My dear Lamb," he says, blinking in the weak light of the sun and gazing about approvingly as though the common sights around them—trees, wall, road—have been arranged specifically for the purpose of looking pleasing. "I've been meaning to ask you whether you wouldn't like to play for the talent show Saturday."

He reaches into his basket, pulls out a slip of paper, and unfolds it laboriously. "Where *are* my glasses?" he mutters, searching his pockets. "Ah, here they are. Now, let me see. We've a *splendid* program this year. I thought you might fit in beautifully"—he points to the paper—"here, between the Hughes-Onslow sisters' gymnastics and Mr. Niven's "When Delia on the plain appears." George Lyttelton, that is. Do you know him? Undervalued poet, and Mr. Niven does a spotless job with it. We'd an audition the other night, tea and sherry and whatnot. Ian was just leaving with his terrier—you know, the one that does the tricks? Races round in circles barking, plays dead, walks on his hind legs? You've seen him? No? Well, quite remarkable. Very clever little dog. And Mr. Niven stuck his head in the door and said he'd do a spot of poetry for us! Oh, dear, that's a bit dull, I thought, but he's quite the elocutionist, it turns out! In any case"—he runs his finger down the paper—"there's no other music, other than Mrs. Ramsey, of course—"

Norris rolls his eyes.

"And I thought we could do with something from the organ." The vicar wrinkles his brow, frowns at the page. "Or perhaps we could put you here, in between Sammy's sword dance and my own poor offering—just a few birdcalls," he adds modestly, glancing up and then hastily back to his paper as he takes in Norris's impassive expression. “Well! No, perhaps it’s as I first thought; you’re better off toward the end of the program, after all, near the raffle. Several ladies will be doing squares of an afghan—I thought I’d have them under the west window, you know, the Wise and Foolish Virgins, but off to the side perhaps, and Mrs. Spooner’s very kindly said she’d sew it all together, she’s so very speedy.” He pauses. “And there’s the bells from the fourth form at Prince’s Mead,” he says faintly. “But that’s not the same as our splendid new organ.” He looks up hopefully.

“I’ll consider it,” Norris says.

“Right!” The vicar waves his arm in a salute as Norris takes Manford’s arm and hurries him away down the pavement. “Something uplifting, I thought?”

As Norris and Manford pass Spooner’s, Mrs. Spooner comes to the door, her hands deep in the pockets of her cardigan. She cranes her thin neck round the door frame to look up the road, which is temporarily empty of traffic, and stops at the sight of Norris and Manford passing on the opposite side of the street, Manford bouncing along happily. He gives her a delighted wave, as though signaling from an airplane. She raises her hand slowly in reply and then quickly ducks back inside. Norris glances behind him and sees Mr. Spooner join his wife at the door, their faces white like two balloons bobbing over their doorsill.

Well, he thinks, it can’t be helped, whatever people want to imagine. What *do* they imagine, though? he wonders. He himself doesn’t know what he’s doing. He doesn’t want Manford to feel uncomfortable, though; he glances at Manford’s face and is about to say something reassuring—though Manford seems perfectly contented, even happy—when he has to stop for Dr. Faber, who is backing his car down his drive in front of them. Dr. Faber drives a Morris Minor, a car far too small for him. He always looks so crowded in it.

Dr. Faber stops the car, rolls down his window, and looks out at them.

"Hallo, Lamb," he says. He smiles up at Manford. "Good morning, Manford. What have you done with your better half?"

Norris glances surreptitiously at Manford and then leans down toward Dr. Faber. "They had a small—difficulty with him at Niven's," he says in a whisper. "I'm just helping matters out temporarily."

Dr. Faber frowns. "What sort of difficulty?"

"Well—" Norris considers how to explain. He leans closer. "He did a spider's web on a cake."

Dr. Faber stares at him a moment and then throws his head back in surprise and laughs. "A spider's web! I'll bet they didn't care for that," Dr. Faber says.

"Well, no!"

"He has an odd talent, I'll say that for him," Dr. Faber concedes, resting an arm on the window of the car, looking fondly at Manford. "Hermione brought home one of the cakes he'd done the other day. Had weeds all over it! In raspberry jam! Absolutely delicious, though. Startlingly good likeness, too, I must say. Good idea of Vida's, to get him that job." He looks up at Norris. "What are you doing with him?"

But Norris feels that Dr. Faber does not understand the problem properly. It *had* been a very good spider's web; anyone could see that, he thinks. But he wants Dr. Faber to appreciate that he, Norris, has stepped in to rescue Manford at this moment; that he's saving him from disgrace. "Mrs. Blatchford was quite upset," he says.

Dr. Faber laughs again. "Well, I'm sure she was," he says. "But it's a talent anyway, whether you do a spider's web or a lot of little roses. Talent," he says, "is whatever comes straight and true from the human heart. With Manford here, you see, it's a direct route." He knocks at his own temple with his knuckles. "Nothing to run interference," he adds significantly.

Norris steps back a pace. Manford is watching a departing lorry, its kite string of black exhaust. "But don't you think," he says slowly, turning back to Dr. Faber, "don't you think that, even with all that talent he has, it would be better if—it would be helpful to know what he thinks? In words, I mean?" He looks at Dr. Faber's face, his mild blue eyes, his heavy jowls, his balding head flushed a healthy pink. "Dr. Faber, does Manford have a language? A word language? And"—he finds himself hastening toward the notion—"why *shouldn't* he speak one day? Just out of the blue?"

Norris is humiliated to see Dr. Faber sigh and then turn his gaze to stare out the windshield of the car at the small garden fronting his house, the yews there clipped neatly into regular waves; I must have said something very stupid, Norris thinks, ashamed.

"They always want to know that," Dr. Faber says, though to Norris it seems as if he weren't speaking to anyone in particular. "It's natural, I suppose." He turns back to Norris. "Those aren't easy questions," he says. "And I haven't got any good answers for you, I'm afraid. But I don't know why he would speak—now, after all this time. There's not much precedent for a mute recovering—or discovering—his voice all of a sudden." And then he squints up at Norris. "You should ask Vida about that, anyway. She claims to know exactly what he's thinking, no words needed at all. Isn't that right, Manford?"

Manford looks up from his interested perusal of the street, meets Dr. Faber's appraisal with a blank look.

Dr. Faber turns his eyes away from Manford and finds Norris's face. "Vida listens with her heart," he says, clamping his fist to his chest and thumping it once significantly. "We should all try it more often."

Norris stands upright as Dr. Faber puts the Morris Minor into gear and waves at him out the window. "Must be going," Dr. Faber calls. "Off to hospital!" He says this last almost gaily, Norris thinks. How does a man who deals so regularly in life and death and the body's terrible betrayals manage to be so unafraid, so blithe? It's all what you're used to, Norris thinks, putting his hands in his pockets. It's whatever is your natural climate.

He stands there, quietly watching Manford, who is ambling slowly up and down the pavement, running his hands lightly through the hollyhocks that crowd the top of the wall. But the next moment, as if in answer to some question Norris has been unable to formulate, the double-decker rumbles into view toward its morning stop before the Dolphin; he sees, with a sudden, odd clarity, two glasses from the night before, tilting precariously atop the stone wall before it. And at this moment, it strikes Norris that perhaps what is called for, this afternoon, is a real outing, not just a ramble round the village or out into the fields. They should go into Winchester; they could have tea at the Wessex. Perhaps they'd bring Vida some chocolates.

But suddenly, though he has nearly started forward, Winchester seems too far away, too dangerously far.

The bus rumbles past them. Manford turns around from the hollyhocks to make shooing motions with his arm as it recedes down the road.

Norris stands morosely watching the bus depart, Manford at

his side. What is he afraid of? That Manford will do something peculiar? Yes, that. You can never tell what he might do. Imagine if he wandered off, Norris thinks with a shudder, like the other night at Southend, and got himself lost in Winchester? But there's something else, too, he knows. It's as if leaving Hursley with Manford would break a contract with the world; Manford is safe, Norris senses, as long as he stays in the village. It's even possible for Norris to imagine now a kind of benevolent fate that anticipates a person's needs and then arranges circumstances to suit them. He believes the world understands that for someone like Manford, someone so innocent, so easily lost, there must be a place where his face is known at every door. Then, should he wander off—indeed, should it be his privilege to wander off—he would be recognized, welcomed, gently returned. In a vague way, Norris understands that this is true of him, too.

Through his stamps he has become an eager and gregarious armchair traveler, a man with a spyglass at the window, even a raconteur. But he wouldn't ever really go anywhere, would he? It isn't in him to leave. It's the fact of the village behind him, its Norman stones and ancient mortar, its known quantities—this is what sets *him* free. For him, at least, just imagining the world is quite enough, as much as he can bear, in fact. His stamps alone show such a proliferation of objects and artifacts: animals and fishes, stars and oceans, seeds and grains and wedding cakes, flowers no bigger than a thimble and enormous monuments, flags and white-bearded monarchs, strangely shaped sailing vessels and the earliest biplanes, kites and tapestries, beautiful native women and tiny cubist paintings, autos and locomotives, cities and deserts and shrines, face after face after face after face, all of it—all of *us,* he thinks—crowding the planet like plants in a jungle, jostling for space, men and women on an endless series of embarkations.

He reaches out and takes Manford's arm. "Let's go," he says, for he feels suddenly stifled; he needs air.

But he feels Manford stiffen slightly in resistance, sees that his face has taken on a look of thoughtful wariness. He stops, looks Manford full in the face; he has only one thing to offer, he knows now: his good intentions.

"I've got something I want to show you," he says then, kindly. "I think you'll like it. And we'll pick flowers for Vida—a great bouquet." He smiles. "Come on. It's a secret. My secret. I'm letting you in on it. Let's not waste another moment, or someone else will stop us."

They turn off the Romsey Road onto the lane that leads up toward his grandmother's cottage. The sky has lifted and a breeze ushers the clouds up higher, disarranging the leaves of the trees that sway beside the lane and turning up their pale undersides. Manford glides along beside Norris, wobbling his outstretched hands with a delicate motion.

When they draw near the cottage, set back in its clearing beneath the canopy of towering copper beech trees, Norris stops at the gate. It doesn't look as inviting as it had in the moonlight; neglect seems to have set in overnight, one stone wall listing dangerously out from beneath the thatch, the weeds formidable, as though threatening to engulf the tiny house. When he unlatches the gate, a pheasant blows out from among the brittle white stalks of silkweed, traverses the clearing at a dead run, and disappears into the woods.

"Squatter." Norris pushes air from his cheeks, making a sound of defeat.

They walk down the path, Norris's gloom growing as they approach the house. He feels uncomfortably hot, too. He pauses to rummage for his handkerchief and realizes in annoyance for the second time today that he has lost it to Mrs. Billy and her watering eye.

He pulls on the latch to the door of the cottage and swings the door wide. Inside, the kitchen is full of a shadowy calm. Norris kicks aside a cache of beechnuts, the prickly cases burst and tangled with filth and leaves. It all looks beyond repair, seamed with moss and mildew. Behind him, Manford claps his hands over his nose and mouth against the sour odor of damp; Norris looks over his shoulder and sees him.

"What was I thinking?" He turns back to face the room.

Manford comes and stands close to him a moment, twin bands of sunlight striped across his chest. He wipes his hands together gently, one on top of the other.

"It will never do," Norris whispers, sitting down on one of the chairs by the table. "She would hate this."

He looks up when he feels Manford approach him. Something about Manford's posture makes Norris think he will be embraced, and he almost begins to adjust himself to receive this kindness, for he can tell, also, that it is kindness Manford intends. But it is much easier than that. For Manford only gazes down at him with a sympathy so full of understanding that Norris is shocked by its intelligence. And then Manford leans down and presses his cheek tenderly to Norris's bowed head, the gesture of a mother to a son.

Under the dense, forgiving, sweet-smelling weight of Manford's head resting against his own—for Manford still smells like a child, Norris realizes, not like a grown man at all—the force of Norris's disappointment and humiliation seems at first to crowd his ribs like a vicious black balloon inflating beside his heart; all of it, *all of it,* his ineptitude, his temerity, his failure to be bold or brave or successful, threatens to extinguish what remains of his ability to be purposeful in this endeavor, to be hopeful; threatens to overtake him altogether. And yet, as they pause there—mysteriously, generously, a faint heat radiating from Manford's cheek through the top of Norris's head—the sensation disperses, and Norris feels it leave him as if the devil himself has just left by a window. He is, quite suddenly, as grateful as he has ever been in his whole life. He puts his arm up awkwardly and cups his palm around Manford's broad, smooth neck.

After a moment, as if he is restless, Manford stands up and extends his hands before him into the whirling sunlight. Norris sees the light shatter and tremble as Manford juggles the invisible matter of air, the fool bewitching the sun. Manford moves through the room, through the light. At a small door a step off the floor, Manford stops, tries the latch, pulls the door open. A narrow flight of stairs curves up into the darkness.

"That's the bedroom," Norris tells him. He turns away. He hears the steps protest beneath Manford's weight. Norris can hear Manford's explorative tread above him. His eyes rest on an old calendar, its photograph pale and faded, on the wall by the window; on a green-checked cushion lying crookedly on the opposite chair; on a single spoon, its bowl blackened, on the floor by the Aga; on the aperture of the window crowded with green.

And then he hears it. The cry is sharp, full of anguish and fear, the pitch high and unnatural, like an animal's.

Like a child's, Norris thinks, springing up from his own chair. A child crying.

NORRIS TAKES THE stairs at a run, crosses the room in two enormous paces, past the gray matter of the bees' nest shattered on the floor, and reaches through the swarm to grab Manford by the arm and drag him back toward the stairs, swinging wildly. Some bees fly into his mouth; he rears back his head and spits, but not before he feels his tongue begin to swell; the pain is fierce. Manford's face, when Norris pauses for one second on the stairs to look at it, is already so misshapen he cannot discern his expression. The bees have stung him all over his head. He must have put his hand right into the nest. Staring at Manford, Norris wonders for a moment if he'd imagined it, the sound. But no, he could not have imagined that. He'd heard it. Manford had made a sound.

As he drags Manford down the stairs, he thinks, Thank God it was a cool morning—they weren't truly lively, or they'd have killed him.

Norris can feel the venom making his heart race, and under his grasp, Manford shakes terribly.

But he cried out, Norris thinks, running out the door. He cried out.

It was the pain that did it.

OUTSIDE ON THE grass, Norris pushes Manford down and tries to roll him, hoping to squash the bees inside his clothes. He feels his own eyelids blossom and swell, feels his lip surge up, stiff and hot. A shuddering pain runs through him. He looks around wildly. A few bees still fly angrily around them, stunned and slowing now in the brighter air. Norris drops to his knees beside Manford, tries to pull his hands from his face. He slaps at the bees at his neck and ears. Hives are funneling up out of his skin, bulbous and hot.

"My God." Norris holds Manford's hands away from his face, the contorted features. "But Manford," he says, close by and breathing hard into his face, "you made a sound. You heard it? You made a sound."

He waits for more, staring at Manford. He is certain that now there will be more, that Manford will open his mouth, and words, rusty and unfamiliar, will fall out.

But Manford says nothing, fights only to free his hands and replace them over his eyes. Norris reaches down and cradles Manford's face, turning it this way and that in disappointment and grief and pity.

"You've been stung," he says. "It's bees. Never before? Never before been stung? It's all right." He takes in a long breath. "But you spoke, Manford. You spoke."

He lets go his hands, and Manford, shaking and cringing, rolls over and draws his knees to his chest.

And then Norris remembers the water.

He drags Manford to the bend in the stream, helps him shuck off his shirt, struggling with the buttons. Manford stands bent over, wagging his head from side to side. Norris, too, hears a singing in his ears, knows it to be the venom. Norris strips off his own shirt as well and takes Manford by the hand. He can hardly speak; his words are thick and furred from the swelling of his mouth and lips. "The water will help," he says. He squeezes Manford's hand, and they step together into the quick current.

Norris won't let go of Manford's hand for fear he'll lose him. He has to push his head down under the water, and Manford fights him then, rearing up, the water running down him as though down a mountain. Norris feels a stone pierce the soft part of his foot but keeps going, wading out deeper, for he can tell that it is better in the water, cold enough to halt the shock. It occurs to him that Manford does not know how to swim, for though at first he tried to free himself from Norris's grasp, now he clings like a terrified child. Norris tries to soothe him, to show him how to cup his hands to run the water over his head. He reaches down, his chin level with the current, and scoops mud from the bottom of the stream, plastering it to his face against the swelling. Manford, trembling, allows him finally to touch him, to put the mud on him in dark, heavy poultices. When Norris steps back, he sees how ugly Manford is, his white shoulders dripping with epaulets of mud, his hat of mud, the dirty water running down his face.

Seeing him there like that, ugly and ridiculous, Norris realizes that though he had never thought it would be easy, trying to win Vida Stephen, he had never once imagined that it would be this hard. He could not have imagined this love, he thinks now, his heart pumping madly from the bee venom and the cold of the water and something else, too—a kind of happiness.

For the first time in his life, he thinks, he has something to lose. He's sure of it.

ON THEIR WAY back to Norris's house in the village, they encounter no one; even the Romsey Road is empty. Norris is grateful for this minor miracle.

Once safely in the house, Norris fetches them both clean shirts—though his own are ridiculously small on Manford—fixes them some brown bread and cheese, and makes a pot of tea.

Manford sits across from Norris at the little table, cramming bread into his mouth. It occurs to Norris that he has never had a guest before. He takes down a jar of Marmite, spreads some on his bread, and places a slab of cheese over the top. He offers Manford some Marmite, but Manford makes a face at the smell, wrinkling up his nose, and makes as if to push Norris's hand away. Norris shrugs. "Suit yourself." They sit there, eating meditatively, and when they finish, Norris clears their plates and takes his seat across from Manford again.

"Your face looks a little better." He gestures across the table. "It's only large still round your eyes." He touches his own face gingerly, feels the swelling at his lip. He peers at Manford critically. "That was a hive you disturbed," he says. "You shouldn't ever put your hand to a hive." He looks down at the table. "Though I don't expect you'll do that ever again."

Manford looks vaguely around the kitchen, his hands winding quietly in his lap. There are crumbs on his face, and a bit of cheese.

Norris leans forward. "You made a sound back there, Manford, didn't you?"

Manford looks away from Norris, squinting up at the low ceiling.

"I heard you!" Norris bangs his fist on the table.

Manford jumps, throws Norris a terrified look. Norris tries to regain his composure. Why am I so—so upset by this? he thinks. But he is. He *is* upset. He reaches forward, puts his hand on Manford's arm. "You made a sound. That means you *can*. You can if you *want* to," he says. He looks at the clock on the wall, its arms fine as hairs, and turns back to look at Manford again. "Don't you see how pleased Vida would be?"

He realizes then that even more than he wants Manford to speak, he wants to return him to Vida with this miracle made manifest. He wants Manford to tell Vida everything he has felt over their lifetime together. He wants Vida to have that gift. And he wants Vida to believe that he, Norris Lamb, has made it possible.

He is instantly shamed by this realization. He puts his head in his hands. What have I become? he thinks. When he looks up again, Manford is gazing at him quietly.

"It's terrible, isn't it, to be a disappointment?" Norris says then quietly. "But you mustn't think I mind. For either of us. We've done the very best we can."

Manford stands then, restless again. Norris watches him wander the room, inspecting various objects—the clock on the wall, the split seam in the gray paper over the plaster, Norris's stiff washing strung over a clotheshorse in the larder, the cup and saucer on the drainboard. Manford pauses at the door to the sitting room, casts a look back over his shoulder at Norris.

"Go on. Help yourself." Norris nods to him.

There is silence for a minute or two; Norris almost forgets Manford is there with him. And then he hears a key struck on the organ, just a single note.

He pushes away his chair and goes to the doorway. Manford is standing in the dark room, facing the instrument. The lace curtains are drawn, their fine work blurred and soft. Norris often plays the organ in the dark, the way his grandmother did when she lost her sight. She told him it had taken her hardly any time to learn to play that way. "My hands have become my eyes," she said, resting a dry palm against his cheek. "You'd be amazed at what I see, Norrie. You would."

He moves beside Manford now. "This was my grandmother's organ," he says. "You know I play in church. She played far better than I do."

Manford raises one hand exploratively over the keys but withdraws it after a moment. Norris leans over and plays a chord for him. Manford looks at Norris, surprised, smiling, his eyes delighted. He splays his fingers, holding them above the keys, tense and excited; he steps back and forth from one foot to the other.

Norris laughs. "There aren't many as like to dance to the organ!" He watches Manford jump around in front of the instrument.

"Look. Here. I'll play so's you can see." Norris crosses the room and pulls aside the curtains, letting a dull haze in through the glass. He returns to the organ and takes his seat before it, playing the opening measures of the *Lyra Innocentium*.

And when he raises his eyes, he sees a movement against the wall beside him, the fluttering accompaniment of Manford's shadows flowing across the faded paper, a hawk or eagle flexing its wings against the old pattern of roses and yellowed trellis-work. The shape of the bird swells as if drawing in breath, lifts its wings, and shakes them.

Norris drops his hands from the keys, spins on his chair, and stares at Manford.

"Of course!" he says. "Your shadows! You could do them in church, at the talent show! That's your *talent,* Manford."

He claps his hands on his thighs, leaps up, and grasps Manford by the arm. "Could you do that?" Norris raises his own hands, sees their shadows leap up to the wall, long and furred. He turns and looks at Manford again.

"Let's take you home," he says. "Oh, let's go home. You look dreadful still, but it's all right."

They let themselves out the back door, squinting against the late-afternoon sunlight. Little puddles shine in the road like tiny bits of mirror, reflective fragments; it must have rained, Norris realizes. Just a shower, while they were having tea. He hadn't noticed.

Norris takes Manford's hand, and this time he doesn't think about who might be watching.

"Hurry, Manford," he says. "We've got to tell Vida. This is a plan."

Eighteen

VIDA SHUTS THE door behind Jeremy and stands there for a moment, her back against the wood. And then, as if she hasn't a moment to lose, she runs up the stairs and into the bathroom, where she runs the water in the bath, violently turning the taps all the way so that the blue-tiled room fills with steam and an explosive cataract of water, the sound of obliteration. She lies in the water for half an hour, throbbing with heat, just her face breaking the surface, her hair billowing out around her in the tub. She lies there until the palms of her hands are wrinkled and her face is bright pink.

And then she remembers about Manford.

She had told Mrs. Blatchford she would stop in and check on him, and then she'd been taken hostage, as she now thinks of it, by Jeremy, and somehow the time has slipped away. She climbs out of the bath and wraps a towel round her and goes to sit, dripping, on the bed to dial the phone and ring Niven's. It's nearly four o'clock, she sees, glancing at the clock.

"But he's not here," Mrs. Blatchford says, picking up at last after ten rings, her tone surprised. "I should have thought they'd have been home long before now. They left hours ago."

Vida feels a chill creep over her. "Who?" she asks. "Who's they?"

"Why, Mr. Lamb!" Mrs. Blatchford pauses as though this should be sufficient explanation, but Vida detects something in her voice, something that makes her alarmed.

"Mrs. Blatchford," she says now, standing up and gripping the telephone. "You must tell me: Has something happened? Why is Manford with Mr. Lamb?"

"Well, I should have thought—" Mrs. Blatchford begins, sounding offended. "Hang on." Vida jumps as the phone is put down sharply on the counter. A moment later there is a deafening crash, the sound of a baking sheet hitting the tile floor. Vida stands by the side of the bed, frozen with fear. What could have happened to Manford? Surely Mr. Lamb would look after him? Surely he is seeing to him? Perhaps—perhaps he's had to take him to Dr. Faber!

She has to sit down now; various angry-sounding noises from the bakery reach her distantly through the telephone. She puts her hand to her forehead. She never should have sent him on to Niven's this morning after his fright over the spider's web. She should have taken him to Dr. Faber's right off, had him seen to; he might have suffered some sort of shock. Oh, she *is* a bad person, she thinks, an irresponsible person, she has no right—

And then suddenly, with an odd sort of relief—as if she had been standing in the middle of the road watching a car speed toward her and then woke to find it had all been a bad dream—it occurs to her that she is behaving very foolishly, has in fact been behaving foolishly all morning, maybe even for her whole life. Her silly worry over whether she might see Jeremy or not at the dairy—just like a schoolgirl! And then seeing him but acting as if she hadn't any mind of her own, allowing him to be the spoiled, angry boy. And then letting him frighten her like that, and jump on her! Her, a grown woman, for God's sake! She ought to be ashamed of herself. She stands up again, this time full of resolve.

Whoever he is, she thinks now suddenly and with a profound clarity, whoever he is, her secret lover—and suddenly the pleasure and pride of it comes over her as never before, like a mantle she has earned—this is not how *he* sees her, a sniveling, foolish woman, dallying with boys the likes of Jeremy. This is not how she wants to appear! She will be better than this.

"Mrs. Blatchford," she shouts into the telephone. "Mrs. Blatchford!"

"I'm right here. You needn't shout." Mrs. Blatchford sounds breathless. "I had to take out the penny loaves."

"Sorry." Vida hitches her towel, trying to regain her composure. "But you must tell me, I—"

"Mr. Lamb came in and had a word with him, and if you must know, I'm all alone here today, Vida," Mrs. Blatchford interrupts her, "and I was worried about him." Her voice recedes for a moment, and Vida clutches the receiver as if to draw her back. Then her voice returns, close by again. "He was so quiet this morning. I thought it best just to have Mr. Lamb run him home. Perhaps he's taken him off for tea? I shouldn't worry if I were you. They left holding hands! I think Manford's quite fond of him."

Vida hitches her towel up again. Mr. Lamb? Holding hands with Manford? But, "He wasn't ill?" is what she manages to say.

"Only a bit quiet. Quieter than usual, I mean," Mrs. Blatchford says. "Don't worry, Vida. He and Mr. Lamb left here together like the oldest of friends, I promise you. I'd no idea, frankly, they were such chums. I'm sure they're just having a ramble together. I'll ring you if I see them pass by."

"Yes. Well, thank you," Vida says. "Thank you, Mrs. Blatchford."

She sets the phone down and realizes she'll have to find the directory for Mr. Lamb's telephone number. She doesn't want to go downstairs in her towel to look for it, so she takes the robe—the robe left by her secret admirer Saturday night—and puts it on. It feels like dressing in water. As she goes downstairs, she catches sight of herself in the long, dark pier mirror, a mysterious and lovely figure, like someone who might have escaped from a painting.

She finds his telephone number and rings his house, feeling suddenly shy. But there isn't any answer, nor at the post office, either. And then, despite herself, she begins to feel alarmed again. She thinks she *will* just call round to Dr. Faber's, only to make sure that he doesn't have Manford there with him, but then she remembers that it's Tuesday, Dr. Faber's day to be at hospital. So instead she runs back upstairs and pulls on some clothes and then runs back downstairs and fetches her umbrella, though it isn't raining, and her first-aid kit, which she keeps in a green canvas satchel hanging over a hook by the door. And then she leaves the house, stepping out into a day that is nearly gone now, afternoon just beginning to cross over toward evening, the new moon low on the horizon across from the sun, and the sky littered with columns of dark birds massing for their evening roost. She thinks she is as prepared as she can be.

THEY ARE COMING round the corner of the lane where the trees meet high overhead like a cathedral arch, Mr. Lamb and Manford, the latter cradling a sloppy bouquet of cowslips in his arms, Mr. Lamb talking excitedly, gesticulating with his hands. When Vida comes in sight of them, she sees Manford recognize her and then start up at a run, barreling toward her through the sweet-smelling air of the lane. When he reaches her, he thrusts the fragrant flowers, dripping their milky liquid, into her shirtfront and embraces her, laying his head against her shoulder. She holds her bouquet with both hands and takes in the scent of him. He doesn't smell like himself. He smells like—like vetiver, she realizes, startled. And he isn't wearing his own shirt. She draws Manford from her shoulder to look at his face again and gasps. The flowers fall to her feet.

But Mr. Lamb, smiling broadly, stoops and retrieves them, and then—more surprises!—leans forward to take her hand and kiss it in a courtly, satisfied way, handing the bouquet back to her!

"Did you have a lovely day?" he asks sweetly.

"A lovely day?" She feels as if she has been spun around in circles. She has an odd memory, quick as a pinch, of holding on to the reins of a little pony at a carnival once, when she'd been only a child; it had run her in tight little circles before the Gypsy man had hurried out into the field to rescue her.

"Yes! Whilst we were off! *We've* had a most exciting time," Mr. Lamb says, as though this were all very ordinary. "And you mustn't worry about his face. It'll be all right by morning. He had a run-in with some bees. The both of us did, I'm afraid." He touches his mouth apologetically; she sees his lip is blistered and puffy. "We've put mud on it, though. That always does the trick. Really," he says, patting her arm in the kindest way, "you mustn't worry. He's quite all right. And we have so much to tell you."

Vida stares at him a moment longer and then returns her gaze to Manford; her face softens. She lifts her fingers to his cheek, and he winces a little, looking balefully at her. "Oh, it must have hurt dreadfully," she says softly. "You've never had a bee sting before."

"I thought so," Mr. Lamb says authoritatively. "I thought he never had, or else he'd have never touched that hive." He nods wisely. "I think that will be the last time for *that*.

"And now—" he says, and as she looks away from Manford and back to Mr. Lamb, she sees that with the arrival of her gaze upon him he has grown suddenly shy again. He touches his hat.

"We've had an idea," he says. "I hope you'll—well, I hope you'll like it."

THEY GO BACK to Southend House, and Vida fixes Manford a Ribena and puts on the telly for him, though he'll have to wait for his beloved Dougal and *The Magic Roundabout*. And then she and Mr. Lamb, by mutual consent, have themselves a large gin—they both seem to need one, for separate reasons. They take their glasses out to the terrace and sit down at the little table in the shadow of the last of the Mercuries. A smile breaks out involuntarily over her face as she gazes at Mr. Lamb's gray head bent over his glass, the hair damp and combed neatly over his scalp, his lip swollen.

"I'm sorry I worried you," he says after a moment, replacing his glass on the table, but he fails to look precisely at her. He seems in fact to be squinting.

"Oh, no," she says quickly. "It was all my fault, really, I—"

"I just thought I'd have him back by his usual time, and there wouldn't be any—" He stops and blushes—a dark red the color of bricks—and looks away toward the garden.

Vida sits up straighter in her chair and stiffens; she feels herself growing alert. After a moment, without exactly intending to, she takes a deep drink of her gin. How does he know what time Manford usually arrives home?

"I saw you," he says then suddenly, turning back to her, "with—*what's-his-name*. The *gardener*."

"Oh! Yes!" Her train of thought is interrupted, and she recognizes with dismay that now *she* is blushing fiercely. Though she is certain that this is conveying entirely the wrong message to Mr. Lamb, she cannot think how to correct the impression. "Yes," she manages at last, feeling defeated already. "I met him at the dairy when I went round to fetch eggs. We were out. Of eggs," she finishes flatly.

She steals a look at Mr. Lamb over the top of her glass. She cannot quite fathom his expression.

"Well," he says quietly.

She moves her gaze away from him, up into the sky over his head. The moon has appeared in the twilight over the banks of yews. It hangs there, tiny and fragile.

She catches Mr. Lamb's eye and he smiles at her, but it is rather a bitter smile, she thinks, and she feels deeply wounded by this. "I don't," she says desperately, "really like him. The gardener."

Mr. Lamb says nothing at this, staring over her shoulder with a bored expression, as if watching an uninteresting program on the television.

She tries again. "He's—aggressive," she finishes. It isn't what she means. What she means is that she is no judge of men.

But it brings Mr. Lamb round. He loses the slightly vindictive expression that has played around his mouth, and now he seems, if nothing else, resigned and quiet. He takes another long swallow from his drink. "Well," he says. "Let's not—" But it seems he cannot go on.

"You said you had an idea," Vida prompts him now, for she is suddenly, unaccountably, afraid that he will leave.

He glances at her.

"Please," she says encouragingly. "Do tell me."

And so he does.

He tells her his idea, that Manford should do his shadows at the vicar's talent show, and at first Vida thinks it's preposterous. But as Mr. Lamb goes on, his voice gathering excitement, she starts to see how perfect it is, really. And then she begins to see it just as Mr. Lamb describes it, how he would station Manford up at the chancel with a light fixed behind him, and how he could do his shadows against the wall over the altar. Mr. Lamb says he will play for him, too, something to go *with* it—perhaps he could work out a transposition of *Carnival of the Animals,* he says. And then she begins to see exactly how it will be—how amazed they will be.

"He'll be a smash. Just you wait. He'll be a smash hit," Mr. Lamb says.

"It's perfect," she says, and she means it. She really means it. She feels so grateful to Mr. Lamb that she could, she could—she almost begins to rise from her chair, lean forward, kiss his hand . . .

But he gets to his feet then, and she feels herself fall back.

He still wears a sad look. But he takes her hand a moment. "I won't say good-bye to him," he says, jerking his head toward the house, where Manford is still sitting; they can hear the sound of the television through the open window. "I'll just let myself out—through the garden."

She opens her mouth, She wants to say something.

One day you will know me, she thinks. And she hears the words as plainly as if Mercury himself had leaned down from his pedestal and put his stone-cold hand to her ear.

But Mr. Lamb is gone before she can say anything. He is descending the steps, his stick swinging ahead of him. He is fading away into the shadows. A deep blue light, sad as a prayer, has fallen over the garden. Vida comes to stand at the top of the steps. The garden appears to be filling with water, the quiet, violet hue of evening, and Vida thinks of the ocean, of Corfu, of her island of happiness, the idea that there might be something still waiting for her in the world. But all she can see, as she looks out over the garden, is a last sight of Mr. Lamb vanishing into the dark recumbent shadows of the oak grove. And before she can call him back, he is gone.

THE GARDEN IS especially beautiful at night. Vida stands in the door of the library near midnight, after Manford has gone to sleep, and pushes it wide open to smell the air. The thin, papery light of the moon plays over the row of Mercuries. She looks up at it and thinks about the astronaut Armstrong stepping into the deep sands of the moon. That night when she had watched it on the telly, she'd thought that the moon seemed so far away. She remembers, with a vague but by now almost unimportant embarrassment, wanting to be rid of her clothes that night, wanting to feel that distant, cold, magical presence on her skin.

But tonight the moon seems tiny, near at hand, a little pearl.

She steps out onto the terrace, wrapping her Oriental robe—*his* robe—around her.

It's funny, she thinks, looking out into the garden, how the architects of Southend hadn't wanted what she thought of as an English garden. Mr. Perry was right. They'd wanted to evoke something else, another world, with a formality more like Italy's; as if it were better to be someone they weren't, she thinks, and to have a garden that proved it! Below her the lawns lie solemn and quiet, laid out in straight lines and diagonals, so that no matter in which direction you walk, eventually you meet up with yourself again, steered back in the direction from which you've come, the lines crossing and interconnecting like the facets of a diamond. In the moonlight the breeze flickers through the trees and shrubs, igniting a silver light among the leaves. The dark, running shadows lie sharp as spear points across the grass. She thinks there can be no place on earth more beautiful than this place. How has it happened?

Once, she would have been frightened to be out here alone at this hour. This garden had felt to her like the end of the world, a place she and Manford alone inhabited, it seemed, a place where no one else would ever come. And yet now, she realizes, it doesn't seem like the last place on earth, but more—oh, more the inside of her own head. Clean and quiet and dark; a map of herself, if she could draw such a thing, or one of Mr. Perry's resurrected buildings, the walls and roof and even the air inside it straightened and restored and blown free of dust.

She can see a light in the window above the stable; Jeremy must be there. She has to laugh at that, the fact that he's come to roost here now, after what he did. She imagines him setting up his things, his few things, whatever they are, in the stable apartment. Often, she thinks, there's surprisingly little we bring with us when we arrive. She had thought he was established with someone else, over there at the dairy. But maybe they've had a parting of the ways, Jeremy and his friend, and she sees that he thought he might have a new arrangement for himself here, with her.

And then she really is amused and sits down on the top step, pulling the robe over her knees. She feels herself smiling from ear to ear.

She is so surprised, still, to have figured it out.

She feels herself smiling into the dark, into the shape of Mr. Lamb standing there, smiling back at her as if to say: Here I've been all along. Here I am. I've been waiting for you.

NORRIS SITS IN his kitchen. After a frantic search he's found Laurence Minor's letter to Vida in the pocket of his trousers. He spreads it out on the table before him, working it smooth with his fingers, over and over again, hour after hour, until it lies flat, though it continues to hold the creases. Laurence's handwriting is faint, barely legible, the script swimming away in places where Norris's fingers have smudged it.

He sits for a long while in his darkening kitchen, thinking. In the fields around him, a fox creeps from its den, runs swiftly through the wood. Fern fronds at the feet of the great trees wind their stems ever tighter against the cool of night, their soft coils curling inward on themselves.

Norris looks up and stares at the empty wall across from him. Hallo, Cupid, you Artful Dodger. And it seems to him only justice, after all, that he should be visited by the notion of his old friend Cupid now, the cherub sitting down at the table across from him, laying down his bow and quiver, his face full of disappointment.

Oh, come, Norris thinks, pushing himself away from the table, disgusted.

Is this not, he thinks, what he had imagined when he'd felt Cupid put a tiny hand to his heart, stopping him in his tracks? Surely Cupid himself had had this experience before—the arrow flying straight toward its mark and then veering off into the wood, landing instead against a tree or deep in the soft earth. Landing nowhere.

But no. Because he'd felt it, hadn't he? Norris Lamb had felt Cupid's arrow. He *had* been struck.

And now—has it all come to nothing? Has he been pierced by love's tiny arrow, only to bleed forever? He'd wondered, even then, when it first began, whether it wasn't too late already. And yet he was given hope somehow. Each time he felt himself failing, something would happen and he could go on.

But there's nowhere to go now, he thinks. I'm done for here. It's over.

He looks down at the letter on the table. He knows what it means: Vida has had an invitation to spend the rest of her life in easy retirement, on a beautiful island, in the company of her family. If he closes his eyes, he can picture her bag on the bed, her dresses folded, the delicate underthings and stockings wrapped in tissue. He can see her hat, placed on the bed by her coat, waiting. He can even see her on the boat; the Strintzis Lines ferry leaves Dubrovnik for Corfu. (He knows this, for he has a stamp of it; there was a handsome series of ferries issued several years back.) And there it is, a white prow breaking the water. He can see Vida at the rail now, her hat in her hand, the wind in her hair, her eyes alight with the wonder of it all. She belongs there, he thinks. It is just as he's always imagined her, like a ship's figurehead. She'd be a painting for all eternity, for every woman who has ever wanted to see the world. If they made it into a stamp, he thinks, it would circulate round the globe. *Maiden Voyage,* he'd call it.

And he is nothing but a criminal, a tamperer with the mails.

He could lie, of course, suggest some mishap, tell her he's never seen a letter so badly damaged, that he's quite horrified by its condition. He could suggest, *imply,* the terrible strain of carelessness that has crept into the mail service, the young people's increasing ambivalence about quality service, about doing a job well. He could speak with passion of the battle, how the Old Guard of the postal ranks fight with every fiber of their bodies, how they attend with heroic vigilance to each letter, each flown soul of a letter.

Yet, he might say, so many mishaps may occur! Why, airplanes veer mysteriously into the Andes, to crash and be lost forever in the muffling white snows! A letter carrier pedaling barefoot down a dusty lane is stricken by a heart attack, his front tire wobbling madly, his spilled cargo lifted at last by an errant wind and scattered across the dry plain. A lorry traversing some serpentine pass disappears in a reckless shower of stone. A letter floats out to sea and is swallowed by a whale. Oh, so many things that may go wrong! How can we guard against each one!

But even if he doesn't confess his crime—*that he has opened and read her mail, that he has steamed open a letter in the back room of the post office*—well, the result will be the same. She will leave Hursley.

And the terrible thing, he realizes, is that she's earned it. She deserves it. He's never felt anything as fiercely as he feels this, though his heart breaks to know it.

And what will become of Manford?

Norris frowns. What about Manford?

A FEW MINUTES later, Norris stands up, folds Laurence's letter carefully, takes his cardigan from the hook in the hall, and puts the letter in his pocket, deep, so it won't fall out. He gathers up his stick from the front door and lets himself out into the night. He stops for a moment at his gate, turns his head to look down the lane. The lights have come on in his neighbors' houses, a blue light here and there where a telly is on, a yellow light over a kitchen sink, a white light blurring behind lace curtains in a bedroom. He doesn't often walk through the village, especially not if he is going to Southend, when he senses a certain stealth is appropriate; but tonight he feels drawn to the pavements and front gardens, the everyday business of the world closing up for the night, his world closing up for the night. Hidden doves rustle in the trees overhead, their soft warbling calls emanating sweetly from among the dark leaves.

He passes slowly before the houses, thinking of Vida—"Come on, Mr. Lamb. Come along with us. Perhaps you'll be invisible, too." No one sees him now; only the eyes of an owl follow him, or a sly cat wending its way into an alley. He looks in a window, sees Mrs. Thompson-Harris asleep over her knitting, sees the Bates boys building something, a model airplane, at the kitchen table; sees Horace the milkman cleaning his shoes at his back step; sees Mr. Blevins stepping across his sitting room in his undershirt, a stack of newspapers in his arms.

AND ANY ONE of them, looking up, might have wondered about Mr. Lamb's walking through the village at this hour. Some of them, in fact, attempting to collect their mail or post a letter or buy a box of stationery, had stood perplexed at the closed door and drawn shades of the post office earlier that afternoon, had wondered what had become of the postmaster, usually so dependable.

Fergus, foul-tempered without his tobacco, had kept his eye out from the forge, begged a pipeful from the odd man lingering there, peering in the window, cupping his hand to the glass.

"Gone out walking with Perry's idiot," Fergus had said, hurrying up whenever he had the opportunity, holding out his pouch for a pinch, as if this news were obligatory trade for tobacco.

"What? Manford Perry? What's happened to Vida?" they'd asked, surprised, and Fergus had shrugged, uninterested now that he had his pipeful. That was all he had to offer.

Even Dr. Faber, stopping round at the end of the day for a box of chocolates for his grandson who was coming to spend the weekend, had paused at the dark post office and wondered about Norris. A little hinge of unease had opened in his thoughts, something unpleasant and unfamiliar, when he remembered seeing Norris and Manford together earlier that day. He liked Manford, as much as you could genuinely like someone so deficient, he'd thought. There was a sweetness to him, an unguarded nature that Dr. Faber, as a physician, found simple and relaxing to confront—no invented symptoms, no distracting terrors about mortality. He'd sworn under his breath, pacing in front of the dark window.

Someone should have given Vida more help, Dr. Faber thought fiercely, and felt suddenly and uncomfortably guilty. Really, she'd been surprisingly intelligent about Manford all these years, if a bit of a worrier. He wouldn't have expected it from a girl in the village, such patience. Even, from time to time, inspiration. Like getting him that job at Niven's. Now, who'd told her that would be such a good idea? He had learned a few things from her, he thought. On her visits to his office with Manford, and the few times he'd been round to Southend to answer some urgent call from her, he'd been impressed by her, by her thoughtfulness. She's had a hard go of it, he decided, and a surprising anger gripped him for a moment. He thought of Manford, unable to lace his own shoes, Vida kneeling at his feet.

Good Lord, you don't hand it round very evenly, do you? he thought.

He'd stared a moment longer through the dark window of the post office, vaguely reviewing the sight of Mr. Lamb and Manford from earlier in the day. They were a likely pair, in a way, he'd thought, surprised.

But he felt tired that evening, uncharacteristically weary. And so he'd set his hat then and turned for home.

There's only so much, he'd thought, any one of us can do.

AND IN FACT no one does look up from his or her business that evening. Norris passes down the pavement, his head wagging from side to side as he looks in every window, curious, as if he has found himself in a foreign country. Aren't the gardens pretty, he thinks, noting the pale strawberry of the foxgloves, the lantern yellow of the butterfly orchid. He counts the ghostly pickets until he reaches the corner and turns onto the Romsey Road.

A few patrons are standing outside the Dolphin, their caps pulled down low on their heads; they turn at the sight of him rounding the corner, watch him until he disappears into the darkness along the street. They down their glasses, think instinctively of their wives and children, resolve to have just one more and head for home. Perhaps their children will be asleep by then, the pubescent girls so startlingly mature suddenly, their breasts budding beneath their nightgowns, their profiles so exotic in the shadows, so like their mothers', traces of forbidden lipstick, perhaps, still on their mouths, blue eye shadow still in a faint smear on their eyelids. How these men love to come upon their daughters like that at night, to touch them tenderly on the head, sweep the hair from their faces, gaze at them. And the little boys, their rooms strewn with toys, one baby arm—scarred at the elbow from scrapping in the street—flung free from the sheets, a soiled plaster dangling by a corner. How sweet they all are.

How quickly the time has passed.

AT THE BENCH in the lane, Norris nearly loses his courage. He could simply leave the letter there; he could go home then and fall into bed, into dreamless sleep. She could find it in the morning, and by then he'd be gone, he thinks wildly, on a packet bound for foreign shores from Southampton—it's not so far to Southampton. He imagines, briefly, that he can escape everything he has set in motion.

She doesn't love him. She never has. She never will. She won't even have the opportunity.

And somehow, oddly, the coldness of this thought steadies him. He sits quietly on the bench, breathing deeply, thinking of all the times he has stood behind the horse chestnut tree here and spied on Vida. Happy memories, they seem to him now.

After a few minutes, he puts his hand to the arm of the bench, pushes himself painfully to his feet. He touches the letter in his pocket. He stands there a moment, waiting. Despite himself, he feels in his heart the old excitement of this errand, of creeping to the low lawns beneath Southend, gazing up at the house, searching for her form against a window. Did she have to be so beautiful? he thinks, a groan gathering within him. There was so much more I could have done. I never even told her how I feel. Such a simple thing.

A breath of wind eddies down the lane, setting up a dark music, castanets in the leaves. A twig cracks sharply, somewhere in the bracken. Then all is silent.

Norris leaves the bench, walks toward the house. One last time, he thinks. I'll go the way I've always gone. Invisible.

VIDA RUBS HER bare foot against the cool, smooth slate of the terrace steps. She glances up at Manford's darkened window behind her and her own beside it, one lamp left on at her dresser, another burning still in the kitchen, at the far end of the house. The randomness of the lights makes the house itself appear like a rocky island, two distant occupants alone, each on their promontory. For a moment, a chill of fear leaping up inside her, she thinks she sees smoke, swirling forms that step forth and gesture to one another, mute and meaningful, full of intention.

But she shakes her head. There they are, her silly old fears.

Everything's all right, she tells herself.

There's no fire in the house. Manford is safe.

She stands up, drawing her robe close around her throat. She looks down into the chiaroscuro of the garden below, the fountain, the gray ribbon of walls, the towering velvet yews and boxwoods, each black blade of grass, the white gravel of the paths, the ghostly entabulature of the grotto.

She sets a foot down upon the first step and then the next, her hand resting on the stone balustrade as though gently grazing the arm of a lover. She holds her head high, looking out over the garden. She sees the light in the stable wink once, twice, as though a form has passed before it; and then there is nothing, just a steady yellow glow as though the room has suddenly emptied, its occupant having quit the closely lit space for someplace darker, for the darkness of the garden.

HOW MANY PEOPLE move in the garden this night? It is hard to tell in the darkness, for the shadows don't hold still for inspection, not so you can be certain, the angle of the moonlight and the presence of even a small wind altering the tableau as if it were the surface of a pool. And of course there are animals, too, a whiskered badger venturing out on purposeful claws, a pair of deer turning in alarm, the thousand silent burrowings of earthworms and snails in the soil, the freakish shape of an owl falling on its cloak into the dark wood. Across the lawn runs a tiny mouse —two; three; no, more. Or are those errant leaves turning and turning?

Jeremy's work, the cleaned flower beds etched neatly and sharply at the edges with a spade. The work of a strong young man only temporarily inhibited by his injury, the hand nursed now tenderly in the other, more tenderly than is necessary perhaps, as he steps from the stable below the garden into the shadow of a sycamore, relieves himself there against the backdrop of the fountain's white noise. A late woolly catkin, having clung on stubbornly past its time, flutters down now from the birch, turning in a gyre, pale yellow. And then a little phantom cloud of white night moths stirs from the wood near Jeremy. He watches them break free, disperse. He steps forward.

There is another footfall at the same moment, so the two cancel each other out, two sounds scored in the same instant. The blackthorn stick descends silently, a third leg making its inaudible step, the interval in the gait.

Does Norris Lamb need this stick for walking? No, but for resting against, for poking and prodding at the earth, a comforting metronome at his heel, a second party accompanying him everywhere. He has raised the stick in anger before, though. He knows it can do the necessary damage if applied properly. There's nothing as stout as blackthorn, otherwise known as sloe, whose black, plumlike fruit flavors gin, the drink you take when you have lost your love, a child, a war.

But Norris is not a man who drinks.

He stands in the high arch between the yews, the poisonous berries glowing a deep red, almost black, among the spiny green. He is scored all over with the fine shadows of the leaves. Even if he moves now you will not trust your eyes. You cannot be certain what you have seen.

And who is the third? The last? The form so unmistakably, even unfashionably feminine, with its full hips and round calf, moving slowly, sedately down the gray steps in the moonlight, the breeze picking up the hem of her robe, fluttering it like white surf at her ankle. She thinks to try it, walking like Manford, her arms reaching as if above the cold spray of the waves, Manford's invisible companions pacing beside her, her eyes closed and head flung back, trusting the current.

And Norris can imagine her maiden voyage begun, her trip already under way, Corfu beckoning. She steps away from earth on the milk white sea of moonlight, the pebbled beach of the garden.

And Norris sees that it is her great sympathy that has made him love her so. Her list-making and storing of provisions, her vigilance through so many nights over the boy's common colds and more, over his whole lifetime of brave, failed endeavor, her exorcism of bats and spiders and other children's cruelties, the thousand times she's thrown a ball or held his hand or soaped his back or trimmed his hair, the way she adjusts the spoon in his hand, the flower in his lapel, his hat against the sun. The way she fits herself up against him at night and holds him, loves him.

Loves him. That's it. That's her reward, her privilege. She loves Manford.

And *she* understands that Manford has been a gift to her, the world rocking in one terrible instant, parting open along a crevasse and swallowing one human being, leaving a baby motherless, only to fill that woman's place with another, a soul so unprepared that it has taken her twenty years to learn what she is made of. And that modesty has made her what she was always destined to become, the heroine of her own tale—the woman who will be at last, before it is too late, the great love of one man's life and the salvation of her own.

NORRIS SEES HER pausing there against the flight of steps, her arms at rest upon the air, her face a tiny white moon.

He sees her. They both do, the two men lurking there at the perimeter of the garden.

But Norris sees Jeremy first.

This is his advantage, that by remaining hidden longer, by waiting, he can recover whatever distance he might have lost in pausing. He turns and runs awkwardly, skirting the edge of the yews, making for the steps of the grotto, where Jeremy now appears, his shoulders rising as he ascends the stair. Norris comes from the dark, something fantastic speeding along the running shadows of the ancient shrubs, a form aggrandized, towering, rising up out of its own darkness. He raises the stick. His eyes show a holy fury, but something else, too. Sadness.

"Down there," Norris hisses, gesturing with the stick back toward the curving stair that leads away from the grotto. "Or I'll give it to you."

"Jesus!" Jeremy backs away, terrified.

Norris hushes him fiercely, prods with the stick.

Jeremy raises his hands in protest a moment and then glances at Vida, motionless and distant at the far end of the garden on the stairs. He had meant nothing. He hadn't even seen her until the last moment!

Norris drives the stick toward him, breathing hard.

"You're crazy!" Jeremy expulses it under his breath like a curse, an evil wind. But he backs away from Norris's stick, down the steps. At the bottom he turns once. Norris stands at the parapet, leaning on it, trying to quiet his jagged breaths.

"This is a crazy house," Jeremy says low. And then he laughs, as something occurs to him. "You won't get any out of *her*, you old bugger." And then he is gone.

VIDA HAS OPENED her eyes to see something move by the grotto, some bent form backing into the shadows. But there is nothing there now. She blinks, takes a breath.

She moves forward toward the grotto and the fountain, gliding down the path, her robe billowing.

For Manford, and for Norris, she is irreplaceable.

If she leaves them, they will mourn her as though she were dead.

She ascends the winding steps of the grotto, unaware of Norris's presence where he crouches beneath her in the recess of the stairs, the relief of a giant shell framing his averted face. She steps to the fountain's edge, presents her palms to the delicate spray from the fountain, feels the delicious chill of it run over her body. She had thought, once, that she wanted nothing between her and the world, that moon waiting overhead. But she knows now that she is already of this world, one miraculous invention rising up out of the sea and shot through with the perfect magic of being alive.

HE WAITS UNTIL she has gone, until she has run lightly down the steps of the grotto and across the lawn and up toward the house, behind the row of Mercuries, their feet raised as if to ascend into the heavens. He sees the door close behind her, a mirror shutting in a wall.

He steps soundlessly from the grotto then, reaches up and closes his hand around the thorny cane of a rose, snaps it off, and brings the beautiful flower close to his face.

He does not know what will happen now when he returns to the house. He does not know what will happen when he rings the bell at the door, presents her with the rose, gives her the letter from Laurence, and makes his confessions. He looks at his pocket watch, tilting the face under the moon to catch the light. It is almost one in the morning, he sees. But it can't wait. He can't wait anymore.

POSTLUDE

"I'VE BROUGHT YOU," he says abruptly when she opens the door, "your mail."

She cannot understand any more of what he is saying at first, for he speaks so low and so quickly.

"This is not how I imagined it," he is saying frantically, standing at the door under the light. "Coming to this. I had thought better of myself, you see."

And all she can think of, looking out at him, is the time, all the time that's passed—the *years* they've known each other.

But his face is so—so sorrowful! This is not what she expects. She had thought, when she opened the door to find him standing there at this peculiar hour, that it was as if he had read her mind. Then—why does he look so miserable? She tries to smile at him.

"Mr. Lamb," she begins, holding the rose he has given her.

"I know it's horrible of me. I know it's late. I'm sorry about that," he says. "But I had to see you. Please."

She leads him to the sitting room off the kitchen.

"Please sit down," he says, and she finds a chair. But she can hardly bear it, the look on his face. He hangs his head.

This is all about the gardener, she thinks wildly. It's all about Jeremy. He thinks I'm in love with Jeremy! "Mr. Lamb!" she begins desperately. "Mr. Lamb!"

But he sighs so deeply she cannot go on; she feels suddenly mortified, as though she does not understand anything at all.

He presses his hands to his eyes. "I've done a terrible thing," he says. "I've broken a sacred trust."

A deep silence falls between them. Vida feels as though hands were closing around her throat, squeezing the breath from her. It is as she suspected; it has been a joke, a prank. An awful, awful prank. She starts to stand up unsteadily; the room tilts. Her eyes fill with tears.

And then he puts an aerogramme on the table. "You mustn't think I've a habit of doing this," he says in a dull voice. "This is the first time. And the last, I assure you. I shan't have another opportunity." He pushes the paper toward her and looks away.

She looks at it, dazed.

"It's for you," he says fiercely then. "I've read your mail."

Read her mail? She does not understand, but he waves a hand at her. "Read it," he says. Bewildered, she takes the letter over to her desk and sits down. And then, after just a few lines, she starts to laugh.

But when she hears the legs of his chair scrape against the floor, she turns around. "Oh, no, Mr. Lamb!" she cries. "No! I wasn't laughing at you."

And isn't he, she thinks now, seeing him standing there, so fierce and so righteous and so brave, everything in the world worth loving? Isn't he the most wonderful man you ever knew? There's not another one like him, not in the whole world.

She crosses the room to stand near him, to stand facing him. She sees his face fall with emotion.

"I had my reasons," he says. "They were very good reasons. The best. I want you to know that."

"But I already do!" she says. "Yes," she says. "Yes, I do."

And she steps up close to him then, so close she can feel his heart beating against her own, just like that day at St. Alphage when he asked her to dinner.

He is warm, and she can feel the heat coming from him. It is what she thought she would feel in Corfu, everything so strange and unfamiliar yet exactly as she'd pictured it in her mind's eye. Exactly as she'd imagined it, the horizon perfectly and gloriously endless, and yet everything still yet to happen.

"Mr. Lamb," she says, and bends her forehead to his lips. "Mr. Lamb."

THE NEXT SATURDAY afternoon, the Saturday of the talent show, Vida ushers Manford up to his bedroom, catches him by the shoulder, and steadies him in front of her. "Manford, do stand still." She fetches him a clean shirt from the wardrobe, helps him into it. She fits a tie round his neck, adjusts the lengths before her, winds a quick knot, and pushes it up neatly into his collar. She takes a pace back from him.

"There," she says in satisfaction. "You look very handsome indeed. You'll cut a very impressive figure." She turns to the bed, smooths the coverlet. Stepping to the window, she pulls aside the curtain, looks out into the garden. Jeremy is there, kneeling in one of the far beds under the sun's last rays. She sniffs. Making up for lost time, she thinks.

She turns back to Manford, who stands with his big hands upon his tie, gazing down at it where it flows over his shirt.

"Don't be fussing with your tie now, or I'll have to do it again," she says, taking his hands in hers and holding them tightly. She looks into his eyes.

"Come on," she says, letting his hands drop at last. "I'll make us tea while we wait for Mr. Lamb."

In the kitchen she lights the burner under the kettle, then slices an apple for Manford and sets it on a plate before him. "Cheese and a biscuit, too?" she asks. "You'll want something in your stomach against the excitement."

Manford lifts a slice of apple gingerly, glances up at her as he takes a tiny, delicate bite.

"Oh, well done, Manford. That was lovely," she says warmly. "Your manners are really lovely now. Fit for the queen—" But quite suddenly she cannot continue. She tries to recover herself, comes and kneels beside him. "You'll remember—" she begins urgently. Manford, munching stolidly, looks at her. She closes her eyes. Of course you will, she thinks. I mustn't be silly.

The bell rings and Vida jumps. "Oh, there's Mr. Lamb!" she cries, winding her hands. "He's early! But he'll have tea with us, perhaps. You don't need to go just yet."

Norris is standing on the stoop in his suit, a plug of violets in his lapel, his hair combed back from his forehead. He looks elegant, and Vida is touched at how handsome he is.

Norris holds in his hand a bottle of champagne, which he thrusts toward her now. "For cracking against the rail," he says.

She takes the bottle from him, holds it close to her breast, her eyes as wide as if she'd slept for days and were now drinking in the light.

He clears his throat. "Well? All ready, is he?"

"Yes, but I thought—" She hesitates. Oh, it is too soon! "Come in and have a cup of tea first, will you? You don't need to go just yet, do you?"

Norris extracts his watch, inspects it with a show of purposefulness. "The vicar wants all the performers there early, for a run-through," he says. "But we've time, I think."

She leads him back through the house, into the kitchen. Manford looks up and smiles at Norris, who places a hand on his shoulder and gives it a squeeze. "He's not nervous, is he?" he asks Vida.

"I don't think so," she says. "I don't know as he understands."

She puts the tea on the table, draws out a chair, and sits down. "Manford," she says, looking at him and leaning forward. "You know what tonight is, don't you? You're to go with Mr. Lamb to the church for the talent show. You'll do your shadows there? I'll follow behind and watch from the audience? And then—"

Manford takes up another slice of cheese. Vida looks over at Mr. Lamb. He makes a motion with his hand as if to say, That's enough for now.

She offers Norris a cup of tea.

"Well," he says after a moment, clearing his throat. "Here we are."

"Yes." She looks down into her cup.

"All set then, are you?"

She nods.

"Remembered everything?"

She nods again, starts to say something, but he interrupts her.

"I'd mind the water, if I were you," he says, looking away from her. "You can't be too careful about foreign water."

"No."

"I've got us two chops, for after the show," he says brightly then. "He likes a good chop?"

"Oh, yes. Yes. That was kind."

She looks up to meet his eyes. She does not want to go now; she does not want to be parted from him, from either of them.

"It's only a look-see," she hears him say then, gently. "Just to have a look. But you must at least see it, Vida. You can't just turn away from an opportunity like that. You've got to—"

"Yes, I know," she says, cutting him off. She does know. She knows he's right—of course, it's what she always thought she wanted. It will be a holiday! But now—well, when Mr. Lamb proposed it that night a week ago, she'd been so touched, almost speechless. And all week he'd been making the arrangements for her, cabling Mr. Perry and explaining it all for her, arranging about the boat, writing Laurence, as if he were an expert traveler! As if he couldn't wait for her to be gone!

Now here it is, the eve of her departure. She will take the train to London this very night! And she doesn't feel sure of anything now. "You're sure you'll be—" she begins.

"Absolutely. In any eventuality. I've said so, haven't I?"

"Yes. But I can't—"

She sees him bite his lip.

His voice cracks. "Should be lovely, this time of year."

She bows her head over her cup.

Though he has not admitted it to himself, Norris fears this may be the last time he sees her. He'd told her that night, when it came to him, how she must go, how she could at least just go and have a holiday. You've never had a holiday, Vida, he'd said. You really must go and stay awhile with him.

And he understands how he's needed here, now, and what he needs, as well. He understands that he can look after Manford as well as anyone besides Vida.

You *must* go, he'd told her. You absolutely must. But he had not appreciated his own vehemence, not until later, when he understood that if she came back, then it would be for certain. Then she would have no doubts.

There's not a minute to spare, he'd told her, and it had felt that urgent. After all this time being so indecisive, he found he could push her away with more force than he'd ever been capable of using to draw her near.

But he had reached out and taken her hands.

It will be everything you've always dreamed of, he'd said. And he had shut his eyes and known it to be true, that he could make her this gift, this most important gift. Not just of a holiday, a trip to Corfu. But this chance to choose for herself her own destiny.

But perhaps he was wrong. Perhaps she would never come back. After all, what does he know about the world? It's all in small pictures, what he knows—his little stamps. He could look at them for hours, but they aren't the same as the real thing.

He could look at her for hours, too. He has so many pictures of her in his head.

SHE WETS HER fingers and smooths Manford's hair, but he twitches away from her.

How like a boy, she thinks as he slips from her hands.

"Never mind," says Mr. Lamb hurriedly, drawing Manford away.

She sees that he wants to be gone. "I've a comb with me," he says. "We'll touch him up right before."

She waits, puts her hand to her neck, an odd pain there. "Norris—" she says. "Norris—"

But he turns to her then, puts a finger to his lips. "Wish us luck," he whispers.

And then they are gone.

"Good luck!" she cries after them. "Manford! Be watching for me, Manford!"

She sees them pass through the gate. They go down the lane together, Manford's heavy frame cumbersome beside Mr. Lamb's narrow one, the two side by side in their unfamiliar suits. At the bench, she sees Manford reach for Mr. Lamb's arm, sees Mr. Lamb take Manford's hand and tuck it under his elbow.

The light in the lane is so beautiful, she thinks, watching how the shadows of the leaves ripple over the two men, the light so gentle and fine. Disappearing into it would be the easiest thing in the world, the sweetest passage, the gentlest vanishing.

And she thinks of the church then, the parish gathered there, the little children leaning over their mothers' laps, the men with their hair dampened, their hands clean, the nails white and sharp from trimming, all their features, family to family, bearing traces of the familiar. There will be flowers, she knows, gathered from every garden. The vicar will be smiling, rubbing his hands, his bald head shining. Lamartine Ramsey, breathless, will have finished her solo, the people grown restless and irritable before the piercing reach of her voice, the ladies of the village crocheting madly beneath the window of the virgins. And Norris and Manford will step forward then, Norris adjusting the light so that Manford's shadow looms up suddenly, huge and dark, against the wall behind the altar, the congregants drawing a collective breath as he pauses there, shifting, his dark shape hunched, unresolved. He will turn to Norris then, she knows, for reassurance. And Norris will steer him, will show him what is to be done.

One by one the shapes will rise up against the wall, the children's mouths opened to tiny Os in delight at the crouching cat, the tattered birds, the arching mongoose, the begging dog. From Manford's hands the fish will swim, the birds soar forth in pairs, the elephant incline his delicate trunk, the giraffe step lightly forward. A low murmur will pass through the people as they raise their eyes, smile, point, motioning to their children to look, look and see! So clever! Who'd have thought it? Isn't it grand!

It will be something to remember always, the night Manford Perry made his shadow shapes in church, all the creatures of the world in stately procession through the vaulted nave of St. Alphage, the children's eyes wide in wonder, Manford become a benevolent Pied Piper, beloved and adored.

It is what she has always wanted for him.

SHE GOES UPSTAIRS then and fetches her cases and Manford's valise. He will stay at Mr. Lamb's; she's already sent over most of his things.

It had been all Mr. Lamb's idea, to have Manford stay with him. "I have in mind to teach him the organ," he'd said. "I think he might just catch on to it."

Stopping round for Manford's belongings the day before, he'd shown her a book he'd been reading, *The Language of the Idiot Savant.* He'd been very excited. "I think he may *be* one of these," he'd said to her, waving the book at her, flipping the pages. "We shall do some experiments, with mathematics and so forth."

He had sat down in the sitting room, his finger on one of the pages, reading bits aloud to her. After a while, she had ceased to hear him, exactly. She had sat very quietly, her hands in her lap, gazing at him, the bright, hot light from the window falling upon his head. Already, it seemed to her, her place in the world was widening, growing brighter and brighter.

She had come to only when his voice had stopped. She'd found him again, her inward gaze sweeping away from the blue, humpbacked promontories of the Albanian coast across the water, the greenish sheen of the shags darting a meter above the sea.

He'd been looking at her.

She'd met his eyes. "'The sun may rise and fall, but nothing shall ever eclipse your beauty,'" she'd said abruptly.

He'd blushed, looked down at his feet. "It's true."

"I never guessed you, you know," she said. "Not till the end."

"I know."

"It's that you were right there, all the while," she said. "I thought it was someone—I couldn't see."

"You don't have to explain," he said. "You don't have to promise."

"I know. You've said so. But I will—"

"No, don't." His face had been pleading. "I'd rather you didn't. I'd rather I could just—hope."

And she'd had to accept this. She loved him for that, especially for that. That he was willing. She felt the absolute freedom of her heart to choose. And she would be changed, she knew, but not as much as she might once have expected.

She had stood, walked to him where he sat in her sitting room, his head bowed. She had dropped to her knees, placed her forehead against his thigh. After a moment he had lifted his hand, rested his palm against her cheek.

"I shall always know where to find you," she'd said, not looking up. "Beacon in the dark."

And he had smiled.

"READY, MANFORD?"

Norris touches his shoulder, waits until Manford looks up and meets his eyes, the immense kindness there.

Norris smiles. "Now. The animals," he says, and raises his hands, sees the strange long shape of his own fingers pour over the stones, his reach miraculously long, as if he could caress each head in every pew, graze each figure in each stained-glass window, Adam with his spade for cultivation, Melchizedek with his offering of bread and wine, Joseph bearing a sheaf of corn, Elijah surrounded by the ravens, David with his crown and scepter,

Ezra poised with quill and book, King Solomon with the model of the temple offered on his outstretched palm, doubting Thomas recoiling from the wound of Christ.

How full the world, Norris thinks, touching Manford's hands, making them rise. How old the stories. How miraculous the ending.

And then he climbs the narrow stairs to the organ, breathes in deep, and begins to play.

DATE			